War of the Gods

Unleashes Fire in the Skies

War of the Gods

Unleashes Fire in the Skies

Book 4 of the Kopaz Series

Dale Groutage

Copyright Material

Dedicated to the Travelers of Life

To my lovely wife, Nancy, and my three exceptional children, Phil,
DaleAnn, and Lane—thank you for your love and support.
We travel our worldly journeys together.
To my Desert Pirate friend, Robbie—thanks! Our adventures in a coal
camp in the 1950s made us who we are today.
We travel on—our journeys are not yet complete.
Two very special people—who gave me life and sent me on the road to
search for hope—are no longer with us. They sit on their lofty thrones
above and smile—their earthly journeys are complete. My father, Fred,
spent twenty-five years in a coal mine. He taught me to never give up.
My mother, Katharine, made our little abode in the desert and our
lives in the ever-present shadow of a bleak existence just a little piece of
heaven.
For all of us who travel on, our journey not yet complete,
there is an old Navy saying:

Fair winds and following seas!

Dale Groulaye

Table of Contents

CHAPTER 1

The Game of a Deathly Riddle

Could it be *déjà vu?* Was the game real? Or was it just a game? After all, who could say what went on at the center of the universe?

"Why have we convened as a council today?" Viracocha growled. The supreme god waited. No one answered. He roared louder. "Why is no one answering me?"

Although Viracocha had strikingly handsome looks and a Mr. Universe body, he commanded the utmost respect from every creature in the universe, especially the primeval gods who sat at the council table as rulers only at his pleasure. He was the image of an eighteen-year-old superhunk. His boyish face, with his shaggy blond hair and deep-set emerald-green eyes, set him apart. He certainly didn't look anything akin to what most humans might consider the supreme god to look like. This was especially true for those who have been steeped in religion from the onset of their mortal existence, taught that god was a white-haired old dictator who looks like Father Time.

Viracocha's voice faded, and all those seated at the council table nervously anticipated what would come next. Their wait was short.

Pounding his fist on the red-diamond table, Viracocha smashed it with such force that shock waves erupted with a booming sound, cracking through the air like a thunderclap in a raging storm. His emerald-green eyes as bright as bolts of lightning, he glared at the primeval gods. Seated in golden thrones at the council table, they ruled the universe. However, at this meeting the order of business was not their continuing rule of the universe but rather the search for an answer to an unsolved riddle.

"The *end* is coming, and here we sit, the riddle unanswered! Why?" shouted the supreme god of the universe.

Gathering his composure, Viracocha looked down the table. No one knew what was consuming his being and affecting his display of emotion, yet clearly something was gnawing at him.

He could not shake one troubling thought. *A traitor sits at my table! Who is it? Is it Dumuzi? Is it Tammuz? Or is it Neptune? They all voted to support Zuron's one-church plan...hmm! Who could it be?*

Even though the thought of a traitor was all-consuming, he held his tongue. With his hands together and index fingers stretched out under his chin, Viracocha gently nodded his head. His mind drifted. *It is not time for a confrontation. I must wait and set a trap. Soon I will know more of who is behind the dastardly deed that is bringing about the destruction of the universe.*

All eyes were focused on Viracocha. His massive golden throne— made from a million pounds of precious metals and laden with tens of thousands of flawless gemstones—was centered at the northern end of the table. The red diamonds, emeralds, sapphires, and rubies larger than basketballs certainly made his throne a seat of beauty, but beauty was not on Viracocha's mind. The War of the Gods was raging full steam ahead, and it was clear, at that most crucial meeting of the primeval gods, that Viracocha's patience was running out. His fist had never before pounded the red-diamond table. Until now, he had used restraint. And like at all such council meetings, he was flanked on his left by his son, Ra, while on his right sat his uniquely beautiful wife, the goddess Neferdor, who looked like an eighteen-year-old supermodel. Her silky black hair and sapphire-blue eyes commanded attention.

Viracocha wanted answers; there could be no doubt about that. But right now, he had only questions. "Why have you not given me the means to destroy Zuron? Why don't I have the ability to focus the destructive rays of Kolar on his planet—Zolob? Why is it that Zuron can focus Lenszar? He has been busy destroying planets. So...we know that he is able to program his GAMMAZEL and then focus Lenszar. That brings up the question, does he have at least one of the secret code words that allows him to program his GAMMAZEL? Evidently he does! My next question is, how did he get the secret code words?"

Viracocha's eyebrows pulled down as his facial expression intensified. "Is it a mystery to you that our GAMMAZEL must be unlocked and programmed so that we can focus Lenszar...that massive lens in the heavens between Kolar and the planets?"

Viracocha stopped. He glared at the gods. His mind was churning with thought. Time passed. Then he spoke his words loudly. "How convenient for Zuron in this deadly game we are playing...he has programmed his GAMMAZEL, so he can focus Lenszar. But here we sit, looking at our GAMMAZEL, which is idle. It sits on the table in front of us doing nothing...why? I'll answer my question. Because we do not have the answer to the riddle necessary to program our GAMMAZEL and focus Lenszar!"

Again, an eerie silence took over. Viracocha was thinking.

While Viracocha was pondering, the god Dumuzi stood. He stood over six feet tall, and he was confident. He looked into Viracocha's eyes and spoke profoundly. "Noble god, we know that the war plan put forth by your son, the god Ra, forbade you to search for the answer to the Riddle of Zuron. We all know that if the wrong answer were put forth and the incorrect symbols dialed into GAMMAZEL, we would lose the war and our planet, Volob, would be reduced to cinder. That puts the responsibility squarely on all of us seated here. We, not you, must come up with the riddle's answer!"

When Dumuzi had finished, Viracocha remained silent for a few minutes, ignoring Dumuzi's comments. It was so quiet that a feather landing on the emerald floor would have made a crashing boom. The only sounds were the flutter of beautiful orange-and-black Verona birds flying in formation back and forth high above the red-diamond table and their serenading heavenly song.

Viracocha lifted his head so he had a full view of all the gods at his table. "Do we not have a nice place to sit and govern the universe?" asked Viracocha. "There can be no denying that a one-carat flawless red-diamond ring would be worth a small ball of gold? You all know that red diamond is the most rare and valuable of all precious gems. Our table is one and a half times the length of an Earthling's football field and more than three feet thick, fashioned from a single, solid red diamond. It is trillions of billions of carats. One would have to compare the value of our table to a ball of gold one billion times the size of Kolar. Now that would be a gigantic ball of gold. Is that not so?"

Viracocha lowered his voice. "The worth of this table matters not if the answer to the riddle remains elusive…is that not also so? Am I the only one who can grasp the magnitude of *our* problem?"

Still standing in front of his throne, the god Dumuzi leaned forward and gently placed his right hand on the tabletop. His fingers tapped. Viracocha rolled his eyes and waited. Dumuzi spoke. "I believe you are part of *our* problem, most noble ruler of the universe!"

"Please proceed, Dumuzi!" snapped Viracocha.

"Your plan to let the human race chart their own destiny was indeed noble by any measure, Your Eminence," replied Dumuzi.

As Dumuzi's words faded, an aura of brilliant green light drifted around the table, much like the aurora borealis that lighted up the majestic northern skies of Earth's atmosphere. But the gods were not holding this most crucial meeting on Earth. No, their pantheon was on Volob, which was one of three planets in the solar system located at the center of the universe.

Dumuzi's face was stern as he continued. "How could you know that religious zealots would step in? And not only have they corrupted the image of 'God' so that humans believe him to be nothing more than an old, long-haired being, but those religious fanatics cleverly use the fear of death and what follows death to control the masses."

Nodding his head slowly, Viracocha asked, "Why is it that the human race has no idea who the true supreme god of the universe is or what I look like?"

Eager to be in the spotlight during the most important meeting ever held at the center of the universe, Dumuzi contemplated his response to Viracocha. "How could any of us know?" he asked rhetorically. "We, that is, all of us who are seated at this table, agreed with your grand plan to let humans chart their own destiny without interference from the gods. Little did we know that keeping our identities secret would result in a mess that has spread to every corner of the universe. Yes, by keeping our identities hidden from the humans, they created their own image of god…this old, white-haired, invisible character!"

Sixty-five gods, not including Viracocha, Neferdor, and Ra, sat at the table, their eyes and ears fixed on Dumuzi. They waited.

Viracocha rasped back, "Do you have your facts straight, Dumuzi?"

There was a slight pause. Dumuzi lifted his head. "You're correct. You did once allow our presence and who we are to be known to a select group of humans in our solar system—those on Kopaz, and then you revealed our existence to a few humans on planet Earth. The royal family of Kopaz and the Egyptians on Earth know who we are." Beaming, Dumuzi said, "We, the gods who sit here at your pleasure, think that may have been a good thing."

Obviously not interested, Viracocha turned to look at Neferdor. She smiled. He smiled back. Then he turned his head back and snapped, "*So?* What is your point, Dumuzi?"

Eager to respond, Dumuzi ventured on. "I do not have to remind us all that the game of war we are playing is not just affecting the gods but all creatures throughout the universe, including humans."

Dumuzi paused. Viracocha motioned with his hand to proceed.

Dumuzi spoke loudly. "So we allowed a few humans to know the business of the gods. Planet Kopaz was a perfect place to try this experiment."

Listening intently, the god Ra was bobbing his head. Sitting to the right of Viracocha, he said not a word but just made head motions. Viracocha noticed the movement from his son. "My son agrees with you, Dumuzi, so I shall ask again. What is your point?"

As if searching, the god Dumuzi mumbled, "Well…you know…ah." Organizing his thoughts, Dumuzi seemed about to say something. He was clearly still formulating in his mind what to say next when Viracocha again slammed his fist on the table. "I'm waiting, Dumuzi!"

Tensions were on the climb, so the god Dumuzi thought he had better have his words perfectly selected. "You know that Prince Kashom traveled to Earth on several occasions. His first visit was to Egypt, where he was given Zanzee by Queen Nefertiti. It seemed to be a good thing, as your son Ra with his daughter Bastet had been there earlier and given Zanzee to the humans."

"Where are you going with this story?" Viracocha wore a puzzled look as he cut Dumuzi off.

At this crucial meeting to discuss a deathly riddle, it seemed that Dumuzi was derailing the scheduled agenda with a tangential story of humans and gods.

Viracocha's glare was a signal to all that the hole that Dumuzi was digging, figuratively speaking, was getting bigger and deeper. At the point when their eyes locked, Dumuzi put his hand to his hair and scratched as if contemplating what to say next.

All waited. "We thought it was a good thing. We thought that Egypt would be a good place to let our presence be known to humans." And as Dumuzi spoke, Ra recalled his visit to Earth over five thousand years ago. Ra's face seemed to take on a glow.

"But," said Dumuzi, "the Theban high priests of Amun Ra eventually took over as evil rulers of Egypt, and we know that was the start of the downfall of humans on planet Earth. So just like all other places in the universe where humans dwell, Earth was no different...except for one small group. There's a small band of humans living in the desert on Earth who are descended from Kashom and who are not letting religion destroy their happiness or fill their every thought with the fear of death and what follows."

Maybe it was the escalating destruction of the universe that consumed Viracocha's mind. Maybe it was the suspicion that there was a traitor at his table.

Not waiting for Dumuzi to finish his rambling, Viracocha's patience snapped like a twig under a heavy foot. "So do you put the blame on me, Dumuzi?"

It was quite strange. As Dumuzi spoke, streaming rays of light from Kolar drifting through the dome above the gods caused an aura of green light to surround Supreme God Viracocha.

Could it be that the rays from the most massive star at the center of the universe, Kolar, filtering through the dome above and striking the solid-emerald-gemstone floor caused the aura of green light? Maybe it was the solid-gold foundation supporting the green-emerald floor that caused the spectacular brilliance. The question lingered. Could the green aura be coming from the floor, or was it another mystery, an omen?

Maybe the light was revealing something and maybe not. For whatever reason, Neptune's face wore a green glow. Omen or not, one thing was for sure. The red-diamond table sat on a green-emerald floor made entirely of flawless gemstone material, three feet thick. Walking across such a floor was a very different experience. Each step was as though floating across a sea of green waters, a brilliance shining through from far below.

About to say something, Viracocha caught his words before they dropped from his lips. His mind, however, he could not stop. *How can I expose the traitor? Is it the green face of Neptune, the sheepish face of Tammuz, or Dumuzi's smirk that reveals the coward who betrayed us?*

With so many questions and so much at stake, Viracocha did not wait for Dumuzi to respond but asked another question. "Are you the one who has failed me, Dumuzi?"

It was an inquisition, and Viracocha was searching for something. He looked at the god Dumuzi and pointed his finger as if it were a spear. "Dumuzi, do you have the answer? It seems you have been working on discovering the elusive answer to Zuron's riddle for a very long time…is that not so? If my memory is not failing me, it has been two million years, so what is your problem, Dumuzi, other than the fact that you evidently don't have the answer. Or do you?"

In sharp response, Dumuzi shouted, "*No!*"

"How dare you disrespect me?" rasped Viracocha. "Do you know that you sit at this council table at my pleasure?"

Dumuzi dropped his eyebrows as his face hardened. His grim expression highlighted his cheekbones as he contemplated his response to the supreme god.

Tempers had never run this high at the council table, even when

Zuron was planning his overthrow of Viracocha. At that time, Viracocha's son, the god Ra, had stepped forward and put forth a compromise that had temporarily halted the impending chaos among the gods that was disrupting the governance of the universe. Ra had presented a winner-take-all tournament between Viracocha and his followers and Zuron and his followers. But the tournament, for Viracocha, had taken a turn for the worse, and Zuron had the upper hand. And so, chaos was building again at the council table of governing gods, but this time the fate of the universe hung in the balance.

"I may sit here at this table at your pleasure, Supreme God, but if this ship sinks, we all sink together!" snapped Dumuzi.

"Hmm…you do have a point, unless there is a traitor among us who would find a warm seat at Zuron's table. Do you have plans, Dumuzi?" asked Viracocha.

There can be no denying that tensions at the council table of the primeval gods were escalating, and Viracocha was getting to the end of his rope, figuratively speaking.

Once more, a deathly silence descended at the council table. The supreme god's question hung in the air like a hot-air balloon. For at least ten minutes, no one said anything. The eerie void of sound was deafening.

Viracocha's patience waned as he waited for Dumuzi's answer to his last question. As Dumuzi said nothing, Viracocha asked, "So, Dumuzi, how did you vote on that most crucial issue that Zuron put before the council, his bullshit one-church idea?"

"Ahh…er…I…er," stumbled Dumuzi, attempting to get out an answer.

As Dumuzi fumbled for words, Viracocha asked in a soft voice, "Dumuzi?"

As Dumuzi hemmed and hawed, the supreme god said, "Please take your seat, Dumuzi. We have heard enough."

Not wanting emotion to dominate the moment, Viracocha turned to face the gods and then leaned forward in his golden throne. He put his hands on the red-diamond table. And in his powerful voice, he repeated his words once more to make his point clear. "Why is it so hard? Are we not intelligent? Two million years have passed. Yet here we sit…the riddle unsolved! It's only a riddle…right? School children can solve riddles, but not the gods? What am I missing? Why have you not given me the means to destroy Zuron? Why don't I have the ability to focus the destructive rays of Kolar on his planet—Zolob? Why is it that Zuron can focus Lenszar? Is that a mystery to you, that our GAMMAZEL must be unlocked and programmed so that Lenszar can be focused not only by Zuron but also by us?"

There wasn't a peep. The goal was simple—the destruction of planet Zolob and, along with it, Zuron's pantheon—yet that most important goal had not been reached, and so Dark God Zuron continued his reign of horror, spreading evil throughout the universe.

There could be no denying that the balance of power in the universe was teetering, and Viracocha had only questions. His focus was on three gods, but he put that aside and changed the subject.

He lifted his head, and his emerald-green eyes landed on Comanzar.

"Where's Quill?" roared Viracocha. His glare at Comanzar prompted an immediate response from the sergeant at arms. Comanzar stood. He stepped to the podium and spoke firmly, looking squarely at Viracocha and Neferdor. "Most honorable supreme god and goddess, Quill is ready to report!"

"Send him forward," snapped Viracocha.

It was only a moment before Quill was at the podium and in the spotlight. Maybe that was why Quill said nothing. He waited. Viracocha's glare intensified as he spoke. "Well?"

Quill stood steadfast, his mind filling with a single thought. *Well, what?*

"Hmm," mumbled the supreme god as he spoke the words loudly. "*Well, what? Is that all you have?*" He was obviously reading Quill's mind.

A stillness surrounded the council table. Eerie sensations dominated the atmosphere. Then Viracocha roared, "Is Mochcom in the outer reaches of hell?"

Calmly Quill replied, "No, most honorable supreme god and goddess. Danny, your royal prince, is traveling the Highway of Time as we currently speak and soon will be in search of Zuron's most heinous disciple!"

"And?" asked Viracocha.

"Most noble ruler of the universe, your royal prince, Danny, has rid Kopaz of evil. The entire Quorum of Goroms, except Gorom Mochcom, reside in hell. I was with Danny when he thrust their miserable carcasses into the Pit of Vulcan, the gateway to hell. The girl dragon, CrystalFlame, stands guard over the Pit of Vulcan so that the evil goroms will never show their miserable faces in the universe again," replied Quill.

"Well done, Quill," said Viracocha, as he wanted all to know that progress was being made.

As the supreme god motioned for Quill to proceed, all were eager to hear more. Quill lowered his voice and carried on. "I travel next to the Scarlet Desert on planet Earth. I will be with Danny at all the right times as he carries out his next mission to rid the universe of Zuron's most heinous disciple, Gorom Mochcom."

This time Viracocha nodded his head as he said, "Let's hope that Danny is successful!" Smiling, he looked directly into Quill's eyes and said, "Good job, Quill, and may the game end in triumph for us all!"

The supreme god motioned with his hand. "Be seated, Quill. I've heard enough!"

It took a few moments for Quill to move out of the spotlight. As Quill took his seat on the golden couch in the dignitary area, Viracocha changed his tone and spoke reverently. "The answer to the riddle is our only hope!" And as he spoke, the massive chandeliers hanging above the red diamond table, glittering with hundreds of thousands of giant diamonds, twisted and sparkled as they shed a twinkling light and heavenly warmth on the gods below, all working on a solution to thwart the impending disaster—a disaster that would bring fire in the skies to even the furthest reaches of the universe and death to all—the end of all life.

Soberly, Viracocha continued. "All that we have...all that matters...all that is good." He paused momentarily and then ventured on, declaring what the final state of the universe could be. "All that is of any worth is at stake if we fail. Our failure will bring an end to the universe as we know it. No longer will the universe be under democratic rule, but it will be subjected to a dictatorship. Is that what we want? An evil dictator spewing horror into every corner of the universe?"

*"We must...*we must forge on!" Viracocha's command cracked like the crack of a gun in the still of an evening, the opening of a deadly battle.

At that very instant, the corps of buglers raised their golden instruments to their mouths and proceeded to trumpet out the call to order. Their rhythmic signal announced the forthcoming of an official proclamation.

The sergeant at arms, Comanzar, stood. He stepped to the podium. "Supreme gods and council members, the war has taken a turn for the worse! Our sky sentinels have detected and monitored greater movement of Lenszar. Zuron has struck! He not only has the ability to destroy a planet but has made the first devastating move to destroy an entire solar system. Somehow, he was able to focus Lenszar on an entire solar system, and now fire in the skies blazes unchecked. Zuron has focused the rays of Kolar on the Nebular solar system in the outer reaches of the Xanthnamus galaxy. All is gone. One hundred billion souls have perished. The entire faction of the human race known as the centurions are no more! The entire solar system is in cinders!"

"Horrible! This will only continue unless you solve the riddle!" Viracocha, his arm outstretched, pointed down the middle of the table. "Sergeant at arms, remind us what Zuron must do to win this game?"

Comanzar took a deep breath. He faced the executive end of the council table and proceeded. "As we all know, most honorable Supreme God Viracocha and Supreme Goddess Neferdor, one GAMMAZEL sits in your pantheon. In fact, it is in front of us on this red-diamond table. Likewise, Zuron has a GAMMAZEL on his planet. You—supreme god and goddess of the universe—can win the war only by unlocking and programming your GAMMAZEL," said Comanzar, pointing to the large golden key-like device on the red-diamond table. "It's your GAMMAZEL that must be unlocked in order to focus the destructive rays of Kolar with Lenszar and destroy Zuron's planet, Zolob." Comanzar looked at Viracocha and continued. "Zuron can win the game in one of three ways."

Comanzar paused to take another deep breath. He returned to Viracocha's question and repeated it. "What does Zuron have to do to win this game? Most honorable Supreme God Viracocha and Supreme Goddess Neferdor, your son, the god Ra, put forth the rules of the game.

I shall repeat them. One, Zuron needs two code words to program his GAMMAZEL in order to destroy our planet, Volob. However, he only needs one code word to partially program his GAMMAZEL and destroy other planets. Evidently, he has one of the code words, as he has managed to incinerate entire solar systems. Two, if Zuron can get the golden key from Neferzul, the royal princess of Neferdor, we will lose the game. If he has the golden key, you will not be able to unlock and program your GAMMAZEL. Three, if Zuron can kill the firstborn male of the new human race with his zedite knife, he will win the game, and we will lose. That firstborn male must come from the union of the royal prince of Viracocha and his mate, the royal princess of Neferdor. You, most honorable Supreme God and you, Supreme Goddess Neferdor, have picked the humans whom you want for your royal prince and princess. Danny and Jeannie have been successful so far. It remains to be seen if Danny can rid the universe of Mochcom. Let's hope that he can. If your royal prince, Danny, can put Mochcom in hell, Jeannie's golden key is safe, and she will be able to unlock our GAMMAZEL."

The supreme god could not hold back his thoughts a moment longer. What was on his mind came roaring out in words of power. "Someone at this table knows the answer. Who among us is the *filthy dog?*" rasped Viracocha. He stopped and took time to look each god in the face directly. And then he proceeded. "How is it that Zuron is able to program his GAMMAZEL? How did he get one of the code words and the symbols? Is there a traitor in our midst giving Zuron the upper hand?"

And so the War of the Gods raged on. Zuron currently had the upper hand in this deadly game, and he was expanding his destructive power. But who, other than the gods, knew or was even aware of this supreme conflict? And who among the gods at Viracocha's table knew why Zuron had one of the code words and associated symbols necessary to focus Lenszar?

CHAPTER 2

The Mark is Missed

⁓

C uriosity has a strange way of foiling even the best-laid plans. Could the love of a little boy, basking in his opportunity to admire the god who was holding him on his lap, have a profound impact on time and space? Zeb's curiosity about the Sun Energy Transformer got the best of him when he was sitting on Danny's lap in those final moments before Jerzom and Danny departed Kopaz. Unknown to Danny, little Zeb fiddled with a knob—a most critical knob on the Sun Energy Transformer, the one that set the destination point in time for the travelers. Their target had been the spring of 1958, but they instead arrived in the fall of 1963, and that created a new set of problems.

They landed in CoalVille, as they thought, right on target. It was just before dawn on a chilly November day. Although the date was obscure, the place wasn't. There could be no argument about that. Danny quickly looked around and then pointed. "There it is—the CoalVille tipple!"

The sun was starting a new day, and its rays filtered around the silhouette of that grand old steel building—the CoalVille tipple—a familiar sight to the son of a coal miner.

Danny mused, *Yes, it is still there. It hasn't moved or taken flight.* His mind froze. *Something is wrong!*

Not entirely aware of his words, Danny began rambling on, sorting the thoughts that were going through his mind. "That thing looks like it is in shambles. All the windows are broken…large pieces of metal are flopping and waving in the wind like fins on a whale." Danny glared at the structure that was used to fill the coal cars with newly mined coal.

It was obvious to Danny. Something had changed. Shaking his head, Danny's mind raced. *This thing looks like an eye-sore relic from the past!*

What the hell year is this? thought Danny. His question was locked in his mind. Jerzom certainly could not answer it.

The wonder of it all was slowly fading for Jerzom. The visions he had created in his mind of the Scarlet Desert were not borne out by the reality before him. The romance, the wonder, the images Jerzom had imagined based on that romantic name—the Scarlet Desert, were at odds with what he saw now. He was staring at an unsightly hulk, a dilapidated old monstrosity of who knew what?

"What is that thing?" asked Jerzom, gawking at the tipple.

He couldn't quite hear what Danny was saying, so Jerzom strained to make sense of Danny's mumblings. "No more coal—mines are shut— tipple is an old hulk—what is going on?"

Then came the crowing, a familiar sound to Danny. *Cock-a-doodle-doo...cock-a-doodle-doo...cock-a-doodle-doo!* The sounds were coming from the backyard of a familiar house, the house next to Danny's old residence.

"Hmm, well, Coal Camp is still here, as Mr. Garetoe's rooster is up and at it early in the morning and letting everyone know it is time to get out of bed," Danny mumbled. "Garetoe's place is about one hundred yards from us," said Danny out of the blue. "I hope Red Rock Creek is not full of water."

Now totally confused, Jerzom asked, "Who is Garetoe, and what is Red Rock Creek?"

Danny wanted a few minutes to gather his thoughts about the place he had been raised in, but there was no time. The tasks at hand took precedent.

He left his friend's questions unanswered as he replied with words of concern. "We have to find a hiding place for the treasure. The sun will be getting everyone out of bed in a few minutes, and if anyone spots us, we'll have trouble."

Danny took off on a sprint and raced to the area under the tipple. He motioned for Jerzom to follow and bring the treasures.

Danny was standing next to a dynamite vault at the CoalVille tipple. The CoalVille Progressive Company, the CPC, had built dynamite vaults throughout the surrounding areas so that the explosives that were used in the mining operations could be stored safely.

"Give me a hand with this," said Danny as he motioned what he wanted.

It took a few moments for Danny to scrape away the dirt on what appeared to be a large flat rock. It was not a rock. It was the concrete lid of a dynamite vault, and Danny's digging had exposed several iron rings attached to it.

Clearing away the three inches of dirt took a few minutes. Both boys grabbed the iron rings set into the concrete slab, and slowly, they swung it aside.

"OK, let's set it down," Danny said.

It was a chore that Danny could have done by himself. Lifting four hundred pounds would have been child's play to him, but including Jerzom fostered their relationship with a spirit of teamwork.

"OK," said Danny, "we got it off."

Perfect for storing something whose value was not calculable, the underground vault could not have been better had it been made to order. It was four feet deep and six by six feet square, and typically; it would take a number of men—at least five stout hunks—to lift the concrete lid and expose the most valued treasure in the universe.

The pit was musty and dank, and happily, there were no unused dynamite sticks lying around.

Smiling, Danny picked up the tin box they had brought with them. He opened it and handed Jerzom a wad of fifty-dollar bills, saying, "We will need this."

"Why are you laughing?" asked Jerzom.

"We stole this money from Mochcom before Jeannie and I left the desert. We were snooping and found it in his house," Danny answered.

And as Danny stuffed a wad of fifty-dollar bills in the front pocket of his Levi's, he laughed louder. "I bet Mochcom shit his britches when he discovered we stole his money."

In a matter of minutes, the treasure—the Sun Energy Transformer, Kashom's golden journal, the sundial key, and the tin box filled with fifty-dollar bills—was securely placed in the vault.

Before they replaced the lid on the vault, Danny grabbed his cloth bag that he had brought with him when he left the Scarlet Desert back in the spring of 1958. He took some clothing out of it.

Fortunately, Jerzom and Danny were about the same size. Danny was more than happy to share with his new best friend an extra change of clothes. The extra pair of pants and shirt that Danny had thrown in his bag before they left CoalVille that awful day in March of 1958 came in handy. Jerzom looked like a CoalVille High School heartthrob in Danny's clothes.

"You're like a high-school football player that the girls want to get their hands on," said Danny as he chuckled.

"Well, if you say so," Jerzom answered.

CoalVille was coming alive. Cars were on the road, some coming and some going, as the people of CoalVille started a new day.

"Good, the treasure is safe. The dynamite vault at the CoalVille tipple is the last place anyone would look," said Danny with a growing smile.

All too aware of the danger of crystallized dynamite sticks that had been lying around, most everyone in CoalVille knew it was better to stay clear and leave well enough alone—to, figuratively speaking, let sleeping dogs lie!

It was only a short walk from the tipple—less than four hundred yards—to Red Rock Creek. Standing on the bank of the dry wash, Danny eyed the streambed. *Hmmm, no water in Red Rock Creek. Forging a river or creek that is dry is of no consequence.*

Jerzom had nothing to do except to wait and watch as Danny made plans.

That there might be no water in Red Rock Creek had not calculated into Danny's decision to wait a few hours to get what they came after—Aerapondes's lock of hair at Jeannie's old house. The cars on the road concerned Danny. Lunch hour, he decided, would be the most inconspicuous time, provoking the least curiosity from casual onlookers.

"We'll wait here in the cover of this cluster of tall sagebrush," said Danny. "It will give us an hour or so to make our plans."

The time passed quickly. Two young men emerged from the banks of the ravine, and as their heads appeared first over the embankment of Red Rock Creek on their climb out, the wind was rustling their unbuttoned shirts. Bulging chest muscles and oversized biceps would scare most anyone from messing with these guys.

Even though Danny's focus was on their assigned task—to get the lock of hair and get Jerzom out—the walk up Main Street was bringing back old memories. With a lump in his throat, Danny looked at his old house as they walked by it. It was different yet much the same. Within a few steps, the edge of the garage came into view. At that moment, he stopped.

Jerzom watched, knowing too well that the sadness dominating Danny's expression could only be from horrific memories of the past.

Jerzom didn't have to ask. Danny pointed and said softly, his voice barely audible over the stirring wind, "Mochcom killed my mom in that building, and I found her."

Jerzom's heart sank watching the young god grieve.

Maybe it was the old garage—the stage of death—that prompted Danny's urgency. Maybe it was instinct, since only a god could know what loomed ahead. But for whatever reason, Danny said, "It is not safe here, and time is running out. We must hurry."

Their walk up Main Street from Danny's old house to Jeannie's took them no more than five minutes. Standing on the edge of the road, Danny had a problem. They were at the spot of the location for Jeannie's old house. The problem was that it was not there. A parking lot stretched over the ground where three houses used to sit—including the old LoneTree house. The CoalVille school district had evidently elected to expand the parking around the old high school building. And in so doing, the old dilapidated houses must have been razed and replaced with asphalt.

Staring, Danny was puzzled. *They tore the houses down!* Yet even deep in thought, Danny's attention was diverted. A car was parked where Jeannie's old house used to stand, and not more than twenty feet from the car stood a person.

Stranger than the missing houses and the parking lot was the horrified look on the young man's face as he held an eight-transistor portable radio to his ear. He was standing on the edge of the road leading from the high school. He was about twenty-five yards from Danny and Jerzom.

Even though his radio was plastered against his ear, the sounds were coming out loud and clear. "President Kennedy has been shot," the radio blared as Walter Cronkite's announcement shocked the world. "In Dallas, Texas, three shots were fired at President Kennedy's motorcade in downtown Dallas. The first reports say that President Kennedy has been seriously wounded by this shooting. More details just arrived. These details about the same as previously: President Kennedy shot today just as his motorcade left downtown Dallas. Mrs. Kennedy jumped up and grabbed Mr. Kennedy. She called 'Oh no!' The motorcade sped on. United Press says that the wounds for President Kennedy perhaps could be fatal."

Danny motioned for Jerzom to follow him as he started to walk toward the young man with the radio. Danny wanted to ask, but he did not. Whoever had just been shot was powerful news and making a fool of himself by asking "Who is President Kennedy?" was not an option. Danny thought, *Hmm, what can I ask him so as not to draw attention to what we are up to and yet get the information I need?*

Staring at the young man with the radio stuck to his ear, Danny said, "How horrible! The president is shot!"

The boy nodded his head but said nothing.

"What day is it?" asked Danny, an ulterior motive at the front of his question.

"November 22, 1963, will live in infamy throughout the ages" was the boy's reply.

"Do you think Pastor Duncan will have a memorial church service in honor of the president?" pressed Danny.

"I don't know any Pastor Duncan. My reverend is Pastor Martin. I like him. He's a good friend and invites me for dinner at his house alongside Bitter Creek in Granite Springs."

The boy stopped and looked into Danny's eyes. "Pastor Martin has a severe limp, and I'm sure that he will need my help this evening because there will be a lot of people at his rectory."

"Oh," said Danny. "Is he there now?"

"Yes, I was planning to have dinner with him this evening, and with this news, I'm sure he will be comforting many who are grieving. It will be a long evening."

Holy shit, thought Danny. *This young man is walking into a trap.* But then he smiled to himself. *That old bastard will be busy, so we can snoop, as Jeannie would say!*

Jerzom could only listen to the strange conversation and wonder why

Danny looked like he was ready to kill somebody.

Pastor Martin, thought Danny. *That son of a bitch! He is using another disguise. He'll think "Pastor Martin" when I get hold of his raggedy old ass and fry it to cinders!*

CHAPTER 3
The Horrors of a Woodshed

S nooping was again the game plan. This time it was not snooping as a treasure hunt but a hunt for the last gorom and anything that would help corner Mochcom and send him to hell. That thought was heavy on Danny's mind.

Hmmm! We're in the right place but at the wrong time. We need to get to the right time for Jerzom to get Aerapondes's lock of hair, but first, I need more information on Mochcom if I am to carry out that part of my mission successfully— killing the last gorom. The danger does not outweigh the risk.

Nothing had changed. The two-rut dirt road was still covered with weeds, old tin cans, and broken bottles. Repeating Tony's words from so long ago, Danny said to Jerzom, "Watch where you step. This is a garbage dump!" as they turned off the main street onto LeRoy's driveway.

Standing in exactly in the same place as it had the last time Danny visited, LeRoy's house was a hundred and fifty feet off the road. It was nestled in a carved-out nook at the base of a small hill. The old rock wall behind the house kept most of the dirt from sloughing off the hill, offering some protection from the elements, yet over the years it had deteriorated, and the dirt was starting to pile up. The dilapidated shack had only one or two asphalt shingles left on the roof.

It brought back old memories—memories that would never fade from Danny's mind. Strips of tar paper that LeRoy had nailed down to keep the rain out had managed to rip loose, leaving unsightly black flags waving to passing onlookers.

There, in front of him, on the ground, another remnant from the past sent chills down Danny's spine.

That old shoe could have been my dad's, thought Danny.

For as long as Danny could remember, his dad would wait to put his shoes on until Hank pulled up in his '54 Ford and honked to let Johnny know he was there.

Yeah, I think every miner in CoalVille wore identical shoes. They must have bought them from the company store, and they only had one brand to pick from. Jerzom noticed Danny's focus on the boot, and that reminded him of the humble beginnings that surely must have been Danny's life as a small boy.

It's like the way Peizar was raised, thought Jerzom as he swallowed a lump that had gathered. *How different and fortunate it was for me being raised in a royal palace.*

When they reached the end of the driveway, Danny said, "Jerzom, we're here."

His words had barely left his mouth when he turned and jerked. Jerzom watched. Danny pointed. "I want to look over there," said Danny. "That bastard is up to something 'cause it looks like there's a bloody handprint on the door of that woodshed."

Now sensing the same emotion as Danny, it was all too clear to Jerzom, with his mind gripped with images of the past. *His reign of murder and death continues.*

Standing in front of the woodshed door, Danny and Jerzom faced each other. Neither blinked as Jerzom said, "I don't have any desire to go in there."

Fully aware of the scene of death that Jerzom had witnessed at the Vassar home when he found little Peizar, Danny understood. "OK."

Silently holding the secrets of its victims, the old woodshed stood against the wind, swirls of dirt dusting it, a monument of evil closed to the world. There were telltale signs of terrible moments. Danny imagined the screams and cries of agony, his thoughts fixed on the tokens and signs left on the walls in the form of dried blood around the iron rings.

The stark reality of innocent children facing a monster was heavy on Danny's mind. *I don't blame Jerzom. There's enough death in the world without seeking more in the dark corners of this woodshed.*

Stepping back and spinning on one foot, Jerzom was not going to peek into a death chamber. He said, "If you don't mind, I'll walk over there," and he pointed to a pile of stacked boards.

Rusted over the years from being exposed to the elements in Wyoming, the hinges squealed as Danny opened the door.

My lord, thought Danny. *Who knows how many have suffered in this chamber of sacrifice?*

In the same formation as the cross to which Eddie had been tied, four iron rings were affixed to the back wall, rope dangling from each one. The casual onlooker might not suspect that the blood-soaked rope was anything but old pieces of strapping material that had weathered in the dry Wyoming climate. A closer look would have revealed that it was blood that had dried to a rusty brown color. And the most observant individual might have perceived that it was an instrument of ritualistic human sacrifice.

Eerily, countless victims had left their mark on the walls of the woodshed. Shaking his head in disbelief, Danny's soul cried with pain as he looked at the many small bloody handprints of children who were now silent. Even though their tales of horror had faded as their little mouths could no longer speak, the bloody handprints screamed out their stories.

"He must bring them to the point of death and then have them in their final moments press their little bloody hands on the walls." Danny whimpered in a low sad voice that was lost in the wind.

The agony, the pain, the suffering, and the horror of it all were staring at Danny. He could all but hear the victims of Gorom Mochcom screaming for mercy as he cut their beating heart from their chests.

"Supreme god of the universe, please help me put an end to this!" Danny said as Jerzom listened just outside the door. Jerzom had walked back toward Danny, and he too had a tale of death that he had uncovered in the pile of wood.

Walking out the door, Danny was met by Jerzom's blank stare.

Danny's words rang with the warmth of a compassionate deity. "The bitter sadness I see leaves me more vigilant, even more ready to carry out the will of Viracocha to bend the arc of justice to the innocent throughout the universe!"

As these sobering words fell from the mouth of the royal prince of Viracocha, Jerzom listened, waited, and then quavered his response. "'The religious monster's victims are buried under the wood. He cut off their hands...little hands. My lord and royal prince of Viracocha, such crimes against helpless children cannot go unanswered by the sword of justice."

Nodding as he locked eyes with Jerzom, Danny said forcefully, "With my last ounce of energy, I will exact justice for their innocent souls."

And with a force that could only thunder from the mouth of a god, Danny roared, "There seems to be no bottom to the pit of evil over which Gorom Mochcom presides, but little does he know that soon he will be at the bottom of the pit of hell!"

The reality of Gorom Mochcom's horror had been burned into Danny's mind as a constant reminder of the evil that consumed that wicked high priest. Danny remembered the last time he had been at this shed as clearly as if he was reliving those horrible moments. Without even thinking, Danny proceeded to tell the story as Jerzom listened.

"Eddie's arms and legs were outstretched. He was tied to four round iron rings on the back wall of LeRoy's woodshed, his arms and legs stretched into an X. He was exhausted from trying to shift his weight from his legs to his arms and then back to his legs. His bloody shirt dangled from his waist, exposing a deep, heart-shaped cut on his bare chest. Jeannie and I lifted his limp body, relieving the tension on the ropes that held him to the back wall of the woodshed. Tony used his knife to cut the ropes that bound Eddie's hands and feet.

"'Be careful now. I think he's free,' I said in a quiet voice.

"We gently removed him from the back wall. Eddie was barely conscious. We laid his limp body on the floor of the woodshed—Jeannie, Tony, and I knelt over him, trying to make him as comfortable as possible.

"Jeannie's canker of hatred that she'd harbored in her heart for Eddie vanished. Her back-alley encounter with him was the furthest thing from her mind. She was a beacon of compassion, helping a young boy who was the victim of a madman.

"'This is horrible. Why would the gods let something like this happen? My lord, look at that cut on the left side of his chest,' Jeannie said as she took a handkerchief from her pocket and wiped the blood that was oozing from it.

"'He's starting to breathe a little more normally. His eyes are starting to open.' I said. Touching Eddie's face, I felt him regain some strength. 'Eddie, can you hear us?' I asked. 'Do you want some water?'"

Danny's voice trailed away. No more words were needed. Danny and Jerzom stood beside each other, right outside of the open door of the woodshed, and their minds were filled with parallel thoughts.

Evil such as that the gorom had committed here, relishing the highest degree of human suffering for the pleasure of a dark god and his disciples, could not be allowed to become the future of the universe.

As the boys stood lost in thought, suddenly, out of nowhere, it appeared. Howling and squealing, a monkey with sharp, pointed fangs raced toward

Jerzom. In its hand, it held an iron ring with a strange, star-shaped object attached to it.

Completely caught off guard, Jerzom froze. His mind was operating in slow motion watching the monkey race over the ground in leaps and bounds.

As the monkey made his final leap, his fangs targeting Jerzom's jugular, Danny swung his arm with his full might, knocking Jerzom to the dirt as efficiently as a prize fighter's knockout blow hurled his opponent to the mat.

And as the monkey was still in flight on his way to Jerzom's neck, it was not only Jerzom who felt the force of the god's strike but also the monkey. He squealed louder than a locomotive whistle announcing a railroad crossing. The creature headed for the open window of the house.

Still holding the iron ring with the star-shaped object on it, the monkey leaped onto the windowsill. And then he was gone as the curtains parted and he jumped through them.

Reaching with one hand to pick Jerzom up, Danny braced his left leg firmly on the ground. Once on his feet, Jerzom said, "You saved my life. Thanks, TRPOV!" Shaking from his tumble to the ground and his brush with death, Jerzom said, "Danny, pardon me, but this is way too much to handle."

Jerzom turned and walked a few steps to get away from the woodshed.

Maybe it was just a coincidence...and maybe not. Looking away, Jerzom could not see the woodshed, nor could he see Danny. Danny's foot was still planted where he had braced it to help Jerzom to his feet.

For some reason, Danny looked down. As a drifting cloud revealed the face of the sun, a flash of light by the toe of Danny's boot grabbed his attention. He bent over and scraped at the dirt. There it was. He picked it up with his heart pounding. Staring at it in the palm of his hand, his mind exploded. *What is this? It has to...the symbols...hmm...from the gods...yes!*

Before Jerzom had a chance to turn again and get a glimpse of Danny's find that so consumed his attention, Danny stuffed the object into the front pocket of his Levi's.

Quickly, Danny shifted his attention from the object he had just put in his pocket to the task at hand—exploring a house of horror for anything that might help the royal prince of Viracocha trap and kill Mochcom. Although there was a personal need for vengeance in the heart of the young god because of the brutal murders of his mother and his best friend, Tony, at the hands of Gorom Mochcom, the fate of the universe depended on Danny destroying the last and final gorom.

The wind died. The sun was bright. Mochcom's house beckoned like an evil chamber of torment, for someone, anyone to come have a look inside.

"Jerzom, we have to go into that house. Something is terribly wrong." Danny stared at the dilapidated house where evil knew no bounds.

The paint on the old wooden siding was peeling away, and after a few more hot summer days and cold winter nights, it would soon be nothing more than a faint reminder of a house. Most of the fence no longer stood but was either lying on the ground or leaning as if it would fall at any minute. The chimney sticking out of the top of the roof had slowly crumbled over the years and was barely poking through the highest location where the four gables formed a point. Garbage was everywhere. With this perfect camouflage, who knew the structure was anything more than a house of horror?

Jerzom nodded. Danny and Jerzom started their walk toward the mysterious edifice.

CHAPTER 4
Pointy-Fanged Monkey

Gazing at the bizarre mess of clutter strewn in every direction, Danny and Jerzom were faced with a challenge. They walked gingerly, and their goal was not to step in a trap.

Mumbling softly, Jerzom said, "Only the twisted mind of a deranged person would have landscaping resembling a garbage dump."

"It's not an accident, Jerzom," said Danny. "He's hiding something, and this stinking mess is camouflage to deter inquisitive passersby."

Maybe it was keen observation by the young god, Danny. Maybe it was fate. Who knows why, but no sooner had Danny spoken than he leaped through the air on a beam of green light, tackling Jerzom, and slamming him to the ground.

Lying at the edge of a thirty-foot hole, Danny and Jerzom heard the sound of crashing boards, garbage, and rocks hitting the bottom.

Covered with dirt, his heart pounding, Jerzom listened to Danny's words. "He *has* booby-trapped this place. I knew it!" rasped Danny.

Danny jumped to his feet and grabbed Jerzom's hand, yanking him to standing. They were only two feet from the edge of a large cavern that had just been exposed. Gingerly, they moved their heads, and as the two looked into a hole of death, it was obvious that it was a trap.

"*Oh my,*" said Jerzom as he looked at what would have been his fate had it not been for Danny.

It was obvious that Mochcom had already been successful with his snare. The first victims of the trap, three skeletons, mingled with sharp, steel-pointed rods sticking out of the ground. That was all that remained of some curious souls who had wandered by but who never had a chance to leave.

Saved by Danny, Jerzom nervously stood on the edge of the pit and looked at it with horror. *That skull is from some unsuspecting stranger who wandered into the yard of Mochcom. Now it looks to the heavens with a rod of steel protruding through it. It could have been me!*

Knowing exactly what was going through Jerzom's mind, Danny nodded and said, "Mochcom is clever. He uses garbage and crap to steer a curious intruder into a trap. Ingenious, I must say. Not many want to walk on garbage when a nice pathway around it is beckoning them!"

Their avoidance of that hole lined with instruments of death was fortuitous. Walking over garbage was not a choice but a saving grace.

"What a stinking mess," snorted Danny as he covered his nose with his shirtsleeve.

Carefully, they navigated through piles of trash and garbage, carefully planning their every step so as to not fall victim to another of Mochcom's concealed traps.

Finally, they were there—the back door was open. Danny was caught in visions of the last time he'd been there snooping, in the spring of 1958. Stepping through the door, his memories gave him a twinge of discomfort. It had been Jeannie's adventurous plan to go snooping. And that they did.

I remember light filtered through the doorway as we peered in. At first, we were hesitant. What a surprise we found!

There could be no denying how unusual it was—especially for three poor teenagers who were all but stepping into a fantastic dream—the dream of finding something of value just by snooping. The house we were peering into was a palace, at least on the inside, a treasure trove disguised by a filthy old house on the outside. It was a combination that was not commonplace in a coal camp.

I remember my eyes darting around the glistening room, decorated with what appeared to be golden objects. I said, "My god, Jeannie, look at this place. It looks like the inside of a king's palace!"

It did. Even though the outside of LeRoy's house provided a perfect illusion—a rattletrap old house—that was not the case. There were golden vases on marble tables and eye-catching medieval tapestries adorning the walls.

Yeah, something was out of the ordinary. It was the sun throwing its afternoon rays through the open door that set the mood of the picture we were staring at.

Crowded together just a few feet inside the doorway, we gaped at the brilliance of the white marble reflecting the streaming light racing around them. What we saw was a kitchen, but a kitchen that could only be in a palace. Staring at the most unusual sight, Jeannie squealed, "Whoa! Get a load of the sink! Are those faucets gold? It sure looks like they are."

"Let's get inside and check this out," I hooted. I grabbed Jeannie's hand and started through the doorway.

"Holy shit…this place is immaculate! There isn't an ounce of dirt anywhere," I said, the first to step inside. "Holy shit again…look at the table and chairs!"

That was it for Jeannie. She had had it with my cussing. Bless her heart. She gave a yank on my arm. I spun around to look at her as she made the motion of washing out my mouth with soap. I rolled my eyes and pretended not to understand. "Danny! Stop your cussing! You don't have to make your point with swear words!"

Of course, that was just the signal for me to have more fun. I pretended to zip my mouth with two fingers, speaking through them. "OK, Princess Jeannie. Your wish is my command." The muffled words came through my cupped hand.

Not only did the walls light up but something more intriguing caught my eye—a yellow sheen. "Holy smokes! Get a load of this!" I said, pointing at it. "It looks like that candle is sitting on a little gold table!'

Holding Jeannie's hand, I gave her a gentle nudge to move toward it. I remember so vividly stroking the gold. "Oh my god! This is worth a fortune! We struck pay dirt!"

Then there was a soft chuckle from the darkness near the covered window in the living room.

Spinning around on one foot, I dropped Jeannie's hand and darted past Tony. The heavy tapestry was swinging back and forth. Slowly it swung back into position and once again stifled any light that tried to get in.

My mind churned with the possibilities. Who had just stuck his head through that window and cackled at us?

Jeannie bolted to my side and grabbed my arm. "What is it, Danny?" she whispered, holding onto me tightly.

As Danny relived those moments so long ago, a shiver of sadness overcame him. It had turned out to be the high-school bullies, Eddie and Terry, who were also snooping. It was different this time. There was no palace to greet Danny and Jerzom as they stepped into the house of Mochcom. Instead, it was a room loaded with filth.

Dirty clothes, dirty dishes, pails of stinking water, animal messes, shovels, and piles of books and newspapers were everywhere they looked. Danny and Jerzom were about to discover a house of filth and stench—an image that had a purpose. Soon it would become evident to Danny that there was more than met the eye, and Mochcom was hiding something.

"Holy rat crap! This place stinks!" snorted Danny. "Look at the stacks of crap he's piled up. What's he hiding?"

Making their way through the stench and garbage in the kitchen, they could only wonder what awaited them on the other side of the doorway in the back wall. They peered into the gloom as their eyes adjusted to the dark environment.

At that instant, the wind fluttered the raggedy old curtain on the window. A sliver of light danced around on the nasty old paint on the back wall and landed on the face of the monkey. His mouth was open, and his fangs showed as he started his shrill squealing.

From the middle of the kitchen where Danny and Jerzom were standing, they could clearly see two doors. One, which led outside, was behind them, and the other one was on the opposite wall, where the monkey was standing. From their vantage point, they could clearly discern that there was a room behind the door the monkey seemed to be guarding.

What that monkey was up to was a mystery. Danny speculated as he said in low growling voice, "I believe it is the same monkey that we found here the first time. Why is that monkey here, and what is it doing?"

Then the monkey darted out of sight. He bolted through the door on the back wall of the kitchen, making a terrible racket as he fled. But before the monkey managed to duck into the adjoining room, Danny saw something. He nudged Jerzom. "That monkey is holding something in its hand…I think it might be something that we need!"

No sooner had the words left Danny's mouth than the noise stopped.

The eerie silence pressed on as the wind fluttered the kitchen window drapes. "Jerzom, follow me!" mumbled Danny.

Walking ever so gingerly, they guarded their movements as they walked across the kitchen floor.

When they stood in the doorway, they could clearly see that the room into which the monkey had just darted into was a bedroom, as the outline of a bed was visible. Yet it was not at all clear what else awaited them there. At that point, Jerzom asked, "What's in there?"

Although the opening was only two feet wide, enough light was filtering through to give a dim glow, revealing another room filled with filth. Heavy drapes hung over the only window, letting almost no sunlight through.

At first, Danny saw nothing in the inky black darkness except the dark image of a bed. Then he spotted something.

Squinting, he started muttering. "Something is reflecting what little light is coming through this doorway—it's like a highly polished mirror on the wall."

It was when Danny was trying to focus on the shiny object that he saw the primate's face. Standing beneath the little mirror on the wall was the monkey.

Danny watched. The monkey stayed still. He squealed no more.

Then, in what looked like a gesture of defiance, the monkey raised his arm with the star-shaped key object.

"That monkey has something. What is it? Yeah, I'm sure we need it," said Danny to alert Jerzom.

Reaching behind him, Danny found Jerzom's hand and said, "Let's walk slowly in and get the door closed so that damn monkey can't escape!"

In moments, Danny and Jerzom were through the small opening and inside the bedroom.

Jerzom moved to the right and grabbed the door. He closed it. Blackness was everywhere.

Jerzom asked, "Danny, this is eerie. Is it safe to be in here?"

Danny said, "*No*, but I think we must. Let's look. Viracocha warned me to stay and find what is in this sanctuary of evil."

The supreme god is communicating with Danny. The thought raced through Jerzom's mind. *Evil is everywhere, and I can only hope Danny will prevail.*

The tenseness of Jerzom's body was evident to Danny, and so he searched for words that would be of some consolation. "Mochcom is in Granite Springs. He's masquerading as Pastor Duncan or Pastor Martin or whoever, and we have at least a half hour."

Reluctantly, Jerzom said, "OK."

Slowly, they wandered into the pitch-black room.

Out of view of Danny and Jerzom, the monkey, like a bronze statue, remained huddled next to the wall beneath the little mirror. With no light to expose his whereabouts, he was safe for the moment.

Managing to get to the window where only a sliver of light made its way into the bedroom, Danny pulled the heavy tapestry drapes back a few inches, letting more light into the room.

Simultaneously, Danny and Jerzom spotted the monkey.

Jerzom asked, "What is it doing?"

Jumping up and down, the creature still held the star-shaped key object in its hand. His fingers gripped the iron ring to which a key was attached.

It didn't take much light to get the little mirror on the wall to show its presence once more.

"There's a hole in the wall. It looks like a star-shaped hole in that metal thing on the wall that is reflecting light," said Jerzom. And as if thinking out loud, Jerzom spoke softly. "Does that thing on the key ring the monkey is holding fit that hole?"

His voice barely above a whisper, Danny replied, "Yes, I think it does. Viracocha has warned me that we need to get it."

With a feeling of urgency, worrying that Mochcom was lurking nearby, Jerzom asked, "How do we get it from the monkey?"

"Jerzom, stand by the door! Don't let him escape, and I'll take care of that little monster," said Danny serenely, so as not to alert the monkey or startle him into making a rash move.

Hearing the rustling in the dark, Jerzom watched the silhouette of Danny at the curtains as his voice broke the silence with a whiff of a whisper. "I'm going to secure the window and pull the drapes back just a crack more so we can see."

"OK, the window is closed," said Danny. "Now what I am going to have you do is gently pick up that pail next to you, the one by your left foot."

Planning was essential for all to go smoothly as clockwork.

"I've got this table in my hands," said Danny in a low voice.

Made of solid-black-walnut wood, it was heavy. Yet for Danny, the table was like a small rock.

With only the splinter of light filtering through the window, Danny's silhouette was all that Jerzom could see as he watched the god effortlessly lift the table above his head.

The monkey had not moved.

Danny was ready. "We need lots of noise. OK, on three, you throw that bucket at the wall where the hole is. I will throw this table. When it breaks to pieces, that animal will drop whatever it has."

There was silence. Then the counting started ever so softly. "One. Two. Three—*go!*"

The table and bucket were on the mark, flying through the air like missiles fired from a fighter jet.

The monkey was startled by the unexpected explosion of the table hitting the solid wall and the clattering of the metal pail. Broken wood flew like shrapnel everywhere. The squealing and howling was deafening. The monkey leaped. He dropped the key ring and bounded onto the bed, jumping in confusion. Realizing he had dropped the ring, the monkey leaped back off bed to get the key ring.

The primate's speed was no match for Danny. Instantly, Danny grabbed a chest of drawers next to the bed and hurled it like a second missile. It slammed into the keys on the floor. Splintering wood and nasty old clothes flew everywhere. The monkey shifted its attack from the keys to Jerzom. Danny's ring was in full swing. The bolt of green light that hit the monkey slammed him into the overturned pail of slop on the floor. Howling in rage, he raced for the window and smashed through it.

When the last piece of broken glass hit the floor, the only sound was a quiet rustling of leaves on the tree outside the window.

That silence was short-lived. "I hear whimpering or something or someone sobbing," said Jerzom.

Danny missed Jerzom's comments. He was looking out the window to see where the monkey was going. The creature ran to the woodshed and darted in.

Maybe it was a coincidence and maybe not. A cloud moved. The sun showed its face. The rays of light hit something on the nightstand that gave off a purple glow.

Slowly, Danny picked it up. "My god, it is Mochcom's black ring! We have it!" whispered Danny in a low voice.

It was the eerie sounds of torment coming from behind the wall that held Jerzom's attention, not what Danny was doing. And since Danny's words were muffled and unrecognizable, the ring was a mystery to Prince Jerzom. He had something else on his mind—the noises coming from behind the bedroom wall.

Jerzom was shuffling through the broken debris at the base of the wall, looking. He spotted the iron ring with the star-shaped key-like device.

Holding the ring in his hand, Jerzom said, "Danny, someone or something is on the other side of this wall."

Danny was fiddling with the black stone ring and did not see Jerzom insert the multipointed key into the hole on the wall and turn it.

Sssssrrrrreeeecccchhh! Ssrrreeeeecccchhhssssaah! Clunk!

The entire back wall of the bedroom moved and exposed a lightless hole.

"Hell, look at that!" yelled Jerzom.

"*Holy Shit, Jerzom!*" hollered Danny. "Do you see what I see?"

Even though Danny was startled, he focused on the glow of two little faces peering out of the inky darkness of what appeared to be a black-marble cavern.

It was not the black ring that Danny had just stuffed in his Levi's pocket but the unfolding scene that revealed why they had been told to find what Mochcom was hiding. Enough light shone in to expose the horror in progress.

Words could not describe the fear in the eyes of the two faces that stared back at Danny and Jerzom. Yet frightened as they were, they remained still. With eyes that never blinked, they focused on Danny and then on Jerzom. Covered with filth and dirt, they were all but unrecognizable as living creatures.

"What or who are they?" asked Jerzom, seeing something that seemed like human faces.

Moving his eyes from the dark, cave-like entrance, he spotted something else on the nightstand next to where the black ring had been. Racing like a bolt of high voltage electricity, Danny's mind made the connection. *That flashlight...is it? Yes, it is Tony's Boy Scout light!*

"Jerzom, hang on," said Danny.

Danny grabbed it. He shone the light into the dark abyss. At that point, he recognized the room. Hidden behind the bedroom wall was the marble-walled room of a palace. It was the same, yet it seemed different. Danny remembered white-marble walls, but that was not what he was staring at. These walls were black marble. The room no longer bore any resemblance to a grand palace. Now it had the essence of a torture chamber with no exit.

Two small, frightened boys were huddled together on the floor. They were pale and gaunt.

Danny's light bounced off the four walls. The room appeared to be square, maybe twenty feet by twenty. A pile of rags on the floor looked like a makeshift bed. A five-gallon bucket in the back corner must have been the toilet. The stench was unbearable, reeking of human waste. There were no windows or furniture.

As he stared at the scene, Danny coped with a pain that wrenched him to his core, his soul aching in disbelief. *My lord, talk about a death hole. Oh, that bastard! How? How? Innocent little boys!*

Danny was no longer silent, as he could not hold back, and not catching himself, his chilling words came forth somberly. "Mochcom traps little kids and keeps them in this dungeon until they are teenagers. He carries out ritual sacrifices in the woodshed." Then, his voice exploding, he roared, *"Oh my God of the universe, I will send that gorom to the depths of hell if it is the last thing I do."*

Frightened by the volume and anger of Danny's outburst, the two boys started screaming at the tops of their lungs.

"Danny, we have to do something," said Jerzom in a quiet, serene voice. "These boys need—"

"I'll take care of this," said Danny, not letting Jerzom finish. In seconds, Danny was standing over the boys. He picked them up, one in each arm.

Until this point, all language had been in the royal language of Kopaz, so the boys didn't comprehend a word of what Danny had just said, only that he had spoken with force. Now Danny spoke to them in English.

"My name is Danny. I'm the royal prince of Supreme God Viracocha, and I am here to rescue you from the disciple of Dark God Zuron."

Jerzom didn't understand English. The boys did. It didn't squelch their fears. Their sobbing continued.

"What are your names?" asked Danny.

They said nothing. Their eyes remained focused on Danny's.

With his arms still held tightly around the boys, Danny walked out of the cave-like room. He positioned his ring finger at the outer wall of the filthy room, drapes flapping in the wind blowing through the shattered window.

"Watch closely, and do not be afraid. Can you do that?" asked Danny.

They nodded their little heads, which were not six inches from Danny's. Their sobbing had subsided a bit.

"Good. I am a god, a good god, and the bad man that put you in there is very evil, and I am going to do this to him. Watch closely."

Before their eyes, Danny's ring exploded the outside wall into smithereens, reducing it to fiery ashes and smoke.

Their little bodies were tense as rocks, and Danny held them tightly, feeling every emotion penetrating the small boys.

"Do you guys believe me when I say I am a god?" asked Danny in a forceful voice.

They nodded, saying nothing.

"*OK, good!*" Danny looked at one and then the other. "I am going to do the same thing to that evil man who threw you in that hole!"

He felt them relax. "You boys are darling little kids, and I am going to take care of you and help you. Do you believe me?"

Their fear of Danny was drifting away as he smiled sweetly at one and then, turning his head, at the other. "What are your names?" asked Danny again.

This time one boy answered. "I'm Danny, and he's Tony, and we are twins."

Danny laughed. "Good! Hello, Danny. Hello, Tony!" He thought, *Danny and Tony…coincidence?*

For the first time, Danny thought he saw twinges of smiles on their faces. He went on. "My best friend's name was Tony!"

They nodded slowly and said, "Our dad was Tony, also."

Hmm, thought Danny, *this is strange.*

The beam of Danny's flashlight was accidently directed into the dark cavern again. Danny saw something familiar. Holding the light steady in his hand, he shone it on the floor next to the pile of rags that had been the boys' bed.

He turned to Jerzom. "Would you hold these brave little guys for a minute?"

"Sure," replied Jerzom, as Danny was already in the process of transferring the boys.

Danny said, "Guys, this is Prince Jerzom. He can't speak English, but he is a good guy, and he is a royal prince from Kopaz!"

That got their attention. With eyes wide open, they studied Jerzom, as he was now holding one in each arm.

Danny walked to the rags, stooped, and picked up a CoalVille Pirate Log. His heart raced as he opened it and read the words silently.

You borrowed
my 55 Chevy
and took Katelynn
to Lover's Lane
and then what
... you Devil?
Tony, I did not
even get a chance
to "Christen"
my Truck!

Your
Best
Buddy
Danny

"Holy shit," said Danny under his breath so that only he could hear. "This is Tony's high-school yearbook!" Danny could not believe his eyes as he turned the page.

My Dearest
Tony
I hope Someplace
in the Vast
Universe You
Can hear me
Call your Name.
We had twins.
I named them
Tony and Danny—
ALL my Love Kate Lynn.

"Oh my lord," he said, speaking in the language of the royals. "These are Tony's sons!"

"What?" answered Jerzom. Though he had no idea what Danny was rambling about, it was obvious that something had changed.

Walking to Jerzom and the boys, two little redheads with freckled faces, Danny asked, "Where is your mom?"

The flood of tears told Danny that they'd witnessed something so horrific that the deepest caves in their little minds hid the secret. Their facial expressions spoke loud, even when the dam of silence between them was greater than Hoover Dam on the Colorado River. He would not make them relive the scene of horror etched in their minds, yet Danny could guess the details. Danny grappled with the horrific image in his mind as he thought, *That monster, Pastor Duncan, killed their mother, KateLynn—maybe right in front of them. My god, how insane!*

"Tony and Danny," said Danny, putting his hand on Little Tony's shoulder, "you will never see such bad things again…I promise."

The last word hadn't yet dropped from his mouth when the crashing sound of a door being slammed open pierced the air.

Loud footsteps in the next room left Danny with no option. "Grab my hand, Jerzom. We fly!"

Danny, Jerzom, Little Danny, and Little Tony flew away on a green beam of light. They exited through the expansive hole in the wall created only minutes earlier by Danny. He had destroyed the wall to demonstrate his powers to two helpless boys, to show that he was indeed a god. Little Danny and Little Tony were no longer trapped in a destiny that would have been more horrendous than words could describe. Now they were on a journey of hope, led by a young god.

Sssscccuuuuuuurrrreee! The sharp sound came from the house as the monkey bared his sharp fangs, a full display of his chilling rage.

CHAPTER 5

CoalVille Tipple and Plans Are Made

Now they had no choice. Although the place was right, the time was wrong. The lock of Aerapondes's hair was nowhere to be found, and yet Gorom Mochcom knew what was going on.

Saving two young boys from human sacrifice was one thing, but discovering who they were was far more than even Danny could conceive. Some mysteries, like the Veil of Time, remained covered until ready to be revealed to those who searched for secrets. Was it fate or just an accident that Danny and Jerzom rescued Little Danny and Little Tony? Yet even more puzzling, could there be a greater purpose not yet divulged? How did Little Danny and Little Tony fit into the picture?

The ride of a beam of green light only lasted a few brief moments, but it was a new experience for those two young boys. Their existence in a hellish dungeon was all they had known for too long. A whole new world was at their fingertips, and boy had it started out with a bang on the ride of their lives.

Danny chuckled and said, "I see you guys like my cool ride!" He could see the smiles on two little guy's faces.

Now standing on firm ground, they said in unison, "How did you do that?"

Danny's chuckle grew louder as he answered, "I'm a god!"

The young god's mind was full, but at the forefront was a single thought. *These little boys are safe forever and will play a role in Viracocha's plan for the human race.*

At the CoalVille tipple, there was little cover, so caution was paramount. Keeping the curiosity of two five-year-old boys in check was a challenge for Danny. As an only child, his interaction with younger people had been limited to a few isolated instances, and for the most part, this was a new experience for him.

Without the constant presence of coal miners milling around and doing their jobs, the sagebrush surrounding the tipple was no longer under siege by stamping feet. It was flourishing, and that was good.

As Danny stood on that hallowed ground, where so many had given their lives for the survival of their beloved wives and children, his mind could picture their faces as they worked to mine and process the coal that powered the trains that were the might and backbone of America.

Gazing at the CoalVille tipple, Danny was sure he saw the faces of coal miners doing their jobs. It was obvious to Prince Jerzom that Danny was deep in thought about something, but what it was he could not see. Danny was looking at the images of miners who had been trapped or buried alive and were now living in the Land of the Dead.

The dynamite vault had been undisturbed for years until Danny gave it a new function as a hiding place for the gifts from the gods. Now this cement hole in the ground, which had been all but retired, had a new purpose. Its old function—to store dangerous explosives that changed the underground landscape of a coal camp and the course of destiny of a band of coal miners—had been replaced with a new function—to hide explosive gifts that could change the universe and the course of destiny for all living creatures.

And during that period of changing functions, large patches of sagebrush had sprung up to make a perfect camouflage blind. Danny was sure they were safe from the observation of curious onlookers busy going about their business in a coal camp on November 22, 1963.

"We need to get out of here. What do we have to do, Jerzom?" asked Danny.

"What do we have to do?" echoed Jerzom as his mind was set in motion. *Hmm, Danny must want something. I wonder what?*

Realizing he had spoken prematurely, Danny said, "Give me a minute, and I will tell you what it is that I need of you."

Everything was new and strange to the two boys. Standing between Danny and Jerzom, Little Danny and Little Tony watched and listened, their curiosity on the rise. And fortunately, all four were hidden by tall sagebrush that kept any unwanted eyes from peering where they were not wanted.

"First," Danny said, "we need to get the treasure out of the vault."

"OK, on three, let's lift," said Jerzom as he and Danny prepared to move the massive cover from the vault. But Jerzom decided it was time for a bit of humor, some entertainment for the two little guys who were being exposed to one of the newest gods of the universe.

"Hey, I thought you were supposed to help," said Danny as Jerzom only pretended to hold onto the iron ring of the lid. Jerzom grinned as he watched the young god effortlessly lift the four-hundred-pound chunk of concrete and set it out of the way.

Little Danny and Little Tony could see who was doing the heavy lifting and who was faking it. "Wow! How did he do that?" The two small boys had no problem judging the weight of a massive piece of concrete used to seal a dynamite vault.

Danny just laughed and pointed to Jerzom. "He was supposed to help!"

With the treasure exposed, it was time to get down to serious business.

The question that Danny had asked earlier hung in the air and also in Jerzom's mind. Yet Danny knew what must be puzzling Jerzom, so it was time. "The dials on the Sun Energy Transformer—we need to set them so that we land in CoalVille in March of 1958," said Danny as he looked at Jerzom and pointed to the treasure.

Danny's earlier question to Jerzom was suddenly not a mystery. He knew what they had to do. "Got it," answered Jerzom. Danny nodded as Jerzom continued. "I have to study my brother's journal. Knowing Kashom, he has recorded every little excruciating detail."

As Jerzom made his remarks and started leafing through the golden journal, Little Danny and Little Tony moved closer to get a bird's-eye view of what the prince of Kopaz was up to.

"Ah ha! Here it is. Kashom says each dial setting represents so many years, and the dials have to be in a specific format." Jerzom beamed as he made sure Danny was pleased with his findings.

"Good work, royal prince," said Danny. "Just don't screw up!"

Jerzom studied each word in Kashom's journal. No one had to tell Jerzom the dangers of a fatal mistake, so he carefully reviewed each instruction at least three times. Mumbling, Jerzom said, "When I see my brother, I'm going to give him holy hell for this!"

"What?" asked Danny. "Is there a problem?"

"No, all is good. It's just that Kashom writes in riddles, and so I have to dig though all the pages to get what he is really saying," grumbled Jerzom, knowing in his heart that soon he could see his brother in the flesh if all went as was written in the ancient journal of Kashom.

As Danny smiled at the two little curiosity seekers, his mind found relief. *It's good that Kashom had the foresight to protect the most valuable information in the universe, for if this information fell into the wrong hands, the war would be lost forever.*

Time marched on. Jerzom continued his work. His heavy eyebrows pulled down over his sharp eyes with intense concentration as he remarked, "But it is more than just the time dials. Somehow, the space dials have something to do with it as well."

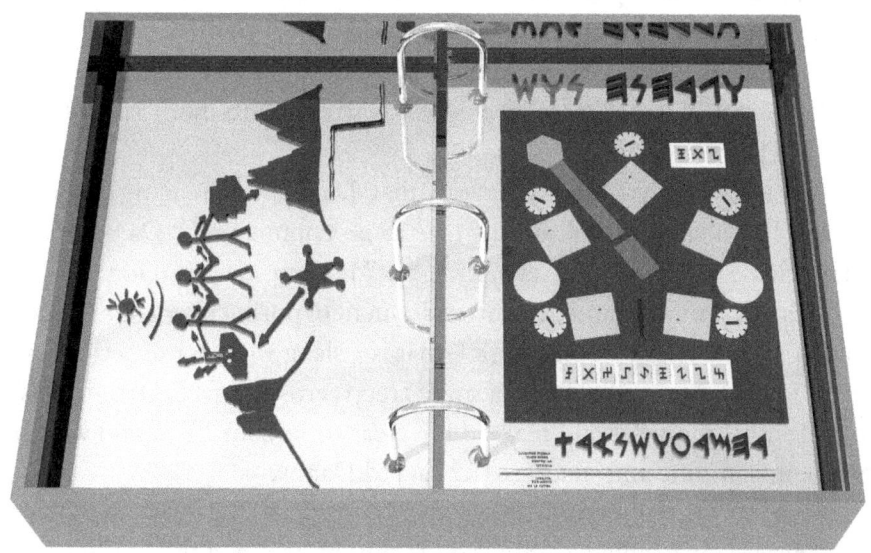

"What is the prince saying?" asked Little Tony.

"I'm not sure. He sounds just like your father did when he was studying all that stuff. To me, it was and is just a bunch of gobbledygook!" said Danny, laughing and making his funny face to the boys where he put a frown on his face, entangled his fingers, covered his face with them, and slowly slid them down to reveal a smile.

The boys laughed. Then Little Danny asked, "Did our dad figure it out?"

"He sure did!" replied Danny, giving each of the boys a high five.

"OK, I've got it. We know one point in time and space—CoalVille on November 22, 1963. So if we get another point in time and space that we know, we are home free! And as you say, Danny, voilà!"

"Voilà, my ass!" said Danny in English. Realizing he had spoken in English instead of the royal language, Danny looked at Little Tony and Little Danny. "Sorry, boys, my English is not for your ears." Danny then looked at Jerzom and repeated his words in the royal language of Kopaz.

Danny's puzzled expression left Jerzom scratching his head in bewilderment. *I just figured this out...what the hell is wrong with him?*

Maybe it's not a good idea to think *What the hell is wrong with him?* when you're dealing with a god—even a god who is your friend. Perhaps it would be more prudent to remember who and what you are dealing with.

"So you're wondering what the hell is wrong with me?" asked Danny quietly. He waited for a response.

It was suddenly clear to Jerzom that Danny was reading his mind. Jerzom had a sincere look on his face as he commented, "Danny, I'm so sorry. Please forgive me. I...er...I...aah..." Jerzom struggled for words.

"It's OK. I understand that the excitement of poring over your brother's golden journals put you on a high—that is a slang word for experiencing a jolt of joy," Danny said as he let a smile creep across his face. Danny paused to collect his thoughts and make them clear to Jerzom. "You said we need two points in time and space, right?" asked Danny.

"Yep," answered Jerzom.

"Here is my problem...the second point in time and space. If we guess and get sent to some unknown place in some weird time...well, you get my point. We are all shit out of luck!" said Danny seriously.

"You are right. What we—" That was all Jerzom managed to say. He was about to add something else when Danny broke in.

Now with a serious look, Danny queried, "Can you leave the dials that deal with space untouched and just change the dials that deal with time a tiny bit?"

"That may work, Danny," replied Jerzom.

Little Danny and Little Tony watched and waited. During their years of imprisonment in a hidden dungeon in a gorom's palace, they had mastered the art of speaking in silent words.

"It is ready," said Jerzom.

The boys were fascinated, and the prospect of going into space and time was better than any tale of fantasy they had created in their minds, whiling away the hours locked in a monster's palace. But their words weren't entirely silent—at least not to the mind of a god—and the hubbub between them did not go unnoticed.

"Flying on a green light *was* cool," said Danny, as he had overheard their private conversation. "If you think flying on a green beam of light is cool, wait for the next ride!"

And so ended their presence on that sad day of November 22, 1963. Little Danny and Little Tony stood between Danny and Jerzom, and all four held hands. Danny was at the helm. He grasped the green bar of the Sun Energy Transformer and turned the key. Then they were gone.

CHAPTER 6

The Riddle of Zuron

"The site of the black pit defines the color of the scent...an interesting riddle provided to us by Zuron. He sits in his pantheon on Zolob and laughs!"

No doubt Supreme God Viracocha was making a point. Yet as Viracocha softly spoke the riddle, he was not laughing. His recital was for a purpose. There could be no doubt as to the purpose of the dark god's riddle. After all, a conquest that would eventually result in a winner-take-all victory was well underway, and the answer to the riddle was still elusive.

Tensions were on the rise. It was not only Viracocha and his wife, Neferdor, that were feeling the weight of doom and chaos descending on them as a smothering final end to democracy in the universe but also the entire Quorum of Primeval Gods who sat at the council table felt the impending loss. No one could predict for sure what life would be like throughout the reaches of eternities if Zuron were triumphant, but the very thought of a bloodthirsty dictator ruling the universe left little to the imagination. Evil, horrors, and abominations beyond description would prevail everywhere.

It was meeting time again, and no one had to guess the course the discussion at the council table of the primeval gods would take. Without a single vacant seat at the table, there could be no question that the decisive point of why the meeting was convened was profound.

"Do you know what is happening? Do you care?" hissed Viracocha.

Glaring at those sitting closest to him, he put his finger on a set of golden plates bound into a tablet sitting in front of him. "Have you read this? Or are you all blind and ignorant?"

While Viracocha was focusing his attention on a large set of golden tablets, Tammuz turned to his right and faced Neptune. Tammuz lifted his hand to shield his face from those who were seated and mouthed some words to Neptune. "Who is the traitor? Someone who sits among us is bringing about our end!"

Tammuz's comments did not go unnoticed by Viracocha. The supreme god reached and grabbed the stack of golden tablets bound by U-shaped fasteners. Large and heavy as they were, it was of no consequence to Viracocha to flick them with his middle finger and send them flying down the tabletop.

As the stack slid to a halt in front of the god Tammuz, Viracocha asked, "Do you know what it says?"

Tammuz took a moment to collect his composure, or at least he attempted to do so. He dropped his hand from his face and looked down the table. Then he looked back up at the supreme god. Their eyes locked. Viracocha glared intensely and waited for a response.

"Ah, er. It has been a while, most honorable supreme god," answered Tammuz.

"Well, at least you are not hiding from me, or are you?" snarled Viracocha. "Your hand is small and offers not much cover when you are looking for the security of being out of sight or invisible! Is that not so, Tammuz?"

Thousands of giant, sparkling diamonds in the overhead chandeliers reflected the brilliance of Kolar, and the dancing rays lit up the red-diamond table as if it were on fire.

A red glow surrounded Tammuz as if he were caught in the spotlight of guilt and was blushing under the scrutiny of an inquisition. But was that the case? He had just asked Neptune a pointed question. Now it seemed that the attention was not on Neptune but on him, so was it the reflection off the red diamond table or the blood rushing to his face?

There could be no denying the gravity of the situation. The end was coming. Viracocha was running out of options. Yes, it was obvious that Zuron had one of the code words and associated symbols. With only the one word, at least he would not be able to score the ultimate victory in the deadly tournament of the War of the Gods. Or would he? Most likely Viracocha was filling his mind with every detail of what the end would look like.

Viracocha spoke the words that were consuming his every thought. "Do you know that Zuron cannot destroy my planet, Volob, without both code words?

The supreme god did not wait for an answer. "But he can destroy every other planet in the universe! So what does that leave us to govern? Please don't answer, as I can answer my own question with one word...*nothing!* No longer will our mission to govern the universe in the name of harmony and good will for all creatures be of any consequence. We no longer can bend the arc of justice to the innocent. We will be like rats in a cage for the eternities, tormented by none other than Zuron!"

To describe Viracocha's golden throne as opulent would be an understatement. It was more massive than a private spectator suite at Dodger Stadium. He leaned forward. "My throne is nice, would you not agree? In fact, my golden throne makes a statement of prosperous exorbitance. It makes an Earthling's ballpark seat of luxury look like nothing but a pittance."

In a forceful tone, Viracocha roared out, "Surrounding the supreme god with extravagance unbounded provides me with a seat of power at the center of the universe without question, but of what use is this seat if I govern *nothing?*"

His focus turned to a vote that had once been held at the council table. "Was it not so long ago, perhaps two million or so years, that we had a vote?" growled Viracocha as he called out a group of gods by name—the very gods whose seats at the table had been moved to the furthest end of the table.

Glaring all the way to the south end of the table, Viracocha looked at that group of gods and snarled, "Tammuz, Ishtar, Dumuzi, Horus, Hathor,

Zeus, Neptune, Plato, Jupiter, Asherah, Osiris, Astarte, Inanna, and Kybele. Oh, how fitting it is to remember that vote at this table. As I recall, you cast the fourteen of the forty-nine votes to support Zuron, or does my memory fail me?"

The winds of Volob were blowing, and the ruling gods were facing not only the displeasure of Viracocha but also their imminent destruction if the crisis was not dealt with quickly. Time as they knew it was almost gone. All that Viracocha could do was forge on in hopes that by some strange circumstance the unsolved Riddle of Zuron would no longer be an elusive string of words that would bring about the end of the universe.

Those fourteen gods sitting at the south end of his table were at the center of a brewing storm.

Viracocha's look intensified. "Ah yes, fourteen of my most loyal gods. You have sat at my table longer than any other, so how was it that you cast your votes against me?" Viracocha snarled.

For over two million years, those words had been locked up inside Viracocha. Perhaps his so-called loyal gods had thought it was over. Little did they fathom that the memory of the supreme god was as infinite as the universe. Viracocha had never forgotten that these fourteen had chosen not to support Viracocha but instead cast their votes in favor of Zuron and his plan to establish one church, the Church of Zuron, for the human race.

"How was it that two million years ago when Zuron and his followers… ah, those votes…let's remember. It was not only the thirty-five who walked their saggy asses out of my pantheon and into Zuron's Black Royal Temple—those cowards who voted to support Zuron—but also, there are fourteen who voted in support of Zuron and elected to sit at my table…is that not so?"

His last words caused a pause. Still almost snarling, Viracocha carefully studied the faces of gods in front of him. "The Black Royal Temple had been only words bandied around at the time the war began. And so what was that all about?"

Hmm, thought Viracocha, *that's a strange look on Jupiter's mug. Why? Why is it that Tammuz's face lit up when I said the words "Black Royal Temple"?*

"How can it be that my master plan was so easily questioned by you, the 'Band of Fourteen'?" The supreme god called out those sitting at the furthest end of the table from him. "For billions of years, it had been unquestioned. You all know it, as I simply stated and declared," bellowed Viracocha.

Pointing at the massive set of golden tablets sitting in front of the god Tammuz, Viracocha rasped, "So, Tammuz, if you can't remember, how about reading what is in front of you, and perhaps your memory will be refreshed!"

As all eyes were on Tammuz, he slowly flipped the pages to the one entitled *Viracocha's Master Plan for the Universe* and began to read.

"All inhabitants of the universe can choose their own courses of existence. They can choose to inflict harm and abuse on their fellow human beings, as well as other created creatures. They can choose to deceive, manipulate, and ravage fellow human beings, as well as other created creatures. They can choose to bear false witness, bully, and impose their wills on other fellow human beings and created creatures. Or they can choose to treat all human beings and living creatures with kindness, love, and respect and help those in need. However, their decisions, how they choose to chart their courses, have consequences. The quality of their existence in the Land of the Dead once they journey down the River Styx will reflect their treatment of fellow human beings and all created creatures that they had dominion over. Ill treatment of fellow humans and creatures will result in howling in miserable agony for the eternities, while good will and kind treatment will result in pleasure and joy throughout the eternities."

A spark of delight glowed in the bosom of each god who had rejected Zuron's plan, and smiles were evident from the executive branch. The supreme god leaned forward and put his elbows on the table. He too felt a quick grin stretch across his face as he said, "Fifty-one, yes, fifty-one saw the foolishness of Zuron's plan, such as it was."

But even for the fifty-one who supported Viracocha and Neferdor, it might not matter now. Deep in Viracocha's soul, he feared that it soon would be finished. Yet even though it might not matter when the war ended and all was gone, right now Viracocha wanted to know why fourteen of his most loyal and trusted gods had voted against him.

Viracocha stopped. He looked on, as if to beckon those sitting at the end of the table to come forth with a rational reason why they had voted against him and in favor of Zuron's plan. Tammuz, Dumuzi, and Neptune just stared back at the supreme god, blank looks on their faces. Their faces revealed nothing. Maybe they had good reasons. Maybe not. Maybe they had been hungry for power at the time they had cast their votes, and that was their way of questing after it…to follow Zuron, who might be a more indulgent leader.

Viracocha spoke firmly. "Why? Why, Tammuz, did you do it? If it will all be over soon, at least give me the pleasure of knowing why you betrayed me? What was it about what you just read that caused a canker to grow in your bosom that prompted you to cast a vote of yea for Zuron?"

Tammuz slowly pulled his mouth to a point of speech, but Viracocha cut him off and snarled, "Slide the tablets to Dumuzi so we can hear his tale of woe, as he is also a member of the Band of Fourteen, all of whom cast a yea vote for Zuron!"

And with the stack of golden tablets that kept the record of all the actions of all the primeval gods who had ever sat at the council table squarely in front of one of the oldest gods at the table, Dumuzi flippantly tossed a few pages of gold over the U-shaped fasteners to the page titled *Zuron's Master Plan for the Universe* and began to read. "There will be only one religion throughout the universe, the Church of Zuron. All human inhabitants of the universe will conform to a strict set of guidelines. Comply with the guidelines and death never comes. Break any of the guidelines and death is immediate, with a final state in the blackest abyss of the Land of the Dead."

"So that was it, Dumuzi? You liked only one church?" snarled Viracocha.

"Most eminent supreme god, as you are well aware, there are countless millions of religions throughout the universe, all worshipping who the hell knows what, and that was our problem. You had no plan to fix it! We knew Zuron would not be triumphant in his quest to secure a majority of votes, so we cast a vote not so much to support him but in defiance of there being no solution to the mess in the universe, a mess caused by these countless religions all based on the premise of a holy endeavor yet in reality driven by the love of money!" snarled Dumuzi back.

"Nicely put, Dumuzi!" said Viracocha. "So what say you now?"

It was evident to some, even if not all, why Viracocha sat silently listening to Dumuzi dig himself deeper into the hole into which he was figuratively crawling.

Dumuzi's snarly little smirk grew and stretched from ear to ear. He knew all too well that Viracocha had boxed himself in with the religious mess in the universe, so he felt obliged to pound the point home. Dumuzi ventured on. "Now it would seem that one church would make things simple. Especially with what had happened…untold numbers of religions sprang into existence—all of which are led by zealots who use the fear of death and what follows death to control the masses and who are primarily driven by the love of money."

His eyes locked with Viracocha's, and being a shrewd god, Dumuzi was careful not, figuratively speaking, to get his foot too near the jaws of a steel trap.

He lowered his voice and continued. "Was it not you, Viracocha, who insisted that the identity of all the ruling gods should be kept from the humans? Was that part of your plan, most honorable supreme god?"

Viracocha and all the gods were listening.

"How convenient!" snapped Dumuzi. "You, Supreme God, gave the religious zealots the green light to go forward! Ah yes. Without knowing who we are, what we look like, and what we stand for, the founders of religious sects realized that almost any god would do. They made one up—an invisible, old, long-bearded, white-haired god and gave him the name—Almighty God!"

Now waving his index finger first at the stack of golden tables and then at Viracocha, Dumuzi stood so all could see. He spoke loudly. "You, Viracocha, gave Zuron the green light. You are the one to blame! Zuron challenged your plan, and thus the vote on Zuron's plan was called. It failed by a two-vote margin, and therein is your dilemma, Supreme God! You recall, as contentions were on the rise because of Zuron's failed attempt to overthrow you, most eminent supreme god, and with such a close split in the votes at this table, a mediator stepped forward, your beloved son, the god Ra.

"Your son's final compromise made sense two million years ago, and it makes sense now. You can't deny that the outcome of the conquest is final. You accepted your son's advice and presented it to us for our approval. It passed. In essence, a war game got underway."

Flipping to the relevant gold plate among the set of tablets, Dumuzi, still standing, began to read the page titled *Ra's War-Game Plan* out loud. "Viracocha retains his position as the supreme god of the universe with the seat of government on Volob for as long as his planet exists. Viracocha and Neferdor will exhort their influence through the royal prince of Viracocha (TRPOV) and the royal princess of Neferdor (TRPON). TRPOV and TRPON shall be gods in training and come from the human race. If valiant, they will have the opportunity to be elevated to seats in golden thrones at the council table of Viracocha and his Quorum of Primeval Gods. Zuron will live in his pantheon on Zolob and wield influence through those disciples he chooses to dwell with humans. A giant lens called Lenszar will have the potential to focus the destructive inferno energy of the star Kolar on either Volob or Zolob."

"*Stop!*" shouted Viracocha, cutting Dumuzi off. "We all know my son's plan. You need not take up our time with your ramblings any longer."

Smiling like the cat that just ate the rat, Dumuzi replied, "You do not like my display of oratory, my going over all the details? Let me have my final word, Viracocha!"

Dumuzi charged on. "We all knew how the vote turned out. As you recall, the vote to approve Ra's plan passed sixty votes to forty. A shout of joy erupted in our council! 'Let the War of the Gods begin!'"

It was time for the supreme god to break his silence. "Hmm, so you and your compatriots could guess the outcome of a vote before we cast it? How clever! It was you, Dumuzi, who just said that. You said that I was the reason for the mess in the universe, that I had no plan to fix the mess, and so on and so on! So knowing, I guess through magic, that Zuron would not be triumphant in his quest to secure a majority of votes, you, along with thirteen of your saggy-assed cohorts, cast a vote simply to complain about what you saw as my failure to solve the mess in the universe caused by these countless religions based on the premise of a holy endeavor yet driven by the love of money! Dumuzi, I don't understand the logic behind your rambling nonsense!"

Dumuzi said nothing. Viracocha's face tightened with an outward show of displeasure as he snarled at Dumuzi. "You must think I am mad or, worse yet, an idiot of your caliber to think that I would buy your simple-minded story. You of all gods could not possibly have known the outcome of the vote before it was cast! If Zuron had won the majority of the votes—thanks to your help—I ask, where would we all be now? With Zuron running the universe, unleashing a reign of *hell* that would make the soul of any god worth his salt weep!"

Viracocha's fiery deep-set green eyes glared at Dumuzi as if they were poison darts. "*You idiot! You spout garbage!*"

Those words from the supreme god had barely left his mouth when the corps of buglers stood and the sergeant at arms stepped up to the podium to make an official announcement. "Supreme God, it is happening now. After two million years, this contest is coming to a final end. *Lenszar has moved once more! It appears Zuron is focusing Lenszar on another solar system!*"

Cutting Comanzar off, Viracocha shouted out an order. "Tell us again how Zuron can win the game! Make it simple so all can understand!"

Comanzar bowed. "Most honorable Supreme God Viracocha and Supreme Goddess Neferdor, your son, the god Ra, as you just discussed, put forth the rules of the game. I shall repeat them. Number one, Zuron needs two code words to program his GAMMAZEL in order to destroy the planet Volob. However, he only needs one code word to partially program his GAMMAZEL and destroy other planets. Evidently, he has one of the code words, as he has managed to incinerate entire solar systems.

"Number two. If Zuron can get the golden key from Neferzul, who is the royal princess of Neferdor, you lose the game. If he has the golden key, you will not be able to unlock and program your GAMMAZEL.

"Number three. If Zuron can kill the firstborn male of the new human race with his zedite knife, he will win the game, and you will lose. That firstborn male must come from the union of the royal prince of Viracocha and his mate, the royal princess of Neferdor. You, most eminent supreme god, and your wife, the supreme goddess, will pick the humans whom you want for your royal prince and princess."

And knowing the gravity of the growing calamity that was threatening total destruction, Comanzar drove his message home. "Zuron has only to accomplish one of these tasks and he wins. You, our supreme god and goddess, on the other hand, need the answer to his riddle, the Riddle of Zuron, to win. The answer needs to be programmed into our GAMMAZEL in order to focus Lenszar on Zuron's planet Zolob and destroy it."

"We have but one option," said Viracocha, "and that is to work harder to unravel the riddle, or we will be reduced to prisoners, rats in a cage for the eternities!"

The supreme god's order was not necessary, but there must have been a reason why he felt it necessary to go over the rules of game in such succinct language.

Eerie as it was, no one at the council table blinked. Yet there was one issue that dominated the supreme god's mind. It was real, and the war was underway. Viracocha could not shake the train of thought on his mind. *How? How could it be that Lenszar has moved? Who is the traitor among us? Dumuzi is too stupid, so is it Tammuz? Or who? Does Neptune have the brains to lead a betrayal?*

CHAPTER 7
Fire in the Sky

They believed they had what they needed. The new place and also the time, so all should be straightforward. With two points in time and space, Jerzom should be able to program the Sun Energy Transformer to where they go next. But progress can sometimes be in the wrong direction if not all is considered. Taking something at face value, one might say, "It was just a matter of time," and another might say, "It was not a matter of time." So what was it?

One thing was for sure. The War of the Gods was raging. And with that knowledge, the urgency of the mission of the royal prince of Viracocha would soon emerge. Yet when decisions impact humans living in faraway galaxies and stretch throughout all eternity, well, it might be worth the time to double-check your calculations, as a mistake in time might be fatal.

And so it was a matter of time before the war was lost—a matter of time to check and make sure they ended up in the right time. Balancing both was Danny's call.

They'd landed at nine in the morning, but the question was, nine o'clock on what day? And where exactly had they landed? Danny was confident that they were in Granite Springs or nearby, as they had not moved the dial that set the place on the Sun Energy Transformer. The date, however, was another story.

Then Danny recognized the place. They were a mile outside Granite

Springs on the banks of Bitter Creek. Finding a perfect hiding place for the gifts from the gods was crucial, and that managed to use up another hour. Fortuitously, another dynamite vault was close by. During the boom years of coal mining in the Scarlet Desert, there had been a need for well-placed dynamite vaults, and that now proved to be a blessing for Danny and the others.

When the treasure was secure, they took off with haste, as time was running out. The walk into Granite Springs took another hour from Danny's mission timetable.

Finally, they were on Main Street, and there Danny realized that they were not, as he had hoped, in 1958. The sleek, modern-looking cars and trucks roaring by gave him his first hint, but then he saw a license plate with a sticker reading "2001." That was a sure giveaway that it was not 1958.

Noon had not yet arrived, but they were hungry. Their pockets were so stuffed with cash that paying for food was of no consequence. And the perfect spot to eat was the restaurant in the lobby of the Grand Hotel at the corner of Broadway and Elk Streets.

"I know the perfect place to grab a bite to eat," said Danny.

It was decided…they would have a well-deserved lunch in the grand old hotel of Granite Springs.

Danny led the way. As he approached the lobby, he turned and looked at Jerzom. "We missed the time again, but we got the place."

"How do you know?" asked Jerzom.

"Take my word for it. I'm right," answered Danny.

The flurry of noise coming from the lobby of the Grand Hotel was anything but normal, and it beckoned to those passersby on the street, inviting them to step in and take a listen. Once inside, the TV grabbed them with the unfolding story.

There was a vacant table in clear view of the large-screen TV. The four travelers sat there and joined the rest of those watching the screen, unable to tear their eyes away.

The giant TV screen was a leap into the future for Danny. He had only ever seen old round-tube black-and-white TVs, which tended to display barely recognizable images, some of which appeared to be in a snowstorm. This was not the television he looked at now.

Holy shit, thought Danny. *Talk about forward progress…just look at the size of the TV, and it's stuck to the wall like a giant talking picture.*

Then it was not the TV that was capturing Danny's mind but the events unfolding before his eyes. *You've got to be kidding me! What the hell is going on?*

Clear as a bell, in vivid bright colors, the screen was filled with images of buildings, planes, people running from collapsing skyscrapers, cars, firemen in strange green clothing, policemen racing everywhere—all of which was foreign not only to Jerzom but also to Danny and the boys.

They were mesmerized by the terrible images on display—and for the reason for those images.

Struggling to keep his composure, Danny could not clear his mind of a single question. *What on earth is going on?*

As he managed to take bites of his triple hamburger and stuff a few fries in his mouth between glimpses of the unfolding attack on the United States, it was not only Danny who stared fixedly at the images unfolding but also a young prince from another place called Kopaz.

"What's happening?" whispered Jerzom.

"I don't know, but it is bad, whatever it is," answered Danny in a hushed voice.

Then he knew. The big bold letters streaming across the TV could not be misread.

> *This is an ongoing news bulletin—the United States is under attack! September 11, 2001 is a date that will live in infamy!*

The rerun of events was continuous. There could be no denying the magnitude of the horrific acts of terror against the city of New York and the peoples of America.

> *This is an ongoing news bulletin—the United States is under attack!*
>
> *7:58 a.m.   United Airlines Flight 175 departs Boston for Los Angeles, carrying 56 passengers, two pilots, and seven flight attendants. The Boeing 767*

is hijacked after takeoff and diverted to New York.

7:59 a.m.   *American Airlines Flight 11 departs Boston for Los Angeles, carrying 81 passengers, two pilots, and nine flight attendants. This Boeing 767 is also hijacked and diverted to New York.*

8:01 a.m.   *United Airlines Flight 93, a Boeing 757 carrying 38 passengers, two pilots, and five flight attendants, leaves Newark, New Jersey, for San Francisco.*

8:10 a.m.   *American Airlines Flight 77 departs Washington's Dulles International Airport for Los Angeles, carrying 58 passengers, two pilots, and four flight attendants. The Boeing 757 is hijacked after takeoff.*

8:46 a.m.   *American Flight 11 from Boston crashes into the North Tower at the World Trade Center.*

9:03 a.m.   *United Flight 175 from Boston crashes into the South Tower at the World Trade Center. The US Federal Aviation Administration shuts down all New York area airports.*

9:21 a.m.   *Bridges and tunnels leading into New York City are closed.*

9:25 a.m.   *All domestic flights are grounded by the US Federal Aviation Administration.*

9:45 a.m.   *American Flight 77 crashes into the Pentagon.*

10:05 a.m.   *The South Tower at the World Trade Center collapses.*

10:05 a.m.   *The White House is evacuated.*

10:10 a.m.   *A large section of one side of the Pentagon collapses.*

10:10 a.m.   *United Flight 93 crashes in a wooded area in Pennsylvania, after passengers confront hijackers.*

10:28 a.m.   *The North Tower at the World Trade Center*
collapses.

"Mr. God, what is going on?" asked Little Tony as he clutched his fork.

"I don't know, Little Tony, but it looks bad!" answered Danny.

Danny, Jerzom, and the boys had their eyes glued to the TV, taking in every detail of the unfolding events, the images recording themselves indelibly in their minds.

"Danny, what do we do?" asked Jerzom as the boys looked at the unfolding horror story on the TV.

Momentarily, Danny said noting. He was deep in thought. *If we don't pick the point in time, the Sun Energy Transformer must gravitate to turning points. It appears that it is drawn to those moments in time where great and devastating events took place, events that changed the course of history. That must be what is happening. We have two dates that defined the course of history: November 22, 1963 and September 11, 2001. Hmmm!*

In the hubbub of excitement and commotion, whatever conversation was going on at their lunch table was lost in the turmoil of noise that was growing louder by the minute.

Yet unknown to all, something other than the events on the TV was about to take center stage, and even Danny had no clue what might be about to overshadow all.

"How long will it take you to figure out the new dial settings, knowing these two dates and the corresponding dial settings for them?" asked Danny.

Carefully, Jerzom gathered his thoughts. "I don't have Kashom's golden journal in front of me, but I'm pretty sure of what has to happen. When we get back to the treasure…well, I think it will only take me fifteen minutes or so. Kashom has made it pretty clear from what I've read in his journal on how to get a new set of dial settings required to transport us to our desired time and place, that is, March 1958 in CoalVille."

Danny said nothing. He listened and waited.

Jerzom continued. "Here is what we have. We know the dial settings for the Scarlet Desert in the vicinity of CoalVille and Granite Springs, which are ten miles apart, and we know the dial settings for November 22,

1963, and for this date, September 11, 2001."

The young royal prince was about to forge on when Danny said, "Good. Let's eat and go!"

There is an old saying: Life is what happens when you are making other plans. And so it was on that eleventh day of September of 2001.

The doors to the lobby of the Grand Hotel stood wide open. Inside, people were packed together like live sardines, but at the open door, people were streaming in and out.

Then it happened. Right before their eyes, brighter than ten thousand suns glued together at high noon, every inch of sky from east to west and from north to south flared up with a light so bright that people standing outside and in the doorway were instantly blinded. Howling with pain, their plight from henceforth would be to forge on, white canes tapping in front of them.

The ongoing explosion, the giant Herculean flash in the sky erupted like ten thousand hydrogen bombs, a new devastation that overshadowed even the tragedy of 9/11.

No more pictures dominated the giant TV. No more words were spoken. There was one fixed message onscreen and nothing more.

THE SKY IS BURNING!
STAND BY...THE WORLD APPEARS TO BE UNDER ATTACK!

Out of nowhere, as all were gawking at the fire in the sky, their hearts full of fear and panic, and their minds full of thoughts of impending doom and the end of the world, Quill showed up. As Jerzom was comforting the boys, trying to ease their fears, he did not see the emissary of Supreme God Viracocha arrive next to Danny.

And likewise, Danny did not see Quill standing next to him until he turned to face Jerzom, and to his surprise, he found himself gawking at Quill.

"What the hell is going on, Quill?" shouted Danny, trying to compete with the roar of noise that was growing like an erupting volcano.

"It's started, Danny! Your time is precious and limited!" said Quill. No one was listening to the dwarf speaking to the young man with bright yellow hair and emerald-green eyes.

"Zuron has managed to focus Lenszar, and he just destroyed the largest planet in this solar system! We have no time to wait!" Quill said with a somber look.

All other eyes were still on the emerging calamity, so no one saw Quill take a knife from his small leather bag. He pressed it into Danny's hand.

Holding it tightly, Danny stared at it, about to ask a question.

Quill interrupted. "It's special. Its handle is a brilliant-green gemstone."

Danny looked at it, and he thought, *An emerald handle!* The blade connected to the handle was most unusual, and the puzzled look on Danny's face prompted Quill to explain. "It's zedite, Danny. In the entire universe, there has been twenty pounds of that precious metal discovered, and you are looking at six pounds of this most rare metal. As you can tell, it's heavy and priceless beyond any description!"

And Danny was still puzzled. With the event in the sky and Quill showing up unexpectedly, Danny's mind was searching. *What is it that I should do?*

In all the noise and commotion, Jerzom had not taken his focus from the ongoing flash, and he was concentrating so hard on Little Danny and Little Tony that he still had not noticed Quill. With so many questions rattling through his mind, Jerzom turned to Viracocha's royal prince for advice. It was then that he saw Quill and the knife in Danny's hand.

Now with intense interest in yet another unfolding event, he listened to Quill's words. "When the beam has lost its power, Black Flight dies only with a strike of the knife, capturing TRPOV'S might!"

Talk about your riddles. Here we go again! That was precisely what went through Danny's mind as he blurted, "Quill, why can't you give me some straight talk in plain English?"

Quill said nothing, and Danny blasted further. "Do you think I understand that? Uh-huh, you have to figure it out! Well, shit, thanks a lot...best friend!"

Quill laughed deeply and gave Danny his don't-ask-me-for-help expression.

However, there were more urgent matters than a beam losing its power over Black Flight.

Quill's look faded into an expression on Danny's face with eyes glaring from deep-set sockets and jawbones locked with an announcement that was changing the universe, as Quill opened his mouth and repeated his message. "Zuron has moved Lenszar and destroyed the largest planet of this solar system!"

And at that moment the Emergency Broadcast System took over and the TV flashed breaking news. *"NASA has taken over the airways. Jupiter is gone! Not only is the United States under attack but our solar system is being destroyed by some outside force."*

Not watching the news coverage, Danny's mind erupted. *Oh, mighty god Viracocha, how long? How long? Guide me to Mochcom, my master and supreme god of the universe!*

Privy to some of Danny's thoughts, Quill said, "Well thought, TRPOV! And now, Danny, it is up to you to make it happen! Time is almost gone."

With a searching gaze of hope, Danny asked, "How much time, Quill?"

Quill's reply was swift and direct. "I don't have the answer." Even though the roar of people in panic was everywhere, in every corner, silence engulfed Danny as he listened to Quill. "Go in haste! Have Jerzom figure out how to get you back to the past!" Quill smiled encouragingly and then said, "I'm needed on Volob. Farewell, mighty prince of Viracocha! May the gods be with you!"

And so it was on 9/11—September eleventh—that the travelers left Granite Springs in the Scarlet Desert of Wyoming.

CHAPTER 8

Lenzar Has Moved, and the Universe Is Burning

Fire in the skies blazed unchecked, and Zuron had his eye on another solar system. So far he had managed to incinerate the solar system Nebular in the outer reaches of the Xanthnamus galaxy. All was gone. One hundred billion perished. The entire faction of the human race known as the centurions were no more! That entire solar system erupted in cinders. Then he destroyed Jupiter. What would be Zuron's next target? Would the Earth be next, or the entire solar system where Earth resides?

An emergency meeting of the Council of Primeval Gods was called. Ordinarily, one might ask what would prompt such an unusual call for an unscheduled meeting, but recent events were so horrific there was no need to wonder.

All sixty-five gods and the three executives, Viracocha, Neferdor, and Ra, were seated at the council table—of course. The very idea of one of the gods skipping out was unthinkable among such an esteemed group of rulers. Who could even imagine a god playing hooky from such an important gathering?

It had to have been interesting, to say the least, for all of the primeval gods to be called into a special council session—something that had never happened, at least not for the last billion years or so.

The supreme god and his wife walked in—the last to make their grand entrances—and took their seats. When they were seated, that signaled all who were standing by their thrones to also take their seats.

Calling the meeting to order was the official sergeant at arms. He stood and declaimed, "The Council of Primeval Gods, with Supreme God Viracocha, his wife, Supreme Goddess Neferdor, and their son, the god Ra, seated at the executive end of the council table, is called to order, with Viracocha presiding. The council is now in session!"

With the announcement of protocol officially carried out, and the meeting opened for the most urgent business, Comanzar took center stage. Not only was Comanzar the official sergeant at arms but over his millions of years of trusted service he was also Viracocha's chief of staff. He walked to the podium and tapped three times on the ceremonial bell. Its elastic resonance created a lasting, high-pitched *riiinnnggg* that dominated the hall for almost ten minutes. In the end, the sound died away slowly to a barely audible hum.

When silence finally descended, Comanzar made a statement. "Supreme God, Lenszar has moved once again. Our sky sentinels have detected not only further movement of Lenszar but also destruction rampant throughout the universe."

"How so?" shouted Viracocha.

"Most honorable Supreme God Viracocha and Supreme Goddess Neferdor, we think Zuron can now focus Lenszar at our solar system, Kolarus. We don't have full confirmation, but if he can focus Lenszar inward, it must be that planet Kopaz is in his sights!"

Now that was not what was expected. Like Viracocha, Dark God Zuron had a GAMMAZEL, which he needed to focus Lenszar on planet Volob. Yet unlike Viracocha's GAMMAZEL, which needed Jeannie's golden key to unlock it, Zuron's GAMMAZEL was unlocked by one of two code words. The Kolarus solar system consisted of three planets that revolved around the most massive star in the universe, the star at the center of the universe—Kolar. The three planets of the Kolarus solar system were Volob, where Supreme God Viracocha, Supreme Goddess Neferdor, their son Ra, and the sixty-five ruling gods dwelled and where the council met,

Zolob, where Dark God Zuron and his cast of gods dwelled, and Kopaz, where the royal family dwelled.

Comanzar continued. "Zuron needs both code words in order to destroy our planet, Volob. He needs only one to destroy Kopaz. Until Danny, your royal prince, most honorable supreme god, rid Kopaz of the evil goroms, the dark god had reason to leave Kopaz out of his sights. Maybe all that is changing!"

Questions abounded, as they always do when the unexpected happens. How could Dark God Zuron have learned the code words he needed to unlock and move his GAMMAZEL and unleash destructive forces throughout the universe? They were the most carefully guarded secret at the council table of the primeval gods—or were they?

"How? How is it that Zuron gets Lenszar to obey his will?" shouted Viracocha.

All watched and listened as Viracocha continued. To the gods, he was still their leader, and maybe he would reveal a course of action that might thwart the impending doom…and maybe not.

"We are *doomed!* I have done all I can. I have relied on you, my faithful council gods, to bring home a triumphant victory. I fear that all is lost, and soon, very soon, we will be nothing more than trapped rats in a cage called Volob!"

Maybe it was just out of contempt for one of the gods who had brought about the collapse of order in the universe. Although Viracocha knew not who was the culprit, he had his suspicions. Maybe it was all he had left. For whatever reason, from the outset it was evident that Viracocha's smoldering anger he had been harboring deep in his inner being was erupting into a blazing outward display of rage.

Looks of utter contempt fell from the supreme god and landed on the god Tammuz as Viracocha demanded answers. "And so, Tammuz, have you conversed with Zuron?"

"No, Supreme God, I have not!" yelled Tammuz.

"You banter around words so freely, as if there were no consequences… is that not so, Tammuz?" snarled Viracocha.

"That is a puzzle to me—what are these words to which you refer,

most eminent supreme god of the universe?" snorted Tammuz.

"Ah! You have a feeble mind of the size of a pissant looking for a hole to crawl into, and that may well be your destination if your recalcitrant attitude does not mend and your recollection is not brought up to date," snarled Viracocha.

The Grand Hall in the Pantheon of the Gods had never yet been the scene of such outward contention, but now anger was rising like a tide about to dislodge a beached ship in distress.

If there was something amiss, it was not evident to Tammuz and most likely also not evident to the throng of gods, whose blank stares surely had something to communicate.

Maybe it was time for clarification? And so Tammuz ventured into that realm when he asked Viracocha what words he meant and let it rest at that.

"I am the only one in the entire universe who knows both of the code words that Zuron needs to win the game!" shouted Viracocha.

The seriousness of it may have prompted Viracocha's next outburst. He roared, "Black Royal Temple! Does that have something do with the code words?"

Now that outcry of three words left a void hanging in the air like a baseball freezing right in front of the batter who would only need to take a home-run swing at that zero-velocity ball to knock it out of not only the park but also the universe.

"So, evidently, Zuron has figured out something and dialed it into his GAMMAZEL…or why would Lenszar move? Why can Zuron use Lenszar to set the skies on fire throughout the galaxies of the universe? Explain to us, Comanzar! Enlighten our minds!" demanded Viracocha.

Since the battle that had just erupted was between Viracocha and Tammuz, Comanzar was caught off guard. Not knowing how to respond the supreme god's command, Comanzar was about to say something, but Viracocha motioned for him to wait for a moment.

It was obvious that Tammuz's confusion and his nonanswer—*what words?*—when asked by Viracocha about the Black Royal Temple might well be genuine.

It was odd indeed. No one moved or said anything. All eyes were on

Viracocha as he was obviously deep in concentration.

Hmm, thought Viracocha. *Does Tammuz have a clue what two of those three words—Black Royal Temple—are all about? Maybe he was just an idiot when he dropped those words in the presence of Zuron, hmm?*

At that point, Viracocha motioned for Comanzar to step back to the podium, and as did, he said, "Comanzar, please restate the significance of the code words needed by Zuron to control his GAMMAZEL and focus Lenszar!"

"Yes, my supreme god of the universe, I shall do so," said the sergeant at arms as he stepped forward and prepared to address the council of gods. With a commanding voice he declared, "With only one of the two required words programmed into his GAMMAZEL, Zuron can unlock his GAMMAZEL. He can then destroy planets in the universe. In the solar system where your royal prince searches for Mochcom, Zuron has destroyed the planet Jupiter," Comanzar reported.

He paused, and then he stole a glance at the gods. It was evident to Comanzar that he had the attention of all, so he continued. "Zuron needs both sacred words in order to program his GAMMAZEL to destroy Volob and your pantheon, most honorable Supreme God Viracocha," reported Comanzar to the council of gods.

His words describing the consequence of one side taking the lead in the War of the Gods brought little consolation. He went on. "Zuron can only be stopped when the answer to the ancient riddle—'The site of the black pit defines the color of the scent'—is programmed into our GAMMAZEL." Then he pointed to the giant golden medallion—identical in nature to the golden key currently in the possession of Neferzul, the royal princess of Neferdor, but much larger. "Also, most honorable Supreme God and Supreme Goddess Neferdor, the royal princess of Neferdor has the key. Neferzul's golden key must unlock GAMMAZEL prior to it being programmed with the symbols that are the answer to the Riddle of Zuron!"

He then pointed to the middle of the red-diamond table. "There is our GAMMAZEL, and it will remain motionless until it is unlocked and programmed. Yet we all know the warning, and I shall clarify it once more. Once GAMMAZEL is unlocked, only the correct symbols will allow Viracocha and Neferdor to win the war. Incorrect symbols will bring instant destruction to us all!"

It was a sobering moment as he concluded his statements. "Yet unlocking our GAMMAZEL with Neferzul's golden key is paramount prior to programming it with the code of symbols derived from the answer to the ancient riddle: 'The site of the black pit defines the color of the scent.' I cannot stress strongly enough that if Zuron manages to get Neferzul's golden key, we are doomed! The game will be over!"

What Comanzar had just said was familiar information to all of the primeval gods. They had known this for two million years. But until now, Zuron had not the capability to focus Lenszar. Something had changed.

And so it was at that special meeting of the Council of Primeval Gods that Comanzar offered an explanation that was taking center stage—the reality of the skies of the universe ablaze, and the simple fact that the answer to a riddle remained elusive.

CHAPTER 9

CoalVille 1958

How interesting the Veil of Time. Jupiter circles the sun—it is still there. All is well. Or is it? Is the unknown dimension of time an illusion, or is it a means of uncovering secrets that will have the most profound effects on the universe for all living creatures through the vast expanse of unending time? Proud Jerzom was, and proud he should be. Jerzom got what they needed—two points in time and space—November 22, 1963, in CoalVille, and September 11, 2001, in Granite Springs. And armed with that knowledge, they were on their way to the past.

It is no longer a case of trial and error, thought Jerzom. *I suspect I have it down pat, as my brother's golden journal instructions are about as precise as they can be, and Kashom is quite clear on how to calibrate the Sun Energy Transformer.* For the young royal prince of Kopaz, all seemed in order.

Their departure from Granite Springs on September 11, 2001, was in the middle of chaos, the sky on fire as Jupiter burned. Trying to be as precise as he could in their efforts to travel back in time, Jerzom calculated the time of their arrival to be the spring of 1958, and the place they wanted to end up in was CoalVille.

They hit their mark, at least as far as the place. The arrived at the bottom of the hill leading into CoalVille. It was three in the morning. The moon was hiding its face, except for a sliver.

"Mr. God," asked Little Tony, "do you do this jumping around all the time? I mean not using a car to go someplace but that green lightning thing?"

Whhoooo…whhooohhoooo came the cry of a great horned hoot owl as if it were encouraging Little Tony to look for answers from this young god.

Grabbing Little Tony's small hand, Danny answered, "Kind of fun, huh?" He clearly was taken in by the innocence of these two little boys, who were now experiencing some joy in their lives.

In the stillness of the night, the lilacs were in full bloom. As black as it was, they were out of sight, but they announced their presence with their fragrance. The scent that the lilacs had full control over displayed with a commanding force the uniqueness of that fragrance, which only Mother Nature could create with her flowering desert bush.

The unseen redolence, the perfume of the lilacs that was on display on that warm night in the hours just prior to first light, also told them the season. The time of year was broadcast by the sweetness of their bouquet.

It has to be springtime, thought Danny as he was swept back in time by the scent of the flowering desert bush. *Yeah*, he mused, *I wonder where that legend came from? The Legend of Sky Fire…hmm.*

He still didn't know what year they had landed in, but with the lilacs in full bloom, it had to be springtime.

Has Jerzom figured out the dials? Danny's mind drifted as they started their walk. *That has yet to be determined.*

In that familiar environment, Danny took charge and guided them as where to go. He pointed where they should go and allowed Tony and Danny to lead the way as they walked in front. That was purposely done. Danny wanted a full view of them.

"What's that beautiful smell?" asked Jerzom.

Maybe it was the stillness of the night, broken only by the occasional interruption of the great horned owl, that made them all so aware of the overpowering scent that filled the air.

"It's a long story, Jerzom, but let me give you the *Reader's Digest* version," answered Danny.

Drawing his eyebrows down to almost a frown, Jerzom asked, "'*Reader's Digest*'?"

"Oh, that means a condensed story!" said Danny. "OK, a long time ago, a Frenchman, Jean-Paul Charbonnel, came to CoalVille to work in the mines. He could find no flowering bushes and hated the desert. He ranted and raved about how ugly it was because it had no flowering bushes, and so he planted and planted and planted."

Laughing freely, Danny said, "Some commoners believed that wild tale of the irate Frenchman, Jean-Paul Charbonnel. When I say commoners, I mean those who came to the Scarlet Desert in search of a place to live and work in the mines—the coal miners and their families."

Danny stopped and made sure Jerzom was listening. The royal prince of Viracocha then went on. "That story—the Jean-Paul Charbonnel story—most residents believe is pretty much a fairy tale. Now let me give you what I believe is the real story!"

Jerzom was all ears as Danny went on. "Yeah, I as well as most everyone who lived in CoalVille think the Jean-Paul Charbonnel tale is nothing more than fairy tale. I believe the real story is in one of the legends of the Kashome people—the Legend of Sky Fire."

Now that perked Jerzom's ears. "The Legend of Sky Fire?" he asked rhetorically.

Danny looked around to face Jerzom. He was walking backward. Little Tony and Little Danny were in the lead. Danny was about to answer Jerzom's question about the ancient Kashome legend, but a strange twist of fate intervened.

The route was so familiar to Danny, he never gave a second thought as to what might be coming, He, Tony, and Jeannie use to walk this stretch of highway, never worrying about oncoming or rear-approaching cars. Danny and Jerzom were on the shoulder of the road.

The road from Granite Springs took a sharp turn before the hill leading into CoalVille. Normally, cars took that curve at a reasonable speed.

It came out of nowhere. A car roaring down the road turned the corner to start up the hill, going at least ninety miles an hour. Little Tony and Little Danny couldn't get out of the way.

The car slammed through them.

Danny screamed "*Nooooooooooooo!*" as his mind filled with images of the boys' shattered bodies splattered over the highway.

Frightened as they were, Little Tony and Little Danny froze in the middle of the road. Shaking uncontrollably, the two boys could not take a step. Danny raced to them and in full motion, grabbed one in each arm and bolted to the borrow pit alongside the highway.

They—Danny and the boys in his arms—hit the ground rolling like a sack of potatoes flying off a delivery truck and ending up alongside the highway as trash.

It was a miracle, and something strange was going on. They were alive, not shattered bodies splattered all over the highway. This truth, although welcome, puzzled Danny.

Danny stood, the boys still firmly in his arms. Walking to a flat stretch of ground on the other side of the incline off the roadway, Danny lifted the boys and looked into their little faces.

On safe ground and feeling their beating hearts and noting that there was no blood, Danny's mind reached to hidden corners searching for answers. *What is going on? Was that a demon? What just slammed into the boys but was like nothing more than the wind blowing around them?*

The puzzle was real. No one had an answer.

"Are you boys OK?" asked Danny as he set them down.

Crying, they answered, "We got run over but the car...it...ah...ah... ah..."

Danny knelt and grabbed their hands. "Are you hurt?"

"No, we are OK," said Little Danny as his sobs started easing.

"Jerzom, let's grab the treasure and the boys and get away from the highway," said Danny as calmly as he could.

Their journey to safer ground at the CoalVille tipple was urgent. They had to hide the treasure. It was fortunate that the sky was bright with starlight and moonlight, making their journey from the road out across the sagebrush a little less perilous. It was a fifteen-minute walk to the CoalVille tipple.

Securing the treasure in a safe haven—in the old CoalVille Progressive Company dynamite bunker—was first and foremost.

Dawn was coming. The sky was getting a little less black. Mr. Sun was not far in the future, and his face shining on CoalVille would soon welcome a new day. Yet sleep was what the boys needed; their little eyelids were drifting downward, and their bodies were shivering in the wee hours of the chilly early morning.

"Jerzom, you take your shirt and wrap it around Tony, and I'll put mine around Little Danny," said Danny, "and then we we'll lie next to them to keep them warm until morning."

His ignorance and confusion weighed on Danny's mind as they all stretched out on the ground, Tony and Danny between Danny and Jerzom. The little boys appeared to be asleep, safely wrapped in the older boys' warm shirts—one from a royal prince and one from a god—leaving the young men to brave the early morning dew bare chested.

Why would a speeding car not smash two small boys to smithereens? It was a head-on collision. It was unnatural. Or was it?

Eyes wide open, staring into the depth of a black sky, Danny searched for answers. *Holy shit, Quill! All the mumbo-jumbo cryptic words that you spouted off about the veil of time being controlled by Aerapondes's ruby ring before we left Kopaz…is that what this is about?*

CHAPTER 10
What's Behind Legends?

Maybe staring into the black sky, just getting a hint of light as a new day approached, caused Danny to reflect upon the weight and magnitude of the mission before him. Maybe it was Little Tony and Little Danny snuggled next to him and the thought of their fate. Maybe it was their parents, Tony and KateLynn, and their final fates. Whatever the reason, Danny sighed loudly. It did not go unnoticed.

"Are you awake?" Jerzom asked as he started a conversation. He also had been staring at the sky.

"Hmm. You can't sleep either?" was Danny's reply.

Listening to the steady sound of the sleeping boys' breathing, Danny talked in a low voice so as not to awaken Danny and Tony as they cuddled together, warm between the royal prince of Viracocha and Jerzom, royal prince of Kopaz.

"It's kind of chilly this early spring morning. I can tell it is spring, but I'm not sure of the month or year," ventured Danny on as he focused on a bright distant star.

It was good that Danny and Jerzom had a few moments to talk. Soon the sun would be up and the magnitude of what lay ahead was also on Jerzom's mind. For now, the hidden mysteries of life in the Scarlet Desert weighed even more heavily on Jerzom.

"Danny, you lived here in this time?" asked Jerzom.

"Well, I think so," replied Danny. "I know it is springtime because of the scent that is filling the air."

Hmm, thought Jerzom, *I wonder where Kashom is and if he is sleeping this morning, also smelling this beautiful scent?*

Everything was so strange to a royal prince from the faraway planet of Kopaz, and Jerzom wanted to hear the story Danny had been about to tell when that ghost car ran through the boys. And most of all, he yearned to know of his brother's people, where they lived, and how it was that the scent of the flowering desert bush was somehow tied to legends of the Kashome people.

Jerzom was about to ask a question, but he was not fast enough, as Danny broke in. The little bodies of Little Danny and Little Tony, trying to keep warm, must have brought back old memories.

"It was awful, Jerzom. Gorom Mochcom killed their father right in front of Jeannie and me. I had a choice to save either Jeannie or Tony. I chose Jeannie," Danny said with a catch in his voice.

Jerzom could see that Danny was struggling to get these words out of his mouth. He was quiet as Danny ventured into the painful past. "Their mother must have been killed by Mochcom, probably in front of them."

Looking at the boys, Danny put his hand on the head of Little Tony and continued. "I cannot believe the evil that exists in the universe—such horrible evil that would take these boys' parents from them and then keep them for human sacrifice."

"Danny, it was the way of the goroms. They got a stranglehold on Kopaz, and my father was oblivious. I and my brother witnessed their wickedness firsthand," mumbled Jerzom in hushed tones. "My dear friend, Peizar, fell victim to the wickedness of those evil goroms."

A morning breeze picked up and rustled the lilacs not more than ten feet from where they lay. It was a gentle sound made by quivering leaves, yet over the sounds of Mother Nature, Danny could hear the sound of hard swallowing as Jerzom spoke.

I never met Peizar but can only imagine what a great guy and friend he was to Jerzom, thought Danny as Jerzom's words recalled the horror and terror inflected on the Vassar family.

Danny paused, took a deep breath, and said softly as not to disturb the boys, "Her name was KateLynn. She and Tony were so much in love. I figure it must have been the night I lent Tony my 1955 Chevy truck that the boys were conceived. Wow. Who would have dreamed that the Veil of Time would uncover the two boys that are sleeping next to us now?"

"Danny, the boys are asleep, and we have a few minutes." Jerzom looked to the sky and then continued. "Would you tell me about my brother and how he helped you and Jeannie escape from Gorom Mochcom."

It was a story Danny wanted to get off his chest, as it was about Jerzom's brother and Tony and that fateful day in the Scarlet Desert when he and Jeannie had escaped.

"Yeah, it is painful, but it is the past, and so much has happened," said Danny as he started to tell of the last few minutes he had lived in the Scarlet Desert.

"We were at the Boar's Tusk, as we knew we had to get away from Mochcom. The Boar's Tusk was significant, as your brother had preprogrammed the Sun Energy Transformer."

Danny paused to reflect on the past. He then ventured on as he recalled the details of that fateful day so long ago.

"I wasn't into reading your brother's journal. Thank goodness Tony was able to figure things out with the help of Jeannie. We spotted a truck coming down the dirt road that leads to the Tusk. It was Pastor Duncan, and then I realized, like your brother, that I had been conned by Mochcom. I was heartsick. 'Let's be calm,' Tony had said, trying to get control of the situation. He ran to the flat rock that Kashom's golden journal was on. 'I think we do what the drawing says. It's our only hope.'"

Danny stopped and looked at Jerzom. They said nothing. Taking a deep breath and searching for the words, he went on, his mind drifting back to those moments, reliving them.

"I pointed my finger right in Tony's face and roared in anger. 'For crying out loud, Tony—*do what?* You're not making a bit of sense. *Come on, guy!* Do something that makes sense, or we're all dead!'"

"Tony's keen sense of judgment was not rattled by my sudden loss of composure.

'*Danny, just listen!* We're going to do what this drawing says to do. We're going to hold hands and hold onto the bronze boxes and their contents. Then one of us will grasp the handle on the transformer. Jeannie will put the arrow into the keyhole and turn it.'

"His hand was trembling as Tony shouted, 'If it works, we will vanish!'

"'You're loony! What the *hell* is that supposed to accomplish?' I was frantically searching for anything that would help. 'That crazy old bastard is almost to the Boar's Tusk. We have about three minutes to do something, or we *die!*'

"At that point Jeannie grabbed my arm and pulled me to the treasures sitting on the rock at the base of the Boar's Tusk on that beautiful sunny afternoon. She said, 'Danny, you must listen to Tony. It's our only hope. Please! For me—just do it!'

"I was not convinced, and I stepped back, pulling my arm away from her. I didn't know what to believe. I screamed at Tony, 'Tony, you're nuts! What the hell do you mean—we'll vanish? You've been reading way too many comic books,' I shouted. 'Get that damn thing figured out. Come on! Get the lead out!'

"Tony calmly took charge. He ripped into me. 'Do you have a better idea? That old bastard tried to cut Eddie's heart out. He'll do much worse to us. You get the answer, Mr. Answer Man? We have two minutes to somehow leave here or be shot by that crazy son of a bitch.'

"Jeannie was crying. Her hands were over her face. I realized we were doomed if I didn't fall in line. At that point, my judgment and strength took hold again.

"Tony picked up on the change coming over me. With a smile of excitement, he screamed, 'I think the transformer will make us invisible!'

"Jeannie stopped crying and waved at Tony. She was so strong. She was Neferzul, and the fulfillment of her mission was paramount.

"She took charge and gave orders. 'Tony, quick! Put the lid on! I told you to do that already! What are you waiting for?'

"Tony responded to her orders. 'OK! Here it is! Now what?'

"'*Merrrrooowwww! Merrrrooowwww!*' growled Zanzee.

"'*Let me see what he's pawing at!*' Jeannie yelled as she ran to her kitty.

"*Wizz binnng! Wizz binnng!*

"She didn't make it to Zanzee. She stumbled and fell helpless to the ground."

If attention was golden, Jerzom was a golden boy. He was riveted by the story he was hearing. He asked, "What happened, Danny?" He was clearly involved in every detail of the story Danny was telling of that awful, horrific day in the desert back in 1958.

"Well, let me go on," said Danny.

"Tony hadn't noticed Jeannie. He was concentrating on the gold tablet Zanzee was telling him about. 'Jeannie, what do we do? Zanzee is warning us!'

"Then his head snapped around to find Jeannie. '*Good lord, Jeannie! Get up! What are you doing? I need you!*' Tony screamed even louder.

"Jeannie managed to stand up and slowly took a step toward Tony. 'Where is it, Tony? What's Zanzee pawing at?' she said in a barely audible voice.

"Tony pointed at the spot on the gold tablet. 'Look at this drawing, Jeannie. Zanzee wants us to look at it. There's a bunch of Spanish on it. We need to figure it out!'

"Tony lifted his head to see Gorom Mochcom in his truck not more than five hundred yards from where they stood. Mochcom's nervous hands rested his rifle on the hood again to steady it. He took aim and pointed it at me. I was jumping and dodging like the best basketball player of all time—not to give him a stationary target.

"I was trying desperately to stay out of harm's way, but Mochcom had his eye on me, and Tony sensed it. He had no choice but to continue as fast as he could to figure out a mystery in the nick of time. I was on my own.

"Tony reeled around to look at Jeannie standing next to him. 'Jeannie, we have to hurry. LeRoy will be here in a second. *He's going to kill us—hurry!* What does this Spanish say?'

"Tony didn't know what to say or what to do. He was terrified and was grasping for straws. 'Watch out, Zanzee!' he screamed as he grabbed Kashom's tablets and pulled them closer so Jeannie could get a better look at the drawing. 'Here it is, Jeannie! Here it is! Look at what it says, and hurry! LeRoy is going to shoot us. He's crazy! He's going to kill us!' Tony kept shouting over and over.

"Tony's eyes said it all. He looked at Jeannie and saw that she was pale, almost fainting. She was holding her beloved cat. Her shirt was covered with blood.

"'Tony, I'm bleeding. I've been shot!' Jeannie cried.

"'My God in heaven, Jeannie!' Tony screamed.

"At that point, I saw what had happened. 'Oh no! Jeannie, give me your hand! Let me help you!' I grabbed her with my strong grip—her blood splashed onto the gold tablets of Kashom. 'Hold onto me, Jeannie,' I said.

"She pointed to where Tony was standing. In a whimpering voice, she said, 'Danny, I have to help Tony. Hold me tight, so I don't fall. I need to look at something. Help me get over to him.'

Quietly, as not to awaken the boys, Danny stood and went to where the treasure was hidden and got Kashom's golden journal. He came back and opened it to a given tablet. Danny continued his story, now with the journal in hand. "Jeannie looked at the Spanish phrase on Kashom's golden tablet. Mayo dioses estar con usted. I didn't know what she was thinking at the time, but now I do. She knew at that point that I was TRPOV and that she was TRPON."

Jerzom looked at the golden tablet in the journal and smiled. "Yep, you are TRPOV, and Jeannie is TRPON, just as Kashom knew one of his descendants would be."

Danny could tell that Jerzom took great pride in his brother and his part in helping the gods. The royal prince said, "Please continue, Danny."

Danny ventured on.

"'Tony,' Jeannie whispered faintly. 'The Spanish, "El reloj de oro encuentra la aguja para la llave de oro," means "The golden watch finds the needle for the golden key." You've already figured this out. It's on your piece of paper...remember. Zanzee is pointing out what Kashom wants us to do. Kashom is telling us to use the settings for the dials that you wrote out on your tablet. It's on the piece of paper you put in your pocket, remember? Do you see what to do?' she moaned.

"Tony sweetly put his hand on her wound. She was trembling. He saw she was bleeding to death, and time was not on their side. He answered, 'Yes, Jeannie.'

"I reeled in horror as Tony took his bloody hand from Jeannie's side. I shrieked in fright. 'Tony, do you have the dials set? If you don't, get the lead out of your pants and get those things set; we won't be the Pirates in the Desert anymore. Crazy LeRoy's lead will make us all cadavers in the desert.'

"Jeannie was so great. She sensed we were concentrating on her and not on the transformer. 'Danny and Tony, I'll be OK. You guys figure out what has to happen,' she said in the sweetest voice she could muster. 'Tony?' Jeannie reached and touched his hand. 'Don't forget to put the brass arrow into the keyhole and turn it. That's part of what needs to happen.' She whimpered, her voice growing ever fainter. She watched Tony while at the same time watching Crazy LeRoy getting closer and closer, his rifle hanging out the window. His truck was almost to the base of the hill from which the Boar's Tusk rose. She touched Tony again. 'Check the combination code.'

"The paper in Tony's fingers containing the code of symbols was quivering in rhythm with his trembling hand. In spite of his body shaking uncontrollably, he forced himself to focus. He had to get the code of symbols on the wheels set absolutely perfectly. Carefully, Tony looked at each wheel on the combination lock and made sure the code that unlocked the Sun Energy Transformer was set correctly."

Danny stopped. He remembered exactly what the code was and set the dials so Jerzom could see. "It was so important that Tony get it right. He did. Here is the code we needed," said Danny as the pointed to the code that had saved Jeannie and him from Gorom Mochcom. "I saved that piece of paper that Tony wrote the code on. I treasure it!"

"'OK, the combination is good,' said Tony, grasping every fiber of his being to concentrate and maintain control.

"Tony then set the five dials that controlled the little shutters over the star points to the exact same positions as indicated on the gold tablet drawing. Tony explained what he had just done. 'This was what Kashom had so masterfully figured out when Mochcom conned him and they used the sun energy transformer to bring them to the Scarlet Desert centuries ago. Setting the dials correctly was paramount in order to get to the point in time and the point in space they wanted to go.'

"Then Tony put the arrow into the keyhole and turned it. It was Tony's eyes that said it all. They lit up like the giant crystal ball in Times Square, New York, on New Year's Eve.

"Zanzee's paw lifted and gently touched her face with his soft, fur-lined footpads. He then jumped from Jeannie's arms. He raced to a large sagebrush thirty feet from her.

"Her heart sank. '*No! Run, Zanzee!* LeRoy will kill you! *Run and hide!* His vulture will hurt you! Run fast, Zanzee! Run away as fast as you can!'

"Jeannie watched her beloved cat run. The anguish in her heart was almost more than she could bear. No one had to tell her the horror and evil that Crazy LeRoy was capable of inflicting. *He's gone. I hope he's safe*, she thought. 'Good-bye, Zanzee! I love you!' whimpered Jeannie.

"Mochcom's truck was fast approaching the base of the Boar's Tusk. His watchful eye caught something.

"We heard Mochcom screaming, '*Damn!* Kashom's cat is here! That damn bird lied to me. He didn't kill Kashom's cat. That black devil is helping them. I'll kill him. I hate that cat!' Mochcom bellowed with rage, watching Zanzee race into the desert.

"Tony was shaking. His eyes could not open wider. They reflected the brilliance of the handle. 'Guys, look at it! The green handle is glowing. We have no choice but to do what the drawing says to do. Come on, Danny. We need to grab all the boxes and hold onto them. We're going to go.'

"I gently held Jeannie and helped her sit next to Tony. 'Jeannie, stay here for a minute. Tony and I will grab the boxes.'

"Pressing her hand to her wound to slow the bleeding, Jeannie sat motionless on the rock. She was getting weaker by the second. She was overcome with emotion as she watched the emerald-green handle of the transformer glow as if surrounded by all the stars of the Milky Way.

"I'm sure she was thinking about how it was a gift from Viracocha! She knew as well as I did that we needed to follow Kashom's advice. We needed to travel the Highway of Time, even if we didn't know where it would take us.

"Boxes in hand, Tony and I raced back to where Jeannie was sitting next to the transformer. She was alive but still bleeding and losing strength.

"'We've got the boxes. Everything else needs to be picked up—grab our canvas bags, everything on the flat rock!' I yelled.

"Silence fell on the Boar's Tusk. *Oh my god!* I thought.

"The roaring motor of the 1948 Ford truck went silent. I watched Crazy LeRoy Nabal jump out, his gun in hand. He was less than a football field's length from where we were standing.

"His hand flew up. He motioned to Black Vulture flying overhead. Vulture dipped in flight. He swooped to his master. '*Help me!*' he yelled. Mochcom's arm waved for his disciple to dive. '*Kill her!*' he screamed louder.

"*Kaboom.* The sound engulfed the air at the Boar's Tusk. It was Monday afternoon, March 24, in the Scarlet Desert of Wyoming. I was shot and collapsed to the ground next to my friends.

"At that point, the supreme god came to my rescue. Spiraling around me in a display of sheer amazement, a green light emanated from my ring and circled my body like a coiled spring of fire.

"My eyes rolled downward from staring at LeRoy and focused on my shirt. My mind was racing. *Why don't I see any blood? Why has the pain gone away? What's going on? I'm not dead—or am I?* Like a phoenix rising from its own ashes, I stood and ran to Jeannie and Tony.

"Tony watched me, and his expression told me his spirit was soaring to the height of the sun. He must have been thinking, *Oh, my great lord in heaven—Danny is on his feet.*

"Then I could see the fear that gripped Tony as he stared at the crazy man orchestrating his next move. In sheer panic, he screamed, 'My god, Danny, do something!'

"I managed to kill Vulture, Mochcom's disciple of death, with my binoculars using them as a sling shot.

"Mochcom pointed a shaking finger at Jeannie. Erupting again, his voice exploded in anger. *'I'm going to kill you, Neferzul!'*

"Mochcom's hand pointed at Tony. He lifted his gun from his side. Panic jangled through Tony's body. He dropped to the ground. I raced to position myself between Tony and Mochcom. With the security of me in front of him, Tony jumped to his feet. He monitored Mochcom's every move.

"'It's the black-haired boy I must stop. I can't kill the prince of Viracocha, but I can kill his friend. He's the brains. I must stop him!' Mochcom muttered. 'I have two shots. I'll use them wisely!'

"Tony was jumping up and down in panic. 'You're alive—thank the god of the rock! Come on, guys. We need the boxes. Grab the boxes, and I'll grab the handle!' screamed Tony. 'I've got one box. Grab the others.'

"But at that point, panic also gripped me. If I grabbed the boxes, I couldn't shield both Tony and Jeannie at the same time. I thought, *My God, what shall I do?* I had to make a decision, and I chose Jeannie and hoped that Mochcom would miss his shot.

"Furious with me, Mochcom screamed, *'You'll pay for this! You killed Vulture! Your friend is going to die.'*

"A loud crack of thunder ripped through the air. Gorom Mochcom's shot did not miss its mark. Tony fell to the ground at my feet. His head rolled in a pool of blood to look at me for the last time. With his dying words, he whimpered instructions to me, his best friend. He always called me his best buddy!

There was a catch in Danny's voice as he searched for composure. "God, did I love Tony!"

Jerzom was still. He waited. Danny continued.

"Tony searched for strength to tell us what to—to tell us Kashom's instructions. His voice was barely audible. 'Grab the green handle,' he said. 'Grab Jeannie's hand.'

"His strength was almost gone. His eyes closed. In the softest of whispers, his last words faded. 'Stand on all the boxes of treasures you want to take.' Then he was lying lifeless on the ground, and he said nothing more.

"My canvas bag with my Pirate Log and a change of clothes hung from my shoulder. I grasped Jeannie's trembling body firmly. 'I hope we're saved,' I said as my mind swirled with so many thoughts—thoughts of my mom, thoughts of my dad, thoughts of their true love. I remember thinking that I loved my mom and that my dad was right about me being a dreamer, about dreaming of finding treasure in the Scarlet Desert.

At this point, Little Danny and Little Tony were awake. They must have been listening to the story, and even though Danny and Jerzom were speaking the language of the royal family of Kopaz, they must have been aware that the story was somehow related to them, as they kept hearing the name "Tony."

Danny, Jerzom, and the two boys sat on the ground, watching the sunrise. The mood had grown so solemn that maybe it was time to change subjects.

"Danny," Jerzom said, "the past holds our memories of sorrow, and the future holds our hope for tomorrow!"

And so the subject changed, but who knew why it changed the way it did. Only time would tell. Maybe it was coincidence, or maybe it was time for a legend that needed to be told. Who would suspect that legends and the telling of legends would uncover the reason of their existence and expose why they're profound?

For whatever reason, Jerzom went back to a question he had asked at the base of the hill leading into CoalVille. "Danny, you started to tell me something about the legends, and I wanted to know the story of why the flowers bloom in the desert," Jerzom asked. With a most sincere look, he stared at Danny and asked, "Danny, could you finish the Legend of Sky Fire?"

It dawned on Danny. *I'd started something, but the car burst on to the scene and ended the story. Like a ghost car hidden behind the Veil of Time, that incident interrupted my telling of the legends to Jerzom.*

"Yes, it's called the Legend of Sky Fire, and some believe it and some don't," said Danny as he proceeded. "All I can say is that 100 percent of the Kashome people believe in the Legend of Sky Fire. Those who are not native to the desert don't!"

Danny stopped. "I will tell the legend in English first so the boys can listen, and then I will repeat it in the language of the royals so you can understand. Jeannie taught the legend to me, so I know it word for word."

Upon finishing the story in English, Danny started again, this time speaking in the language of the royals.

The Legend of Sky Fire

As seen from far away, in springtime, the desert is ablaze with a thick carpet of scarlet paintbrush. Was it always this way? The answer is no!

There was a time when the ancients who lived in the Scarlet Desert saw only a bleak landscape. And why was that? There could be no reason to ignore the gods in their generosity, as they wanted the ancients who lived in the desert to have a home of splendor. But dirt, dust, and wind had dominated the barren landscape for eons.

What could the gods do? Could they ask Sky to kiss the ground and bring on a new beginning? Could they have the Winds of Change blow away the mountains of parched rock and sand and erase this desolate habitat?

Sky kissed the ground but to no avail. The desert remained bleakly barren. At her failure at such a formidable task, weeping in sadness, tears fell from the face of Sky, and where they fell, a blaze of splendor sprang up throughout the desert, covering it with scarlet paintbrush.

Sky was so happy, she told the gods to look down at the Scarlet Desert, now ablaze with a red carpet. Smiling down, the gods took note of the work of Sky, but then they saw the arid corner without bloom.

Nestled among the hills was the blight of shiny black ribbons of coal that mocked Sky's tears of joy. Desolate and parched as the hills had been, their only hidden beauty were strips of inky blackness, yet all void of the scarlet brush. There could be no bitter sadness more wrenching to Sky, whose tears turned to fiery hail in defiance of the hills adorned with the blight of coal. And from that hail of fire came new life, and that is why the desert bush with the sacred name of "lieloc" blooms months early in the springtime of CoalVille, showering all with its scent. The gods smiled, but when the ancients changed the name of the flowering vine to "lilac," the gods turned their faces away, and the sacred name of lieloc was lost on the winds of time.

Listening closely to each word, Jerzom asked when Danny finished, "Ah, do you believe that, Danny?"

Danny laughed. *"Yes! Absolutely!* Some say that the fiery hail from Sky fell in early February. And that is why the lieloc bushes bloom long before the scarlet paintbrush springs to life as a red carpet on the Scarlet Desert. Who knows for sure if that is the reason? But I think that is the real story."

Danny's gaze at the lieloc bushes caused Jerzom to stop and wait. And then, with a perplexed look, Danny said, "It is strange that these are the only bushes that bloom so early! Hmm."

The boys looked at the Scarlet Desert bushes and pointed. "Mr. God, is it *lieloc* or *lilac*?"

The sun had risen and was shining just above the eastern horizon as Danny contemplated the boys' question. "Well, let me say this. The ancients have no doubt that that is what happened," said Danny with conviction, "so I will stick by my story and call them *lieloc*, as it is a sacred name and revered by the gods."

Repeating what Danny had said to the boys in English, he made similar comments to Jerzom in the royal language. Now that response prompted a question from Jerzom. "Who are the ancients?"

As Danny had lived in the Scarlet Desert his entire life, he was more than willing to tell of the culture he had been schooled in by Jeannie. "Oh, they were of countless numbers a long time ago. But that is a mystery also. When your brother, Kashom"—Danny looked directly at Jerzom—"and Mochcom landed in the Scarlet Desert, the people who had lived in the desert for thousands of years had all but died off. Who knows why? There were only a few left, fewer than five in number. Some say the Spaniards brought European diseases that killed them. Ah…you probably have no idea who the Spaniards and the Europeans were. Well, they were visitors to this land a long time ago."

There was a long pause. Danny's sincere look caused Jerzom to listen intently, as he wanted to grasp every detail about his brother's life in the desert.

"Actually, since your brother's people have lived here for centuries, I would also consider them the ancients! I believe that Jeannie also came to that same conclusion."

Noting Jerzom's undivided attention, Danny went on. "OK, back to the story. Let me see if I can make some sense of what I'm telling you. Jeannie is extremely proud of her heritage and told me many times about the Legend of Kashom and the Legend of the Boar's Tusk. She had me memorize the Legend of Sky Fire…I have no idea why she did that. I just told that one, so let me continue."

Danny stopped to gather his thoughts and then charged on. "First, I'll tell you the Legend of Kashom."

The Legend of Kashom

In his new home in the desert, Kashom met the ancient inhabitants who lived there and fell in love with the daughter of the chief, a gorgeous girl who was called Star-of-Night. His wedding gift to her was a lovely golden medallion with a blue sapphire–colored star-shaped gemstone at its center. Kashom and Star-of-Night had a beautiful daughter, Moon-of-Day, and a son, Yellow Moon. Their daughter had soft white skin like the petals of a rose, silky black hair, and sapphire-blue eyes. She was entrusted with the golden key. Her beautiful features marked her as the Chosen One, fated to redeem her father's honor and restore him to his rightful place as heir to the royal throne of Kopaz. She was the second keeper of the key and was given the sacred name of Neferzul.

Jerzom was all ears as Danny told the story of what had transpired so long ago. Yet the realm of time was a question. It hung in the air like a hummingbird, wings beating ninety miles an hour but going nowhere.

"Danny, sorry for interrupting, but how long ago did this take place?"

He hesitated at Jerzom's question. Danny looked to the sky and then at Jerzom and said, "Centuries ago!" He paused again, collecting his thoughts.

"The Veil of Time that Quill talked about is a mystery. It's a dimension that holds secrets that we are not yet privy to. Maybe soon we shall unlock the secrets of time."

And as if in a trance, Danny continued, "Yes, maybe soon we'll find the answers."

With that, he charged on.

Against his father's wishes, Yellow Moon, a young warrior, went hunting for Desert Eagle. He took Moon-of-Day on the hunt with him, but she mysteriously fell into a crevasse and was lost forever.

Kashom and Star-of-Night mourned the loss of their daughter. They had another daughter, Skip-with-Wind. With Moon-of-Day's death, she became the next keeper of the key. Because she did not have shiny black hair, sapphire-blue eyes, and soft white skin, she was not given the sacred name of Neferzul. Kashom said he could not be restored to his rightful throne until another who looked like his murdered sister, Aerapondes, came forth from his bloodline.

The new Chosen One will have shiny black hair, sapphire-blue eyes, and soft white skin like Aerapondes and Moon-of-Day. She will be called Neferzul and will hold the golden key of Neferdor. Together with her partner, the male who holds the golden watch of Viracocha, they will travel the Highway of Time, redeem Kashom's honor, and be thrust center stage on the battlefield of the gods.

Thus, the golden key has been passed down from generation to generation in the Lone Tree family.

Skip-with-Wind gave the key to her daughter, Ripple-in-Pond.

Ripple-in-Pond gave the key to her daughter, Golden Cloud.

Golden Cloud gave the key to her daughter, Clear Water.

Clear Water is Jeannie's grandmother, and she gave the key to Soft Wind, Jeannie's mother and now Jeannie has it.

The Kashome people wait for the supreme god Viracocha and his wife, Neferdor, to reveal their emissaries, TRPOV and TRPON.

TRPOV will be designated by Viracocha's gift of the golden watch.

The Neferzul who is in possession of the golden key of Neferdor at the time when TRPOV is gifted the golden watch of Viracocha will become TRPON.

Viracocha told Kashom that, as part of his purgatory, if he is to regain his royal status, he must aid TRPOV and TRPON in the fulfillment of their missions, declare to them who they are, and let them know they will be valiant warriors for Viracocha and Neferdor in the battle of deities.

Smiling, Danny finished what he had to say. "And so you see, Jerzom, your brother fulfilled the mission that he had been given by Supreme God Viracocha. He revealed to Jeannie and me who we are—TRPOV and TRPON. He guided us to the gifts of the gods, the priceless treasures required for time and space travel. And because he has been valiant in completing his mission, he will be restored to royalty in Kopaz!"

Jerzom broke in, his excitement evident in every word spilling from his mouth. "Danny that is so *cool*, as you would say! You have no idea what it means to me to learn of my beloved brother, who was scorned by our father."

"Yeah, hopefully we'll meet him soon. Now for the Legend of the Boar's Tusk. In a land far away—in a time long ago—a young prince lost his honor. He left his royal family and lush tropical homeland in disgrace because of lies told by an evil high priest. The young prince, whose name was Kashom, ended up in the Scarlet Desert."

Stopping briefly, Danny wanted to emphasize a point that Jeannie had done so many times before. Danny quoted Jeannie, "So many times when we were alone, Jeannie would tell me the legends, and she would say, 'You must not forget this.'" For a moment, Danny paused to collect his thoughts so he could say precisely the words of the legend.

"Yellow Moon, an old man, climbed to the top of the Boar's Tusk and looked down at the young man—his father—Kashom—and said in a loud voice, 'Father, it is finished—the keys unlock the bottomless pit by the star of the chamber!' Then he thrust himself from the top of the monument and fell to his death at the feet of his father."

Danny stopped. Jerzom said, "Go on!"

It was obvious to Danny that these stories of his brother's life in the Scarlet Desert were a treasure to Jerzom. He watched Jerzom lying on the desert sands and looking to the sky as he listened.

Danny proceeded. "At that time, Kashom's son was a very old man; however, your brother is forever young, eighteen years old, just like Jeannie, you, and I are. It's a precious gift from the gods for those who are privileged to travel the Highway of Time."

With their eyes locked, Danny concluded. "You know the outcome of both these legends."

"Yes, you are TRPOV. Jeannie is TRPON. And I have touched the treasure hidden in the secret chamber of the Boar's Tusk." There was still time. Mr. Sun was not yet fully awake. So Jerzom asked more. "Danny, you just told me the Legend of Sky Fire, but you haven't told me what it means. What's it about? Do you have any idea what the legend means? Or if it is to be used for something?"

Danny's face showed signs of puzzlement as he answered. "Jerzom, that's a mystery. As I said, the ancients believed it. The Kashome people believe it. They are the ones who have kept the Legend of Sky Fire alive and tell it so that each generation has a full knowledge of it. Maybe soon we will find the answers to the mystery of the Legend of Sky Fire."

It was obvious to Jerzom that Danny was deep in thought, and most likely, it was the mystery of the Legend of Sky Fire that was on Danny's mind. Danny paused. Jerzom waited and listened. The little boys also waited. Like Jerzom, their curiosity was aroused.

Danny added, "The newcomers to the Scarlet Desert said it was a meteorite shower and not a fiery hail of Sky's tears. Who knows the mystery or why the Kashome people have preserved this legend for so long? Maybe it has to do with the gods."

Moments of silence drifted in as they looked to the sky, and then Danny said, "Maybe soon we'll find the answer."

That last statement, an answer to his question that really said nothing, was identical to the answer to a previous question that Jerzom had asked about the Legend of Kashom. He had asked how long ago it had taken place. And that hit Danny alongside the head like a baseball bat!

He jumped to his feet, startling the little boys. "Viracocha told me personally what's going on. Without the presence of the ruby ring, the portal of reality remains closed! That's it!" With a somber look, he looked at Jerzom and said slowly, "We need your sister's ring."

Legends. What are they, and do they have an impact? What's behind them?

CHAPTER 11

A Lock of Hair

Could it be that the fear of death and what comes after death have been the two single mysteries that religious zealots have used since the dawning of time to control the masses? That is what Viracocha and the Council of Primeval Gods surmised.

Maybe it was that these countless religions, each with its own view of the divine, was at the core of the question posed by Supreme God Viracocha. "Who are all these gods that these religions have chosen to worship?"

And also puzzling to Viracocha was that the countless religions that sprang into existence over the eons had formulated their own unique answers to three questions: What was before life as a human in the preexistence? What is the purpose of being a human? What comes after death?

There could be no doubt that Viracocha had seen through the zealots, whom he believed had tied the answers to these questions to the mysteries of death. How was it that the mysteries of death had allowed the religious throngs to flourish for ages when the Land of the Dead was not a mystery to the supreme god of the universe and his council of gods? Why was that? Could it be that the answer to that mystery involved a lock of hair?

Jeannie, Danny, Kashom, his people, and Jerzom understood this mystery of the Land of the Dead. They were fully aware that the lock of hair of one who resided in the Land of the Dead could unlock the pathway that led back to the Land of the Living. Yet even understanding that mystery of death, Danny and Jerzom had another mystery that they were dealing with—they were in the process of deciphering the mystery of the Veil of Time.

The Veil of Time was strange indeed. It could hide the human side of existence and leave one to wonder why it was that others were present yet not present. Throughout the ages it had been so. There were those who explained this Veil of Time by surmising that those who are present yet not are mere ghosts. In fact, the ancient celebration of All Hallows' Eve commemorates the ghosts and goblins that both live among us and yet do not.

The sun was finally shining down, shedding its warmth on two little guys who had worn only shirts from Danny and Jerzom as blankets throughout the chilly night. They were up and ready to go.

There was no longer any need to be covert as they walked from the CoalVille tipple through Red Rock Creek and into the streets of CoalVille, as it seemed something was going on. The Veil of Time was hiding the presence of Danny, Jerzom, Little Danny, and Little Tony from all who were busy with their daily lives in CoalVille.

As Danny, Jerzom, Little Danny, and Little Tony climbed over the three-foot embankment of Red Rock Creek and emerged into the back streets of CoalVille, the date on a passing car's license plate told Danny the year.

"Jerzom, it's the spring of 1958! You got the Sun Energy Transformer programmed perfectly! Good job!" said Danny as he watched the car speed away and fade from view as it rounded the corner of Main Street, which separated the lower camp from the middle camp.

"This is really weird," said Jerzom. "Why is it that we are here yet not here? These people can't see us," said Jerzom as two grade-school-aged boys walked right in front of him, clueless that a royal prince of Kopaz stood less than two feet from them.

Maybe it was too complicated for Jerzom. Maybe it was just the way it was.

Danny took a stab at explaining what he thought was going on. "OK, I lived in this time. I left, and now I am back, so I can't be two places at once, and since you and the boys are with me, all of us experience the warp in time that paradox causes." He stopped and asked, "Are you following, Jerzom?"

"Yep! Ah...er...I think so," the royal prince of Kopaz answered.

"Well, like I told you last night, Viracocha told me personally what's going on. 'Without the presence of the ruby ring, the portal of reality remains closed!'" Danny grinned, clearly cheered, knowing he had figured out the message from Viracocha. "And like I said to you, I need your sister's ruby ring to open the portal of reality!"

Strange as it was, the four ventured to Jeannie's old house and walked in. There was her mother.

Staring in utter amazement, Danny's mind pulled images from the past. *She looks exactly the same*, thought Danny. Soft Wind was tall, thirty-three years old, and beautiful, with long, shiny black hair and deep-brown eyes.

Busy cleaning and making the little house a piece of heaven in the Scarlet Desert, Soft Wind walked right past Danny where he stood in the kitchen. Then she entered the living room. Turning and following her, Danny watched Soft Wind sit on the old couch next to the window, resting for a minute between her chores.

Danny dropped his eyes from looking at the couch and now gazed at Jeannie's mom, his thoughts continuing to tumble. *How can the Veil of Time be so weird? This is goofy! I'd like to talk to her and tell her all about Kopaz and Jeannie.*

It was so real. Soft Wind was now sitting on the living room couch, its hand-sewn patches marking each repair over the years. Danny remembered a story that Soft Wind had told Jeannie, which Jeannie had later told him. *It was the first time she told me about her sacred name.* "Well, Jeannie, the father of our nation is Kashom. And you know that you're part of the legend. Your real name isn't Jeannie—it's Neferzul, which means Beautiful Keeper of the Golden Key."

Then Soft Wind got up from the old couch, walking past Danny, Jerzom, and the boys. It was obvious the boys were fascinated. They all watched Soft Wind go to the kitchen cupboards. Her hand reached into the pot cupboard next to the stove. Soft Wind scooted the stacked pots and pans to one side, looking for her favorite coffee pan. She spotted it— speckled white paint on blue porcelain.

Soft Wind pulled open the cupboard drawer next to the sink. She reached and took out a neatly cut piece of white cheesecloth. Her fingers held a prized possession, an old silver spoon.

Danny pointed to the spoon and said to Jerzom, "It once belonged to Kashom's second daughter. It has been passed down for generations, and Soft Wind inherited it from her grandmother."

Mesmerized could not have been a better descriptor that defined the look on Jerzom's face. He wanted to reach out and touch the silver spoon.

First she spooned the right amount of fresh-ground coffee into the cloth, tied it closed with string, and tossed it into the boiling water. It was a matter of minutes until the aroma of fresh coffee filtered through the air into the living room.

How weird, thought Danny. *I can smell the coffee.*

Soft Wind walked back through the living room door with her cup of coffee and a small plate with a slice of banana bread on it, balancing them perfectly. She sat them on the coffee table.

That old handmade wooden coffee table, with its layers of paint, sat as a monument in the living room. And if the walls could speak, they would tell stories of Soft Wind and Jeannie's countless discussions of ancient legends. Its shabby appearance reflected its hard years of valiant service. For as long as it had been the centerpiece of support for countless coffee cups during those discussions, the old coffee table was vigilant.

Maybe it was supposed to happen, and maybe it was just a coincidence.

Danny, Jerzom, and the boys watched Soft Wind stand and go to her secret hiding place—a hole hidden under a throw rug on the living room floor. She rolled back the rug, lifted up a loose board, reached into the hole, and brought out a bronze box that she kept there.

She opened the box and took out two goatskins with writings on them in the native language of Kashom. For a few moments, she stared at them in silence. Holding them with both hands, Soft Wing looked fondly at the legends, and she must have been thinking of her lovely daughter, Jeannie.

Shooting in every direction, Jerzom's mind was filled with warmth and happiness as he thought, *Oh my, that is my brother's handwriting!*

Setting the bronze box on the table in front of the couch, Soft Wind sat again and relaxed.

The afghans folded neatly on the back of the couch looked inviting. Soft Wind must have felt a twinge of cold air drift thought one of many cracks in the walls of the old house, because she reached for one and covered her folded legs on the couch.

It was like a movie on a big silver screen unfolding the story of Jerzom's brother's life in the Scarlet Desert. Jerzom looked on as each new chapter furthered the plot.

Soft Wind leaned forward and reached for the bronze box. She took out a pouch. She opened it and removed the lock of hair. She held it in ceremonial fashion, drawn across her cupped hands on outstretched arms. Contracting her fingers around the lock, she squeezed it. Retracting her arms, she released her fingers and gently took the hair from her left hand with her right. She replaced the lock in its pouch, returning it to the bronze box.

Jerzom's eyes followed Soft Wind's every movement, and he asked Danny, "Do we just take the lock of hair?"

"Yes, we do," Danny responded.

CHAPTER 12
Someone Else's Lock of Hair

I s stealing a crime when the existence of every living creature in the universe depends upon the stolen object? That's an interesting question, especially when there is no way to talk to the person who owns what you want and you have no way to get it except by stealing it. But maybe it is not stealing. Perhaps Aerapondes's lock of hair belongs to the royal family, and the royal prince of Kopaz is just reclaiming it.

They got what they came for—Aerapondes's lock of hair.

As they walked out the door and started making plans, Little Danny and Little Tony surprised Danny and Jerzom with a new challenge.

Tugging on Danny's pants to get his attention, Little Tony said, "We have my mommy's and daddy's locks of hair."

How could Danny not want his best friend, Tony, and Jeannie's best friend, KateLynn, back from the Land of the Dead? It was a decision the royal prince of Viracocha would have to make shortly. It was unlike their earlier decision to enter Mochcom's house, discovering two little boys trapped in a dungeon of death and rescuing them. No, this time entering Gorom Mochcom's house for a second time would be set in motion by a motive—a most noble and very important cause.

The War of the Gods was raging, and planets were being blown to smithereens. Time was running out, and yet Danny would lay down his life for his friends who had fallen victim to Mochcom. The supreme god might levy severe consequences for deviating from his mission, but that was a risk he was willing to take.

"Tony, Danny, where are the locks of hair?" asked Danny.

"Where you found us." It was not the answer Danny wanted to hear.

When you are a god, decisions fall on your shoulders and, in essence, the buck stops with you. And so it was with Danny.

He turned to Jerzom. "Although we have what you came to get—your sister's lock of hair—we are not going back to Kopaz...yet."

Walking back through the minefield of booby traps that Mochcom had prepared for intruders was once more Danny and Jerzom's challenge—except this time, they had two little guys to keep safe.

"It's the third time I've walked through this stinking pile of garbage," said Danny. "Look at all this crap and garbage Mochcom has strewn in all directions...decaying animal carcasses and you name it...makes me want to throw up."

There could be no doubt that Jerzom had similar reactions to the filth they were navigating through as he listened to Danny's next comment.

"When we get what we came for, I think it will be our last."

"I hope so," Jerzom answered.

As they tiptoed through the garbage, they heard a sound of horror—*ssscccccccrrrrreecchh*—ripping through the air as a black vulture showed up.

Attacking in a ruthless dive of vengeance, his single focus was the royal prince of Viracocha's ring.

Slamming into Danny with the force of a diving warplane, the bird hurled Danny to the ground, razor-sharp talons digging deep into his right forearm muscles. Despite the unbearable pain, Danny managed to cup his fingers and make it impossible for Black Vulture's sharp beak to snatch the ring from his hand.

Suffering so horrific a pain, Danny's strength ebbed, and he was almost no match for the Black Disciple of Mochcom. With his forearm pouring blood profusely, Danny aimed his ring at the bird, which was now trying to rip at his head to take his eyes out with his knife-sharp beak. With his left hand trying to protect his eyes, he managed to steady his ring.

The beam of green light did nothing. His ring did not work.

Each passing moment, the situation was growing direr. Figuratively speaking, if a course correction was not enacted immediately, Danny would no longer have his ring. It would be the end not only for Danny, Jerzom, and the boys but also for quite possibly all who lived in the universe.

As Mochcom's black bird of death, Black Vulture, sat on top of Danny in a pile of garbage, Jerzom made the boys back up and huddle. He wanted them as far as possible from Black Vulture.

Not in a million years would Danny have expected Black Vulture to be in the picture again. At the Boar's Tusk on that fateful day of March 24, 1958, Danny had already killed Mochcom's black bird of death, Black Vulture.

Danny's mind was racing. *Somehow, time is at the center of this puzzle. The date must precede March, or is this vulture an offspring of Black Vulture, or is it a reincarnation, or what?*

While Danny engaged in a raging struggle in a heap of garbage, Jerzom raced with all his might to help. Fortunately, the bird's focus on Danny's ring was relentless, and Jerzom was not Black Vulture's target. Finding Danny's leather bag tied to his waist, Jerzom retrieved the knife.

He shouted Quill's instructions. "When the beam has lost its power, Black Flight dies only with a strike of the knife, capturing TRPOV'S might!"

Danny listened.

Confused by the presence of Jerzom and the unknown instrument in his hand, Black Vulture's hesitation gave the prince the moment he needed.

With the knife in Jerzom's hand and its point in the feathers of Black Vulture, Danny aimed his ring's beam of green light at the handle. The knife flamed, and Jerzom drove it into the bird's flesh.

A fiery knife, exploding with wrathful energy deep into the heart of Black Vulture, was the bird's final doom.

His bloody feathers smoldered on the ground.

Danny's ring had back its power, and he was able to restore his arm with the gift from the gods as the beam of green light closed his slashed muscle, even though it had been opened to the bone. He had barely time to finish using his ring prior to an unexpected new challenge.

The unexpected happened in clockwork fashion as if orchestrated by some unknown force. The familiar screeching cries of the monkey came from nowhere.

Jerking his head in one direction and then another, Danny saw nothing. *Where in the hell is that creature hiding?* From behind a fifty-gallon steel drum, the monkey sprang. The boys were his target, and his leap was perfect. He landed on Little Danny, and sinking his fangs into the boy's arm, the monkey darted away, dragging his prey in his mouth.

With no option, Danny pointed the beam from his ring like a surgical knife at the back leg of the creature. It worked. A bloody leg dropped to the ground, and the monkey dropped Little Danny.

Racing with the full speed of a god, Danny scooped up the boy from the ground. Unconscious, Little Danny had suffered more than a bite to his arm.

And in the voice of a god, Danny roared, pointing his ring at his target. "Mighty god of the universe, if it be your will, let my ring save this child."

The power of the gods was on display again. Little Danny's head moved. His eyes opened, tears pouring from them as he said through his sobs, "Did you kill him?"

And before Danny could answer this simple question from an innocent child, something else grabbed the attention of the royal prince of Viracocha. From the corner of his eye, he saw Mochcom exiting his house.

There was no Veil of Time covering Black Vulture, and so Danny's instant reaction was to use his ring on Mochcom. As the evil gorom walked toward his dead bird, which lay on the ground, a pile of smoldering, burnt feathers midway between Danny and Mochcom, Danny lifted his ring finger, and a beam of green light shot across the space. It penetrated the body of Gorom Mochcom with no effect, other than provoking a chanting howl. "Prince of Viracocha, I know you are here, and your doom is in the making—the sacrifice of the firstborn male child. You know what I talk about, do you not? *Haaa! Haaaaa! Haaaa!*" The madman's laugh pierced the air in a horrifying singsong chant that left Little Danny and Little Tony screaming with fright.

Mochcom's chilling words caused Jerzom to jerk. *Is Gorom Mochcom talking about the boys, Little Danny and Little Tony, or does that evil disciple of death have someone else in mind?*

Yet it was not only Jerzom left in the dark by Mochcom's rant but also Danny. Amid the chaos and confusion, Danny had not a clue. His mind was racing. *What the hell is that evil creature talking about? What or who is the firstborn male child?*

Maybe it was unintended, and maybe it wasn't. For whatever reason, Mochcom's words about killing the firstborn male child took second place to the urgency at hand. "Jerzom, we have to act quickly!"

The monkey was nowhere in sight. The mood turned eerie.

Observant Danny was, and that was all it took, as he said, "He can't see us or the boys, but he knows we are here."

Wondering, however, what the depth of the Veil of Time included, Danny was taking no chances. "Jerzom, get the boys. We need to get what we came for and get out of here. That monkey is not hidden by the Veil of Time. I think Gorom Mochcom can't see us, but he knows we're here and can command his evil servants to carry out his will."

Even though Danny was sure Mochcom was unable to see who was in his sanctuary of death, Danny took no chances. Watching every minute motion of Gorom Mochcom, Danny motioned for Jerzom to take Tony, and he held Little Danny.

With his free arm, Danny picked up a piece of iron pipe and hurled it at Mochcom. It flew through him as though he were a ghost.

At the end of its trajectory, the pipe, cartwheeling end over end, slammed into a fifty-gallon tank with the booming sound of a base drum in the Macy's Thanksgiving Day parade.

Mochcom didn't flinch, clearly oblivious to extraneous sounds, and so Danny said, "Let's get the locks of hair and get the hell out of here!"

Wandering back through the house, Danny thought, *I hope this is my last trip to this place of horror!*

"Shit," said Danny, "he has the wall closed, and we don't have the monkey's key!"

"Danny," said Jerzom quietly, knowing the boys were frightened, "blow the damn wall down like you did the other one."

"You're right, Jerzom. It's people who are trapped in the time warp—not physical objects. *Stand back!*"

Kaboom, and the wall was gone.

"Good job, Danny," said Jerzom, using some of the slang he had picked up from his new friend. "I said, 'Blow the damn wall down,' and you did it!"

Tony's Boy Scout flashlight was still in the stinking garbage on the floor where Danny had dropped it. His intention had been never to subject his hand to such filth again, but he had no choice. "Holy shit, I hope this is the last time I touch this thing!"

He paused. Then, with a chuckle, he said in the language of the royals, "Sorry, Tony, but your piece-of-shit light is staying in this garbage hole after we use it to find your hair."

Jerzom laughed. "Let's hope!"

In English, Danny asked Little Tony, "Where are your mother's and father's locks of hair?"

Without speaking, Little Tony pointed.

Danny shone the flashlight on a small cardboard box, and the beam fell on a leather pouch. Danny grabbed it and was about to bolt for the door when he saw what appeared to be the edge of a rolled-up piece of paper sticking out of the top of the pouch between the two drawstrings. He pulled on it.

Danny's face said it all as Jerzom watched the young god read the note. Nothing could hide the horror emanating from Danny's outward expression of the inner emotions tearing at his soul.

"You *fucking bastard!*" howled Danny.

Fools!
You take
me for an
IDIOT?
" No Hair
— No Tony
— No Katelynn

Forever!"
Ha Ha

The young god dropped the paper on the filthy floor and stepped on it as he motioned for the others to follow him.

Ironically, they walked out the kitchen door as Mochcom was walking in, and they walked through him.

CHAPTER 13

Jerzom Is Going Home

As the clock ticked away, could there be serenity? When singing a lullaby to a new baby, a young mother might want nothing more than for time to stand still and give her that treasured moment as a gift that would last forever.

But in contrast, however, to a mother wanting to hang onto treasured moments for an eternity, when the bugles trumpet and the cavalry charges, would a soldier want that moment of war to last forever? Now consider these two moments are one and the same, the mother singing as the soldier charges. Consider the question: Even though there are times of great joy that some would like to last and cherish forever by somehow stopping the clock, would it be reasonable, on the other hand, for those hoping to preserve moments of joy at the same time hope that time would stand still and give an endless rerun of the bloody ravages of war? It's an interesting question, since this is most likely is not what most would want—hope that joy would last forever and at the same time hope that misery would last forever.

Yet could there be both—new life in a faraway land and a raging war that threatened the existence of every creature in the universe, even that drowsy newborn? Is this food for thought?

Bonds of friendship had strengthened, and the incident at the Pit of Vulcan, when Jerzom was sure he had lost his honor forever by attempting to steal the golden watch from the royal prince of Viracocha, seemed now like a faded memory from a distant past. The redemption of Jerzom's honor was at hand, if he so chose.

Leaving the house of horror without what they had come to get, it was time to move on. As they meandered back through the piles of garbage on their way to the road, Danny and Jerzom wanted the dreaded secret of Tony and KateLynn living in the Land of the Dead for all eternity to remain secret from Little Danny and Little Tony.

It was time for light talk. The woodshed was on their way, and in a matter of minutes, if all went as planned, it would be like an image in the rearview mirror of an automobile racing down the road to a new destination. However, the house of horror, the woodshed, was still three hundred feet in front of them.

Light talk continued. "My dear friend, I thought that when Tony was killed by Mochcom I could never find one to replace him," said Danny, looking at Jerzom.

Words were not needed. The bond of friendship that had been forged between Danny and Jerzom was most profound.

"My royal prince of Viracocha, beyond my wildest imagination I never dreamed I would have as a best friend a god who will sit at the council table of the primeval gods!" Jerzom said, struggling to make a statement that would not offend the young god.

"Our journeys have just started, my friend, and soon we shall venture to a realm of existence that is beyond human understanding, but first we have work to do!" Danny replied.

Moving his eyes from Jerzom, Danny looked at Little Danny and Little Tony. "Would you like to get your mother and father back?"

There could be nothing that made a heart soar like an eagle more than the smile on a little boy's face. And when that smile was multiplied by two, a soaring eagle had no limits.

"Can you do that, Mr. Danny?" asked Little Tony.

Little Danny held back a smile and listened as his brother said, "I thought they were dead!" It was his way of asking for more, knowing that a god was standing in front of him.

"Well," said Danny as he laughed freely, "I don't *think* we can get your mom and dad back...*I know we can!*"

There were a few smiles and sounds of laughter as Danny watched the reaction on the faces of the sons of his best buddy. And his mind was filled with the thought, *Tony...I can't wait to see you again!*

That thought was fleeting, as something at center stage could change all. Now, more seriously, Danny said in a quiet voice, "The War of the Gods has started, and time is not on our side."

The reminder was real. The bleeding leg of the monkey lay on the ground not more than ten feet from Danny, Jerzom, and the boys. Who knew if that sharp-pointed-toothed creature were lurking somewhere near?

A fight to the death was no hindrance to the loyal servant of an evil man.

Rrrraaaarrrrraaarrrraa! Mochcom's monkey squealed from his hiding place. Someone had kindled his vengeance not once but twice— superhuman or godly, it mattered not. His target was in sight.

Danny's mistake was taking his eye off the proverbial ball—the woodshed. Crouching on the roof, the monkey lay in waiting. At the moment Danny glanced at the two little boys, the monkey leaped and flew through the air. Danny's ring was his target.

Bony, furry fingers succeed in ripping it from Danny's finger as the monkey's sharp teeth sank deep into Danny's forearm. The pain was excruciating, and it was too late. The monkey was leaping away with the source of power that controlled the fate of the universe.

It was not the whirl of Kopaz, but it was close. In Kopaz, at the athletic games of Zor, Jerzom had been the only royal prince to ever win a gold medal. And to this day, no one has broken that record of Jerzom in Kopaz.

One never knows for sure why things happen. Why was Jerzom a skilled athlete? And even more curiously, why was his Olympic achievement in the sport of what was called the whirl of Kopaz?

Jerzom picked up an iron ring that lay in the dirt at his feet. And with his skill as the gold medalist of Zor, he swung his arm back, and in a victor's fashion, ready to stand on the winner's podium, flung it through the air.

The iron ring struck the monkey in the neck like a guillotine, and his furry head rolled from his body as he was making his final leap over the picket fence and his getaway.

Lying in the dirt at the base of the fence was the head of a monkey, eyes wide open.

Jerzom walked to the headless body of that monkey-like creature, and he pried open the fingers of whatever it was and retrieved Danny's ring.

Stretching his arm out with his palm up, he handed Danny his priceless gift from the gods.

There were no words profound enough to express to a newfound friend the message that was hidden in Danny's heart. "Thanks, Jerzom!"

Despite the simplicity of Danny's words, the royal prince of Kopaz knew in his heart the feeling of gratitude that the young god had for him.

Walking down the driveway for what Danny hoped would be the last time, he turned to look at the filthy old house and woodshed. His mind was caught for a moment as he thought, *The horror...the evil...and the suffering that has been carried out here will forever be on the pages of history, yet hope is a good thing, and maybe those who have fallen victim here will see justice bend toward them!*

It was a marathon walk back to the CoalVille tipple, and that was not an option. Planets were at stake, and time was the enemy.

"Grab my hand, Tony, and you grab Little Danny's, and then Jerzom's. We fly."

Gathered at the dynamite vault, Jerzom, Little Danny, and Little Tony prepared to leave.

"You guys, Danny and Tony, I want you guys to mind Jerzom. You will travel far, and then you will be in a palace called Kopaz. There you will live in a royal palace. Are you ready for that?" As he was speaking to the boys, Danny had to turn his head to hide his tears.

He put his hand to his face to wipe away his tears but smiled when he heard a loud "*Yes!*" from two little guys who showed no more fear.

Putting his arm around his new best friend, Danny said, "You have your sister's hair and—" He could not finish what was tumbling around in his mind. *Tell my love I can't wait to hold her in my arms again.*

Choking up, Danny said, "Your place of honor is forever."

It's funny how friendships are forged. Jerzom wanted his best friend, Peizar, back. To that end, he chanced a dangerous course when he elected to steal a golden watch. The young god who owned that watch was now his best friend.

Danny was far from elated to be alone, but it was necessary. He alone must carry out his mission—to rid the universe of the final evil creature, the black disciple of Dark God Zuron.

As he thought of his final journey in the Scarlet Desert, he said, "I think you need to get out of here. There is something going on I fear is not right."

"My royal prince of Viracocha…the gods be with you!'" said Jerzom as his voice struggled to put words together.

And then, squeezing Danny's hand, as visible tears trickled down his cheek, Jerzom said, "Jeannie will be most anxious to get a report. I'll give her your love."

And then they were gone.

Could there be both—new life in a faraway land and an endless raging war that threatens the existence of every creature in the universe, even a newborn? Was this food for thought?

Like the crack of a gun in the stillness of a quiet evening, rolling thunder from an approaching springtime desert storm found Danny staring at the spot where his newfound friends were no more.

CHAPTER 14
Is Earth Next?

I t seems that when a foregone conclusion is just on the horizon, all hell will break loose or those facing the impending doom will just sit back and let it end life as they know it. Could this be the case here? Was there hope for the universe, or was it too late?

"*How? How?*" bellowed Viracocha. "*How* could you let this happen? Do you know how many planets it will take to tilt the tide of this war? *Oh hell*, the tide has already turned. What do we do?"

He must have been feeling hopeless, as if fate had stepped in, even in the Pantheon of the Gods, wielding the sword of doom that would end his dynasty, keep him from being supreme god forever. Panic was about to take center stage.

Blank faces stared back. There could be none at the council table of the gods who would slough off the gravity of the unfolding events that threatened the outcome of the war with Zuron.

"I want Quill here *now!*" yelled the supreme god.

It would seem that tensions at a table surrounded by the gods who rule the universe would be rather nonexistent and only a serene environment would exist. You would think that the creators of the universe would work in harmony as they planned and managed the affairs of all they had set their hand to creating. Why would there be contention?

It did leave one to wonder, unless Jupiter was only the first of their creations to go up in smoke, and it mattered not to them that now not only had countless other planets been reduced to smoldering cinders but also entire solar systems. Would their creations going up in smoke before their eyes be cause for concern and bring about contention? Just maybe!

"I find the complacency here rather disturbing. First, I am not the only one who will lose if this conquest goes not in my direction," growled Viracocha.

He looked at Jupiter, who was seated not more than three thrones away. "Do you, Jupiter, find it amusing that your namesake planet is no more?"

Cordial, yet reserved, Jupiter answered, "No, Supreme God, I do not!"

Now glaring with his deep-set emerald-green eyes, Viracocha proceeded, pounding his fist on the table. "Then what do you plan to do about it, Jupiter?"

Gently placing his hands on the red-diamond table, his elbows and forearms resting on the armrests of his golden throne, Jupiter made a profound statement. "Viracocha, who among us is privy to that most guarded knowledge that creates the calamity that is befalling us all?"

After a pause to contemplate his response, Viracocha spoke methodically. "What did you say? Or were my ears fooling me?"

"I said, how did Zuron get something that he was not privy to? Or, more profoundly, was it not you, Supreme God, who had control over the two code words? It appears, most assuredly, that he, Dark God Zuron, must now have at least one of them…is this not so?"

Ignoring Jupiter, Viracocha changed the focus of conversation. His face hard, he looked at all the gods and said, "'The site of the black pit defines the color of the scent.' I have yet to hear anyone venture the answer to this deathly riddle." Then turning back to Jupiter, he said, "Jupiter, you have surely been at my side for longer than I can remember, yet you have your tongue tied when it comes to riddles."

Waiting for a response from Jupiter, a god who Viracocha felt was more interested in fencing than survival, was off the table. Their conversation abruptly ended. Jupiter said nothing. And so it was that an unanswered riddle once again reared its face with deadly consequences.

Maybe it was that for eons the setting of the pantheon had been taken for granted. Maybe over the billions of years the gods had lost their perspective of who they were and why they were there. History suggests that seems to happen at seats of government.

It's hard to imagine such a place. Consider walking on a blue-diamond floor. Now picture that floor to be the material of the most famous diamond of all—the Hope Diamond. It's immense. When you're at the Smithsonian and look at it under the glass display case, you might say, "Wow! This thing is huge!" Yet if the Hope Diamond were dropped on the blue-diamond floor of the Pantheon of the Gods, it would be as a speck of dust.

Now imagine walking over this floor and peering into what looks like a large football stadium. It is oval—one hundred yards wide and two hundred fifty yards long. The blue diamond floor is at the crest of this unusually shaped meeting room. You can see golden stairs surrounding the entire oblong opening. There are fifty stairs leading down to the floor of the meeting room where the red-diamond table is located. As you descend the golden stairs and step onto the floor of the oval-shaped room, your feet rest on a three-foot-thick floor of glistening emerald gemstone that is supported by a solid foundation of pure gold. Light from Kolar filters through the sky dome and hits the mirrored surface of the gold. The light is reflected back through the gemstone floor, creating a heavenly aura surrounding the gods at work.

Yet this is but one of thousands of rooms at the Pantheon of the Gods. What else might you see if tours were allowed? You might find the decor of the grand dining room to be of impeccable taste. But feasting at the table of the gods would certainly be a highlight of the tour, especially if it were a special occasion with foods that only gods are allowed to eat. Yet, maybe to the gods, the foods that have been set before them since time began have lost their savor.

One has to wonder, when you're sitting in a room larger in size than ten city blocks of New York, what's in the other rooms? Why so big? What goes on here?

Certainly, those are valid questions, but the gods of the universe can do and have what they please, so the questions have no merit. That is, unless all of that grandeur and greatness of their domicile goes up in smoke. They might ask, where will we go and what will we do when our pantheon is no more?

Trumpets blasted. The council's spokesperson stepped into the limelight and announced with force, "Supreme God Viracocha, Quill is present!"

"Send him in," yelled Viracocha.

Quill spoke not a word as he waited for instruction.

"Your report...let's have it!" shouted Viracocha.

"Supreme God Viracocha, Gorom Mochcom yet lives," reported Quill.

"Hmm. Is that it?" asked Viracocha.

"No, Supreme God. Mochcom no longer has Black Vulture or his evil monkey! He has but one line of defense left, and that is his black ring from Zuron."

"Any more?" asked Viracocha.

"The young prince of Kopaz, Jerzom, is home, and he has a lock of Aerapondes's hair," replied Quill.

"That is good!" said Viracocha. "With the lock of hair, I can retrieve Aerapondes from the Land of the Dead, as she is the only one who can bring about the final demise of Mochcom, Zuron's disciple. She must hold my zedite knife when it is thrust into the beating heart of Mochcom as he lies on the top of my high tower when my glory is at its high point. Others can help her hold my knife, but the hand of Aerapondes on my zedite knife is required. Yes, we do make progress."

Quill's news brought a smile to Neferdor's face, knowing the first Neferzul would soon be back from the Land of the Dead.

"Quill, keep up the good work. Help Danny achieve his mission! Go and do what you can do," Viracocha said as he dismissed Quill.

After Quill departed, Viracocha turned to one of his council gods. "Neptune, do you know what comes next?" he snarled.

Like a fog, silence hung everywhere. The light of the chandeliers suspended above them could not compete with the silence that filled every morsel of space in the council room of the gods.

"No, my lord. We have failed you, and now the final calamity is about to befall us," replied Neptune.

"Yes," said Viracocha, pointing. "Look yonder through the sky domes and witness the display. The blackness of that distant sky is coming alive."

The explosive display of brilliance lighting up the cold void of space to the east of Zolob meant that there was now nothing but ashes and cinder in the place of what used to be a planet called Neptune.

CHAPTER 15

Wandering Back and Forth in a Void of Time

One could ask whether living with ghosts might be strange.

An interesting question, and yet if most were asked the question in a slightly different way—would you like to live with ghosts?—they might hesitate.

For Danny, being back in CoalVille in the spring of 1958 was bittersweet. He'd watched his beloved parents, Darla and Johnny, as they were busy living, or so it seemed. He wanted to talk to them as they were coming and going, but they were as the living dead. They had made their journey down the River Styx. That could not be denied.

Wandering the streets of CoalVille all alone, those memories of his life in the Scarlet Desert seemed so long ago, and they were Danny's treasured moments he wanted never to let go. As he walked by his old house for at least the tenth time, it was as if an arm reached out and said, "Come on in."

It was late. In the wee hours of the night, his heart ached, and he wanted his warm bed. The back door was open, and so he ventured in. It was dark. There were no signs of life. He opened his bedroom door, walked in, and closed it behind him.

He took his Levi's off and crawled into his bed. It was old times, and it felt good.

The night lingered on. He drifted in and out of sleep. It was if he had returned to the past. Surely, there could be no denying that fact. Danny was in the past. Yet, it was different. Danny was trapped behind the Veil of Time in a void of reality.

In the stillness of the black night, a sliver of light made its way through the bedroom window as a cloud drifted away from the moon, exposing its face. For a brief moment, the illuminated cracks in the plaster on his bedroom walls took on ghostly shapes that danced in rhythm with the flickering moonlight.

His eyes sprang wide open from the security of sleep. He was reliving the past. It was the recurring nightmare of screaming cries for help coming from a hole deep in the figment of Danny's imagination—followed by a loud bang.

He stared at the eerie figures—watching them fade into pitch blackness as the moon's light once again was concealed by the ever-moving clouds of the dark night.

The demon of remembrances hiding in the cobwebs of Danny's mind was pulling him into the depths of depression. He was caught in the realm of reliving those dreadful nights after the death of his father.

Drifting in and out of sleep in the blackness of night, he wondered if daylight would come.

The first rays of light stretched across the sage-covered desert, painting it a bloodred scarlet on Tuesday morning, the eleventh day of March 1958.

Thank god, it's morning. I hate dark, black nights. God, why can't I just sleep?

Danny watched the sun through his window peek over the eastern horizon and start its daily climb into the skies over CoalVille.

Holy shit, is this real, or am I trapped in time with no way out? What month is it? Is it February or March? Dad was killed in late February, but he is here... or is he? Heavy thoughts for the son of coalminer caught in a time warp. Could it be that a time warp had a strange way of shifting time as if time had no point of bearing? The portal of reality remained closed as Danny struggled for answers.

With those first rays of light, the wind on the Scarlet Desert picked up speed. It rattled the windows of his bedroom. He laid on top of the threadbare covers of his bed, listening to the sounds they made. Crisp March air whipped through the small crack of the opened window and across the nightstand next to his bed. Papers from a school assignment that Danny had left so long ago next to his bed fluttered from the stand and skittered spider-like over the floor.

Noises coming from the kitchen sent a chill of sweet-bitter remembrance through his being. He got dressed and ventured out. There they were, deep in talk.

"Hi, sweetie! You're up early. Boy, do you look like a million dollars. Wow—why would I ask for anything more? The best sight in the morning for an all-American boy—*a beautiful lady* with nothing on but a red-satin nightshirt!"

Darla walked from her bedroom with her nightshirt hanging no lower than midthigh. "Hey, that's enough to make a guy stay home from work!" Johnny blew Darla a kiss and motioned for her to come sit on his lap. "Boy, sweetie, we sure do have fun in the pale moonlight. Can't wait for the weekend—just two more days!"

"Johnny—shh! Danny is still sleeping. I'm not dressed, and I don't want him up!" She smiled. "Oh, Johnny, you're so handsome. Where'd you get that strong body, those beautiful eyes, that cute little nose?" She gently took his face in her hands and kissed him. *I just love him! He's tall and has such bright yellow hair and deep-set brown eyes. He's the love of my life!*

"You're just trying to butter me up. That's OK—be my guest. How's Danny doing, sweetie?" Johnny said.

"Oh, he's just great. All he can talk about is the upcoming Superior Grizzlies basketball game. Coach Bollas sure thinks the world of our son. He believes Danny is the best player on the team, and the CoalVille Pirates will beat the Grizzlies and be state champions this year," Darla said with pride, thinking about her boy.

"Honey, do you want me to make three eggs and toast this morning? Hank will be here in a few minutes to pick you up, so I had better hustle," said Darla.

"Sure, sweetie—that sounds like a great breakfast! God, I love that boy. We sure have fun in my red Chevy. I think Danny gets a bigger kick out of it than I do. This weekend I think we'll go racing through the desert. Wanna go, sweetie?" Johnny looked at his wife for confirmation. He didn't have to.

"Sure, honey. You think that you and Danny are going to have all the fun? *Nooooooo waaaaaay!*" Darla said as she stood next to the coal-burning stove, cooking Johnny's eggs and bacon.

No sooner had Johnny finished the last bite of his breakfast than he heard the honking horn of his friend's car. "Gotta go, honey. Hank is here— he's early! Oh, and get the crystal vase polished up—I'll bring twenty-four red roses home tonight so we can have a rich-man's dinner. Give me a kiss. See ya later, sweetie. I'm off to the black hole!"

Oh no! He doesn't have his lunch pail. I better catch him before he gets out the door. Darla circumvented what could have been a disaster—her husband at the bottom of the mine with no lunch.

"Honey, don't forget your lunch pail. It's in the fridge," she said. Just before he reached for the back doorknob—he made an abrupt turnaround and headed back to the fridge.

"Got to hurry! Hank's awaitin'!" Darla heard Johnny call out to her as he raced to meet his friend.

"I love you. Be careful, honey. I hate that you have to work in that awful coal mine." Johnny didn't hear what Darla said. He'd already bolted out the door and was headed for Hank's car. She heard the 1954 Ford motor purring as it drove off, Hank and Johnny in the front seat.

Strange indeed the conversation was between his parents. They were talking of him being there. They were talking about a ball game that he had already played. As he was listening, his mind erupted. *My god, what is going on? This could not get any weirder if someone wrote a fantasy tale of the living dead!*

The problems Danny faced were many. Without Aerapondes's ruby ring, he was trapped in a time warp. Without the gifts from the gods, the Sun Energy Transformer, he was trapped in CoalVille. He was trapped with no way out of either predicament.

Yet even stranger, it was the period in time in CoalVille that he was trapped in. It was a time warp with a finite dimension that he wandered around through over and over and over. He would relive events not once, not twice, but over and over. He never knew what point in time he would be in next.

His only hope was that the portal of reality would open before the time warp randomly changed, shifting into a reality before his dad would make his last trip to the coal mine. Time was running out, and he had no idea when it would end. Danny needed Aerapondes's ruby ring on her finger and her presence in CoalVille to unlock the warp. He didn't have either. Her ruby ring was in Kopaz, and Princess Aerapondes was in the Land of the Dead. Without Princess Aerapondes wearing her ring and standing with Danny, the portal of reality would remain closed, trapping him in a time warp.

CHAPTER 16
Yellzor the Ballplayer

Loneliness can close the walls in on you and bring out the boogey-man when it's in the middle of the night and when there's nothing but darkness surrounding you. It's funny how your mind races around in those situations and searches for something—anything—that might make the demons go and hide.

It wasn't long ago that Danny felt he was at the helm of the ship *Discovery*, sailing along on the seas of hope, headed for a shiny horizon with the love of his dreams, Jeannie, and his big furry friend, Yellzor, by his side.

Danny was all alone now, with no one to talk to. He was surrounded by images of ghostlike people from his past. He could see and hear them talking, but they had no idea he was there. To while away the hours, he had walked the main street of CoalVille at least fifty times. It had started to grow dark as the sun dropped to the western horizon in search of its resting spot for the evening.

Pulling into the parking lot outside the gymnasium of the CoalVille high school, the faithful fans were parking their cars and heading for the bleachers. Danny had nothing to do, so why not take in a ball game?

Wandering into the men's locker room, Danny watched as his old teammates got suited up for the big game. Danny spotted his locker.

Maybe he wanted to be part of a team. Maybe he was tired of being alone. For whatever reason, Danny remembered the combination of his locker and opened it. His basketball uniform was where he had left it. He suited up and followed his teammates onto the gymnasium floor.

As Coach Bollas always did, he called a team huddle to give the Pirates a pep talk just before the starting buzzer. Danny joined the huddle. No one saw him, but he heard all.

"OK, team, we have to win tonight. If we do, we're on our way to the playoffs. The Blair Town Wolverines is a tough team, but we can beat them. When we beat them tonight, we have one team left—Superior— and if we beat them, it's on to LaRayme for the state tournament. The Wolverines are fast, aggressive, and a well-coached team. We had luck when we beat them last year. They only have three new players since we faced them last. They're disciplined, but their weak point is their guard. He's inexperienced—so Robbie, when that guard has the ball, you get behind him and stick your hand right next to his—the one he is dribbling with—and he will lose control, and then you fly after the ball, and it will be all over. We'll have it, and, Robbie, don't look back as you head for the basket! OK, let's have a *Pirate cheer!*"

"*On, CoalVille! Go, Pirates, go!*" shouted the team and all who were in the gymnasium in unison.

"We got it, Coach Bollas," Robbie and his teammates said at the same time.

Coach Bollas looked at the large garnet ring that he wore. Standing next to him, Danny heard Coach Bollas say softly, "I wonder where Danny is? I remember he had a ring—a large emerald ring—it must be worth a fortune!"

He'd never sat on the bench. Danny had played every minute of every game. Walking with those teammates who would be sitting on the sidelines, Danny had a pain in his heart, knowing he was just a spectator.

Two minutes before game time, the cheerleaders ran out on the floor to get the crowd revved up. Jeannie was not leading the cheering squad. The band played the school song—"On CoalVille Pirates"—and the pep squad started the crowd singing.

On CoalVille, on CoalVille,

On to victory!
We're the Pirates of CoalVille.
We're for our school.
Loyal we will be, rah, rah, rah!
We'll stand by you,
While you're fighting
For our high-school fame!
So fight, Pirates, fight, fight, fight!
We'll win this game!

Then the band played the national anthem. When they finished, the game got underway. The Wolverines scored first. But the Pirates were on the scoreboard less than thirty seconds later. First the Wolverines led and then the Pirates. The lead went back and forth during the first half of the game.

The half-time buzzer sounded, and the teams exited the gym floor, heading to their locker rooms.

"You guys are doing great. We're only down by five points—forty-five to forty. Robbie, that guard is catching onto the hand movement that you're using to get the ball away from him. In this next half, get in front of him, pivot to the right, and then to the left. He won't figure out what you're doing until it's too late."

Danny concentrated as Coach Bollas instructed the Pirates how to win. His heart pounded with agony. He wanted to be part of the team. *I need to help. If I were there, Coach Bollas and the team would be counting on me. How can I help?*

Eerie as it was, Danny walked with his team and Coach Bollas back to the basketball court.

In his mind, Danny could hear Jeannie cheering her lungs out. *She used to watch me walk through the doorway onto the gymnasium floor, and then she'd get the crowd going. The crowd, the band, the pep club, and the cheerleaders would all stand and clap to the rhythm of "On CoalVille Pirates" to cheer us on as we entered the gymnasium and took our positions on the basketball court.*

The game started. Danny was not going to sit this half out. Watching from a bench was more than he could stand. He stood and ran to his team. To his surprise, someone else was there.

Yoooooowwwwweeeeellllll! The sound filled Danny's ears.

"Holy shit, Yellzor, what are you doing? You'll frighten everyone!" yelled Danny.

That certainly was not the case. Only Danny saw the giant wolf. Yellzor's howling was silent to everyone but Danny.

Strange as it was, a big high-school boy with shaggy yellow hair and emerald-green eyes raced to his friend and tackled him on the gym floor. It was a sight. The wolf and Danny rolled around like a boy with a big toy as Danny said, "Boy, are you a sight for sore eyes!"

And again, Yellzor let out a howl. *Yoooooowwwwweeeeellllll!* The furry beast greeted the young god, whom Yellzor had missed as much as Danny missed him.

It was more than a bit strange to Yellzor, as he had never been in the middle of a basketball game. Yet it seemed like time to have fun. With a few instructions from Danny, the wolf was ready to play ball.

"Yellzor, when that ball is tossed from one of those players with the blue jerseys on, you run like hell and bat the ball with your paw before the other boy can catch it. Got it?" yelled Danny over the noise of the crowd.

Yhhheeooooollllll! was the response.

"OK," said Danny, "not only do you bat the ball in the air, you bat it to me!" Danny further coached his furry teammate. "You see, Yellzor, it will be my job to tip the ball to the best Pirate guys, and then we'll win!" yelled Danny making a victory sign with his index and middle finger raised high in the air.

Rrroooooooooo was Yellzor's reply, as if to say "Got it!"

And so in the second half, the basketball took strange midair trajectories that were unexplainable to all the team players, Pirates and Wolverines alike, as well as the coaches, fans, and cheerleaders. But that didn't matter to Coach Bollas and the Pirates. They were winning, so whatever was causing the ball to fly through the air so weirdly was fine with them as long as it helped them run up the score. And that they did. The Pirates won by a whopping thirty points.

It was amazing how a ball headed for the basket, yet not on target, suddenly dropped through the net. Yellzor had found his game. Although Danny and Yellzor were in a time warp, they found that they could have an effect on nonhuman objects, and the giant wolf was having loads of fun. Who knew why it was happening? When Yellzor hit the ball in the air at midcourt, it appeared his giant paw was passing through a transparent object. Yet something was going on. Energy from his paw somehow affected the ball's trajectory. As he swiped at the basketball from midcourt, Yellzor then raced to the basket and waited for the ball to arrive. When in range, the giant wolf leaped in the air, and the energy of his swift paw was on the mark. If the ball was not headed for the basket, Yellzor made sure his paw got it through the hoop.

Of course, there were fiery objections from the Wolverines' coach, but who could argue? The referees had no choice except to count the points.

After following Danny to the locker room, Yellzor waited patiently in the hallway outside the dressing room for his best friend to get dressed. It was a strange sight—Danny, a young seventeen-year-old, six-foot-three-inch ballplayer, walking alongside his six-foot wolf.

Once dressed, they made their way to the gymnasium door. Back in the gym, the crowd was pumped, and the noise had Yellzor's ears standing straight up.

Responding to Danny's command, the wolf stood on his back two legs and stretched out his right front paw. Danny gave him a high five and said, "We did it!" Then a flash of movement caught his eye.

A young boy was pushing people aside as he raced for the door. It was obvious. The boy's face wore nothing but panic. Just as he was about to dash out the door, he turned his head for a quick backward glance.

Following the boy's unnatural behavior, Danny eyes were trained on his strangely alarming movements. He saw the man the boy had jerked his head to get a bearing on. His long, black filthy coat and his limp were unmistakable.

"It's him!" said Danny.

Even had he not been in a time warp, the sound of Danny's voice would have fallen on deaf ears, as those around him were uttering the victory cries of fans celebrating a Pirate win.

Outside, the moon was bright, and the stars were twinkling as Danny and Yellzor made their way through the parking lot en route to Main Street.

Then a shadow caught Danny's attention. The silhouette of a young boy wearing a white T-shirt racing for the back alley was chilling. The shadowy figure limping after the boy caused Danny and Yellzor to change direction and head to the unlit dirt roadway behind Jeannie's house. In an outright sprint, Danny and Yellzor ran to the entrance of the alley. They looked. They saw nothing.

Where did he go? thought Danny as he dropped his hand from Yellzor's back and squinted into the darkness, void of movement.

CHAPTER 17

Back Alley Déjà Vu

As he stood at the mouth of the alley, Danny's hand fumbled with something in his pocket. Danny clutched Jeannie's note. He didn't have to take it out. His mind had an imprint of it burned into an indelible image.

My Love—He is my Hero! He puts his Life in Peril for All of US. Soon the Gods will Set us Free as a New Human Race is Underway!

Farewell My Love! May Viracocha and Neferdor Speed you on your quest to rid the Universe of Evil.

Jeannie LoneTree

J L
D R

He went over every word as if the note were in front of his eyes. *Hmm. She uses the words "All of us"!* The glaring words were riveted to his mind. *"A new human race is underway." What is she saying? She's telling me something.*

With the moon on the rise, his heart pounded, and he loved her more deeply. Her way of telling him something had always been her hinting at little secrets, obscure events that exploded into giant realities.

Yet as he rehearsed her final words to him, the noise from the back alley leading down behind Jeannie's house sent a chilling feeling up his spine. It was an eerie déjà vu—Eddie stalking Jeannie after a game.

No, thought Danny. *It's not Jeannie, and it's not Eddie. Another family lives in Eddie's old house, and Jeannie is gone. Who is stalking whom?*

Even knowing that it was a teenage boy running for his life, Danny couldn't shake that story Jeannie had told him.

It was after the basketball game, remembered Danny. *Two shadowy figures skulked under the bleachers—they watched events taking place as Jeannie, Tony, KateLynn, and I were talking moments before all the lights were turned off and the gymnasium doors were closed and locked. They waited under the seats and peered through cracks between the bleacher stands.*

This night was all so much like that night so long ago. Noises in the night after another basketball game brought back old memories. Images flashed through his mind like a TV drama. It stretched on, but it was only moments in Danny's mind.

They were the last to leave. Terry's hand pushed the bar on the exit door. It opened with its familiar grinding sound. Leaving the dark gymnasium, they would have spotted Coach Bollas walking with me and Coach Smith toward the high school. It left them free to stalk Jeannie.

Jeannie told me the story so vividly that it was like a horror movie. *When she walked by, Eddie jumped out of the shadows and grabbed her. He flung her backward, stepping in front of her, and held firmly to her arm with a tight, pinching grip.*

"Hi there, cutie!" Eddie muttered as he stood in front of Jeannie, blocking her path. His flashlight shone brightly into her eyes.

Her eyes flew open. Her heart dropped like a rock descending to a bottomless pit. "My god! Who are you?" she screamed. Blinded by the light, she couldn't see his face.

His free hand touched her face. "Pretty white skin…my daffodil…oh, so soft and sweet. I'll bet it smells luscious and so soft to the touch!" Eddie rasped in a slow, singsong voice.

His black shadowy figure was featureless, but his voice was a dead giveaway. "It's you! Eddie! You bastard! Get away from me! What do you want?"

His hand brushed over her lips. "You know what I want! I want my little daffodil! Eddie won't hurt you. We'll have some fun! Won't we?" Eddie muttered as he reached to grab her.

Jeannie's hand swung from her side and grabbed his, and she pinched it with all her might. "You son of a bitch! Get your filthy hands off me," she screamed.

But that was then—Jeannie being stalked by bullies—and this was now—an unsuspecting boy being stalked by the Prince of Darkness.

Sensing his master's tension, Yellzor took Danny's hand in his mouth and gently let him know he was there.

Together they ventured down the alleyway. They saw nothing. After walking the length of a hundred yards, the pitch-black dirt alleyway broke out into the open. It was catercorner from the house across the street from Danny's.

The streetlight in front of Danny's house attracted miller moths. They were flying in tiny circles under the bright lamp. It was Mother Nature's way of building the food chain. Chasing the fluttering moths, bats were having a feast.

It wasn't the bats, and it wasn't the miller moths that were being caught and devoured, that grabbed Danny's attention. It was a young boy. This was not the teenage boy from the basketball game. He was nowhere in sight. This was a much younger boy, a little blond-haired kid with a stick standing at the base of the streetlamp.

At that point, Danny chucked to himself. *That is what I used to do. I thought I could catch a bat flying after moths with a stick by waving it in the air and knocking the bat to the ground.*

"Little guy, it can't be done!" That was the advice Danny wanted to tell the boy.

Then something strange caught Danny's attention. Danny spotted a shadow moving alongside the row of cottonwood trees across Main Street from where the yellow-haired small boy was chasing bats. It was slowing moving toward the boy who was under the streetlamp.

To Danny, there was only one objective. *That shadowy figure is stalking the young boy and does not want to scare him so that he flees to safety, escaping the grasp of doom.*

Instantly, Danny was prepared to make a move. He clutched the fur on Yellzor's neck as if to warn him to not make a sound. Danny had Mochcom's black ring and was jolted by inner thoughts. *He's defenseless without his ring, and he has no idea I'm watching him watch his prey.*

Then it happened. Danny was positive Mochcom had spotted him and Yellzor. The gorom stood still for a minute and stared at Danny's hiding place.

Does he know I'm here? The fear pressed on Danny's mind. *Are we still in a time warp?*

The sound of a foot stepping on a tin can changed everything. Could it be that was what happened? Mochcom looked away from where Danny and Yellzor were crouched behind a lilac bush.

At the end of the row of trees, like a rabbit hiding from a coyote, the boy wearing the white T-shirt emerged from his cover and darted back into the alley.

Mochcom changed his target from the yellow-haired small boy to the teenager with a white T-shirt. He started a fast wobbling run, moving as fast as he could manage, but then he stumbled on a limb that had been broken off by the wind.

The crashing sound across the street startled the little yellowed-haired boy who was sure he would catch a bat. Small as he was, his instinct was sound, and he started running for the house next to Danny's.

Meanwhile, back up the alley and within moments, Danny heard a door slam shut.

Thank god, that teenager must have made it home, thought Danny.

Danny searched for the yellow-haired boy. *He is gone,* thought Danny. *Evidently, he lives in the house next to my old house.*

That lingering thought hung in Danny's mind.

Weird, thought Danny, *I don't remember a little guy like that living next to me. I wonder who he is and why he was out so late all alone. He can't be more than five years old!*

Time stretched on. For fifteen minutes, Danny and Yellzor waited behind their cover of the lilac bush. Silence was everywhere. Not even the sound of an evening breeze cut through the air. All trace of Mochcom had vanished.

Within fifty yards from the back door of his house, Danny had a choice to make. *Hmm. Should we wait longer for Mochcom…or has he gone? Does he know where we are, or are we still in ghost land?*

A stream of cars came into view. Bright lights on, they approached the row of trees alongside Main Street. Car after car showed no sign of the Prince of Darkness.

Damn…that bastard got away! thought Danny.

Now that was a really weird thought, for if Danny had confronted Mochcom, would he have been a ghost or a man? Up until now, Mochcom had been in ghost land, as Danny was caught in a time warp. So maybe the entire matter was just fleeting gibberish…or was it?

Danny gestured for Yellzor to follow. They approached the back door of his old house. *Tonight, I'll have a friend sleeping with me…if he can fit on the bed!*

As Danny stepped through the door with Yellzor by his side, a lingering thought hung in the air. *Where did Mochcom go?*

CHAPTER 18

Back to the Past

W hen the unexpected happens, most often it catches by surprise those who are least suspecting. As it turns out, nothing in life can be for certain, and even the gods can't see into the future. The course of existence for all can be steered in a given direction, but the details of events along that journey unfold as unpredictable happenings that we call surprises!

Danny was tired of being among ghosts with no interaction. It was clear what was happening. Viracocha had made it indelibly clear. They were in the royal library of the palace of Kopaz. In a flashback, Danny's mind heard Supreme God Viracocha's voice as if it were yesterday. "The ruby ring of Neferdor was once worn on the finger of the supreme goddess, Neferdor. It holds a secret. Without the presence of the ruby ring, the portal of reality remains closed!"

At that time in Kopaz, it was not only Danny and Quill who saw the supreme god standing in their midst but also Jeannie.

As Danny walked up the stairs of his old house, his mind was full. He wanted Jeannie. He wanted the ruby ring to be in CoalVille and lift the veil of time that was keeping him trapped in world of ghosts.

The full moon seemed even brighter as Danny wrapped his fingers on a glowing doorknob that was acting like a mirror for the man in the moon. Danny's heart sank a bit as he turned the handle while noticing the warm evening light.

His thoughts of Jeannie were stuck in the front of his mind and wouldn't go away. Knowing she was safe in a land far away in the loving care of her grandmother, Queen Neferapondes, gave him comfort, yet he missed her dearly.

As Danny stepped through the back door into the dark kitchen, he had not only Jeannie on his mind but also his parents. *My ghost parents must be in bed. God, I hate this! Stuck in a time warp with no way to escape.*

Hesitant, Yellzor was not sure if he wanted to follow his master into the unknown expanse of a black room in an unknown house.

"Come on, Yellzor. It's OK," said Danny, knowing his wolf had second thoughts.

"Where's the light switch?" asked Danny rhetorically, knowing his words were not heard by any.

"Hi, Danny." A voice pierced the air the moment the lights came on. "I see you haven't forgotten where the light switch is located!"

"*Holy shit!*" screamed Danny, as he instantly spun around to see where and who had just spoken.

Staring in unbelief, he heard people yell, "*Surprise!*" as he gawked at Johnny and Darla.

"Oh no! Are you guys real, or are you ghosts playing tricks?" These were the only words Danny had in response.

"We are real, son! And guess what?" Danny's parents—no longer ghosts—said to Danny.

Those words—*And guess what?*—lingered. Danny was about to say something, but he didn't get his words out before his parents said, "We have visitors!"

Two people walked through the doorway between the kitchen and living room. They had their arms intertwined and were obviously in love, as could be seen by the smiles they were showering on each other.

Instantly, Danny's face was filled with anger. He shouted, "Jerzom, you bastard, how could you? Jeannie…I…I…why…why?"

The young god did not stop his wrath. "You were my friend! I thought you were my best friend, and how have you repaid me? You bastard!"

Mixed-up words dropped from Danny's lips in garbled fashion.

"I've got the ruby ring, and the portal of reality is now open," said Jerzom, trying to remain calm. He had dropped his arm from around the waist of the girl next to him.

Jerzom's words did not register. Danny had one thought on his mind, and that was sending his fist into Jerzom's face. Danny's clenched fist was well on its way and found its mark as he decked Jerzom. "How could you do this to me after all I've done for you? You bastard!" roared Danny again in a fit of rage.

You might say tensions were on the rise. As Danny was about to unleash a wrath of words on the girl, she screamed, "*Dad, stop!*"

Now that figuratively decked Danny. No sooner had the girl shouted at him than another couple came through the doorway.

Staring at the pair, feeling as if he were going crazy, Danny could not believe what he was looking at. "Are you Little Danny?" he asked the boy who had just entered. And before the boy could answer, the girl he had his arm around—a young, eighteen-year-old girl identical to the girl who had just walked out holding Jerzom's arm, and who had called him "Dad"—said, "Hi, Dad!"

My god, what is going on? thought Danny.

To any casual observer, it was obvious. Or was it? Why would the first young girl upset Danny and then call him "Dad"? But then to add to the unfolding drama, in stepped another young girl who was identical in looks to the first girl and also called Danny "Dad."

Shaking his head, Danny was about to say something. However, the odd procession was not finished. To Danny's surprise, through the doorway between the kitchen and living room—the doorway that Danny had gone through a million times when he lived there—in stepped another couple holding hands.

By this time, Jerzom had managed to roll over onto his side. He was silently watching, for fear of getting another punch to his jaw.

A few snickers were coming from the other side of the kitchen. Danny looked at his parents. The snickers stopped. Danny was totally dumbfounded. Then his parents screamed in bloodcurdling sounds, "*What is that?*" Their faces were white with fear.

Yooooowwwwwwooooo! howled Yellzor.

Yeah, you might say the unexpected was happening. It was time for someone to narrate what was going on, and that was Jeannie's job.

That he had been totally caught off guard was the understatement of the century, as Danny tried to find a safe footing by backtracking. He had no place to go, as he figuratively took his foot out of his mouth and said, "Yellzor, behave."

With Danny in a compromising position, he tried another tack. He pointed and laughed. "Don't be scared. He's my big yellow wolf, and he's a sweetie!"

Jerzom was still lying on the floor, as the blow from Danny's fist had nearly knocked him cold, and the royal prince of Kopaz was in a dazed state, his nose flowing with red blood.

Danny quickly walked to Jerzom. He didn't wait. Danny bent over, grabbed Jerzom's hand, and yanked him to his feet. "I'm so sorry, Jerzom! Please forgive me!"

Danny's soft words to Jerzom were short-lived. Something was happening that needed explanation. Looking at Jerzom, Danny said, "What the hell is going on?" He obviously had not put two and two together to figure out that Princess Aerapondes must be present with her ruby ring.

Jerzom said nothing.

Danny was trying to make sense of the bizarre situation when something else happened. The young girl who had had her arm locked through Jerzom's just moments earlier gave Danny a giant hug.

"Holy shit!" Danny's favorite words dropped from his mouth. And maybe rightfully so, as it was Danny who had jumped the gun and smashed his best friend to the ground without knowing the facts. Yet that brought up a good question—what were the facts?

Danny's mind was still swirling with that thought. *What the hell is going on?* And then he heard a familiar sound.

"Hi, sweetie," said Jeannie as she stepped through the door, knowing Danny was sick with foot-in-mouth disease. "Looks like you are having trouble," she said, a smirk growing on her face. "You just knocked out our son-in-law, making you make a fool of yourself!"

Danny didn't care. She was a sight for sore eyes. His grin emerged as he said, "OK, you got me. So what in the hell is going on?"

It was Jeannie's turn to talk. She could not wait to get her words out. "Once Princess Aerapondes was back from the Land of the Dead, we decided to have Jerzom and his sister with her ruby ring travel from Kopaz to CoalVille. I just couldn't bear to not be with you any longer, and I wanted you to see our family! So we all traveled the Highway of Time, and here we are!"

Prior to Danny's entrance, Jeannie, Aerapondes, and the entire crowd had showed up with the ruby ring and opened the portal of reality. Jeannie was able to explain to Danny's parents, Johnny and Darla, a mystery that had plagued them. She told them the connection Danny and she had with the gods. She explained the mystery of the gold note—how Danny inherited supreme power as TRPOV in union with TRPON—that had been left on their blanket the night of their honeymoon at the Boar's Tusk so long ago.

With a few snickers and Jeannie pointing, she explained, "I see, my love, you need some introductions. That is Jerzom. You just decked him! He is married to Little Jeannie, our oldest triplet. This is Little KateLynn, our second-oldest triplet, and she is married to Little Danny, whom you know. They are all sweet eighteen, and legally married," said Jeannie giggling.

Shaking his head, it dawned on him. *Her note to me! "My Love—he is my hero! He puts his life in peril for ALL of US. Soon the Gods will set us free as a new human race is underway. Farewell my Love! May Viracocha and Neferdor speed you on your quest to rid the universe of evil.*

Jeanne lifted her arm and motioned for all to come and get introduced. One by one, several eighteen-year-olds came through the door between the kitchen and the living room.

But Jeannie wasn't done talking, and her smile was growing with each word. "This is Jeanondes, our third triplet, and she is married to Little Zeb. This is Little Tony, and he's married to Princess Aerapondes, and she has her ruby ring, so that is why your parents are no longer ghosts in a time warp!" Jeannie said as her little smile grew to a giant smiley face.

Then her smile died. "Princess Aerapondes was the only one brought back from the Land of the Dead by Supreme God Viracocha. The fates of Tony, KateLynn, Peizar, and Merapondes remain unknown," said Jeannie.

At first, "*Wow!*" was the only word Danny could manage as Johnny and Darla stood in the background snickering. Then he said, "Everyone...I mean...all of the girls look identical!"

Once more, Jeannie snickered and said, "Maybe we inherited our looks from the goddess Neferdor!"

It was just Jeannie's way of letting Danny know that she knew the grand scheme of things, and he was, as usual, in the dark.

What Danny did not know was what had happened earlier. It had happened during the basketball game where Danny and Yellzor were the star players. Earlier that evening, the throng of teenagers had descended on the Robertses' home and made proper introductions to Johnny and Darla.

"Danny," said Jeannie, "come here." She pointed to the living room. Jeannie knew that Danny wanted some private time with her. With a little grin, she asked, "Would you kids mind if Danny and I had a minute to ourselves?"

Once they were alone, she stood with a hand on each of his cheeks. "I thought I would die, my love. You have no idea the pain in my heart as you ventured on to save us all."

He looked and listened, and then she kissed him. It was also a moment of déjà vu.

In a sweet embrace, he held her next to him. Her beating heart spoke loudly as her longing look of love shone on his face. Now their bonds of strength grew stronger as their journey continued. Once the impoverished children of coal miners, they'd walked a lonely road, and now within their reach were golden thrones at the council table of the primeval gods.

"Do you remember what happened on this old couch?" asked Danny as he looked at the old stove pipe coming out of the living room stove, making an S-shaped curve into the chimney.

Jeannie smiled. "Yes. Not quite as good as the royal palace...would you agree?"

In the excitement of it all, someone had been overlooked. At that point, Quill emerged onto the scene.

"Where is the little guy?" Quill asked, his voice full of concern. Not waiting for an answer, he charged on with a booming voice. "Did you not know that two are playing the game of war?"

Danny's instant jolt of energy caused him to race to Quill's side. His tutor was about the most serious person Danny had ever known. *What is up? Evil is afoot, and something is wrong!*

And as all listened, Quill drove home his point, repeating the supreme god's words. "Remember what Viracocha said! 'On top of my high tower, when my glory is at its high point, the first Neferzul will thrust my knife of zedite into the beating heart of Mochcom as he lies on the Shroud of Goroms with a finger bone of my wife's first prized possession deep in his throat! The war is lost when the firstborn son of the new race is sacrificed with Zuron's knife of zedite that is thrust into the boy's heart at the base of Viracocha's high tower when the full moon is at its high point!'"

"*Oh no*, he's gone!" screamed Little Jeannie, the oldest daughter, as Jerzom's heart sank.

CHAPTER 19
Sacrifice of the Firstborn Male

Skulking in the shadowy back alley of CoalVille on that bright moonlit night in early spring 1958, Mochcom spotted his prey.

The moon was not yet where it had to be. For the sacrifice to take effect, it had to be carried out precisely as the dark god would have it. It was a full moon that evening, and it was headed for the necessary position—right smack in the middle of the sparkling ribbon of the Milky Way that stretched across the middle of the dark black sky.

For those who know about mice, it is well known that a mousetrap is a simple device. It is constructed from a small piece of wood with a spring mechanism on it. Like with any trap, there has to be bait. A nice piece of cheese will do, that is, if you are a mouse looking for a snack. Innocent as the tempting piece of cheese looks, it all changes when the mouse decides to have a bite and puts his nose on the bait—*snap!* And it is all over.

Trapping the one person in the entire universe who could change the course of destiny of all living creatures for the eternities might not be unlike trapping an unsuspecting mouse. But who was this person who alone had the potential to impact the universe?

Could it be a little boy trying to catch a bat?

Mochcom was puzzled. *Where did he go? He was after a bat, not unlike the one I hold in my hands.*

Yet it was not just the boy that Mochcom was racing to find. Time was short, and the Prince of Darkness was also racing the clock, especially with what he knew about this most special human sacrifice and how it must be carried out.

"The royal prince of Viracocha is here but did not recognize the firstborn son of the new human race. Soon that will change, and I must have completed my most prized task for Zuron." The words fell softly from Mochcom's mouth and were lost among the sounds of the gentle evening breeze rustling leaves on the row of cottonwood trees. Mochcom's voice was as concealed as his movements as he stalked his prey.

With its broken wing, the innocent little bat had no place to fly. It flipped around helplessly under the streetlight. That was the enticement that the Prince of Darkness knew would bring his prey to where the trap would spring on him.

Monitoring from a short distance, Mochcom watched and waited for his game to take the bait. It did not take long. The boy came, and springing like the fatal snap of a mouse trap, Gorom Mochcom had his prize in his grasp. "How did you hide from me, my little sacrificial lamb?" Mochcom rasped softly as he grabbed DannyR and wrapped his hand over the boy's mouth.

His old 1948 Ford truck was ready to go. Their destination—Boar's Tusk—was half an hour away, and with only an hour to complete his most sacred assignment from Zuron, Mochcom was all too aware of the ticking clock.

The sharp fingernails on Mochcom's gripping hand dug deeply into DannyR's flesh. Crimson blood oozed from under each nail, making tiny red rivers flow down the small boy's arm.

Only four and a half, DannyR could not fight the large gorom, and his screams for help were lost in the filthy cab of the Ford truck as it headed for the desert in the late evening hours.

Wooooooop…wooooooop…wooooooop! VultureTwo's wings flapped as he flew in front of his master's truck. *Rawaarrrrr…rarrrarreeee!* he screeched as he watched his master, Lord Mochcom, through the windshield.

"How convenient Zuron has made it for me," snorted Mochcom, slobber dropping from his mouth. "He has given me my first vulture's son, and he is a good one! Soon all will be over, and I will be at the center of the universe, on a golden throne, sitting next to you, most glorious Zuron!"

Mochcom tapped his bloodstained fingernails on the Bakelite steering wheel of his 1948 Ford truck in rhythm with the thoughts of grandeur racing through his consciousness. "In less than an hour, all will be mine!" Mochcom said as he smiled and watched VultureTwo through the windshield fan the air with his wings to propel his flight.

"He thought he killed my only Black Disciple of Death. *Haaaaa! Haaaaa!*" spouted off Mochcom as DannyR lay helpless on the floorboards of the old truck, tightly bound with ropes.

Mochcom leaned over, grabbed a corner of the duct tape that was on the boy's mouth, and yanked it off. Screams from the shrieking vulture right outside the open window filled the cab of the truck.

"Your grandfather is an idiot! *Hahaaaaa!* He had no idea Black Vulture had a son!" he yelled, and DannyR screamed louder.

"I want to hear you scream, my little lamb, for soon your screams will be silent for the eternities. *Hahaaaaaaaa…hahaaaaaaaaa!*" roared Mochcom.

It was time. Mochcom's ability to transmogrify his body, or change in appearance or form, especially strangely or grotesquely, was his gift from Zuron, and he loved it.

"I just love to transmogrify my body," he said as he changed to a hideous-looking wolf-like creature with the face of a man covered with wolf hair.

"I've enjoyed my life, masquerading under the disguises of innocent people over the centuries of time in the Scarlet Desert, but now I'll be Lord Mochcom once more and rule as the gorom of Kopaz, and all will cower before my wolf face as I rip out their jugulars with my pointy white teeth!"

The pain in DannyR's arm was unbearable. His heart sank into a hole and fluttered as terror gripped his soul and sent rippling twinges racing around his body.

As he was bounced around on the floor of the truck, clouds of dirt were all he could breathe, and his head was being battered with every pothole the truck rattled over.

Mochcom reached an arm down and stroked his long, bony fingers through DannyR's sun-colored blond hair. "Do you like your daddy? Who is he? You better tell Mochcom—I will hurt you unless you help me. It will be our little secret, my little lamb," the high priest said as he drew his words out, mumbling in an eerie, singsong voice.

"Let me touch your chest! I'm going to do the Capacocha ceremony with the marking. I'll finish with the heart removal! *Haaaahaaaaa… hahaaaaa!*"

Bouncing over each rock and hitting the holes in the old dirt road meant the truck's headlights wavered up and down on the two ruts in front of the old Ford truck.

Then in the headlights, it was there. Mochcom screamed as he saw the Boar's Tusk come into view. "*Soon*, my little lamb!"

It towered in front of him. Although it was night, the moon was rising behind the Boar's Tusk, shedding its cool light on the tower, making it look like a reaching silhouette, stretching as if to touch a lone cloud drifting quietly in front of the moon.

"How stupid! The royal prince of Viracocha thought the only way to win the War of the Gods was to extinguish fire in the skies! Little did he know that killing the firstborn male of the new human race was the means to a much easier victory! *Haaaahaaaaa…hahaaaaa!*"

Staring at the rock formation, Mochcom's mind exploded with rapture as he roared out, "In less than an hour, the war will be finished, and I will be the head priest of the Church of Zuron! *Yes!*"

CHAPTER 20

Quil Reports to the Council—Again

Could there be a meeting of the gods at which that old saying "All is well" turns out not to be the case? What about miracles? Perhaps, but who knows? A dull knife could have cut the tensions that had thickened to the point of no return and were moving to center stage at a lightning-fast pace.

The official spokesman, the sergeant at arms, called the meeting to order. "Arise all. Supreme God Viracocha and Supreme Goddess Neferdor enter!"

All stood until Supreme God Viracocha and Neferdor had taken their seats at the head of the table. And all eyes were upon them. Viracocha glared as his head rolled from side to side. Not one god was absent from this urgent, special meeting.

"Do any among you have the answer, by chance?" were his first words.

There could be no doubt what was on the mind of the supreme god—the balance of power and the control of the universe. Left without options, he could only share his deepest thoughts with his fellow gods and goddesses. Soon, if the war was lost, his thoughts would no longer matter, no matter how he expressed them. All would be over for the Council of Primeval Gods who had ruled the universe since the beginning of time.

Viracocha looked down the table at those seated as he spoke. "Do you know that doom is moments away? I have been with you for eons, and who would have ever dreamed that it would end? My heart is heavy. I must take the blame. Zeus argued with me when I put forth my plan to let the humans chart their own course of destiny. I wanted no interference from the gods. So, as a condition, I made it very plain that the humans would never know who we are, what we look like, and how we govern. That was my downfall, and I must stand here today and apologize to Zeus for his wisdom that I did not grasp!"

Out of sheer frustration, Viracocha's fist slammed onto the tabletop. His head reared back. He stood. He roared with vengeance. "A miracle for the gods is needed...do you not agree?" Viracocha waited. Silence was everywhere. Then he continued. "That is a foolish idea, but that is what it has boiled down to. I have to laugh just thinking about a miracle for the gods!"

Viracocha pointed at the guest throne, not more than fifty yards from his, and said, "Quill, give us a report!"

If tension could talk, the room would be abuzz with clamor. Quill stood. He walked to the podium. Quill took his pace behind the podium and proceeded with his pronouncement of the status of the War of the Gods. "Zuron has one of the key words and has used it to move Lenszar. With the movement of Lenszar, Jupiter, Neptune, and many other planets have been vaporized. The new human race has begun. The firstborn son has arrived—the son of Prince Jerzom and Little Jeannie. She is the oldest triplet of the royal prince of Viracocha and the royal princess of Neferdor. The war will be lost if Zuron either secures the second code word or if his disciple, Mochcom, ritually sacrifices the firstborn son of the new human race with the zedite knife of Zuron. Mochcom, Zuron's disciple, has captured this boy, the firstborn son of the new human race. Time is gone!"

"You bring us good tidings, Quill. Now how about the bad news?" rasped Viracocha.

A flock of white doves flew into the grand council hall and circled the meeting. "Is this an omen of a brighter future?" asked Viracocha, but then a swarm of black ravens swooped in and overpowered the doves. "Hmm. I see. What now, Quill?" The supreme god pressed on.

"Viracocha, ruler of the universe, we have but one course," replied Quill.

"And?" The supreme god took his seat and placed both hands on the table, palms turned up.

Quill still maintained his dignity. Deep in his heart, he knew the end was all but upon them. Yet his respect for the gods was unwavering.

"Most benevolent god, our only course is this. We must rid the universe of Zuron's prince of darkness, Mochcom, thus eliminating his ability to sacrifice the firstborn son of the new human race. That task, ridding the universe of Zuron's prince of darkness, can only be accomplished by Princess Aerapondes thrusting your zedite knife into the beating heart of Mochcom on the top of your high tower when your glory is at its high point. Solve the riddle so you, most honorable supreme god, can destroy Zuron's planet, Zolob."

Formidable indeed were the tasks facing the humans working to become gods. Did any of the gods show a twinge of panic? If so, how would they have displayed it? That might have been the question on Viracocha's mind as his face turned rigid and his glare swept over those assembled like a steel sword ready to strike.

"Hmm. Well put, Quill," said Viracocha, and then he looked to the gods and spoke to them as a group. "Complacency? Will your ineffectiveness be the defining statement of your character when Volob is but a cloud of vapor?"

Viracocha turned to Quill and said, "Quill, fly! *Go!* Fly as fast as you can. Help Danny! I don't think Zuron will destroy Earth as long as Mochcom is there. It is our miracle, if there is such a thing!"

And with that, the meeting ended.

CHAPTER 21
A Race with Death

There could be no panic as dire as the one they were facing, the panic brought about by the kidnapping of a small child. The sacrifice of the firstborn son of the new human race at the hands of Mochcom would mean the ushering in of evil throughout the universe.

"*Where is he?*" screamed Little Jeannie as her voice intensified to sheer cries of horror.

Racing to the door and bolting out, Jerzom was gone. "*Danny! Danny! Danny!*" screamed Jerzom. There was no answer.

There are times when someone is present for good reason. Quill's assignment was stark and direct as he left Viracocha's presence with the god's orders: "*Don't come back until all is finished!*"

It was like a spark—the time it took for Quill to travel from Volob to the Scarlet Desert. There could be no lingering questions as to the urgency of the moment or the task at hand. The sacrifice of a four-and-a-half-year-old boy was center stage. Time was almost gone.

Within moments of leaving the Pantheon of the Gods on Volob, Quill was standing next to Danny and Jeannie. His voice roared like a volcano as he bellowed, "*We fly! In half an hour, it will be over!*"

Making last-minute glances and looking at who was needed, Quill was fast and efficient in his survey. "I'll take the girls—Jeannie, Little Jeannie, Jeanondes, Aerapondes, and Little KateLynn!"

He turned to Danny. "You take the boys—Jerzom, Little Danny, Little Tony, and Zeb."

He stopped. Jerzom was gone. Quill yelled, "*Zeb, get Jerzom in here now...go!*"

Danny was all too aware that Mochcom would win if chaos reigned among those on the side of Viracocha. No doubt, it must have been one of the reasons Supreme God Viracocha wanted Danny as his royal prince, as cool heads were paramount at the moment of supreme crisis. And if ever there was a crisis, it was now, and Danny knew it.

"At the Tusk, my friend, we shall prevail," Danny said calmly to Quill and all who were listening.

In moments, they were off. High in the black sky, two green beams of light streaked across the expanse of open space. Danny and Quill each had a string of passengers. Danny took the lead holding Jerzom's left hand, and in turn, Jerzom held onto the first group of skyward travelers. Likewise, Quill had his passengers holding hands, and he held tightly to the hand of the lead passenger, Jeannie.

Showered with moonlight in every direction, the desert was an expansive vista of gentle rolling hills covered with purple sage. It was an awesome sight from passengers in the sky headed for the Boar's Tusk, but the beauty of the Scarlet Desert was the last thing on their minds. No, it was a little boy trapped by a monster.

And there it was. Jutting into the sky as if reaching to kiss them as they swept by it stood the Boar's Tusk. It towered as the Scarlet Desert's monument, Viracocha's high tower.

At the base of the Boar's Tusk, Vulture Two stood. His gangly neck supported his featherless head adorned with bright-red wrinkled skin like his father. Vulture Two's bobbing beak moved in stride with each careful step. He was standing next to Mochcom, who had positioned two poles in the ground three feet apart.

Four iron rings were attached—two on each pole. Suspended between them, as if making a cross, a small boy hung, helpless in the hands of a monster.

"My little lamb, you are ready, I see," rasped Mochcom as he finished tying DannyR's wrists to the upper rings and his ankles to the bottom two.

Sobbing uncontrollably, DannyR's little face was lit with moonlight. Mochcom had positioned him that way on purpose.

"In a few minutes, it will be over!" roared Mochcom as he looked to the sky at the two circling beams of green lights spiraling around the top of the Tusk.

What Mochcom did not comprehend was that their purpose in spiraling was twofold. They intended to alert someone on the ground that they were there, and they were seeking to locate the appropriate spot to land.

Quill pointed. He signaled where the landing site should be. And unknown to all, at least as far as Quill surmised, he waved at a silhouette on the ground. Whoever it was waved back.

But Danny saw the silhouette and noticed it waving at them. A wave from Danny prompted a second wave, a gesture like a high five.

All was ready.

Mochcom screamed, *"Go!"*

With fully outstretched wings, VultureTwo maneuvered himself into the air. He took to the skies and flew out of sight.

In his flight, he stretched out his razor-sharp talons, as they were perfect knives, ones that could cut deep into an enemy's throat.

Their landings were perfect. Quill was closer to the base of the Tusk, not more than fifty yards from where Mochcom was conducting his ritual sacrifice.

Danny was ten feet further out.

There could be no hiding Jeannie's expression of panic. Her eyes, as large as the moon making its way through the Milky Way, were shiny with tears, which poured like the Yellshome River down her cheeks. She could not speak as emotion gripped the foundation of her soul and wrenched her with a pain so intense that her senses were dulled. Even when she had been in the dungeon of the great pyramid, she had never known such gripping pain in her heart as her terror over the impending fate of her grandson. The firstborn of the new human race was at the center of a death scene, and that exploded her emotions like an atom bomb.

Her mind had only one thought. *My God, it will be over. The war will be won by Zuron, and my beloved little DannyR will be no more!*

As the matriarch, she grasped the girls' hands, as they all were equally as upset and frightened. Searching for comfort was like looking for air in the wind as they wrung their shaking hands and hoped for a miracle.

Comfort could not be found, for before their very eyes, the monster of the universe was cackling and in the process of unleashing a horror like no other. If successful, it would strike instantly every corner of the universe and make the exploding planets seem like child's play.

From the corner of his eye, Danny caught a glimpse of a flash of red movement behind the nearby bush. His head jerked to look. Jerzom caught Danny's movements and looked also.

Strategically placed on the other side of Mochcom, there was someone in the darkness. The question was who.

CHAPTER 22
The Arrow of a Prince

Three minutes and it would be all over.

Reaching into his pocket, Danny grasped the black ring of Mochcom.

With thoughts of victory, he managed an inner smile as his mind was basking in glory of possessing Mochcom's best defense. And with that inner smile, his mind raced on. *You son of a bitch, you. I'm going to cut deep into your chest and pierce your heart with the knife of the gods and feed you to the demons of hell!*

Jumping into the open and standing erect, Danny bellowed, "You die, and then you fry in the Pit of Vulcan and roast in hell for the eternities!" His bare chest and muscles shimmered in the moonlight as Danny raised his arm into the air and let the moonlight strike his emerald ring.

A minute clicked by, and to Mochcom's delight, the game clock was running out with his victory in sight.

It was his turn to rattle sabers as Mochcom rasped, "You are finished!" He roared as he raised his knife above his head. *"Royal prince of nothing... you are in the throes of defeat. Viracocha has picked a loser!"*

At that point, Danny's ring exploded with a vengeance, sending a bolt of raw energy at the Prince of Darkness.

Nothing happened, except laughter.

Mochcom's screeching laughter ripped through the night air like the death chants of a victor celebrating his battle win. Mochcom was encircled with an armor of purple light from his ring that he displayed with pleasure.

What? The question raced through Danny's mind as the grasped the ring in his pocket and looked at Mochcom, who was in the final stages of his mission to end the War of the Gods.

It was interesting how things were playing out. Danny had been sure he had the upper hand when he found Mochcom's black ring. Evidently, it was an imitation, as Mochcom was still able to defend himself against the royal prince of Viracocha's emerald ring. Evidently, it was Mochcom's way of grinding salt into a wound, figuratively speaking, as he knew Danny would want vengeance after the horrific murder of his mother. Laughing at Danny was an outward showing of the diabolical nature of Mochcom, as if to say, "I gotcha. You thought you had me…you thought you had my ring, but all you have is a fake ring…you idiot!"

Yet it was interesting how things were playing out. Could it be that Mochcom's train of thought and focus were diverted momentarily by his so-called victory dance when he decided to spitefully rub it in, crying, "*Viracocha has picked a loser!*" Who knows, but just maybe that precious moment Mochcom wasted changed the course of history. That momentary diversion allowed a communication to take place via a flash of light. Yet it was not only the flash of light that Mochcom missed seeing but also the moment Mochcom took to bask in glory that gave Jerzom time to observe something very unique.

Cleverly observant, the young prince from Kopaz noticed something interesting. Mochcom's left arm lifted, and there seemed to be something strange going on with the spiraling purple light around his torso. Only obvious in the dead of night when the beam of light was most noticeable, one who was observant could detect a flaw!

Time was running out. Less than two minutes remained, and the war would end. Evil would prevail, and good would vanish from the universe.

Danny was in front of Jerzom. It was funny how things worked out. Danny had seen a silhouette on the ground just prior to their landing. He suspected that only he and Quill were aware of the stranger on the ground. Yet, unknown to Danny, Jerzom motioned to the silhouette in the bush behind Mochcom. Jerzom used his knife to reflect the moonlight.

With Mochcom's back to the large sagebrush and his moment of basking in a so-called premature victory dance, Mochcom never saw the flash of light.

But at that moment, Danny did. Now he asked himself a crucial question. How could they orchestrate the defeat of a monster that had the upper hand?

Mochcom let all know he was at the brink of winning the war and handing the victory to Zuron as he howled, "It's over. The gods have lost, and Zuron is the victor! I have but one fatal blow to make, and then I will laugh with pleasure when your miserable bodies are ashes in hell! When the firstborn son of the new race is sacrificed with Zuron's knife of zedite that I thrust into the boy's heart at the base of Viracocha's high tower…yes, when the full moon is at its high point, and then *all is done!*"

Jerzom waited. He could not tell Danny for fear that Mochcom might overhear their plan. Jerzom's only hope was that Danny would understand what to do in the nick of time.

Danny's back was to Jerzom. Jerzom had but one hope, and that was that the royal prince of Viracocha was vigilant. Jerzom put his trust in Danny as to the final moments of knowing what to do and then to make the correct crucial decision. In effect, he allowed him to take charge as a god.

All that the girls could do was watch and hope. Jeannie, Little Jeannie, KateLynn, Jeanondes, and Aerapondes huddled in fear as the scene of horror unfolded before their eyes.

At that moment, Jeannie spotted outstretched black wings high in the sky, gliding in front of the moon.

My god, it's him. What shall we do? Is it over? The bitter fear of defeat raced through Jeannie's mind, knowing her encounters with Black Vulture in the past. Now it was as though it was destiny. She cried inside as she saw the hand of Mochcom lift to the sky, a knife of zedite clutched in his fingers.

Her mind screamed with agony. *Oh my god, we are finished. After all we've been through, it comes down to this.*

She could no longer hold back her cries of defeat as she convulsed with utter pain in every morsel of her being.

In her state of torture, she was not alone. Her daughters wept openly, as did Prince Zeb, Little Danny, and Little Tony. They could do nothing except watch in utter horror as the final moments approached.

There was only one way it could be done. The sacrifice of the firstborn of the new human race had to follow a strict set of rules. It had to be. Mochcom had to raise his left arm with his ring above his right hand holding the zedite knife of Zuron. The light of the high moon must mix with the purple beam from Mochcom's ring and strike the handle of the knife. The sacrifice could only occur at one moment in time. Mochcom waited. With the point of the knife on DannyR's chest, right over his heart, the moment was now. All that was needed was the moonlight and purple beam to strike the handle.

Yet Jerzom's keen sense of awareness monitored the spiraling beam of purple light around Mochcom's torso as the high priest lifted his arm. Squinting and waiting, Jerzom's moment was in the making as he focused his concentration on the purple light. His mind was ready. *It's only his* torso *that is protected by the purple beam of light.*

At the crucial moment, a sword came flying toward Danny, flung by someone only Jerzom had noticed. He had used his knife to reflect the desert's moonlight, and the improvised communication had been perfect. Spinning through the air, the sword was on target.

Startled by the *sssswwwwwiiiiiisssssss* noise cutting through the desert's night air, Danny reacted. In moments, the object would whizz past Danny. He was ready. He had an idea. He leaped in the air on a beam of green light. He was a god, and he acted like one. Danny had waited for what seemed like an eternity to wreak vengeance on the monster that had brutally killed his mother and best buddy, Tony. It was that time, and Danny could only hope that the arc of justice would bend toward the innocent and that the balance between good and evil would tip to the better good of humanity.

Flash…flash…flash…flash…flash! A spinning object reflected the bright moonlight with each revolution.

At that moment, from the corner of his eye, Jerzom caught a glimpse of a black streak falling from the sky. His head jerked to look.

Now, VultureTwo was where Mochcom wanted him to be—above and behind Danny—diving from his location above the Boar's Tusk with the wrath of the destroying a superhuman. With his wings tucked tightly against his body, and his talons perfectly outstretched, his dive was underway. Like the torpedo from a German U-boat striking the blind side of a British warship, VultureTwo's attack was perfectly executed.

At the very instant that Mochcom's hand was starting to thrust his knife into the heart of DannyR, Danny was above Mochcom's head, propelled by a beam of green light.

Jerzom's bow had been readied, and figuratively speaking, it was aimed at the Achilles heel of the disciple of Zuron. It was vulnerable, as Mochcom's defense had exposed the sweet spot, and the young prince of Kopaz had one thing on his mind. *My son will not die!*

With the precision of Priam's son Paris, aided by Apollo, who wounded Achilles in his vulnerable heel with an arrow, Jerzom's arrow found its mark—Mochcom's right thigh. Mochcom's torso was all that was protected by his beam of purple light. Who knows why, but his arms and legs were unguarded and unprotected targets.

Howling screams filled the midnight air as the arrow penetrated the fleshy muscle and sunk deep into the large bone of Mochcom's leg. Mochcom bent over in agony but was unaware of what would happen next.

In a split second, Danny had caught the hilt of the whirling object—a razor-sharp steel sword—in midair. The *flash...flash...flash...flash... flash* of its spinning trajectory, reflecting the bright moonlight with each revolution, had captured Danny's attention. And with the precision and speed of lightning, Danny's arm swung the sword and sliced through Mochcom's arm, and the hand with his black ring fell.

Twitching, the bloody stump of what used to be an intact arm fell to the ground, and blood oozed from the severed end to stain the desert sand a crimson red. In like fashion, Mochcom fell to the ground. The moment when he must thrust his zedite knife into the heart of a small boy had passed. Mochcom's mission now was to get the ring of power from his detached arm.

His eyes were no longer on a zedite knife about to strike a boy's heart, but instead they fell on the twitching fingers of a severed arm lying in a pool of crimson blood spotlighted by a full moon in the Scarlet Desert.

It was not completely over. VultureTwo's forty pounds of muscle traveling sixty miles per hour struck Danny's back like the death blow of an iron ball from a pirate's cannon.

VultureTwo was perfect in his execution. Danny fell to the ground with his head landing on the severed arm of Mochcom. With his head lying on the ground, Danny's eyes were not more than six inches from that quivering hand. He witnessed another something pull the black ring from a twitching finger, and his mind erupted with suspicion. *Did Mochcom get his ring back?*

Chaos ensued. VultureTwo's plan was being carried out flawlessly, or so he thought as he stood erect, the black ring in his beak.

Dropping his zedite knife, Mochcom reached, desperate to snatch his ring from Vulture's beak.

It was too late. From his position on the ground, Danny was swift a second time, and he swung the mysterious sword. As it circled through the air, it not only severed the head of VultureTwo but also the other hand of Mochcom as it was reaching for his ring of power. Mochcom's last-ditch effort failed, and his quest for horror ended.

Then out of the darkness, someone spoke. "Good, work, little brother!" The voice came from someone standing next to Danny, who was still lying on the ground.

The silhouette reached out a hand out toward Danny. Danny reached and grabbed the hand. As he was being pulled to his feet, Danny said, "I thought it was you, Kashom."

"Good work, my royal prince of Viracocha," Prince Kashom said as the moonlight lit up a smile on his face.

Kashom turned his head to Jerzom. It was the first time in centuries that he had seen his beloved brother. "Well done, little brother," said Kashom as he looked at his little brother, who was now a young warrior. Kashom laughed, and he finished his train of thought and put them to words. "Damn! I didn't think your archery skills were that precise!"

"Who me? Archery skills? Damn, I thought maybe yours had rusted with age, my royal brother," Jerzom answered Kashom.

There could be no words for such a reunion. Jerzom was at the point of lunging through the air to get his arms around his brother. And in a moment of excitement, that was exactly what he did.

It was a sight indeed—two brothers, whose reunion after of so much time apart was defined by smacking body blows. And try as he might, Jerzom was not quite up to knocking his beloved brother to the ground. It didn't happen.

"Better build your muscles a little bigger if you want to get one up on me, little brother," belted out Prince Kashom with a few laughs as he had braced his body for Jerzom's smack.

Hugging his older brother with a bear hug and showing off his ripped muscles, the younger prince said in response, "Yeah, and I didn't think you were auditioning for a spot as the champion sword twirler in the universe! But I see your skill has not rusted at all!"

The bear hug was but a moment in time. Jerzom dropped his arms from his brother and raced to his son. Like the proud king of a new prince, Jerzom displayed their son to his mother, Little Jeannie. It was a miracle, and all knew it!

Time can wait for some things but not others. The reunion of two royal princes and the touching moments of relieved young parents holding their only son, the firstborn son of the new human race, were both short-lived.

"Kashom, do you have rope?" asked Danny.

"Yes, my royal prince," answered Kashom. "Jerzom and I will make sure the monster is tied and bound so that the demons in hell cannot free him."

"Good, let me know when you've secured him, as there is one last pleasure I shall derive this evening." Danny smiled with pride at capturing the vilest human to walk the face of the Earth.

For Mochcom, his fate was sealed. On the morrow, at high noon, his trip to the outer reaches of hell would start at the top of the Boar's Tusk. Vultures in the Scarlet Desert were no more.

A little boy was in the arms of his mom. His father sat next to them.

Aerapondes, an early victim of his evil, now waited to carry out the final demise of Mochcom.

Quill asked Kashom, "Do you have the Shroud of Goroms?"

"Yes," Kashom answered.

Even though he was armless, Mochcom was tied and bound. No one would sleep that night at the Boar's Tusk. The prize was the prisoner, and guarding him with all their might was top of the order.

The pleasure Danny had just mentioned to Kashom was holding Kashom's special descendent in his arms. Holding Jeannie tightly, Danny's heart found tranquility.

"Jeannie, tomorrow at noon it will be finished," said Danny with tears in his eyes as he looked at his partner.

CHAPTER 23

The Last Gorom

Although Mochcom was all but finished, no one let down his guard. At stake was the fate of the universe, and it was playing out on the Scarlet Desert of Wyoming in the spring of 1958.

It was a long journey through time. Thousands of years ago, an institution, the Council of Goroms, had been created to assist the royal family of Kopaz. And as the years went on, the Quorum of High Priests had become more powerful, and their influence reached beyond the government of the royal family. In effect, they became the de facto rulers, and the royal family were puppet rulers.

It's interesting how conversation around a bonfire has a way of bringing out many puzzling stories that otherwise would be just assumed to have happened by chance. And so it was on that evening following the capture of Gorom Mochcom.

There really hadn't been time for a family reunion. Or was it a reunion? There were children. There was a grandchild, whose terrible fate had been averted.

No one would sleep, including DannyR, who was not about to shut his eyes. The comfort of his mother's arms was what he wanted, and that was what he got.

"He's ready, my royal prince of Viracocha," said Kashom as three brave stalwarts stood like sentinels over Mochcom not more than ten feet from

Danny.

"Good! Well done! Viracocha is pleased. He has personally told me this very evening that we all have met his expectations," Danny said as he contemplated his next move.

Jeannie walked to where Danny and Kashom were standing. They were in what appeared to be a serious discussion. She looked at her great-great-great-great-grandfather and asked, "I am curious, Kashom. How did you get the golden key of Neferdor from Mochcom?"

"I thought you might be curious," answered Kashom as he smiled. "Your cat helped me!" Kashom reached and scratched Zanzee behind his ears as Jeannie snuggled her precious cat in her arms.

"Yes, at the precise moment I discovered the evil deception of Gorom Mochcom, Zanzee came to my rescue. Mochcom had your golden key in the pocket of his leather skirt. I knew it was there from the circular bulge it made. But I knew if I attempted to get it, his black ring would send me to the outer reaches of hell. I did not know what to do. Then it happened. Mochcom looked to the sky. Maybe it was to acknowledge Zuron and to get some recognition from the dark god for his success in getting the golden key. Who knows why the gorom looked to the sky, but at that moment of letting down his guard, Zanzee came out of nowhere and took a death grip on Mochcom's throat. For some reason, as he reached to dislodge Zanzee from his jugular, the Black Disciple's black ring came off his finger and fell to the ground. I did not see that happen, but I took advantage of the opportunity Zanzee had created. I picked up a large log that was fortuitously at my feet and, with all my might, swung it into Mochcom's legs, breaking them both. Mochcom fell to the ground. I pulled his loinskirt off and sprinted into the desert. By the time Mochcom had figured out what had happened and recovered his ring from the dirt, Zanzee and I were long gone. I had the golden key back and vowed never again to let it fall into Mochcom's hands."

As Jeannie and Danny listened to Kashom's incredible story, she snuggled Zanzee even more tightly in her arms and loved him even more.

"I asked my mother many times how you got the golden key, but she did not have the answer. I've always been curious, and now I know!" Jeannie said, a huge smile erupting on her face as her heart swelled with love for her protector, Zanzee.

Kashom reached and touched Jeannie's arm. "I'm so proud of you, Jeannie. You are like a daughter to me…a twin to my sister Aerapondes and my first daughter Moon-of-Day. Jeannie, you are the third Neferzul and are of my bloodline, and I cannot say strongly enough how proud I am of how you handle yourself and what you have accomplished! And I might add, the gods are pleased, and soon you will meet Supreme Goddess Neferdor, who looks exactly like you!"

There was something bittersweet reflecting in Kashom's mind: *My sister, Merapondes, is not here. I think I know why.*

What could Jeannie say? She had an idea of what was troubling Kashom. It was obvious. The horrific death of Merapondes by the hand of the evil goroms will forever be etched on Jeannie's mind. But she also knew that the forces of good were setting a new standard for the universe, and so she had hope that in the vastness of time that Merapondes would not remain a prisoner in the Land of the Dead. But the fact was that one very special member of the royal family was not in the Scarlet Desert on that warm spring evening of 1958. There were no words to describe the feeling in her heart. She looked to the sky, a tear rolling down her cheek.

With the moon shining brightly on Kashom's face, sweetly Jeannie said, "Kashom, I know in my heart that all of the royal family will soon be reunited for the eternities."

The towering Boar's Tusk was a bright silhouette in the glowing purple night's sky as the full moon seemed to be painting the desert with an omen of hope. Kashom smiled at Jeannie and nodded in response to her words.

Princess Aerapondes had walked to Kashom's side and was holding his hand. They were quietly conversing about the harrowing events that were changing the course of destiny for all living creatures throughout the universe. It was a sight to behold…a brother and sister making up for lost time. But time was marching on, and Mochcom had not yet met his demise. The course of destiny that could change the existence of all living creatures throughout the universe was not yet complete. The next day's sun was not at its high point. Mochcom's heart was still beating, and there was no zedite knife lodged in its black depths.

Beaming like the Cheshire cat, it was hard for Quill to hide his emotions. Yet he knew deep inside that he must remain vigilant. He would not fully display his pleasure in the efforts of Danny and Jeannie and how proud he was of them until the morrow, when Mochcom's final moments had come.

Danny walked fifty yards to where the girls had huddled in a group around DannyR and were busy in girly talk. "I have yet one task at hand, and it is most likely not for young girls to witness, so I advise you all to stay here," said Danny.

Jeannie's heart was pounding. She was proud. Danny was her hero and savior and she wanted to let him know. "Danny, just a minute. I...er...ah...ah...I want..." Jeannie tried but the right words would not come out.

"Yes, Jeannie?" said Danny as he looked at her face glowing in the moonlight.

"I just love you." Racing to him, she was in his arms.

"We did it, my love, and I can't stop crying just thinking of our trail of tears, but I see the horizon of hope has turned to a victory of eternal joy!" Jeannie said through sobs of emotion such as her daughters had never seen from her.

For three daughters to see their parents so in love and joyfully witnessing the fall of evil was the sight of a lifetime, especially in the Scarlet Desert on a chilly spring evening.

Knowing all too well that victory was at hand yet not in hand, Jeannie was anxious for Danny to carry on. "You have more?" she asked.

He said, "Yes!"

"Then our love can wait until we can bask in it with nothing but a bright future on the road stretching through the eternities ahead!" said Jeannie with delight. She dropped her hands from his cheeks.

Reaching into his pocket, Danny tightly grasped the one last item needed to prepare Mochcom for his final farewell.

Standing together over Mochcom, Kashom, Quill, Jerzom, Zeb, Little Tony, Little Danny, and the royal prince of Viracocha were about to inflict Mochcom with a pain he will carry with him throughout the ages of endless time.

"We're ready, royal prince of Viracocha," said Quill.

In ceremonial fashion, all but Danny knelt with their right knees on the ground and their right hands on Mochcom.

The gorom's eyes shot wide open. For the first time in his existence, Mochcom's face was riddled with the horrifying look of terror. His body was so tightly bound with leather thongs that breathing was a chore. The tide of horror orchestrated by Mochcom had turned, and figuratively speaking, justice was knocking at the door of the most horrendous, evil creature that had gripped the universe with a reign of terror. His body tensed to a hardness not unlike solid granite as his doom grew closer. The stumps of his arm stubs were bound across his chest.

Kashom opened his hand. A black obsidian knife glittered in the moonlight.

Danny looked on with a smile and said, "Prepare this monster's mouth!"

If screams were possible, the night air at the Boar's Tusk would be as a horror house on Halloween, but Mochcom's mouth had a black volcanic-glass knife stuck in it, so no screams ushered forth. He could make no sound but only gurgle.

"Good," said Quill as he witnessed that bloody mouth, the shiny knife wedged between the teeth of Mochcom's upper and lower jaws.

"The time is now," said Danny as he pulled a white object from his Levi's front pocket with right hand and stretched out his left to receive another object from Quill.

Quill stretched out his arm, proffering a metal ball to Danny. Quill looked at Danny with a smile and said, "We are ready, my royal prince of Viracocha. It is time. Here is the zedite ball from Viracocha."

Danny took the metal ball from Quill and then looked at Mochcom. The gorom's mouth oozed blood from the volcanic-glass knife lodged in it. Mochcom's eyes reflected the moon's rays as if they were screaming for mercy.

"Are you ready, Danny, most noble prince of Viracocha?" asked Quill.

"Yes," answered Danny. "With Viracocha's zedite ball, we give to Mochcom the horrifying suffering he inflicted on each and every one of his victims, so he will experience their pain, their sorrow, and utter torment of hell they experienced at his monstrous hands!"

The royal prince of Viracocha placed the finger bone that he had once pulled from the bottom of the pool at the base of Yellshome Falls and plunged it deep into the throat of Mochcom. Danny held the bone steady with his left and lifted his right high above his head, his fingers grasping the zedite ball.

Bam! The sound filled the air on top of the Boar's Tusk as the pearly white, sharp finger bone was jabbed deep into Mochcom's throat.

His body exploding with pain, Mochcom convulsed and tried to scream once more. His efforts were in vain.

Reaching into the old filthy coat of the gorom, Danny pulled Zuron's zedite knife from its place in an inner pocket. "How nice of you to give this to me!"

"Yellzor," yelled Danny. "Guard him through the night!"

His beast obeyed and howled with delight. *YYYOOOOOOWWWWWWWW!* He took his place as the official guard of the most prized prisoner in the universe.

And now it was not just the face of the moon. Like a giant portrait in the black sky over the Boar's Tusk, Danny was sure he saw the supreme god smiling down.

A bonfire was blazing at the base of the Boar's Tusk.

The carcass of VultureTwo lay beside the bound body of Mochcom. Soon both would be wrapped in the Shroud of Goroms as piles of ashes.

There were jokes and snide remarks about the Black Bird of Death, and Mochcom could only sit and listen. His reign of terror and horror had ended, and his final journey to the pit of hell was in preparation.

"Danny, we are starving," said Jeannie as she snuggled next to him on a rock at the edge of the fire.

Danny reached in his pocket and took out fifteen twenty-dollar bills. He laughed as he raised them so Mochcom could get a glimpse from his dirt bed and said, "We're going to have a feast tonight on your nickel!"

Handing the money to Quill, Danny said, "Take Little Danny and Tony, and go to Granite Springs. Go on a streak of green light, and get some food…there are some all-night markets with great food."

Danny got a puzzled look, and Quill said, "What?"

Folding the thumb of his right hand, Danny lifted it to his lips, rubbing it back and forth—clearly in a deep state of thought.

Quill got a little uneasy, thinking he had done something to offend the young god. He asked, "Is there something that I've done to offend you, my lord?"

Maybe it was because it was almost over. Maybe it was the late evening and that Danny had had so much on his mind in the past few weeks and just the magnitude of their accomplishments was a subject of thought. No one could deny that Danny was center stage, changing the outcome of the War of the Gods. At this point, Quill could no longer read Danny's mind. Danny was a god, and there could be no question that the supreme god was pleased. Why would he not be? Danny had willingly done all that was asked. And then maybe it was just Danny relaxing.

Quill waited as the royal prince of Viracocha continued his deep state of thought. Then Danny looked at Jeannie and then at Quill. She smiled and nodded back at Danny. So it looked as if all was settled as Danny spoke with a clear voice so the royal princess of Neferdor could hear him.

"Quill, I know you have a great mind, and I don't have to write this down, but Jeannie and I would like you to get five pounds of kranski kielbasa…but do you think you can remember that?"

"Sure," replied Quill. "If you and Jeannie like kranski kielbasa, I can't wait to try it, whatever it is!"

Danny reached into his pocket, grabbed a few more fifty-dollar bills, and stretched out his arm to Zeb. "Zeb, remember, you are Jerzom's right-hand man, and oh, by the way, your right hand looks fantastic!"

Zeb took the money and smiled. For the first time, he remarked about something that happed a long time ago. He looked at Danny intently and asked, "When you were holding me, Mr. God, and I was a little boy, did I screw up the Sun Energy Transformer?"

Danny burst into laughter and answered his friend, Zeb, who was now his son-in-law. "Nah! You were just having fun, and Jerzom and I did just great…it all turned out! So off to town to get goodies! Don't forget the

Pepsi and peanuts!"

He looked at Little Tony but didn't have to say a word as Little Tony smiled and said, "Got it! Marshmallows, hot dogs, chips, and lots of other goodies!"

Then Little Tony added, "Kranski kielbasa, marshmallows, hot dogs, chips, Pepsi and peanuts, and lots of goodies!"

Quill screwed up his face. "I'm sure glad that Danny and Tony are going with me, 'cause Zeb and I sure in the hell don't know what all that stuff is!"

And with that comment by Quill, Danny motioned for Zeb, Little Danny, and Tony to go with Quill. They were off, streaking across the Scarlet Desert on a beam of green light. Their mission was the food, and their destination was Ben's Market. It didn't take long.

"We got it," hooted Quill as he and boys landed upon their return from Granite Springs. "Lots of goodies, including five pounds of kranski kielbasa for a long feast at a bonfire at the base of the Boar's Tusk in the Scarlet Desert of Wyoming. Our victory over evil will mark this place as sacred ground for the ages, and this hallowed ground on which we now stand will be a symbol of good over evil from now until the end of time."

The night hours whiled away. The food was good, and the stories by the bonfire were precious.

Kashom and Jerzom caught up on many years of lost time.

As the night rolled on, the great horned owls that lived in the Scarlet Desert provided a chorus. *Whoooooo! Whoooooooo!*

Midnight was upon them, and the fire kept them all toasty as the creatures of the night continued their serenade.

Quill told interesting stories when questioned. When asked by Danny, "So, Quill, have you over the years been Kashom's tutor or what?"

"The short answer is yes, and the long answer is no," replied Quill. "You see, Danny, you are the royal prince. Yet your success has had some help along the way, and that was Viracocha's will." Quill looked at Kashom and then at Danny.

Now Jeannie's ears perked up. She had longed to know of her great-great-great-great-grandfather, but sitting next to this handsome eighteen-year-old by a bonfire at the base of the Boar's Tusk had left her speechless, at least for a while. She wanted to ask questions. She wanted to delve into the past. But all that could wait.

These were touching moments for the children of the royal family of Kopaz as Prince Kashom and Prince Jerzom talked to their little sister, Princess Aerapondes. In the realm of the god's time, it was thousands of years since Kashom had seen his beloved sister. But time was different in the Land of Kopaz, and because of that difference, three of the children of the royal family of Kopaz had time to reflect on events that had defined their lives. They set the tone of the evening—catching up on old times and filling Princess Aerapondes in on the centuries, at least for Kashom, of life she had missed when she lived in the Land of the Dead. Jerzom had stories of his youth in the Land of Kopaz and his beloved friend, Peizar, who now dwelt with Merapondes in the Land of the Dead.

Jeannie's heart was full of joy as she listened to the royal youth of Kopaz exchange touching stories of defining moments in the history of the universe. Yet, when Jerzom talked about Merapondes and Peizar, there was a pang of sadness in her heart.

Jeannie did manage to interject one question. "Quill, it was Kashom's journal that pointed the way, and I'm curious," she asked, looking at Quill. "Did you help him with that?"

"Yes, Jeannie, that was part of my assignment from the supreme god," answered Quill.

Holding Danny's hand as they sat on the rock and tossed sage wood on the fire, Jeannie added, "Do you think about our journey, Danny?" She squeezed his hand.

The warmth of the fire made his answer easy. "Yeah, it has been something we can write a novel about," answered Danny with a chuckle.

CHAPTER 24

Noon Ceremony on top of the Boar's Tusk

Small talk and precious stories of years in the making drifted on as the sun showed a sliver of its face above the horizon. The warmth of a new day overwhelmed the warmth of the fire.

Now it was a matter of formality. Mochcom's final sendoff was, figuratively speaking, set in stone by the supreme god.

"On top of my high tower, when my glory is at its high point, the first Neferzul will thrust my knife of zedite into the beating heart of Mochcom as he lies on the Shroud of Goroms with a finger bone of my wife's first prized possession deep in his throat!"

It was mystifying, and Aerapondes was confused. *I'm not about to bring up the idea that one of my finger bones is to be stuck in his throat!*

Obviously, Danny knew what was troubling Aerapondes, so he volunteered an explanation that only she would know what it meant. He said, "Princess Aerapondes, I suggest that it be not just your hand on the knife but the hands of all the girls whom this monster has harmed…so that means Jeannie, Little Jeannie, Jeanondes, Little KateLynn, and you."

Aerapondes could not bring herself to look at Mochcom, let alone think about orchestrating his demise.

"Don't worry about the bone. It's taken care of," Danny said as he repeated his support. "And not only the girls but also the boys will participate. We'll make the final farewell for Mochcom and his sendoff into hell a family affair!"

Looking at Danny, Jeannie thought, *He has a gift for making the load a bit lighter for those who have had a heavy lift for so long!*

Looking passionately at the royal princess, Danny thought, *It is a heavy load she has carried. And I know she had a good idea what the finger bone is about.*

Since Danny had already smashed the finger bone deep into the throat of the high priest, no more needed to be said on that subject. It was done in accordance with the instructions of Supreme God Viracocha.

And maybe Danny had done that finger bone thing when he did so that Gorom Mochcom would spend his last night in the land of the living going through pure hell, with a throat so wracked with pain that breathing was a chore. Knowing that Mochcom had a few more hours to endure excruciating pain because of his severed arms and the white finger bone lodged deep in his throat gave Danny a little solace. He looked directly into the eyes of Mochcom. *You bastard. I hope for the sake of my mom that she somehow sees your miserable being in pain and agony for your dastardly crimes against humanity!*

That interchange between Danny and Mochcom was brief. Danny had other items to take care of, as opposed to staring at a miserable monster on his way to hell.

Gazing at the rising sun, something was perplexing Danny, so he asked Quill, "Why the Shroud of Goroms? And what the hell is it?"

Kashom stepped forward and for the first time displayed something most unusual. He said, "This is it."

Never one to take a flimsy answer, Danny asked, "Yeah...so what the hell is it?"

Quill laughed as he said, "It is a story. So are you up for it?"

"What else are we going to do for the next four hours except listen to *you!*" said Danny with a hoot. He watched the sun as it kissed the horizon and then drifted higher so it was fully in the morning sky.

Quill was center stage, and he had a story to tell. "OK, here goes. The very first goroms, thousands of years ago, knew what they were up to...evil!

Their reign of terror would send them to the outer reaches of darkness in the deepest abyss of hell, so they wanted more."

It was an odd statement, but Danny just nodded, so Quill proceeded. "Now you know the only way, at least that is what you've been taught, is that a lock of hair is needed to bring a loved one back from the Land of the Dead. As it turns out, while a lock of hair works, so would anything that identifies you and only you, preserved from your dead body after you have departed to the Land of the Dead. And so, for thousands of years, every single gorom that has been alive has had a large chunk of tanned hide preserved and sewn into this shroud."

It was making sense, and Danny asked Kashom, "Can I see it?" It was brought out and displayed. "Holy crap," said Danny. "This looks like the work of Adolf Hitler!"

"Yes," answered Quill, "and the goroms were hopeful that Dark God Zuron would win the War of the Gods and use this Ancient Shroud of Goroms to bring back all their evil souls from the Land of the Dead."

It was clear as Danny nodded. "Yes, and so when Mochcom's ashes are wrapped in the Ancient Shroud of Goroms and thrown into the Pit of Vulcan, and CrystalFlame is at the helm guarding the mouth of hell, then all of the goroms for all time will never be able to show their evil faces again!"

"You got it!" said Quill.

As the sun moved higher in the sky, the time to deal with Mochcom was growing nigh, and everyone's anxiety was on the rise.

"It's time," said Quill. "Danny, you and the boys take Mochcom to the top of the tower, and I'll take the girls."

It seemed like a well-rehearsed play to everyone as they stood on the Boar's Tusk, Viracocha's high tower in the Scarlet Desert. It was especially strange, so Jerzom asked his brother, "Why is it flat up here?"

"You noticed!" answered Kashom.

"Yeah," said Zeb, "I don't even live here, and this is strange indeed to have no less than a perfectly flat area four hundred feet in the sky. It looks like a dance floor.

Laughing, Kashom said, "My son, Yellow Moon, made it a long time ago. Maybe he thought we needed a dance floor to send Mochcom to hell!"

There were chuckles, laughs, and snickers from all except one. Mochcom lay on his back on the Ancient Shroud of Goroms, with his dead bird and severed arms next to him. His body wracked with pain, his face was dark with agony as he choked on the blood trickling down his throat from the obsidian knife and finger bone lodged in his throat.

His options were gone.

Standing over Mochcom, first Aerapondes wrapped her fingers around the zedite knife of Viracocha. Then others followed, their hands covering her hands, until all joined in. It was only a few moments more until Viracocha's glory, the sun, would be at its high point. At high noon in the Scarlet Desert on this glorious day, Viracocha would watch from his planet, Volob, and would bask in delight. However, it would be a dreaded and fateful day for Mochcom and Zuron in his pantheon on planet Zolob.

His eyes expressed his terror the only way he could as all held the point of the knife steady on the gorom's chest, right over his heart.

Laid out on the Ancient Shroud of Goroms, with his severed arms and a dead bird alongside him, Gorom Mochcom had only moments as Aerapondes, Jeannie, and all the girls and all the boys held Viracocha's zedite knife. Thirty seconds and it would be over. Anxiety built to a crescendo as the sun inched higher.

At the very instant that Viracocha's glory reached its high point, they plunged Viracocha's zedite knife in unison into Mochcom's beating heart. And with the fiery blast of an atom bomb, the brilliance of the sun's rays penetrated the precious gemstone handle of the zedite knife, and Mochcom's body erupted into an inferno. Then there were only ashes—no vulture, no severed arms, and no Mochcom, just ashes.

At that very moment, a thundering voice boomed throughout the Scarlet Desert. "Well done, Danny, my royal prince!'"

Quill could wait no longer to utter his proud remarks. Above the Scarlet Desert in the glory of the noonday sun atop the high tower of Viracocha, he stretched out his arm and pointed to Danny and Jeannie as he spoke. "In the expanse of unending time and over the eons of eternity, we stand in awe and wonderment before these two."

A slight breeze was all that competed with Quill's words. He continued. "None! No! None in the entire universe could have done what these two have just accomplished. The royal prince of Viracocha and the royal princess of Neferdor will stand forever as beacons of justice in their quest to rid the universe of evil. *Well done, Danny! Well done, Jeannie!*"

Accolades were always hard for Danny, so he waited for Quill to finish. Then he smiled and added a few words of his own. "Not without standing on the shoulders of many, to mention just a few: Quill; Kashom; my best buddy, Tony; Jeannie's best friend, KateLynn; Jerzom; Aerapondes; Merapondes; and Peizar, who gave the ultimate—their lives—in the battle of good against evil; as well as the queen, Neferapondes; Tony's mom, Rose; Jeannie's mom, Soft Wind; and my beloved parents, Johnny and Darla."

A shiver of sadness ran through Danny's body as he spoke of his high-school friends, Tony and KateLynn. Jeannie noticed. She stepped to his side and grasped his hand. She squeezed it softly, knowing a pain was still in his heart.

And then in perfect form, Danny added, "OK, everybody, we're going home. We've done what was needed to be done, and we have the Shroud of Goroms and the ashes of Mochcom and his evil black bird," said Danny as they finished and prepared for their journey to Kopaz. "But I still have one stop to make!"

Yet, as he was speaking, the sky above them suddenly roared into fire. The blast was more intense than a million Hiroshima explosions.

"We have problems," yelled Danny. "*Grab hands! We fly!*"

And so it was that on that sunny day in 1958 at the top of the Boar's Tusk.

CHAPTER 25
1955 Chevy Headed for Kopaz

Astark doom was in the sky. Not only was the explosion of Herculean magnitude creating a sheer panic in civilizations throughout the world but the chance of being caught in a twist of fate was also the reality staring Danny, Jeannie, and all who were with them head on.

Serenity was elusive as a butterfly in the middle of what was transpiring. Yet if Danny and Jeannie could not maintain their leadership of their small party of humans who were the start of the new human race, all would be lost forever.

Streaking across the deep-blue skies of the Scarlet Desert, they were back in CoalVille moments after Mochcom's sendoff. Quill was furious with Danny for diverting their plans to travel back to Kopaz and instead making a detour and taking them all back to CoalVille.

"Danny, we have huge problems! Is it not obvious to you? We need to go!" yelled Quill. "The planets are exploding, and who knows when Earth will be next!"

Who was in charge was obvious.

"You don't run the show, and you are not the captain of this ship, Quill," shouted Danny.

Their voices were all but lost in the shouts, the cries, the cars smashing into other cars and buildings, and the total chaos that was erupting.

Standing in Danny's old front yard, Quill put a few yards of distance between him and the royal prince of Viracocha. In the time that he had known the young god, Quill had understood the relationship—he was a tutor, and Danny was a god.

Danny did not want war with his tutor. How could Quill know that? He couldn't. For someone of extraterrestrial origin, it was a hidden mystery.

The bonds between father and son and mother and son that were forged on their journeys over the road of sorrows and trail of tears could only be known by those travelers who had made it through that voyage of earthly life.

At the very moment that Danny threw open the front door, a car slammed into the fence and flipped over in the front yard, landing on its top with all four of its wheels spinning freely. The travelers in the car were no longer on earthly roads but on the boat sailing down the River Styx.

"Mom! Dad!" yelled Danny. He saw no one. He raced to the bedroom. They were not there. He raced into the kitchen. No one was there. "Mom! Dad!"

His heart pounded. *Where? Where? Where are they?*

By this time, the whole Kopazi party was in the house, and tensions were on the rise. The sky exploded into ever more violent displays of a heavenly firestorm.

"*Danny!*" screamed Jeannie. "*Where are you?*"

Whatever planet has bit the dust at the hands of Zuron, thought Quill, looking to the skies, *soon the sun will be hidden behind a veil of dust and the Earth will freeze.*

The open garage door Jeannie saw through the kitchen window grabbed her attention. Her memory of the horror of being in Danny's kitchen and following him to the garage to find his mom exploded like the planet in the sky. Jeannie's heart sank. *My god, I hope not!*

Running out of his bedroom and bolting through the door leading to the kitchen, Danny ran smack dab into Jeannie and would have knocked her to the floor had he not grabbed her just as she was starting to tumble. Danny lifted Jeannie from the precarious position he had just put her in.

Jeannie saw, as if in a daze, the red flowers. Just as they had always been, there were the geraniums on a windowsill. Yet it was not the geraniums that caught her attention but the garage.

"Danny, your mom and dad are in the garage. We have to get out of here...*now!*" blared Jeannie at Danny.

Not only did Quill realize the emergency that threatened to destroy all that had been accomplished but Jeannie did too, and she was the one person who could yank Danny's attention in the right direction immediately. And that she did.

Throwing the back door open and bounding down the stairs in three leaps, Danny was on the ground. Jeannie was left behind. Realizing his exuberance had left her at the top of the back porch, Danny turned and said, "Sorry, Jeannie. You OK?"

"Go, Danny. We have to get out of here!" she yelled and waved him toward the garage.

They were in the garage, both his mom and dad. Danny saw them immediately. "Dad, Mom, we have to go!" yelled Danny, elevated concern in his voice.

Johnny had his truck door open and was about to jump onto the front seat when Darla screamed, "Johnny, Danny is right! We can't stay any longer!"

When everything of any value that you ever had only came after an uphill struggle, you treasure even the smallest items that have come your way. And so it was with Johnny Roberts.

"Not without my truck," yelled Johnny.

Time was swiftly marching on, and time was running out. When the skies were exploding, who could argue with the urgency of this impending doom, unless you wanted something?

Now Jeannie, Little Jeannie, Aerapondes, Little Tony, Little Danny, Kashom, Jerzom, DannyR, KateLynn, Zeb, Kashom, Quill, and Jeanondes were in the garage—as well as the Shroud of Goroms packed with the ashes of a black bird of death and a monster.

It didn't matter. The numbers before him would not change Johnny's mind. If he was going, his truck was going, and that was that. Even Danny could not argue that point with his father.

At that point, Danny had no choice. "Jump in everybody," yelled

Danny. "Jeannie, Mom, and DannyR are in the front with Dad and me, and everyone else is in the back. *Let's go!*"

And through the darkening skies of the Scarlet Desert, a beam of green light propelled a 1955 red Chevy pickup loaded with passengers through the gathering cloud of ashes collecting in the skies above. They streaked through the fallout of planets that were no more on their way to Kopaz.

And so it was on the last day of Earth in CoalVille during the spring of 1958.

CHAPTER 26
The Royal Palace

I t was most unusual. In the entire history of the royal palace, nothing like it had ever been in the royal gardens. Why would there be a red 1955 Chevy pickup in Kopaz? There were no roads, no gas stations, and certainly no garages to overhaul engines. Maybe that was why it was so unusual to find a pickup parked outside the entrance of the royal palace.

The landing was perfect. The weather was most inviting. On the grassy lawn not far from the entrance to the royal palace, Queen Neferapondes stood where all the waving travelers who had just arrived could see her.

It wasn't that she couldn't wait to see her granddaughters, her newest grandson, and a couple of newfound friends—twin boys who had ventured from the Scarlet Desert to Kopaz with Prince Jerzom. No, it was someone else the queen was waiting for.

It had been a very long time, but now Queen Neferapondes's aching heart was well on the mend. She could not take her eyes off Kashom, who was standing tall in the back of Johnny's shiny red pickup.

He saw his mom. His heart pounded. Leaping over the side of the pickup truck, Kashom hit the ground running and raced into the arms of his mother. "I'm home, *Mom!*"

There could be nothing more exciting for a mother than to have a son return with honor. She wanted to see his face. Gently, she put her hands on his cheeks and pushed him away bit so she could look into his eyes. "*Oh,*

Kashom, you have no idea how my heart is feeling as I look into your face and see my son once more!"

Within moments, all had left the truck except Johnny.

Just because it was unusual didn't stop a throng of curiosity seekers from descending on it. They gathered around, but their questions were foreign to Johnny. In a few moments, people were snooping everywhere—in the cab, in the bed, underneath it, in the glove box, and wherever they could find to explore next.

Proud as he was, Johnny had shined and waxed his truck in the noonday sun, and it looked like it belonged in the Macy's Thanksgiving Day parade in New York City. The oak flooring in the bed looked brand new. Without a scratch anywhere, it most likely never had a heavy load placed in it.

There were three teenagers sitting on the Naugahyde front seat. You could tell by the size of their wide-open eyes that they thought this truck was cool! With their hands on the Bakelite steering wheel, they must have been dreaming of going for a test ride.

Johnny didn't have to speak their language. The romance of cars has and always will be a language in its own right.

Turning his head, Danny thought as he looked back, *Oh, Dad, you are in hog heaven!*

Staring at the moonie hubcaps, a young boy watched a party of people who had just arrived walk into the royal palace. The moonies were a perfect convex mirror and captured not only the scene of visitors entering the palace but also the image of a royal prince from the Scarlet Desert who had been absent from Kopaz for a very long time.

"I've been busy trying to get all the rooms ready for everyone," Neferapondes said to her oldest son as her mind raced in all directions trying to find a topic of conversation, but she was struggling.

"Oh, Mom, I know you so well. You're always fretting about visitors and how the arrangements will be…I guess that is just a mom thing," said Kashom as he chuckled freely.

She laughed. "Kashom, there is so much I want to hear from you. You have no idea the pain in my heart that never went away when you were taken from us."

Not missing an instant of what was transpiring between the queen and Kashom, Jeannie felt her spirits lift to the height of the sun, not the earth's sun, but a giant star overhead called Kolar.

But then she overheard a conversation taking place between Quill and Danny.

"I had no idea what your life growing up in CoalVille was like. Please forgive me, Danny." Quill was searching for the right words.

Danny said nothing. He looked at Quill and listened.

"I was concerned about how long it would be...you know, if Earth was next? I was ah...err...I...I just wanted all of us to get out alive," Quill stuttered as he tried to make sense.

"Quill," said Danny, "I knew that Lenszar was focusing the energy on our solar system and...I..."

Danny had to collect himself to forge on, and Jeannie was all ears.

She dropped her attention from Kashom and Queen Neferapondes totally as she moved to Danny's side. She grabbed his hand. She had a pretty good idea of what he was about to say, but she wanted to hear it from him.

The young girls and the guys were messing around in the entrance to the royal palace. Only Danny, Jeannie, Quill, Neferapondes, and Kashom were walking down the hallway toward the royal library.

Now it was not just Jeannie and Quill who were paying attention to the royal prince of Viracocha but also Neferapondes and Kashom.

"Lenszar was moving," said Danny in a sullen voice as he stared out of one of the hall windows, "and I knew there might be just a small window of time...and yes, I did not know, and do not know, the fate of Earth."

He stopped and looked at Kashom and then at the queen. "I did not want to take a chance. I wanted my parents out of there," he went on. Danny choked a bit as he went on. "My dad and mom have gone through hell, and it was not just a Mochcom hell. It was the hell of my dad spending most of his life in a hole two thousand feet below the ground and my mom worrying each and every day, wondering if he would come out alive. And one day, he didn't."

For a moment, there was silence—a deathly silence—as Danny paused.

All were listening intently. Then he spoke quietly. "The one thing my dad was able to get for himself was his 1955 Chevy truck. He worked extra hours every day for three years in that hellhole just to have a prize he could call his own."

"Danny," said Quill. "I feel your pain and understand. Again, please forgive me."

Yet Quill was all too aware of something that Danny was not. Maybe it was because of Danny's love of his parents and all that had transpired over the years in CoalVille. Maybe the supreme god did not want to add more pain to the memories of the past that were still so strongly on Danny's mind. For whatever reason, the supreme god had shared with Quill the consequences of what happened to those who lived in the Land of the Dead and were retrieved without locks of hair.

With a look of sadness on his face, Quill thought, *I can't tell Danny.* And so, trying to control his emotions, knowing that at some point in the near future, the royal prince of Viracocha would come face to face with a new reality, Quill simply listened.

"It's OK, Quill. With the universe exploding as we speak, we have something more pressing to take care of." Danny squeezed Jeannie's hand and smiled down at her. "We have three hours to dispose of the Shroud of Goroms and the ashes of Mochcom and his black bird," said Danny seriously.

The queen interjected. "Take care of what has to be done, and then you will have nice clean beds to lie in this evening. My staff will see to it."

"Yes," said Danny. "That is kind of you, my dear queen, and so we charge on to halt this War of the Gods before it is too late."

CHAPTER 27

The Final Gorom in
the Pit of Vulcan

"Hey, Dad, do you want to see a for-real dragon?" asked Danny
as his father was still messing around with his truck and
group of teenage boys whose lives in Kopaz never exposed them to such a
wonderment.

Spinning around, Johnny saw Danny and waved. "What? A dragon?
Sure!" replied Johnny. "These young guys are having fun, and I'd take
them for a spin if I could tell them…or talk to 'em."

Danny jumped in and made an introduction he had missed. "Guys, this
is my dad. His name is Johnny, and he will take you all for the ride of your
life when we get back!"

Kozar, the boy who seemed to be the leader of the pack, asked, "This is
your dad? He is cool, and yeah, we want to go for a ride. But what are you
guys doing now?"

Laughing, Danny pointed to the Vulcan Mountains on the distant
horizon. "Johnny wants to see a dragon! We'll be back before you guys go
to bed. It will be late, but that thing"—Danny pointed to the truck—"has
lights, so a short spin is in the works!"

Preparations were all but taken care of. Quill had made sure of that.
He'd guarded the Shroud of Goroms containing the ashes of the last

gorom with his life, as this was the final victory over evil, and nothing would spoil that.

Maybe it was just the excitement of having his parents with him. Maybe it was the excitement of being with Jeannie again and knowing with all his heart that he would not have to leave her to chase after goroms again. For sure, Danny was elated. Yet elation is fleeting, even for Danny.

Working in a hole in the ground two thousand feet deep with a bunch of guys whom your life depends on day in and day out creates a unique bond. Johnny and his buddies had their own slang, and some of it was not appropriate for ladies. Maybe that was where Danny picked up his coal-camp slang that Jeannie was always threatening to wash out of his mouth for, even if that meant soaping up the mouth of the boy she all but worshiped.

"All right, got that piece of shit wrapped up in a bigger piece of shit that has all the crap from the ages in a nice little package to send to hell," said Danny as he threw his hand in the air for a high five from his dad.

"OK, Danny, how do you get this, as you call it, 'piece of shit' to where it boards the boat to hell?" asked Johnny.

"Grab hold, Dad. We are on our way!"

And in the night sky they went: Quill, Kashom, Johnny, Danny, and the Ancient Shroud of Goroms—not to leave out the big yellow wolf, Yellzor, who gave a howl to let all know he was going to see CrystalFlame.

A beam of green light streaked across the Milky Way, and they all headed for the Pit of Vulcan.

CrystalFlame was ready. She was vigilant, and no doubt the streak of green light alerted her that Danny or Quill were on their way with more black souls to toss into hell.

From high in the sky, Johnny looked down and was like a kid with one thought on his mind. *Holy shit, this is a kick-butt ride compared to my '55 Chevy.*

In moments, they were at the Pit of Vulcan. Their welcome was anything but normal, as CrystalFlame was standing erect on her hind legs, making her tower into the air three hundred feet, and her fire-breathing landing light for Danny was the perfect marker.

"Hey, we're here," shouted Danny. "Good girl, CrystalFlame! You certainly showed me right where to land on this dark night."

Her response—*rrrrooooooooooorrrrrrrrrrraaaaaaaarrrrrr!*—was most definitely memorable for Johnny.

Of course, Yellzor had his own greeting for CrystalFlame. *Yyyoooowwwell!*

They had time—at least fifteen minutes—as the moon had not yet risen to beyond the point of no return.

"Dad, you and Kashom hold down the hatches as Quill, Yellzor, and I do the honors of letting Mochcom and that gangly throng of friends he's wrapped in get their first glimpse of what hell is all about!" Danny motioned for CrystalFlame to lower her head.

In only a few seconds, the dragon had her head over the roaring Pit of Vulcan. No one could say why, but for some reason, the volcano was unusually active that evening. Maybe it was the delight of the door of hell opening for a visitor.

"On three," said Danny as he and Quill each took hold of opposite ends of the rolled up Ancient Shroud of Goroms, swinging it back and forth in rhythm with the dragon's head swinging and spewing fire with each breath.

And like clockwork, the shroud holding the remains of Mochcom and his Black Bird flew into the air, one hundred feet above the molten lava.

It hit, and with an explosive display of boiling, roaring lava, for an instant the Shroud of Goroms burned brighter than ten thousand neon signs on the Las Vegas strip.

Danny yelled, "Happy days in hell, and good riddance!"

It was over. CrystalFlame took her place of vigilance, and for the eternities, she would make sure that the Quorum of Goroms never showed their evil faces again.

A thundering sound cracked through the air. "Good work, my royal prince of Viracocha." The voice sent a jolt of joy through Johnny as he and his son stood at the edge of the volcanic pit and looked down at the gurgling lava.

And as they stood there, a face shone in the western sky as the supreme god made himself known to all. Viracocha's voice ripped through the air once more. "You have a good son, Johnny, and you're a good father!"

Johnny's heart swelled, knowing Danny had fulfilled his mission. *Yeah*, thought Johnny, *it all started so long ago at the base of the Boar's Tusk, but then to see it all end at the top of the Tusk is way beyond the comprehension of a coal miner.*

Johnny stood for a few more minutes, clutching his son's hand and remembering those special moments with Darla on that night, his honeymoon night, at the base of the Boar's Tusk. *Yeah, Darla and I were young lovers. The gold note, the emerald ring on a gold chain, and the golden watch were a mystery—but no more!*

Wow, thought Johnny, *my son inherits supreme power!*

Maybe Danny could read his father's mind. Maybe it was just time to go. For whatever reason, Danny let his father's hand go and pointed to the sky.

Danny said, "We fly!" He put his dad at the head of the line, and soon they were all in the air again on a beam of green light.

It's my son at the helm now, thought Johnny.

And flying through the air to a strange world called Kopaz, Johnny couldn't get those thoughts to leave his mind. He kept taking a trip back down memory lane to a special evening in the Scarlet Desert when he was eighteen years old.

Tightening his fingers on his son's hand, Johnny's mind kept seeing the image of the gold note he and Darla found on their honeymoon at the Boar's Tusk. They had discovered it in the morning, lying next to them. He tensed as the message on the note flashed through his mind, once more remembering the warning. *Reveal the secret to no one until they reveal the source.*

So much had happened since that fun spring night in 1940.

It was a mystery to me for all those years, thought Johnny, sailing on a beam of green light being guided by his son. *Hmm. That note so long ago changed everything.*

The image of the gold note in Johnny's mind was so real that he felt like he could reach out and grasp it in his hands. The mystery of the note had never vanished, but the reality that was happening he could not deny stemmed from the note.

Gifts from the Gods

❖ The boy will have emerald-green eyes and sun-colored yellow hair. He shall be called Danny, and endless time shall be his gift.

❖ The emerald ring he must have with him always and guard it with his life.

❖ The golden watch holds a secret. Reveal the secret to no one until they reveal the source.

❖ Disobey any: condemnation will fall upon him.

❖ Obey all: he inherits supreme power as TRPOV in union with TRPON.

SGV

There was much Johnny didn't understand. He only obeyed, and being a simple coal miner was maybe a good thing. He squeezed Danny's hand more tightly as his mind drifted. *Events are taking place that are changing the universe, and boy am I proud of my son, Danny.*

Johnny happened to catch a glimpse of his and Danny's hands clasped together as they were flying over Kopaz.

Johnny's mind burst into doubt. *My hand…my god, what is happening? Why?*

Johnny jerked, but Danny didn't notice.

CHAPTER 28

The Gods Are Summoned

"It's time, Danny," said Quill.

Standing not more than twenty feet from Kozar, the boy who waited patiently for Johnny to return, Johnny knew that he wanted his ride.

Danny hadn't noticed until now, but now it was obvious, and Danny didn't have a thing to say. He stared at the face of his dad and searched for a few words.

Maybe it was the moonlight. Maybe it was all the excitement. Maybe it was just being with his dad once more after his beloved friend had ventured to the Land of the Dead.

"Danny, we don't have time to wait any more," said Quill as he drew Danny's attention from his father.

Turning quickly, Danny could sense that something was up but wasn't quite sure what. He looked into Quill's eyes and asked, "At the council table?"

"Yes," answered Quill, as he suspected Danny had gotten the message also but was just waiting for his father to get settled.

Danny gazed into the sky, and he was sure the stars were not just twinkling as stars normally do but that the distant flashes of light were a sure sign that not all was well in the universe. Danny was center stage in the War of the Gods, and with his mind rolling around on several subjects, he seized on one thought. *The war is raging even though Mochcom is in hell with his entire band of bastards. There must be more going on, and I have yet to find out more secrets of the universe.*

But it was not just that the sky continued to burn that captivated his inner thoughts—it was more. *What is going on with my dad? What?*

Quill must have known. He looked sad as he turned and reached for Danny's hand, which the boy had lifted toward his dad. Being only four feet tall, he had to stretch, but standing on tiptoe, Quill stopped him, and he managed to grasp Danny's hand. Danny looked down.

The night birds were at it again. Their serenading love ritual was in full swing, and their choice of location—the royal gardens in the courtyard—was a nice place to fill the air with music to accompany the aroma of the flowers that were closing their faces for the evening.

"Danny, would you get Jeannie?" Quill's face wore a look of not only urgency but also concern.

"Yeah, Quill, I know we need to go. I'll get Jeannie. It will only take a moment," said Danny as he took off at a sprint toward the palace.

Opening the passenger door, Johnny motioned for Kozar to jump in.

Danny was just walking through the massive wooden doors leading into the Grand Hall when he heard his dad's truck engine start. It was only a moment, and then Johnny was doing wheelies on the lawn of the grand courtyard.

For sure the gardeners would be busy in the morning fixing the bushes and flowers that were open season to the wheels of the '55 Chevy.

For a fifteen-year-old boy who had only traveled by horse and carriage until now, it was quite a ride. Kozar's face could not have been happier had he been accepting an Oscar for most entertaining and novel action device in a movie.

Fortunately, Jeannie was in the Grand Hall, so Danny did not have to go searching for her. He yelled out, "Jeannie, we are leaving!"

She got the message. Darla and Neferapondes were down the hallway a bit. Although Darla spoke only English, Neferapondes was doing quite well with sign language.

When they were walking out the door and into the royal courtyard, they saw Quill standing alone, not more than fifty feet from them. He motioned to them, and they approached him. Quill pointed to what appeared like a large star in the sky.

"That is the planet Volob. It circles Kolar, just as Kopaz does. It looks like a star, but it is not, and that is where our presence is needed ASAP," said Quill. "Danny, you take Jeannie, and I'll follow. We fly!"

They took off. Danny looked down. From high in the sky, Danny saw two old faces looking up with aging curiosity. *My god, what is happening to my parents?*

CHAPTER 29

The Voices of Gods

When you're invited to sit at the table of the primeval gods and it is the very first time in billions of years that new members have been invited, what is the protocol? Although this is an interesting question, there are many others: Do you offer solutions to perplexing questions? How do you deal with decisions so profound that the very existence of the gods could be at stake? How do you deal when the outcome may be an immense monstrosity? Do you sit there and keep your mouth shut?

Those are interesting questions. What are the answers?

Danny knew he had done all that had been asked. He had eliminated the evil and horror that had plagued not only Earth but also Kopaz. Danny hadn't quite figured out where Volob was in the universe yet, but from what Quill had said earlier—that it circled Kolar, just as Kopaz did—he suspected it was part of the solar system of the gods. Despite Danny's great accomplishments with his partner, Jeannie, who was faithfully next to him for his entire journey, were there still those who viewed the newcomers, the royal prince of Viracocha and the royal princess of Neferdor, as something other than heroes?

Where in the universe had Danny, Jeannie, Yellzor, Zanzee, and Quill just landed? It looked like the sun. Was it? There could be nothing more bewildering and unusual than what was before their eyes.

Immediately turning to Quill, Danny asked, "Where are we?"

He had no sooner finished his question than Danny caught a glimpse of what looked like the most magnificent white stallion that had ever existed. It wandered out of the lush bushes, which had giant purple flowers hanging from them. Now a painter would have loved this scene, for it was unique, like no other setting in the universe. That image on canvas in brilliant oils would surely demand a handsome price.

Yet it wasn't the stallion or the magnificent flowering bushes that seized Danny's attention. It was the horn.

"Quill, holy shit, is that a unicorn?" asked Danny as the white animal made its way toward Yellzor.

Before Quill could answer, another question rushed to the front of Danny's mind as he watched Yellzor bounding over the grassy lawn area to greet whatever it was that was coming his way. And greet they did. Now Yellzor's tongue was large to say the least, but licking a unicorn who was in turn licking the rough fur on the wolf's neck was not normal…or was it?

And so Danny's second and third questions were out of his mouth before Quill had answered his first. "Do they know each other? Are they friends?"

Now Jeannie was just waiting to pounce but thought she would have a little fun first. She held her tongue and just snuggled Zanzee in her arms, lifted him to her face, and nuzzled him.

Quill answered, *"Yes…yes…yes!"*

Danny had no reply other than "And?"

It was time. Jeannie pounced. "Oh no! My wonderful Danny boy has turned into a blind cyclops! And not only blind with the only eye you had and now with no eye to see but a tongue that can say only *and* like the scarecrow searching for a brain?"

That was it for Danny. He blurted, "Jeannie, don't give me that pile of shit! You have no idea where we are or where these crazy creatures are coming from." He was talking to her but was looking at something else.

Danny's eyes were locked on a black stallion with a human head, shoulders, arms, and hands emerging from the same bushes with their giant, three-foot-wide purple flowers. *Holy shit*, thought Danny, *that thing is a Greek centaur!*

He turned to Jeannie. "You talk to that thing that is galloping right at us!"

She shook her head. "*Nope!*"

The decision to start the conversation was not Danny's. Galloping at a full sprint, the creature with the head and upper body of a human and the body of a horse stopped less than two feet from Danny.

Its long curly blond hair covered its ears. Its face was stern and tanned from being continuously in the rays of Kolar. Its eyes were a dark navy blue. It said, "You're wanted. Hop on. Danny, you ride me, and Jeannie, you ride WhiteHorn."

Quill motioned for the white unicorn to come to him. "Stand still," said Quill. Locking his fingers together, Quill made a stirrup with his hands and said, "Jeannie, hop on!"

Looking like a princess in a fairytale, or the goddess of love, Jeannie mounted the unicorn, her fickle smirk starting to grow.

Watching Danny standing next to the human-headed creature, Jeannie snickered and barely managed to get her words out between her choked-up laughter. "Danny boy, are you going to be a nice cowboy, get on your pony, and ride?"

Danny really had had it with Jeannie. He knew he was no match for her, but he tried anyway. "Jeannie, I'm going to…" That was as far as he got as Danny watched the giant purple flowers turn a dark red and start to fall to the ground.

"Get on," said the human head on the horse's body.

With Quill and Zanzee on Yellzor's back and Jeannie and Danny on the two creatures of the bush, they were on their way racing across a landscape like a new-world Disneyland.

Snakes with rat heads were slithering in tall red grass. Water flowed uphill and splashed backward over rocks. The river they were on the banks of glittered like a stream of pure white diamonds in the light from a noonday star brighter than a million of the Earth's suns.

As they rounded a bend in the river at full gallop, the building came into view. Walls made of pure white and yellow gold, solid emerald and blue sapphire, and inlaid with designs of red diamond glowed as if in the center of a spotlight. Somehow, that halo of ever-changing colors was lights created by the heavenly star shedding its rays on the building as if on the starring actor on a Broadway stage.

There was no way to speculate on the immense size of the building. For as far as you looked west, it was there in sight. For as far as you looked east, it was in view. One could only conclude that it was nothing short of gigantic.

Trumpets were blasting. Drums were pounding. Flags were flying, and the doors leading into the Pantheon of the Gods were directly up a flight of stairs that reached a thousand feet into the sky.

As Danny and Jeannie dismounted, they said in unison, "Wow!"

Still sitting on Yellzor's back, Quill remarked, "Maybe you had better get back on—that is, unless you want to walk for the next several days to get where we are going."

Jeannie pulled her hands over her face and spread her fingers so two sapphire eyes were all that was visible. Then she blinked and said, "You screwed up, Danny...better get back on your pony!"

Danny had to chuckle at that. "Jeannie, why the hell did you follow me and jump off WhiteHorn?"

She laughed. "You jumped off FacePony first, Danny boy!"

And so up the long flight of stairs they went. The doors that had been closed were opening almost ceremonially as music played and thousands of white doves flew as a cloud in and out of the doorway. It looked to be a thousand feet tall and five hundred feet wide. A casual observer probably would not have recognized the opening as a door, let alone a doorway, to the inner sanctum of the Council of Primeval Gods.

Inside the doorway was a whole new world. It was like being indoors yet outside. It was immaculate. There wasn't an iota of dirt anywhere, but animals with shiny black-and-white fur were grazing on flowers of every imaginable color. It was strange indeed to see a bearlike animal with spotted black-and-white fur eating flowers and then to watch the flowers reappear.

Past a giant enclave where water fountains and lily ponds dotted the floor, there was a wall with a circular window.

They made their way to that wall, and the window opened. It was one hundred feet in diameter. They stepped in. Amazingly, there were rows of couch-like seats made of what appeared to Danny to be white leather, silk, gold, and precious gemstones, all fabricated into a material.

"Now we ride the tube," said Quill. "Take a comfortable seat, and we will emerge in the Grand Council Hall."

It was a few moments to relax. Danny had a question for Quill, who was sitting on the couch opposite from where he and Jeannie were seated.

His face sunk in lines of great concern, Danny asked, "What is the matter with my parents?"

Maybe it was just riding on the tube in the Pantheon of the Gods that prompted the question. Maybe it was his love of his parents. One thing was for certain—Johnny and Darla were changing.

"Danny, I didn't know if you noticed. You must have," said Quill in a clear voice of concern.

Quill looked at Danny and slowly explained. "What happened is that Johnny and Darla were both in the Land of the Dead. You intersected a point in time. The problem was that it was back in time. It was prior to their trip down the River Styx. And then you took them on the Highway of Time."

"What can we do, Quill?" asked Danny, clearly distressed.

Quill took a deep breath. He didn't answer Danny's question directly but proceeded to talk about their final departure from the Scarlet Desert.

"If you recall, Danny, I was quite upset just prior to the point when we left the Boar's Tusk for the last time. You had decided to go to CoalVille. I knew why you were going, and I also knew the consequences. Maybe that is why I was so upset and wanted to leave."

It was then that Danny realized that Quill only had good intentions. *My god,* thought Danny, *I rebuked Quill when he wanted to bypass CoalVille...I was wrong! Quill knew consequences I did not and was caught in a dilemma—head for Kopaz from the Boar's Tusk and leave my parents behind so I would not see them grow old, or let me fetch them and then suffer the consequences!*

Quill described the sad reality. "I don't think there is anything short of visiting the Land of the Dead and retrieving their locks of hair."

Now that was strange to Danny. "Their locks of hair? I thought one had to bring a lock of hair to get a soul from the Land of the Dead?"

"Yes, that's true, Danny," said Quill. "You need a lock of hair to match the one that is there. You see, hair has a molecular chemistry that is unique to that one individual. In fact, it is the physical record of the entire bloodline of that person, and that is why hair is used to identify a soul in the Land of the Dead."

Gazing at the empty couches on the tube as it traveled along its way to the Grand Council Hall, Quill collected his thoughts. He then added his final comment. "There are locks of hair for both Johnny and Danny in the Land of the Dead. With it remaining there, and they are not there, your parents will grow old at a very accelerated rate before dying. Then they will be lost forever."

My God! thought Danny. *What have I done? I only wanted them out of CoalVille before the end of the world. My God, why?*

"Is there anything, Quill?" Danny choked on the lump that had lodged in his throat.

"Viracocha is the only one who can authorize the removal of hair that resides in the Land of The Dead," Quill said as the tube came to a stop.

Hearing the entire conversation, Jeannie had no words. She gently placed her hand on Danny's and let her soft fingers touch his.

Shortly, what Quill said when they got on the transportation system in the Pantheon of the Gods—that they would ride the tube and shortly emerge in the Grand Council Hall—was fulfilled.

They were at the Grand Council Hall of the Gods. Through a round window-like doorway, similar to the one they entered, Danny, Jeannie, Quill, Yellzor, Zanzee, and the two horse-like creatures exited the tube.

Stepping through the doorway, Danny could see no one. He could hear loud voices, but where they were coming from was a mystery.

As Danny, Jeannie, Quill, Zanzee, Yellzor, and the two horse-like creatures were walking across the blue-diamond floor that had been laid on a foundation of yellow gold, its beauty and magnificence were lost. Danny's mind was shattered. He was trying to comprehend that he had taken from his parents the opportunity to live again.

They were moving toward what appeared to be a large elliptical hole.

It was through that opening that the voices were emanating.

And as clear as a bell, a voice that could only come from a powerful god said, "I'm your only son. My name is Ra, and my question for my father, Supreme God Viracocha. Why do you bring these earthlings to our table?"

A baseball bat could not have hit Danny harder. His heart sank. Walking next to him, Jeannie tightened her fingers so that they intertwined with Danny's.

They were just coming to the edge of the elliptical opening. It was like standing on the north rim of the Grand Canyon. Looking down, they could see the gods. Sitting at a red-diamond table that was at least one hundred and fifty yards long and fifty yards wide, they were busy.

The stairway leading down to the table was like the bleachers in a football stadium. Yet unlike bleachers, the stairs were not used as seats. They were pure gold, and each layer of stairs wrapped around the elliptical opening.

From where they stood, they could see the red table on the green-emerald floor was catching light from somewhere, and it reminded Jeannie of light from the white-topped waves on Jackson Lake at the base of the Grand Tetons when the sun was reflecting from each whitecap.

As they started their descent down the long stairway, the voice of the supreme god's son, Ra, became louder with each step. "Why does my father do this? Are we to be humiliated by humans at our table for a reason?"

At that point, a deathly silence fell on the council of gods, and the only sound was the footsteps on the stairs.

CHAPTER 30

Ancient Mysteries Unraveled

It made no sense to Danny. He was valiant; there could be no denying that. Even the gods would have to, at the very least, recognize his efforts to rid the universe of evil. Or would they?

The newcomers, Danny and Jeannie, were on the last stair leading to the council table of the primeval gods. As they stepped off onto the emerald-gemstone floor, Danny and Jeannie were the center of focus. Perceptive as he was, Danny looked around the table and discerned only puzzlement from the gods, except for those seated at the executive end. Viracocha and his wife, Neferdor, were not looking at Danny and Jeannie; they were in what appeared to be a private conversation. The god Ra was glaring at Danny.

Holy shit, thought Danny. *What have we gotten ourselves into?*

At that point, the sergeant at arms stood. A troop of buglers raised their golden instruments to their mouths and proceeded to trumpet out the call to order.

All gods stood, except Viracocha, Neferdor, and Ra, as they constituted the executive council of the gods and had no reason to stand.

As the bugle sounds faded, Viracocha said, "Show our newcomers their positions!"

That was Quill's responsibility, and so he carried out the order.

It seemed like a walk of a lifetime, a walk that would never end. Finally, they were at the end of the long table—the end diametrically opposite where the executive council sat. Danny and Jeannie stood next to their seats. Two dilapidated chairs that looked as if they had seen better days were positioned next to each other.

Danny looked at the two wooden chairs.

Viracocha waited until Danny and Jeannie were standing at their seats and then gestured. "All! Please be seated!"

Amid all the golden thrones, these flimsy wooden chairs made a statement, and Danny thought about saying something as the chair legs wobbled under him. He held his words, but his mind was not still. *They stuck us in these?* mused Danny to himself, never suspecting the god Ra was already at work to welcome the newcomers in his own way.

Jeannie grabbed his hand and whispered, "Danny, just hold on!"

"*Silence!*" The command cut through the air as Ra pounded his fist on the table in front of him.

Pins could be dropping, and all would hear their *tinkle tinkle* as they bounced on the solid-green-emerald-gemstone floor.

Even Jeannie winced. She could not kid around anymore. *The War of the Gods is real*, she thought. *And there is something amiss at this council table.*

Because they did not know what to do or what to expect next, Danny and Jeannie sat quietly. Fortunately, it was in Danny and Jeannie's favor that the War of the Gods was raging. Who knows for sure, but just maybe that was why attention turned from the newcomers to the dire situation that was exploding the universe into chaos.

Protocol was in order. Viracocha took center stage.

"Do I have to ask one more time why I am surrounded by idiots and a group that has been increased, just maybe, with those two at the end of the table?" The supreme god growled and then asked, "Should this be renamed the Council of Imbeciles?"

His voice rose, and his fist pounded with a force that sent shock waves down the table as Viracocha shouted, "*The riddle...oh, the riddle! Who has the answer to the riddle?*"

He stopped. He glared all the way down the table. His eyes, like daggers, landed on Danny. Viracocha's arm lifted, and his finger shot out like a poison dart at Danny. He spoke in a singsong voice. "Do you have the answer to the riddle?"

Even though Danny was six-foot-three-inches tall, the little wooden chair with short legs in which he sat made him seem like a dwarf.

At first, Danny was totally caught in a state of stupidity. He was dumbfounded. He said nothing.

"I'm waiting!" said Viracocha, drawing out his words.

Maybe it was coincidence. Maybe it was fate. For whatever reason, at that point in Viracocha's inquisition of Danny the buglers stood and blasted out another ceremonial concert of sound. The sergeant at arms, Comanzar, stood. He stepped to the podium.

"Supreme God, Zuron has struck again. Fire in the skies blazes unchecked." With both hands on the podium, the sergeant at arms leaned forward and pronounced, "All humans in the entire universe except for those on Kopaz are gone!"

Ra burst into the conversation. "What solar system?"

"Sick...no, not sick...*stinking sick!* You are *all* sickening!" yelled Viracocha.

His fiery-green eyes were on the gods once more. "Tammuz, Ishtar, Dumuzi, Horus, Hathor, Zeus, Neptune, Plato, Jupiter, Asherah, Osiris, Astarte, Inanna, and Kybele—have you not solved it yet?"

Viracocha waited. Those gods who were now the focal point of Viracocha's inquisition sat at the end of the table where Danny and Jeannie were and wore dead-giveaway looks.

"*Answer me, you imbeciles!*" shouted the supreme god.

No one said anything. Supreme God Viracocha had never resorted to calling the gods at his table imbeciles and idiots. Could it be that the end was coming and Viracocha was without options?

Danny watched that group of gods—those sitting closest to Jeannie and himself—keep their faces blank as no one flinched. Surveying the expressions on their faces, a thought drifted through Danny's mind. *They look like the cat that just ate the canary. What's up?*

"Why is it so hard? *The site of the black pit defines the color of the scent!* Yes, the unanswered riddle...the elusive riddle...the riddle I want the answer to!" shouted Viracocha.

Maybe it was something familiar. Maybe not. Maybe it was just the right time for the riddle to come up. Danny's ears perked up, yet at the same time, the god Ra was off on a shouting spree again.

"Was it Earth and the Earth's solar system that was fuel for Zuron's bonfire in the skies?" shouted Ra.

All eyes turned to the supreme god's son, Ra.

Danny felt a paw on his leg. It was Zanzee. *Is he trying to tell me something?* thought Danny as he managed to steal a quick glance at Zanzee stroking his pant leg.

Danny seized the opportunity to ask Jeannie for something, ever so cautiously, as the gods were in a shouting match.

Comanzar shouted to Ra, "*Yes! Earth is gone and four billion humans!*"

"Jeannie do you have your colored pencils and pad of paper?" Danny whispered from the side of his mouth.

Knowing the delicacy of the situation, Jeannie nodded slightly and handed her pencils and paper to Danny under the table.

As stealthily as possible, Danny scribbled something on the paper.

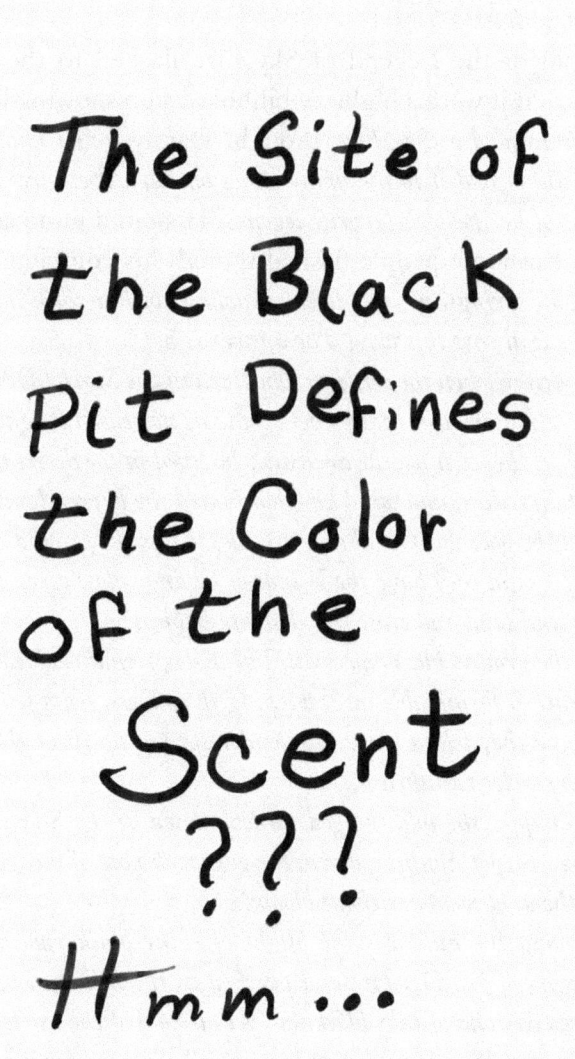

The Site of
the Black
Pit Defines
the Color
of the
Scent
???
Hmm...

As Danny was looking at the riddle, Comanzar shouted back to Ra once more. "Fire in the skies! Zuron is unleashing a hell of fire in the skies!"

It was those words—fire in the skies—that sent Danny's mind into a marathon race for answers.

The legend, thought Danny. *Yes! The Legend of Sky Fire! That has to have something to do with it!*

Every detail of the Legend of Sky Fire flashed to the front of his consciousness as if it were a highway billboard sign showing him the way.

Hmm…the Legend of Sky Fire, thought Danny. *Yes! I know it by heart! So long ago, Jeannie told it to me many times on our adventures in the Scarlet Desert. It is one of her people's favorite legends.* His mind lit up as the ancient legend of the Kashome people flashed though his consciousness. *As seen from far away, in springtime, the desert is ablaze with a thick carpet of scarlet paintbrush. Was it always this way? The answer is no!*

There was a time when the ancients who lived in the Scarlet Desert saw only a bleak landscape. And why was that? There could be no reason to ignore the gods in their generosity, as they wanted the ancients who lived in the desert to have a home of splendor. But dirt, dust, and wind had dominated the barren landscape for eons.

What could the gods do? Could they ask Sky to kiss the ground and bring on a new beginning? Could they have the Winds of Change blow away the mountains of parched rock and sand and erase this desolate habitat?

Sky kissed the ground but to no avail. The desert remained bleakly barren. At her failure at such a formidable task, weeping in sadness, tears fell from the face of Sky, and where they fell, a blaze of splendor sprang up throughout the desert, covering it with scarlet paintbrush.

Sky was so happy, she told the gods to look down at the Scarlet Desert, now ablaze with a red carpet. Smiling down, the gods took note of the work of Sky, but then they saw the arid corner without bloom.

Nestled among the hills was the blight of shiny black ribbons of coal that mocked Sky's tears of joy. Desolate and parched as the hills had been, their only hidden beauty were strips of inky blackness, yet all void of the scarlet brush. There could be no bitter sadness more wrenching to Sky, whose tears turned to fiery hail in defiance of the hills adorned with the blight of coal. And from that hail of fire came new life, and that is why the desert bush with the sacred name of lieloc blooms months early in the springtime of CoalVille, showering all with its scent. The gods smiled, but when the ancients changed the name of the flowering vine to "lilac," the gods turned their faces away, and the sacred name of lieloc was lost on the winds of time.

It was this sentence that grabbed him: *And from that hail of fire came new life, and that is why the desert bush with the sacred name of lieloc blooms months early in the springtime of CoalVille, showering all with its scent.* That sentence hit Danny like four thousand tons of bricks. *Yes! That's it! My God, the answer! It is in there someplace…what is it?*

Now there was no stopping him. Danny was fumbling and writing furiously with Jeannie's pad of paper on his lap. In a state of panic, he scribbled as if all depended on his finishing, which it did.

The Legend of Sky Fire had to do with a scent. Danny's mind was racing against the clock. He drifted into thought as Jeannie's hand rested on his leg under the table. She held her breath as if that would help Danny.

He wrote on the paper, "CoalVille." *Hmm…CoalVille is the site of the black pit.* And with a twinge of sadness, briefly his mind drifted. *It was that black pit—the coal mine—that buried my father alive.*

Yet in the dire situation of the universe erupting in a blaze of fire, those thoughts of his beloved father were short-lived. Time was running out, and the riddle remained unsolved. Danny quickly charged on, as all depended on the elusive answer to the Riddle of Zuron.

Even in the middle of the unfolding doom of the universe, nothing escaped Viracocha. Picking up every thought in Danny's mind, the supreme god was focusing. His mind was exploring what was going on there. *Zanzee…CoalVille…Legend of Sky Fire…what the hell?*

Danny whispered ever so softly as he thought out loud. "Hmm. So CoalVille is the site of the black pit. OK. CoalVille is the name, but what does it have to do with the answer to the Riddle of Zuron? What does the name 'CoalVille' have to do with the scent, and how does the scent define the color? Yeah, the color is the answer to the riddle!"

He fumbled with the colored pencils. *Let me see…three Ls. How? Hmm. Can I rearrange them?*

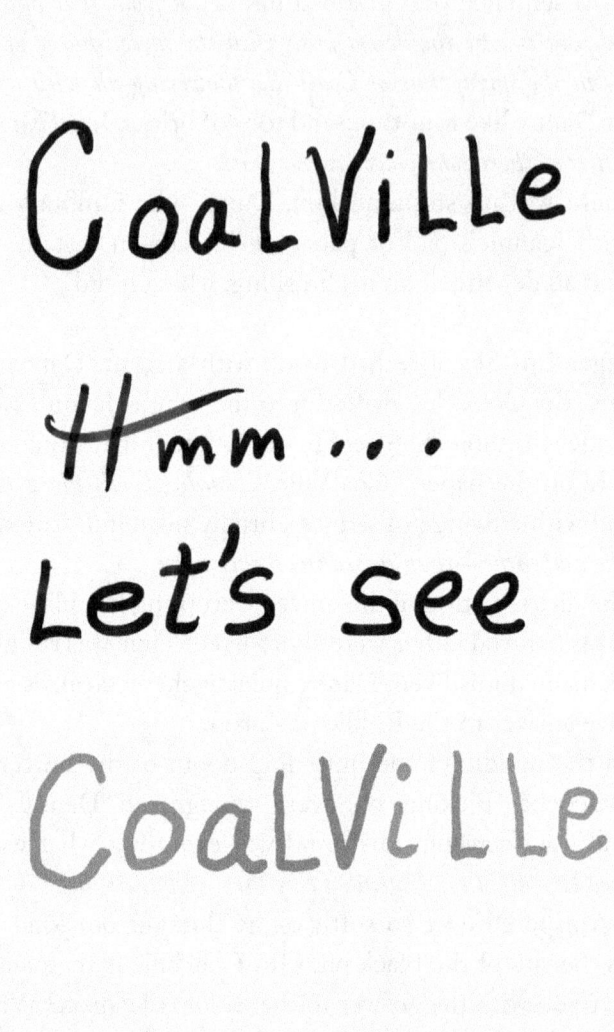

His mind wandered through corners and crevasses it had never known. *Holy Shit!* Danny thought. *I can rearrange the letters. The letters of CoalVille can be rearranged as "LavLieLoc."*

He scribbled on the pad of paper a note for Jeannie. She looked. She stared. Her face went blank.

Jeannie,
it is Simple
CoalViLle
and
LavLieLoc
have the
Same set of
Letters!

Is this it? My God, I have it! His mind exploded as he wrote his conclusion on the paper.

He plopped the paper on the table so Jeannie could see his second note. She nodded.

Jeannie,
The answer to
the Riddle
Comes from
an Anagram!

LavLieLoc
The answer
is Lavender
Look:
LavenderLieLoc

Danny didn't know the name of the god who sat in the golden throne closest to Jeannie, the last throne at the end of the long table. He had red hair and a long, pointed nose. His eyes, framed by bushy eyebrows, were set on high cheekbones, and he had a long neck. He stretched his neck further as he tried to get a glimpse of Danny's note, and he bobbled his head but was unable to see the writing on the paper.

He wasn't the only curious onlooker. Zanzee, sitting on Jeannie's lap, put his little head forward and gawked also. He stuck his paw out and tapped Danny's bare arm as if to give his approval.

Oh my gosh! thought Jeannie. *I don't know if he knows what he is doing. This is crazy…or is it?*

As Comanzar was babbling away about something, a shout rang out in the council hall of primeval gods!

"*My God*, it's *lavender!*" shouted Danny. "*Yes! It's lavender!*" His second shout was even louder, and Danny stood, filled with jubilation.

If pins could have been heard dropping on the floor during the last silence, at this moment, cotton balls would have struck the emerald-gemstone floor with thuds of thunder.

"*How dare you?*" screamed Ra. "*You traitorous dog, you!*"

Snarling like a rabid wolf, Ra glared at Danny and pointed his finger venomously. He growled, "You come to this table. You insult us! Your smirk will be on your face for eternity in *hell, you filthy pig!*"

Ra was not finished. Still in the spotlight, still making his case, he forged on. Viracocha looked askance at his son next to him. His wife, Neferdor, reached and grabbed Viracocha's hand. All eyes were on Ra.

Maybe it was that Danny looked as if he could be Viracocha's identical twin—handsome beyond description. Maybe Ra was jealous of that fact, as he looked nothing like his father. Indeed, he was rather ugly. Ra was short and had thinning, scraggly brown hair that looked like dried straw. Most likely, Ra would give anything to have a head of beautiful shaggy blond hair like his father, which was identical in every way to Danny's beautiful shaggy blond hair. Or maybe it was just the fact that at Danny's first council meeting, as the newest god at the table, he offered the elusive answer to the Riddle of Zuron that had evaded the primeval gods for eternities.

Seldom, if ever, had the god Ra risen from his throne. He was there to support his father, and that he had done for millions of billions of years. For him to stand was most unusual, as it was for the god who was second in command in the universe to enter into a most serious conversation and be consumed by rage.

Standing in front of his golden throne with his hands on the table, the god Ra pressed his chest out like he wore a medal of valor and bellowed in a voice full of vengeance, "On your way to hell, your nose will wipe every inch of the floors of this pantheon. *You are nothing more than a swine with its nose in filth!*"

As Jeannie sat next to Danny in the old wooden chair, her hands tensed to a knot as the god Ra unleashed his wrath. She felt that her heart was no longer in her chest but was sinking into a bottomless pit. She could do nothing, as it was Danny who was digging the hole deeper and deeper. She knew they were both headed for the bottom of an abyss.

CHAPTER 31

The Traitor Disclosed

There is something familiar to those who watch the Academy Awards each year, and it is the red carpet. There is no doubt that being on the red carpet is a distinct honor that few are afforded and an opportunity for which most would do anything.

The long run of red-diamond table in the Hall of the Primeval Gods, however, might not afford the status of supercelebrity to one walking on it. At least that was the central issue on Jeannie's mind.

Danny suddenly stood during the dressing down he was getting from Viracocha's son, the god Ra. Caught off guard, Jeannie was all but sure they were done for when Danny's last shout sent Ra into a rancorous tirade. Yet that was minor in comparison to what Danny was doing now.

Oh no! What are you doing? The thought seared through Jeannie's mind as Danny jumped on the flimsy wooden chair on his way to his target—the top of the red-diamond table.

Standing totally erect on the red-diamond table, he started walking. Although no one present viewed it as such, Danny was like David facing Goliath, and he walked on. Every eye from every god had only one focus, and that was the human walking through them on what appeared to be a kamikaze mission.

Jeannie squeezed poor Zanzee so tightly that he must have felt that the end was in sight for him also. His little paws wanted to claw, but he held back and instead started purring.

It was odd indeed. On one end of the table was a cat purring so loudly that all could hear. Right smack in the middle of the table was a six-foot-three-inch young man with shaggy yellow-colored hair, not unlike Viracocha's, emerald-green eyes, not unlike Viracocha's, and a show of stamina unlike anything that had transpired at the Council of Primeval Gods—ever.

She had no options left. Danny was on his own, and Jeannie could only watch and wait.

With each step, Danny's engineer's boots, with their metal taps on the toes and heels, made a distinct sound that had never been heard in the grand council hall.

Click-tap...click-tap...click-tap sounded with each step he took.

Danny was now midtable. GAMMAZEL was right before his eyes. He had no idea what it was or what it was used for, but it looked nearly identical to Jeannie's golden key—except it was not three inches in diameter, but thirty feet across.

Holy shit, that is a big key, thought Danny as he walked by it. The image of Jeannie's key flashed in his mind as he tried to compare the two. *It looks like Jeannie's, except for the writing in the middle of it, and that damn thing is thirty feet across. Holy shit! That is huge!*

The reflection of the thirty-foot golden key in the red-diamond tabletop caught his attention. *Wow! The key looks like it is sitting on a red mirror. What is this for?*

But as he walked by, Danny missed seeing the device at the base of the giant key and its reflection in the mirrored surface.

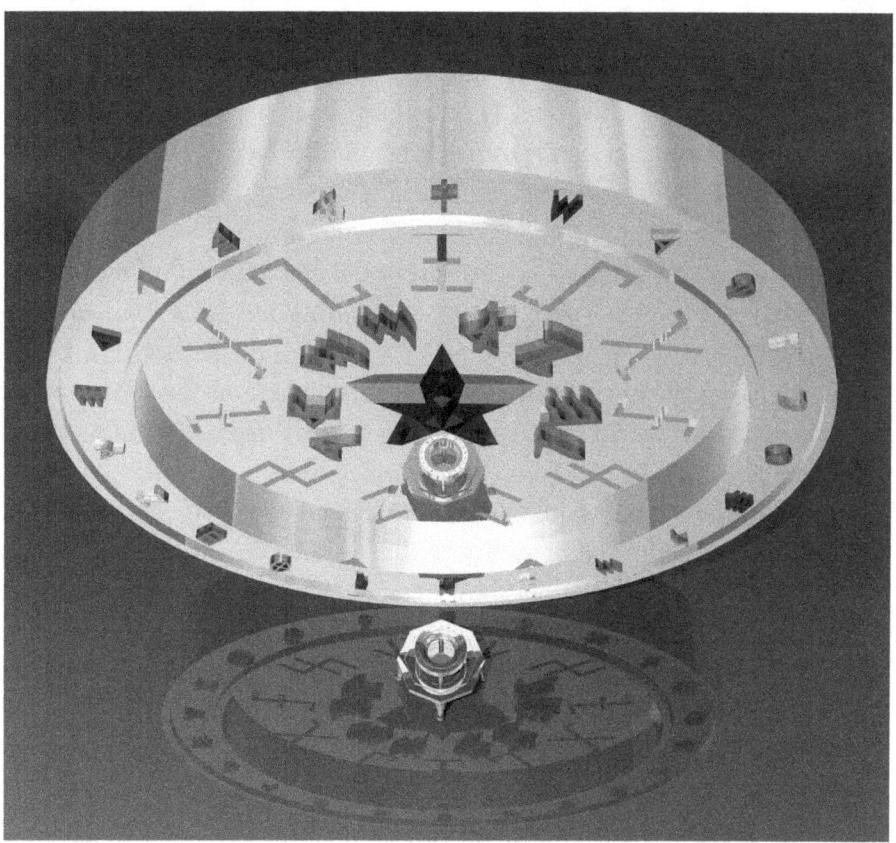

There in a throne just to the right of the giant key was what appeared to be a little dwarf man. If he stood, Danny surmised he would be no taller than three feet. His nose was round and had a wart on the end of it. His eyes were so deeply set it looked as if they were hiding in holes.

It was not what he looked like or how small he was that drew Danny's attention but the apparatus that his hands were clutching. It was a system of levers labeled with mirror-image symbols attached to the giant golden key.

But all of this happened in a second, as Danny gave the giant golden key but a passing glance as he walked by on his way to the other end of the table.

He had now walked seventy-five yards. He never looked back. Maybe if he had, he would have had second thoughts about what he was doing.

Jeannie was all but ready to die. She no longer had her hands on Zanzee. For the cat, that was good, as he wasn't being squeezed. No, her hands were now over her face. It must have been an instinctive reaction by Jeannie to throw her hands over her face in the face of extreme fright.

My God, Danny...please stop! was the single thought that kept replaying over and over in her mind.

Danny was now twenty-five yards from the executive end of the council table. Silence was everywhere, except for the *click-tap...click-tap...click-tap* of his shoes.

Ra's glare grew more intense with each step, and it was as if he were counting the *click-taps* in anticipation of his unleashing a deathblow at the right moment.

The supreme god waited. His ultimate control kept his son from any premature action, and so Viracocha waited for the reason of this extraordinary display of courage—or lunacy, whichever it turned out to be.

Danny was ten yards away from his target. He put his hand in his pocket and grasped an object with his fingers. With that object in his grip, Danny's mind took off and relived that day at the woodshed.

Jerzom had turned and walked a few steps to get away from staring into the horror of a woodshed that was a chamber of human sacrifice.

Maybe it was just a coincidence on that day in CoalVille...and maybe not. I don't think so, thought Danny.

When Jerzom had looked away, he did not see the woodshed, nor could he see me. It was my foot that was still planted where I had put it to help Jerzom to his feet.

For some reason I looked down. Fortunately, a drifting cloud revealing the face of the sun caught a flash of light at the toe of my boot. It grabbed my attention. I bent over and scraped the dirt. There it was. I picked it up with my heart pounding. Staring at it in the palm of my hand, my mind exploded. What is this? It has to... the symbols...hmm...from the gods...yes!

I know what it is, and there can only be one reason why Mochcom had it. Someone gave it to him, and evidently Mochcom dropped it in the filth around his home and lost it.

Ra lifted his hand to strike Danny with the might of a god and send him down the River Styx on a speedboat. It didn't happen.

"*Stop!*" yelled Viracocha as his eyes watched Danny's every facial expression.

Those at the table witnessed not Danny stopping, but Ra. Danny was where he wanted to be. Standing not more than five feet in front of the second-most powerful male god in the universe, Danny pulled his hand from his pocket and threw the object onto the table.

Clink...tink...clink. Clink. Tink. Tink. The object flipped around and then found a resting place smack in front of Ra.

Only the eyes at the executive end of the council table were positioned to view the object. There was a hubbub of whispers at the other end of the table coming from the gods closest to Jeannie. She couldn't make out their words.

Watching the goddess Neferdor told Jeannie something. The supreme god's wife rarely displayed emotion, but her eyes opening to the size of silver dollars surely meant something.

Jeannie's mind was shooting in every direction. *What is it? What did Danny throw on the table? What are you doing?*

All eyes were on Danny, and every god, goddess, and Jeannie had just one thought. *What did he just throw onto the table?* A strange eerie silence was gathering. The hubbub of whispers was slowly fading, and the gods were watching the episode unfold.

That silence was short-lived. Danny's voice could be heard as loud as an announcement coming over the loudspeaker system at Dodger Stadium.

"*Who is the traitorous dog…who?*" shouted Danny.

No one talked. The pressing silence after Danny's last shout closed in like the grip of a vice squeezing its prey into submission.

And like the thundering crack of a cannon slicing through the stillness of a quiet evening, Danny's voice boomed once more as he roared, "*Who!* I ask again, who is the *filthy pig among the gods?*"

And then there was another voice that joined Danny's. "*Answer him!*"

howled Viracocha.

The god Ra said nothing.

And with the voice of a god, Danny shouted, *"Your nose…not mine…yes, your nose will wipe asses for the eternities in hell…you slimy, wretched, stinking hog!"*

At the other end of the table, a young girl's heart came out of the hole it had been hiding in and started beating again.

Viracocha stood. He leaned forward. He looked up at Danny's face. Locking eyes with Danny, he asked in a loud voice, "What did you say?"

"Lavender!" boomed Danny's commanding voice. "The answer to the ancient Riddle of Zuron is 'lavender'!"

CHAPTER 32
Black Temple Explodes

Their eyes never moved. It was almost like a staring contest, but that was not the case. The supreme god of the universe engaged in a staring contest? Or was it? At least that was what it appeared to be. Viracocha remained standing, his two arms forward with both hands on the table as he leaned into a position where his head was looking directly at Danny's.

It could have been cause for concern, especially after previous comments had more or less belittled Danny. But now the tide had turned, and standing on the red-diamond table looking down at Viracocha was a quite unusual way for a human to interact with a god.

Yet was he human? Danny certainly came from humans, as did Jeannie. Had humans ever been at the council table of the primeval gods? The answer to that question is "Absolutely not!" There were at least sixty-five voting members prior to Danny and Jeannie's arrival. But the question remained whether Danny and Jeannie would have a vote at the council table.

One word filled the hall with a thundering resonance.

"*Well?*" Viracocha's voice cut through the silence, as he demanded a response.

One thing was different, however. This time, Viracocha's glaring green eyes were matched by Danny's glaring green eyes staring back at him.

The supreme god studied every minute expression on Danny's face, and the young god from the Scarlet Desert answered, "*Well, what?*"

What came next was beyond the comprehension of the sixty-five voting gods at the council table. They had no vote. Viracocha just overrode them with his next command, and it was directed at Danny.

"*Do it!*" yelled Viracocha.

Who knows why Viracocha ordered it? Maybe it was because the Quorum of Primeval Gods had failed Viracocha for millions of years. Maybe it was Danny and Jeannie's unwavering determination to rid the universe of evil and their triumphant victory in their latest quest. Who would ever know? But for whatever reason, you might say, "It was most unusual!" Surely, there had never been a human at the council table of the primeval gods. But now there were two newcomers—children of coal miners from the Scarlet Desert of Wyoming—seated among the ruling gods of the universe. And from what had just transpired, Danny was no mere human! He was indeed a god with the unwavering respect of the supreme god of the universe. Danny and Jeannie might never have cast a vote at the council table of the primeval gods, but Danny had just trumped them all. He was carrying out an order that had not been ratified by a majority vote from the quorum of gods. Their voices in this matter did not matter to Viracocha. It was Danny and Jeannie, and only Danny and Jeannie, who were center stage on the War of the Gods. The baton, figuratively speaking, had been fumbled by the Quorum of Primeval Gods for who knows how long, certainly millions of years. Now that baton was in the hands of newcomers—a young god and young goddess. Danny and Jeannie were in command, and the rest of the gods had no say in the most crucial decision ever made concerning the fate of the universe.

It was a long hundred-and-fifty-yard look that Danny gave Jeannie as he turned from staring into Viracocha's face to give a smile to the smiling eighteen-year-old girl sitting in a small wooden chair at the south end of the council table.

At that point, when Danny stared down the table at Jeannie, it hit her like a ton of bricks!

"My god," she whispered to herself. *It is time. It is time to do it!* That was her revelation. She reached into a secret corner of her mind and pulled out the conversation she had with her mom, Soft Wind, so long ago as they sat on that old couch in their living room.

My mom was so right! Danny just figured it out. He used the Legend of Sky Fire to solve the riddle! What else did my mom say that night?

Although Jeannie and Soft Wind had not talked for what seemed like forever, their conversation shot through Jeannie's mind in a matter of seconds. Every detail of their conversation flashed through her consciousness as if it she were reliving it.

"In just a minute you can go to bed, but I am not through!" said Mom. "Jeannie, there is one more vital thing you must know," said Soft Wind, with a most serious look. "There is another function of your golden key, and it may be the most important one!"

My heart pounding and eyes wide open, I blurted, "Mom, you are scaring me. Do I need to hear all of this stuff?"

Without a moment's hesitation, Mom emphatically said, "Yes!"

Growing tenser by each ticking second, I had no options left. My mother was not about to let me, her only daughter, be exposed to the gravest of dangers with no knowledge of what lay ahead.

"Can I hold your hand?" asked my mom.

I moved from my chair to be next to Mom on the old couch, and we held hands. Soft Wind continued. "I just told you that your key must be a part of a set of keys that unlock the bottomless pit by the star of the chamber. Evidently, that sacred statement in our legends has something to do with unleashing the power of the sun, which leads to the essences of what our people seek—the Pearl of Time—eternal youth. But there is more!"

"More?" I asked. I was sure I looked utterly bewildered.

"Yes. It is not only the power of our sun that your golden key unlocks but also the power of the star at the center of the universe. That star is called Kolar," said Soft Wind with a smile as if to convey to me how proud she was that her daughter would be one of the gods and goddess who resided in their pantheon on Volob, the Herculean planet that revolved around Kolar.

"Are you sure, Mom?" I asked, even more puzzled.

Looking as serious as she had ever looked, Mom said, "Yes, your key unlocks GAMMAZEL. And you must only reveal this when—and only when—the answer to the Riddle of Zuron is revealed."

Butting in, I interrupted. "Mom, this is crazy stuff! What is GAMMAZEL?"

Soft Wind paid no attention. "We do not know what GAMMAZEL is. And this is the warning I must give you, Jeannie, that you must hold this secret and not reveal it to Danny or even the royal prince of Viracocha until you know the answer to the Riddle of Zuron."

"Mom, you are really scaring me. Zuron is the dark god, and now I have to know the answer to an ancient riddle?" I blurted. Then I added, "How will I know that the answer to the riddle is the correct one? And what is this Riddle of Zuron?"

The afghan had fallen to the floor. The lights of a passing car were dancing once more across the old plastered walls of our living room, and the cracks were like figures in the dance.

It was a bit chilly, so Mom reached and grabbed the afghan that had been covering her and tossed it over our legs. Then she said, "We do not know the ancient Riddle of Zuron. Only the gods know that. And you will know the answer is correct, as it has something to do with another of our legends, the Legend of Sky Fire, which you know and which I will not bother telling you again, as I know you are tired."

Jeannie was elated. Her mother's warning to her so long ago on that night of legends was all coming into focus.

Yeah, my mom spoke clearly. "Mochcom and Zuron are the only ones who know about the connection of the riddle's answer to fire in the sky! Evidently, Kashom overheard Mochcom say something about the riddle and that the answer was connected to a scent and fire in the sky!"

I kept listening. Mom continued. "Kashom knew that at some time the Neferzul who would help solve the ancient Riddle of Zuron would come from his posterity."

And then with conviction, Soft Wind made her point. "Jeannie, you are that Neferzul. Kashom wanted to do all he could to help you succeed in your mission, which is essential if the supreme god Viracocha is to be triumphant in winning the war! And to help you, the Kashome people have told the Legend of Sky Fire. It was Kashom who first told this legend. He did it to help you solve the Riddle of Zuron.'

Boy was I as confused as I thought on that night so long ago? This is way too much, as this Night of Legends has turned into much more than I had ever imagined.

I said, "Good night, Mom." I skipped off to my bedroom.

And then it exploded into Jeannie's mind. It made sense. It was what her mom had said. "Yes, your key unlocks GAMMAZEL. And you must only reveal this when the answer to the ancient Riddle of Zuron is revealed."

Holy umping jabeebees! My golden key unlocks GAMMAZEL, and that is the giant golden key in the middle of the red-diamond table!

But that was not all. Something else was needed once GAMMAZEL was unlocked.

Sometimes old habits came in handy. For as long as Danny had known Jeannie, she was never without her small canvas bag with papers and pencils. Today was no exception. Jeannie opened her bag and started fumbling through her stuff.

Hmm…where is it? she thought. *I know I have it.*

She spotted what she wanted—a piece of paper that Tony had written something on when they were still searching for hidden treasures in the Scarlet Desert so long ago. Maybe she had kept the paper as a keepsake to remind her how neat a friend Tony was.

"Ah…there it is!" she whispered.

And the faces of the fourteen gods sitting closest to her, those who had fallen out of grace with Viracocha for casting their vote with Zuron, lit up with interest. Most likely, they had one thought that dominated their minds: *What is she doing?* All were listening as Jeannie whispered, "Ah… there it is!"

They might have not known what she was doing, but Jeannie did. She plopped the piece of paper on the red-diamond table in front of her.

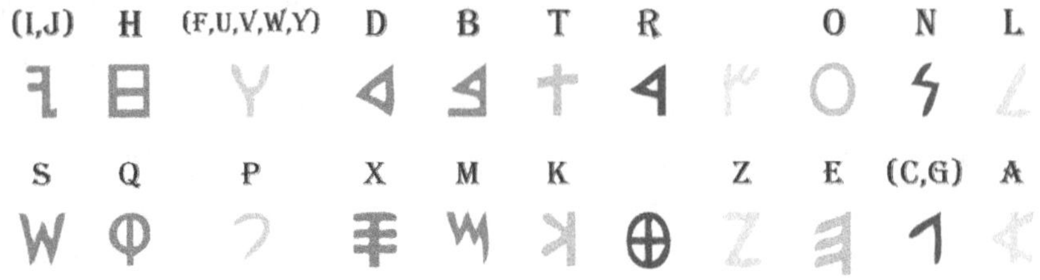
(I,J) H (F,U,V,W,Y) D B T R O N L
S Q P X M K Z E (C,G) A

"OK," Jeannie said out loud. "What are the symbols for lavender?"

It only took her a moment, and she had it down. "There! Thank you, Tony!" she said, waving the paper in the faces of the gawking gods. And at the south end of the council table, a code of symbols was revealed.

Danny and Jeannie were about to start an incredible journey. The elation must have been beyond any feeling that either Danny or Jeannie could have previously dreamed of. It was a moment of glory that would trump any other moment in the history of the universe.

Maybe brainwaves work on the same network when it comes such to monumental feats.

Jeannie's smile was growing, and her mind was going wild. *There is synergy and teamwork going at the council table of the gods. Danny solved the ancient Riddle of Zuron, and I am going to unlock GAMMAZEL with my key.*

Jeannie stood, stepped up on her wooden chair, and stopped to make sure Zanzee was secure in her hands, and they leaped onto the red-diamond table.

There was no stopping her smile. As she started her walk down the tabletop to the center, where Danny was also headed, she stopped for a moment and looked at a god who was smiling at her.

What's with that guy? thought Jeannie.

He caught her glance. *Hmm*, thought Tammuz. "What words? Black Royal Temple?" he said very softly to Jeannie as she walked by.

He's a weird one. The thought passed through Jeannie's mind as she caught his words.

How could she know? This was the first time she had been at the Pantheon of the Gods. How could she have any knowledge of an earlier conversation between Viracocha and the god Tammuz, when tensions were on the rise?

Viracocha had grilled the god Tammuz in front of all his peers. "What words? What about those three words—Black Royal Temple?" Viracocha had roared. Indeed, the supreme god's questions stirred the emotions of the gods and especially Tammuz. Behind the questions of Viracocha was the implication that he was a traitor. But that had just changed, and so had the smile on Tammuz's face.

Jeannie could care less about a black royal temple or that weird duck of a god that got all tangled up in words with the supreme god.

Jeannie had rhythm on her mind, and that was her sole focus.

Her boots, like Danny's, had cleats on the toes and heels that made a distinctive sound: *click-tap…click-tap…click-tap*.

She listened and paced her steps so that the rhythm she made was in sync with the music of Danny's boots: *click-tap…click-tap…click-tap*. The sound of victory grew louder as Danny and Jeannie made their way to center stage.

For some unknown reason, Yellzor wanted to be center stage also. He'd been rolled up in a giant ball of yellow fur behind the wooded chairs but popped his eye open and took notice when Jeannie jumped onto the red-diamond table.

In two bounds, he was on the table also. As a giant wolf, of course he had a long stride, so catching up to Jeannie took only a matter of seconds. And then he walked at her side.

They were almost there. Danny lifted his arm and pointed. Ten more steps each and they would be midtable.

GAMMAZEL was right before their eyes, located precisely in the middle of the red-diamond table, both from length and width standpoints.

The strange little god with the round nose, complete with wart, jumped on his golden throne. Standing on the seat, he readied himself for his next leap, which would put him on the table.

Flying from his waist like a referee's arm throwing a penalty flag in an important Super Bowl game, Danny's arm made it clear that the little god should stop, but he backed up his gesture with a verbal command. "*Sit!*"

Most likely, in his entire tenure of sitting at the council table of the primeval gods, the god Zipzor had never been called out by a human. But Danny was not human. He was the god, along with Jeannie, in charge of winning the War of the Gods, and no little dwarf god with a round nose was about to interfere with the most important event that had ever taken place in the universe. That honor was Danny's and Jeannie's alone. They were the new gods at the council table and apparently had command and unquestionable authority. Zipzor just got ordered to stay in his seat.

That subtle little move didn't get past Jeannie.

Now standing next to Danny, she managed to say through her smile, "So, Danny boy, do you know how to work this thing, or do you have to ask that little god to jump on the table again?"

Most likely, in the entire history of the meetings of the council of the primeval gods, there had never been a show that so demanded laughter, and laughter there was at Jeannie's comments.

And through the laughing outburst from the seated gods, filling the air with noise, Danny focused and said, "Jeannie, do you have the symbols?"

"Yep!" was her reply.

"Well, holy shit, I thought you had lost it when you crawled under the table, *girl!*" said Danny though his chuckles and giggles. "Yeah, when I was putting it to the god Ra for being a traitor, you ducked out of sight!"

She paused as if she didn't have a comeback, but she did. She was just timing it right. "Danny, you can't cuss in front of the gods!" That comment by Jeannie brought out a few more laughs from the gods, but not from Viracocha.

"Get with it!" came the command from the executive end of the table.

Jeannie sat down. She took off her right boot and dislodged the pin located in the heel of it so that it could be pivoted, revealing her golden key. Giggling, Jeannie looked up from her sitting position and said, "You don't know how to make that thing work…but neaner—neaner—neaner…I do!"

That didn't stop Danny, "Yeah, here I was saving the universe, and you were hiding and crawling away!"

At that comment, however, a booming voice cracked through the air. *"You haven't saved anything yet!"*

Viracocha was still in charge, and his statement had just confirmed that.

Maybe it was meant to be. Maybe it was just a way of bringing Danny down to Volob. Who knows? Whatever it was, the urgency of the situation just got worse.

The trumpets sounded.

When silence descended following the blast of rhythmic bugling, Comanzar made his statement. "Supreme God, Lenszar has moved. Our sky sentinels have detected that not only is Lenszar moving again but it appears to be focusing on planet Kopaz."

"*Go, Danny! Go!*" screamed Jeannie. "I'll put my key in GAMMAZEL to unlock it," she said.

"Where's the paper?" he yelled back, as he had no idea of what she had just said about her golden key and GAMMAZEL.

Jeannie was racing to the giant golden key. She looked for where she would place her key. She spotted the place. *That is it!* Jeannie thought. *It looks similar to the sundial key that my golden key works with.*

At the base of GAMMAZEL there was a golden object much like the sundial key that Danny, Jeannie, and Tony had found in the Scarlet Desert of Wyoming in the spring of 1958. This device, however, did not have Roman numerals, but it did have an exact set of colored gemstone symbols that were identical to the outer ring of symbols on Jeannie's golden key.

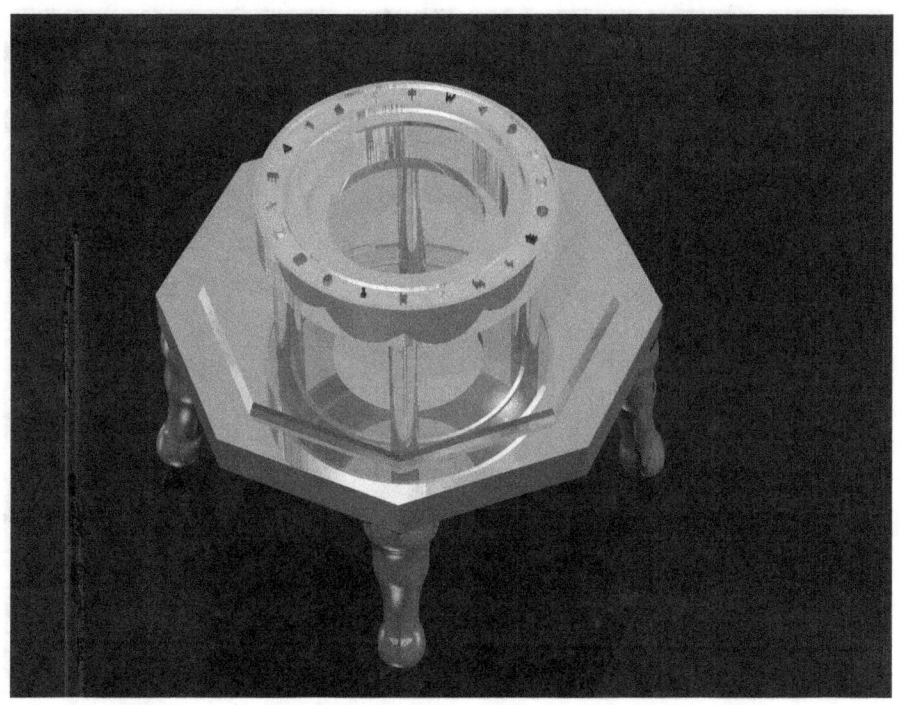

She lined up the symbols of her golden key to match the symbols on the perimeter of the round indentation and dropped her golden key into it.

"There, my golden key is in place!" she said.

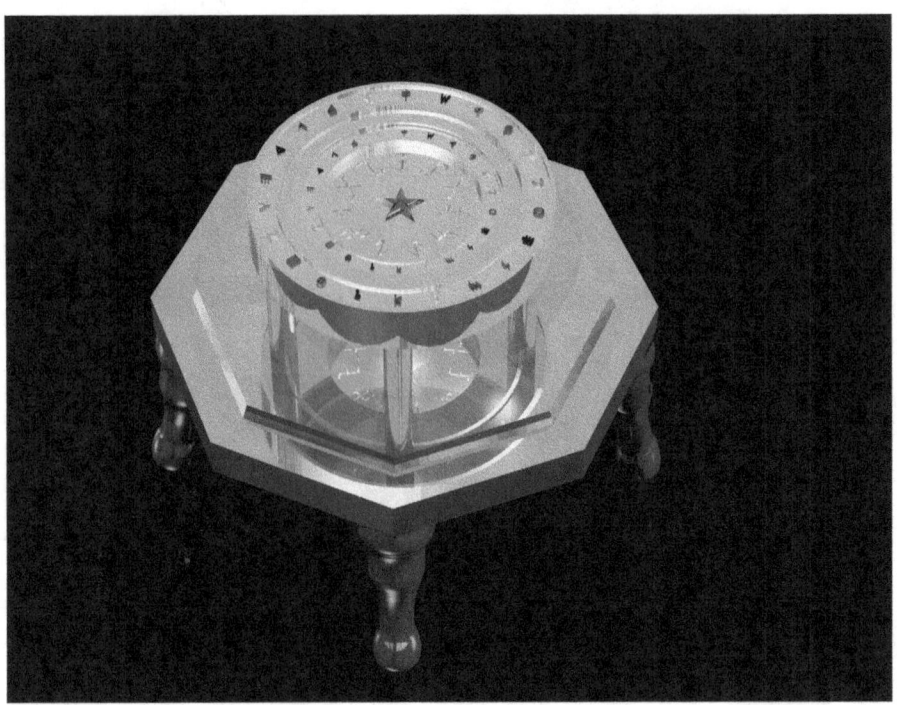

At the very moment that Jeannie's words faded, the trumpets blasted and sounded off again. Comanzar stated, "Supreme God, GAMMAZEL is now unlocked, armed, and ready for the code of symbols."

Danny was stymied. He had no idea what had just happened, but his complete befuddlement primed him for a comment from Jeannie. "Danny boy, hang tight. We're *ready to rock and roll!* So get ready to roll this baby round and round!"

"*Go! What are you waiting for?*" yelled Viracocha.

Seized by the god's urgency, Jeannie screamed, "Here! Here is the code of symbols! As I give you them one at a time, you spin that baby!"

Standing at the edge of GAMMAZEL, Danny grabbed it with both hands. Unlocked by Jeannie's golden key, it now rotated freely on some sort of ball-bearing system, so it spun like a wheel.

As Danny spun the giant golden key, the rays of Kolar shone through a slit in the roof of the pantheon. It was no ordinary slit but a gap filled with yellow diamond, so the slice of yellow light struck one of the mirror-image symbols, shining through it, and displaying its image on the red-diamond tabletop.

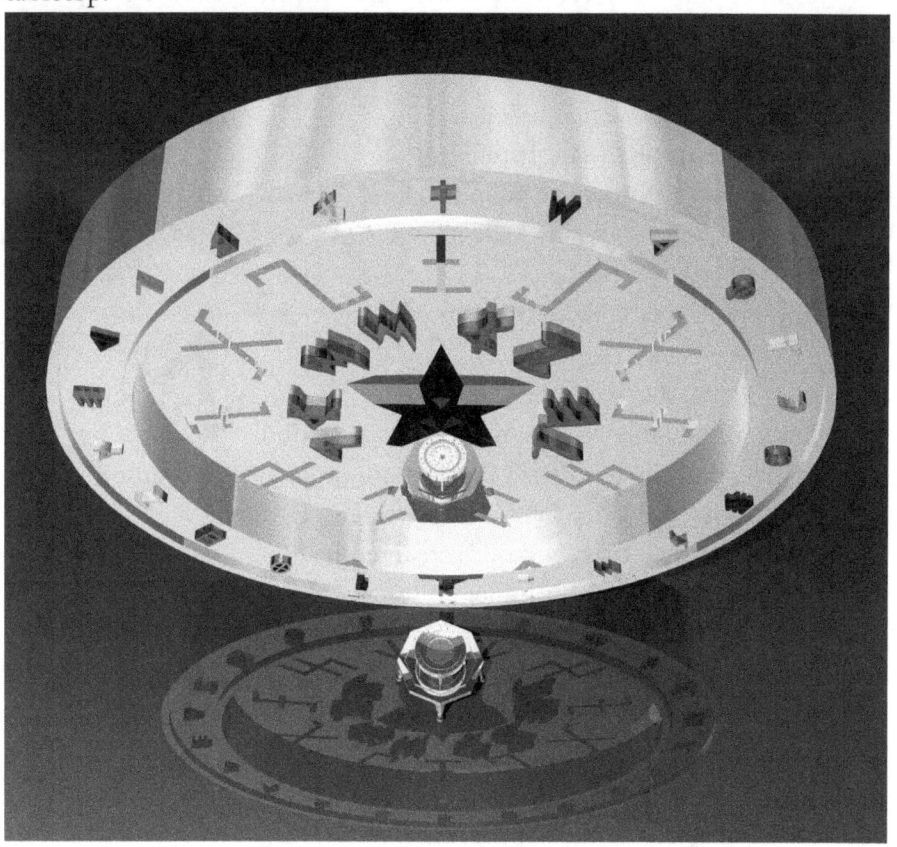

"Danny, spin it to   ," said Jeannie as she showed him the first symbol.

Spinning GAMMAZEL to the position where the first symbol aligned with the pointer on the red-diamond table, the light coming through

the yellow-diamond slit in the roof of the pantheon formed the
mirror-image symbol on the table.

"Jeannie, pull the lever with that symbol on it!" yelled Danny as he
pointed to the brilliant image formed by light on the table.

"Got it!" she replied and did it.

"What is the next one?" asked Danny.

"Here, it's this one," said Jeannie.

"Good," said Danny as he pulled on GAMMAZEL, spinning it to align

the pointer on the table with the symbol   .

There on the table was the mirror-image symbol   .

"Jeannie, pull the lever with that symbol on it!" yelled Danny.

"We just did that one, Danny. Don't screw up, or the war is lost. I just
pulled the lever with that symbol!" screamed Jeannie.

"Don't argue with me, Jeannie. Pull that damn lever! JUST DO IT!"

"OK, I did it!"

Maybe, sometimes, there is a gift that comes out of nowhere. Maybe
that was the case.

As Jeannie pulled the same lever, the corps of buglers put their golden
trumpets to their mouths and blasted out a rhythmic signal, announcing
the forthcoming of an official proclamation.

Comanzar made a statement. "Supreme God, Lenszar has changed
direction! Our sky sentinels have detected new movement from Lenszar.
Now it appears to be turning away from planet Kopaz."

Danny took a deep breath as his mind relaxed. *Thank God! This thing
is working!*

For as long as the gods had convened at their council table, they had
never witnessed such an event. Their hopes and dreams were not fading.

Jeannie also had thoughts. *Wow! Danny knew what he was doing. I'm sure glad he didn't listen to me.*

"What's the next one, Jeannie?" asked Danny, his demeanor a little cooler now.

"Here is it," said Jeannie.

Rolling GAMMAZEL to   , the   mirror-image symbol was displayed. Danny said, "Pull the lever with that symbol, Jeannie."

And she did it. Step by step, Danny rotated GAMMAZEL to the appropriate symbol for each letter in the answer to the Riddle of Zuron: lavender. As he did, one by one the mirror-image symbols were displayed, letting Jeannie know what lever to pull next. She had pulled six levers and was down to the last two.

When he had dialed in the seventh symbol—the   symbol on GAMMAZEL—Jeannie put her hands on the lever associated with this mirror-image symbol and pulled it. At the moment that Jeannie pulled the seventh lever, the trumpets blasted again.

Comanzar made the statement. "Supreme God, Lenszar has focused! Our sky sentinels have detected further movement of Lenszar, and it is now focused on the planet of Dark God Zuron—planet Zolob!"

They were down to the last symbol that corresponded to the final mirror-image symbol.

The formality was not interfering with the jubilation that was building. For millions of years, Viracocha had waited for this moment. He was now only one symbol away from the ultimate victory.

The excitement was not limited to the gods. Yellzor let out a howl. *Yyyyyooooooooolllllllooooooollllll!* It rocked the entire room.

"*Good boy!*" yelled Danny as he smiled glowingly at his beast.

There had never been such smiles of joy on young gods' faces as there were right now on the faces of Danny and Jeannie.

"Come on, Zanzee! You have to help Yellzor!" hooted Jeannie.

The cat's reaction was instantaneous. Zanzee let out a roar no one thought possible. *Rrrrrraaaarrrrreeeerrreeerrrr!* That brought a round of applause from all except the god Ra. His silence was all that he had left to offer.

With only one symbol left, anticipation was growing as they waited for the final climatic event of the War of the Gods.

Danny looked at Viracocha.

The supreme god nodded and said, "DO IT!"

"The last one, Jeannie! What is the last symbol?"

"Here it is, Danny," Jeannie said. No one could deny that the young goddess had just arrived at stardom.

Danny dialed in the last symbol:

He walked to Jeannie's side and motioned for Yellzor and Zanzee to come forward.

They did.

With Danny and Jeannie's hands on the lever for the ⌐ mirror-image symbol, and Yellzor and Zanzee's paws over the young gods's hands, it was time.

The gods' eyes were not on Danny and Jeannie. No, they were looking to the sky through the giant star window in the roof of the Pantheon of the Gods.

"On three," said Danny. "One…two…three!" They pulled the lever.

The flash was blinding to the point of literally almost destroying the sight of every eye looking skyward. To call what the gods were currently witnessing a massive explosion would be a huge understatement.

The explosion that took place as Zolob, disintegrated by the focused rays of Kolar through Lenszar, erupted into a monumental inferno that trumped all explosions in the universe throughout the ages. It was a spectacle unlike anything that had occurred since the dawning of time.

There was a standing ovation by all, except for one, as the cry rang out, "The war is over!" and this was proclaimed by all, except for Ra.

"*Well done, my royal prince!*" boomed Viracocha.

His wife followed suit. "Well done, my royal princess!"

And so there were symbols that matched the answer to a deathly riddle that won the War of the Gods on that balmy day on Volob.

CHAPTER 33
Out

When someone upsets the apple cart, apples roll. Now that is a simple little expression that describes situations in our lives as they might occur. You might even say it is a way of expressing frustration.

However, when someone has been with you through thick and thin and that someone is flesh and blood, the apple cart being upended might not lead to apples rolling but something of much more value—like a head!

Whose head was going to roll was not much of a mystery after Danny and Jeannie got done with the traitor among the gods, no less a personage than the supreme god's only son, Ra.

Exactly what was this strange-looking medallion that looked like it was half of something? Not only that, but where had it come from, and how had Danny gotten it?

The two newest gods were seated, once more, in their flimsy wooden chairs at the south end of the council table. However, their presence was no longer simply tolerated, as it had been prior to planet Zolob going up in smoke. Evidently, they had earned a little respect.

Zanzee sat on Jeannie's lap again, and his purring was welcomed by all the gods who now could sit and relax in their pantheon until the end of who knows what, as time had no ending. Their conversations had to have centered on the great victory they had just achieved, which would go down in the history of the universe as the war that was won by humans who became gods.

Jeannie had a thing about petting Zanzee when he was on her lap. As she stroked him, she asked Danny, "Where did you get that thing? And how did you know?"

"That's a secret, Jeannie," answered Danny, his fickle grin about to show.

"Don't give me that pile of shit, you rascal!" said Jeannie laughing as all around joined in.

"You know better to cuss and swear, especially when you are in the company of gods," replied Danny.

"Yeah, OK. Where did you get it?"

Obviously curious, the gods—Tammuz, Ishtar, Dumuzi, Horus, Hathor, Zeus, Neptune, Plato, Jupiter, Asherah, and Osiris—also took an interest. Although they had once voted in support of Zuron...well, that was eons ago, and they hoped that time might erase all mistakes. But that was not so with Supreme God Viracocha. However, with the war now over, they felt a little more at ease. Three goddesses—Astarte, Inanna, and Kybele—who had also voted to support Zuron joined in with their question, which they asked in unison with the eleven gods. "Yeah, Danny, where did you get it?"

Maybe they were searching. Maybe they were sincere. The fact was that Danny had something that only three people in the entire universe knew existed.

"Gorom Mochcom!" answered Danny. "And the question I had—how did Mochcom get it—hung on me like a million-pound weight."

Danny's stillness took center stage, and all eyes were on him, even those at the executive end of the council table, as the young god broke his silence. "Suffice it to say, I knew!"

The celebration was over. It was time for a trial.

Normally, when a crime is committed, a trial and evidence are required for conviction or exoneration. This is done because there are the tipping scales of justice, and whatever the case turns out to be, an unbiased result tilts toward innocence or guilt.

The half of the golden medallion never left the red-diamond table. There it was in full view the entire time that Danny and Jeannie worked to incinerate planet Zolob.

"Neferdor, did I give you something at the time that our son, Ra, formulated a compromise to settle the dispute that had erupted?" asked the supreme god of his wife.

"Yes, my beloved husband. You gave me this."

"What is that object I gave you?" pressed Viracocha.

"It's half of a medallion with a code word on it," answered Neferdor.

He was the prosecutor examining a witness, kind but very firm. "Hmm. And where is the other half?" the supreme god asked.

The goddess Neferdor, who looked like she could be Jeannie's twin sister, gazed down at the other end of the table. Jeannie was happy. There was no question.

Neferdor answered the question. "It was given to our son, Ra. Like me, he was never to reveal it to anyone, not even you, my wonderful husband." It was a sad moment.

Normally we do not think of gods or goddesses as having emotions, especially ones that would make them cry. That was not the case. Neferdor's eyes were streaming rivers of tears as she looked past her husband to her son.

"Can I hold your half of the medallion?" asked Viracocha of his wife.

Saying nothing, Neferdor handed it to him.

Viracocha reached and picked up the other half that had been lying on the table.

He held them in the palms of his hands, facing upward, exposing the medallions so all could see.

There could be no question what was going on.

"If no one but three gods had ever seen these objects, who but the three would know what they are?" asked Viracocha. He sighed and continued. Although he had to do it, there was a twinge of remorse in the supreme god's voice. Glaring down the table, Viracocha asked the gods, "Who knew both sets of symbols?" He spoke out loud the sound for each code symbol:

 and the sound

for each associated code word: **Basilikḗ and Oikía**.

Shaking his head, he answered his own question. "Only I!"

"I gave one side of the medallion to Ra, the side with the code of

symbols ◁ ⟨ W ꟾ ∠ ꟾ ⴹ." Again, Viracocha repeated the sounds of each symbol.

He looked at his wife as he continued. "To Neferdor, I gave the side

of the medallion that had the code of symbols O ꟾ ꓘ ꓕ." And likewise, he repeated the sounds of the symbols.

He had to make such a clear point that his judgment would be indisputable when placed on the scales of justice. "Only Ra, other than myself, knew the code of symbols on his half of the medallion, and only Neferdor, other than I, knew the other code of symbols on her medallion. So how did Danny get Ra's medallion with the code of symbols?"

Silence hung after that question, but it was short-lived.

"With Zuron having only one of the code words and the associated symbols, he was able to move Lenszar, destroy other planets in the universe, but he could not destroy our planet, Volob." There was a long pause as Viracocha, only a few feet from his son, glared at Ra. Still looking directly at his son, Viracocha asked, "So how did Zuron get your medallion, Ra?"

There was no answer to the supreme god's question.

"You see," said Viracocha as he stopped, turned, and looked at the god Tammuz, "I was wrong."

The supreme god hesitated, but then he proceeded. "I suspected Tammuz was the one. When Zuron also shared a spot at this table, Tammuz dropped the words *Black Royal Temple* not once, not twice, but who knows how many times?"

As Viracocha shook his head, Tammuz had a strong feeling of vindication and joyfully felt relief that he need not fear a wrath coming his way without cause.

"So I must take the blame, also, for not coming to grips with the reality that my son, Ra, would do such a thing, for I failed to question the destruction of the planets as a consequence of betrayal."

Viracocha's temper changed as his mind could clearly visualize his son's deceit. Once more, he turned to look directly at Ra, who sat in his throne to Viracocha's right. The god focused his glare.

"How?" roared Viracocha. "You were right before my eyes, filthy with devious acts of treason, and I saw it not. How? Yes, how did I miss it? You hatched your scheming plan millions of years ago but perfected it not so long ago. You, miserable rotten creature that you are, used your own daughter, Bastet, to charm the Egyptian royals with a cat your mother gave you. You wretched beast, you thought your plan was clever. Yes, you used the Egyptians to develop, test, and hone your plan to dethrone your father. The Theban high priests of Amun Ra conspired with the puppet rulers and brought Egypt to its knees. And did you smile with pride, marveling at your handiwork when the high priest Herihor strangled the poor Egyptians for the sake of money and power? You must have beamed with your success as you watched the evildoers operating under the guise of religion, the

Theban high priests of Amun Ra, topple the royal rulers of Egypt. With that success under your belt, you put the final element of your plan into effect right next to me on planet Kopaz. Your goroms. Your high priests, again under the guise of religion, conspired to stifle the royal family of Kopaz. You filthy monster!"

Viracocha's words brought a lump to Neferdor's throat as she looked to the two people at the far end of the long table for comfort. Perhaps the two newcomers would fill this pain in her heart and heal the wound that she never saw coming.

Although tensions had never been higher at the council table, not even when Zuron was conceiving his evil plan, justice had to take her rightful place. It was a solemn moment. There could be no hasty rush to judgment without cause, for Viracocha's own creed was set in stone: *We bend the arc of justice to the innocent and to the hearts of those who stand for good.*

And as he dropped his hands and placed the two halves of the medallion on the red-diamond table, he said, "There is a final certain test that no one can argue with."

He moved the two separate pieces close to each other. "Only two pieces in the universe will fuse together as they touch." Viracocha said. "Let's see."

And in a voice of supreme power, Viracocha roared, *"Guilty!"*

Viracocha turned his head. His glare intensified, and his emerald-green eyes were as fiery darts that penetrated to the core of Ra's soul. Looking into the eyes of his son, he passed judgment. "There is no judgment swift or final enough to balance the evil you have wrought upon creation throughout the universe. The depths of outer darkness have no corner black enough to house your wretched soul. Your dastardly deeds will be the haunting chains of bondage that will wrap your miserable being in a coal-black tomb in the bottomless pit of the abyss of hell!

Ra's evil soul was twitching with an explosive rebuttal, but locked in the confines of his pathetic body, his countenance displayed no remorse.

"How fitting an end for you. How ironic! Your demise brought about by a cat that was a gift from your mother, the son of a coal miner, and an innocent girl who had a vision of hope!" Ra's father's words echoed through the council hall, making a moment in the annals of the universe.

Swiftly pointing his outstretched arm, Viracocha's final words bolted from his mouth. "Depart to your prison of perdition in the furthest reaches of the universe. *Begone, you traitorous dog!*"

And as Ra vanished from the council table of the primeval gods, Viracocha looked over the remaining gods and shouted, "*Out...I say out!*"

CHAPTER 34

A Lonely Walk

It was unexpected. The question of why the supreme god had ended with an outburst in the way he did had to have weighed on Danny and Jeannie, as it was a turn of events that came out of nowhere.

Where would they go? What would they do? Certainly, those questions would be on their minds as they walked out of the council room and up the long set of golden stairs to ascend to the main floor of the Grand Council Hall.

What was interesting was that the same two horse-like creatures accompanied Danny and Jeannie as they exited the council of the gods and headed for the door leading out of the pantheon.

Quill was not there, but Zanzee and Yellzor were with them. This time, however, they did not ride the horse creatures. They all walked together as a group.

Jeannie spotted the circular window that was the doorway into the tube. She pointed and speculated it was at least a ten-minute walk to reach it, and so they had time to talk.

Multicolored birds, some green-and-blue, others yellow-and-brown, were gathering in flocks of their own kind. Oddly, they were circling in cloud-like formations by the tens of thousands, yet there were no bird droppings that would normally be the telltale signs of birds flying around in a house.

"Danny, how did you know?" asked Jeannie.

She waited, and he just kept walking. "Come on, Danny. Say something," she said in earnest.

"Look, Jeannie, I have put my heart and soul into this quest. You know that," Danny said with a forlorn look on his face. "I've done all that has been asked, yet I am so confused about what is going on." They stood in front of the circular doorway to the tube. "Do you know where we are going? Do you know what we are doing? Do you know where this tube thing is going to take us? Do you know where we are going to sleep tonight? Do you—"

"Stop it, Danny!" yelled Jeannie as she cut him off. "Look, I've told you many times that hope is a good thing, and do I have to go through our whole history to remind you all the hope that came our way?" asked Jeannie.

They were on the tube. They were going someplace. Who knows where? They had no idea.

After half an hour, the thing came to a screeching stop. It was at that point that the centaur and the white unicorn said, "We've been asked to let you ride, so please get on!"

"Well, that's encouraging," remarked Danny sinisterly.

"Danny, *please*," said Jeannie. "Let's just go where these guys take us and...well, have hope!"

It was something that was bound to happen. Danny had proven himself and was not about to play second fiddle to anyone. "Look, Jeannie, we've gone through hell for a cause, and we *won!* Do you think I'm going to play dead, let some other nerd take credit and be the one?" asked Danny.

"What are you talking about?" Jeannie asked with a puzzled look.

Danny never answered her question. He decided to do something else instead.

Jeannie was riding WhiteHorn and Danny was riding the centaur. Things were so weird, they decided to have fun.

As they exited the pantheon, Danny said, "You guys, I want speed, and I want *fun...so get on with it!*"

And that they did. Danny and Jeannie spent an incredible afternoon galloping though the hillsides around the pantheon. For hours and hours, they played in a make-believe world. It was magical. It was like being in a fairyland with real fairies. Strange little people with cellophane-like wings flew in and out of the trees. Large turtles with eyes that looked like sparkling blue diamonds surfaced, making what appeared to be small islands in the ponds.

The hours drifted by. At one point, a giant bat invited them to go for a ride. From her perch high in the air, Jeannie said, "As long as I have Zanzee, I feel safe on this creature. How about you, Danny?"

He laughed and stuck one finger in the air. "I've got my ring as a safety net! And if that don't work, well, Yellzor will make a soft landing!"

That was all it took. Yellzor let out a howl that made the giant bat do high-speed cartwheels in the air.

It was the ride of a lifetime, and it went on for hours. Two gods, a cat, and a giant wolf rode on a Herculean bat as if it were normal.

It was going on late afternoon, which would be about five in Earth time. It was time for a rest.

Sitting on a rock fence made of a crystalline material that continuously changed color, Jeannie snuggled next to Danny. She sensed he was lost in thought. *Earth is gone and all those billions of people, and for what reason?* Holding onto his arm, she felt it go hard as a rock. She looked at his face. It looked as if it had gone someplace in search of answers. Maybe he had. Danny did have a lot to think about. Maybe it was an impending doom that he was trying to find a way around.

Danny stared as his mind drifted. *How do I ask for help? Do I just say to Viracocha, "Can I go to the Land of the Dead and get the hair?" Hmm.*

"I know what you are thinking, Danny," said Jeannie. "I wouldn't if I were you. I would let it go…hard as it seems!"

"Why, Jeannie?" he asked.

"I just have a premonition, Danny. That's all." Jeannie moved her hand from his arm to his face and asked, "Can I get a kiss, my love?"

Locked in an embrace, they were startled when someone said, "You're wanted."

CHAPTER 35
Back to the Council Table

It's those times when you least expect it that something happens, like it or not. Maybe that is why we swing from one extreme to another. Maybe if everything went exactly as we wanted it to go, we wouldn't be happy because it really wasn't what we wanted. Who knows?

The one thing for sure is that when you are forever young and have just intervened and redirected the climatic outcome of the War of the Gods, could it be that your troubles are gone and your place in history is set in stone. Who knows? Yet who wouldn't want to be in those shoes?

The ride on the tube and their travels back to the central oval room where the governance of the universe took place seemed a lot faster this time, as Danny, Jeannie, Quill, Yellzor, and Zanzee headed back to the council hall of the primeval gods. They arrived next to the red-diamond table in less than ten minutes. Who knows why? It was just the way it was.

Quill motioned for them to take a seat as he pointed. It was a bench made of a beautiful lavender gemstone material that Danny hadn't seen the first time he had been there. From his vantage point, he had a full view of the south end of the council table, as he was not more than fifty feet from where he and Jeannie had sat earlier. Danny mused as he sat on the bench, Jeannie holding Zanzee, and with Yellzor and Quill next to him. *I know this bench was not here earlier.* He looked at the south end of the council room. *Hmm…nothing is there. The entire south end of the council table has no wooden seats or golden thrones.*

Being in the elliptical meeting room was strange, as no one else was there. It was as if they were the only spectators at a teamless football game.

An hour went by, and nothing happened. Jeannie speculated that it was now early evening. Quill had left the room. Now it was only Danny, Jeannie, Zanzee, and Yellzor.

Thoughtfully, Danny gave Jeannie a curious look. "Jeannie, did you notice this beautiful lavender bench that we are sitting on? This thing is gigantic, and it is catching rays from Kolar streaming through the sky dome above, making it look like a glowing seat of power, something about to come alive!"

A voice startled Danny and Jeannie.

"He's ready," said Quill out of the clear blue. "And you are right, Danny, the most beautiful lavender bench is made of the most precious gemstone material in the universe. The one you are sitting on was not here earlier. It is here in your honor, yours and Jeannie's, to remind everyone who it was that won the war!"

Then Quill smiled. "We'll board a private vehicle in a moment and then go to the designated spot."

What the hell is the designated spot? thought Danny.

If an airplane could be out of this world, well, that it was. The private vehicle was a flight machine beyond normal imagination. Its seats were heavenly material made of who knows what? They were like the leather seats of a brand-new SUV but with the appearance and texture of gold, and yet they were soft to rest on.

"Are we in heaven or what?" asked Jeannie as they took their seats.

Not only was the seating special but the decor was equally intricate, with carvings of gold, inlaid precious gems, exotic wood trim, and leather appointments of a design that Lexus would love to borrow.

In moments, they were there. It was a library-like room that again was like a mirage of wonder. The bookcases, the couches, the tables, the chairs, the candelabras, the chandeliers, and the crown moldings would certainly make the Palace of Versailles look like Mochcom's woodshed.

Quill took a seat in the hallway, where he would wait until summoned.

Entering, Danny said, "Wow...nice digs, Viracocha!"

That prompted a laugh from the supreme god. "You have earned a level of respect from me that allows you to say such a thing." He paused and looked at Danny with a smile as he added, "If anyone else except Neferdor, you, or Jeannie said, 'Nice digs, Viracocha,' well, that person would find himself in a fiery pit forever."

Viracocha smiled and then went on. "I have much to say and not much time. But we will have the eternities to get acquainted and just enjoy each other's friendship."

If ever Jeannie's heart had taken off like a rocket, it did then. *Oh my golly, did I hear him correctly?* The thought raced to the front of Jeannie's mind. *Did he just call us friends?*

Unannounced, Supreme Goddess Neferdor walked in. She came to Jeannie's side and said, "Viracocha has something for you, but afterward, I'd like to show you your quarters and have wardrobes laid out for your inspection and acceptance, if that is OK with you."

"Ah, sure! Tha...that's fine!" Jeannie beamed in answer.

"Come, sit," said Viracocha as he motioned to Danny and Jeannie.

There were only four in the room—Viracocha, Neferdor, Danny and Jeannie. At the table they sat, not much was visible, as whatever was there was under a cover of some sort, something like a golden blanket.

Now that they were all relaxed, the conversation started. "Danny and Jeannie, I am so proud of you. You filled my and Neferdor's vessels of expectation to overflowing. If the universe ever owed anyone something of priceless value, it is you!"

Danny didn't know what to say. Yellzor, resting at his side, just yawned. Jeannie had Zanzee in her arms, and both looked like the cat who just ate the canary. When the supreme god compliments you in such overwhelming terms, what do you say? Is there anything you can say without making a fool of yourself? Danny knew he couldn't. He remained still.

It was Jeannie who offered something, and she spoke softly. "Most gracious god and goddess, for our debts to you, Danny, and I speak for him, and I will do what is asked and will do it with willing hearts!"

"I know that, Jeannie. You already have!" said Viracocha. "In four hours, we will have a special council meeting, so I want to let you know what to expect."

Now Viracocha's expression hardened, and his eyes glistened. He flipped his shaggy yellow hair back as he spoke profoundly. "The most prized position at the council table of the primeval gods is that of Keeper of the Book of Life. It is the position most coveted as it, in essence, governs the gift of life. Since the dawning of time itself, gods of all sorts have quested after this most prized position. It has never, and I repeat, *never* been given to any god."

Oh my god, thought Danny. *You have got to be kidding!*

"No, Danny, I'm not kidding." At that point it was clear to both Danny and Jeannie that he had just read Danny's mind. "It's you and Jeannie who have reached for and obtained this position. No one else has ever come to the level of excellence that you, my royal prince and Neferdor's royal princess, have shown the entire universe. It's you and you alone who rightfully deserve this most prized honor," said Viracocha in a crystal-clear voice that demanded nothing but respect.

Sitting on the throne between Danny and Jeannie, Viracocha put his right hand on Danny's shoulder and his left on Jeannie's. "Never have I met such brave and valiant souls as you two. I'm proud to have you be the Keepers of the Book of Life with control over the gift of life."

There was a quiet moment, and then Viracocha lifted the golden blanket and exposed what looked like two boxes. They looked heavy. They were shimmering and shining as if they were the most precious items ever.

"I won't let you see them yet," Viracocha said as he flipped the blanket over them again, "but later there will be time for that. I only wanted to prepare you."

Danny's heart swelled with pride. From CoalVille to the Pantheon of the Gods was one thing, but to feel the friendship of the most powerful person in the universe, and one who just put the ultimate trust in you, was kind of hard to fathom.

"OK, so it is done. You will be presented for confirmation, and that is that!" said Viracocha, and then he called for Quill to come inside the grand library of the pantheon and be seated at the visitors' golden couch on the east wall.

"OK," he said as he turned to Danny. "You do have my zedite knife, do you not?"

Oh shit. A bolt of fear shot through Danny's mind. *What did I do with it?*

There was a little snicker coming from someplace. Danny suspected it was Jeannie or Neferdor, but wasn't quite sure.

"Do you have it?" Viracocha asked once more.

Now he was uncomfortable. It was becoming clear that Danny was in a predicament. "Ah…er…ah, I think I must have put it someplace," he mumbled.

At that instant, he felt something. *Is that Jeannie's finger?*

At any other time, there would be no question as to who was having a little fun. Now he wasn't quite sure, but he had a good idea of who was taking advantage of the situation. This was a different situation, as he had never been in a private meeting with a god, let alone the supreme god.

"Damn it, Jeannie," said Danny, a grin growing on his face. "Hold on, Viracocha," said Danny as he laughed out loud. "My partner is taking advantage of the situation, and I have to put a stop to it!"

Laughter erupted from all. Maybe that was a good thing. Tension at the pantheon had grown to overwhelming proportions and had dominated the mood, and no laughter had graced the halls for a long time. Who could have ever known what would bring laughter back to the Pantheon of the Gods?

Now it was Viracocha's mind drifting. *Yeah, it seems that war can do that—kill laughter.* On the table in front of him was Danny's hand. Taking the opportunity, Viracocha put his hand over Danny's and said, "War is a laughter killer, but that is all history, so laughter is good!"

Since all were concentrating on Danny, no one saw the bag being placed on the table. Yet there it was as Jeannie said, "Guess what?" Actually, no guessing was necessary. Jeannie already had her hand in the bag. "You asked if Danny had your zedite knife, and I must confess, I look after my *love*, and so here it is."

She placed it on the table. "Not only your zedite knife but also Zuron's knife and the zedite ball."

"Wow!" said Viracocha and Neferdor simultaneously. "Do you know the value of those three items?"

Viracocha looked at Danny and repeated his question. "Do you have any idea of their worth?"

As Danny fumbled for a response that wouldn't make him sound like he was a complete dunce, he managed to say, "A...a lot?" It was all but a rhetorical question.

"Hmm, you might say that. Yeah, a lot," said Viracocha as he laughed freely. "Danny, what you see on this table is all of the zedite in the entire universe. You know our star, Kolar, is one thousand times the size of your sun. Well, think about a pile of gold that is one million times as large as Kolar, and that would not even come close to the value of these three objects!"

Then the supreme god paused. He put his right index finger on the zedite knife that had once belonged to Zuron and said, "Danny, the value I just talked about pales in comparison to what you and Jeannie have done. It was you, Danny, that took this knife from Zuron. Without this knife, the dark side will *never* have control of the universe. That, my young god, makes this prize priceless. You cannot put a value on the quality of good! You and Jeannie have set a standard in the universe that has never been reached. Evil is contained as long as we own this knife!"

Now the snicker grew even louder, and Jeannie jumped in. "Better thank me, Danny, for saving your six o'clock 'cause if you had lost these, you would have been in hot water!"

And with that comment, it was time to move on. Viracocha stood. He motioned for Quill, who had been waiting patiently on the visitor's golden couch, to come forward. "Quill, show Danny to his quarters and make him comfortable, and like Jeannie, let him inspect his wardrobe and all that stuff."

Viracocha and Neferdor walked toward the door, and just as they were about to leave, he casually said, "The council will convene in three hours."

Yet something was gnawing at Viracocha. He stopped. The supreme god turned to look squarely into Danny's eyes. The two faced each other, but it was Viracocha who spoke first. "Danny, how did you know?" It was a profound question. Viracocha's mind was searching. *How did Danny know that my son, Ra, was the traitor?*

With no delay, Danny responded, "My answer is most likely the same as my question to you, Viracocha. How did you know?"

Although Danny had reached the status of being able to read most minds, there were a few whose thoughts were sealed to him, including Viracocha, Neferdor, and Jeannie. But that was not the case for Viracocha. Assuredly, Viracocha could read the boy's thoughts even as Danny mused, *Walking down the red-diamond table was a risk worth taking, even though I faced the wrath of lightening from the finger of Viracocha striking me with each step at every moment! Yes, how did Viracocha know not to wield his sword of discernment? How did he know not to unleash on me instant incineration with the eternities being my future in the depths of hell?*

Viracocha's nodding head clued Jeannie that he was following Danny's every reflection on that singular event that had changed the course of destiny for all living creatures throughout the universe.

"Hmm. Yes, the correct answer, Danny. When balance teeters throughout the universe, when everything hinges on the correct answer, no other will do!"

He smiled at Danny and Jeannie as he said, "See you both in three hours!"

CHAPTER 36
An Aching Heart

Having no idea where his living quarters in the Pantheon of the Gods were, Danny let Quill lead the way. One thing did, however, cross his mind. *I hope Jeannie and I are not separated.*

Danny's personal transportation vehicle had his name embossed on the side in large gold letters. As he and Quill got in, he had to stop and look. *Hmm, someone has been busy.*

The interior was unlike anything Danny had seen. It was personalized just for him. The seats had both his first and last names—Danny Roberts—embroidered in striking brilliance. Awed, he looked at the detail. Traveling at over a hundred miles per hour, it was only a matter of minutes before they were in front of an entrance. Above the doorway was a sign:

Residence of

Danny Roberts

Quill held the massive golden door open, and Danny stepped in. "Wow! How big is this pad?" asked Danny.

More formal than he had been in the past, Quill answered, "My lord, this is not a 'pad.' It is a penthouse, and it is one million square feet, in Earth measurements."

"Hmm. Nice!" said Danny as he looked around. "One million square feet. Nice!"

The room he was in was not unlike the Grand Council Hall, as the floors were made of green emerald three feet thick laid on a three-foot foundation of solid yellow gold.

The benches looked to be of white gold inlaid with gemstones, and there were solid gold statues of stately looking men who Danny suspected had some place in the history of the universe.

"There must be a hundred couches in this room, Quill," Danny said as he turned and pointed to one closest to them.

"You will need them, Danny. Trust me," replied Quill.

Although Danny was mesmerized by the grandiose ambiance of his new living quarters, his mind was someplace else, and Quill knew it.

"Danny, my friend, what is it that troubles you?" was Quill's direct question.

There was a longing look on the face of the royal prince of Viracocha. Quill could not discern what was on the young god's mind, but he knew it was very concerning.

Danny asked, "Do we have time to go to Kopaz?" The young god then placed his right hand on Quill's shoulder and looked him in the eye. "My parents will not be here before Jeannie and I are confirmed as members of the Quorum of Primeval Gods, and it troubles me."

"Only if we hurry, Danny," answered Quill. As he looked at Danny, Quill had many thoughts of his own. *I know what is troubling my friend.*

And when the word *friend* came to his mind, Quill became tense. Quill's mind seized on the new reality. *He's now one of the most important and powerful gods in the universe.*

Maybe that was what bothered Quill. When Danny was a god in training, things had been different. *Danny's elevation places him almost beyond friendship, and it saddens me*, thought Quill.

Nothing gets by the son of a coal miner. Danny immediately said loudly, "Quill, our friendship is way beyond status!" Quill looked at him as Danny charged on. "Who could have a better friend than you? And don't forget that!"

Before Quill could formulate a comeback, Danny said, "You know the way, so let's get the hell out of here and head for Kopaz!"

Maybe it was a welcome relief for Quill to get out of the pantheon.

Maybe it was what Danny needed after being at the center of a storm, such high-stakes drama unfolding more rapidly than he wanted. For whatever reason, as they left the pantheon, their sense of friendship and bonding was stronger than it had ever been.

With Quill navigating, they arrived at the Grand Courtyard in front of the royal palace in what seemed like a second.

No one was there to greet them. Danny and Quill quickly walked along the garden pathway leading to the massive wooden door at the entrance of the Grand Hall. The doorman saw them coming, and the right-hand door was open by the time Danny and Quill were there.

Danny and Quill walked in. On the other side of the Grand Hall stood Queen Neferapondes. Her look was telling. Danny had an idea. He was shaking inside.

The three met at the center of the hall, and the queen stretched out her hand to touch Danny's face. She had tears flowing from her eyes.

"I'm so sorry, Danny," said the queen. "We have only a short time left. The moments are now precious, and I don't know what to do."

His eyes swelled with tears, as he knew what was heavy on the queen's heart. "Can I see them?" Danny said as his hands wiped away the tears that he could not control.

It was like a reverent funeral march as the three walked down the hallway that led from the back door of the Grand Hall.

"Your parents are in the library, Danny," said Neferapondes.

In moments they were there. All of the family was with them. It was their new family, and Darla loved being around the granddaughters and the little guy, DannyR.

It was worse than Danny could have imagined. They were old beyond recognition. His mom was able to stand, but just barely. She had Aerapondes help her to her feet. Johnny sat on the white leather couch, but he was unable to stand. Age had overcome them.

It was as if his heart had been lost in a hole someplace. Danny felt a hollowness that he had never experienced.

"Hi, Mom," he said. "How are you doing?"

He had to turn his head as he wept. He did not want his mother to see him in that state.

For the next half hour, Danny tried to contain his emotions as he talked to his mom and dad. They talked about old times in the Scarlet Desert. They talked of going to Granite Springs and laughed about Danny staring at the jewelry in Paul's Confectionary on Main Street. They talked about Danny always dreaming of finding pirate treasure in the Scarlet Desert.

Time was marching on. Each moment, Danny saw his parents grow dimmer. He so wanted to stay with them, as their hours were limited, and soon they would return to a boat that would take them to a place where they had been with the others who had departed—the Land of the Dead.

That thought, that dreadful thought, would not leave Danny's mind. *Because of me, they will live for eternity in the Land of the Dead.*

Danny turned his head so his mom could not see him weep.

The decision to stay with his parents until the end was out of Danny's control. Perceptively, Queen Neferapondes gently placed her hand in Danny's. "You are a god, Danny, and you are needed on Volob. Your parents' families and I will comfort Johnny and Darla until they board the boat on the River Styx." With tears in her eyes, the royal queen said, "It will be OK, Danny. It will be OK."

Yet deep in Danny's heart, he knew it was the last time he would ever see Johnny and Darla. It was a bittersweet moment. *My parents travel to a place I cannot venture, and my love waits for me as we shall share an eternity as gods bending the arc of justice to the innocent.*

"Danny, it's time. We have to get back to the pantheon, as Viracocha is expecting us," said Quill, knowing that time was an enemy and slipping by and that it cared nothing for dying parents or the arc of justice.

Darla looked at her son for the last time. "You go, Danny. You are needed elsewhere, and just remember—they were good times in the Scarlet Desert. No, they were the best of times." Darla could no longer hold back her tears, knowing it was the last time she would ever see her only boy.

She turned her head so Danny could no longer see her face.

The pain in Danny's heart was like a bolt of lightning ripping to shreds the memories of a coal miner, his wife, their only son, and their life in the Scarlet Desert.

As Danny and Quill walked out of the royal library, all eyes followed them. It was Danny's new and old family—the queen, a new daughter-in-law, Aerapondes, and her husband, Little Tony, Jerzom and his new wife, Little Jeannie, and their son, DannyR, Prince Zeb and his wife, Jeanondes, Little Danny, and Little KateLynn, and Danny's parents, Johnny and Darla.

It's the last time I will see him. That was Darla's only thought as she caught her final glimpse of the young god as he disappeared with his tutor through the open door. Now the pair was out of sight, and all they could hear were footsteps in the hallway leading to the Grand Hall of the Royal Palace.

And so it was on that important day of high-muckamuck godly meetings at the center of the universe.

CHAPTER 37
Welcome to the Gods

Normally, we would be aware of something that is very, very precious, or so it would seem. It is usually those things that are most valuable that stand out and are considered most notable for our attention. Is that always true? Take, for instance, the gift of life. Is that very, very precious? What is it? Is it earned? Who gets it? How do you get it, and who has control over the gift of life for all creatures throughout the universe?

Now there are a handful of thought-provoking questions. Maybe the gift of life is a mystery. Maybe it isn't.

Quill and Danny were back from Kopaz. Despite the most unbelievable event that was soon to redefine Danny's existence, he was sad. How could he not be? His parents were no longer youthful teenagers in the Scarlet Desert. Even when they had been young and struggling against all odds in a bleak existence, they had something that could not be purchased at any price—they were youthful and loved life. Now even that was all gone. In those final moments that Danny spent with his parents, Johnny and Darla had no doubt put on a front, trying to make the most of life, but that was not the case. They were old, decrepit people who were dying. With feeble minds, there could be no fronts. Age has a way of taking away dignity, and that it did with Johnny and Darla. But they had no idea their dignity was gone.

"Quill, which of these two outfits should I wear?" asked Danny as he was preparing for the upcoming extravaganza extraordinaire.

"That one," pointed Quill as he spoke firmly. "That will make you look, as people on Earth used to say, like a million dollars!"

And that it did. His robe was cut so as to make his chest muscles stand out like a prizefighter's. His arms, likewise, were revealed through the sleeves as sculptured works of art worthy of a god.

There was just the right mix of jewels and gold to make his appearance not gaudy but rather bold and dashing.

His loin covering was of the finest leather and embossed with patterns of warriors. It demanded respect yet showed enough of his legs to let all know that he was equal to Viracocha in every respect. He was one of the two ripped studs of the gods. There could be no denying that a close look would be required to tell Danny from Supreme God Viracocha. They looked like identical twins.

"That's it, Danny!" said Quill, "You're ready!"

In the waiting room just outside the Grand Council Hall, Danny met up with Jeannie.

"*Oh my! Just look at you,*" said Danny when he saw her. "Jeannie, I am worried that some other dashing guy will see you and want you all for his own." Danny went to throw his arms around her.

"Danny, *wait!* We have to get through this ceremony, and then your hands can go wherever they want, but for now, you can't ruffle my clothes." Jeannie giggled willingly.

And a sight she was. Her gown was made of heavenly material that flowed around her body, revealing yet hiding every mystery that was inviting to any onlooker's eyes. Her teardrop earrings were blue diamonds, each the size of the Hope Diamond. Her low-cut dress line revealed just the right amount of bosom. It was adorned with an octagonal blue diamond two inches across and encircled with white diamonds in a platinum setting.

No princess or queen could compete with Jeannie as she was on her way to take center stage at the most important event the gods of the universe had ever hosted.

As Danny and Jeannie strode like the royalty they were into the council room of the primeval gods, trumpets sounded and drums were beaten. Dancers were orchestrated in choreographed performances that demanded nothing but praise for their excellence.

At the north end of the red-diamond table, now there were four golden thrones of a magnitude and stature that surely had to be the seats of power for the four supreme gods of the universe.

Viracocha and Neferdor were standing behind the two middle thrones. As Danny and Jeannie were escorted to the executive end of the table, Viracocha indicated where he wanted Danny and Jeannie to stand.

Prior to Danny and Jeannie taking their seats, Viracocha said, "I don't know about you Danny and Jeannie, but the whole TRPOV and TRPON thing sounds goofy to me, so your names are your titles, and that is how they appear on your thrones: *Danny* and *Jeannie.*"

He didn't get to finish before Jeannie blurted, "*Oh, thank goodness!* Danny and I are thrilled you got rid of the formal gobbledygook."

"Good, whatever 'gobbledygook' means. I'm glad you approve," said Viracocha.

Not one god was absent. They all stood. They all faced the executive end of the table.

"Please sit, Danny and Jeannie," said Viracocha.

It was like what goes on in the wardroom of a battleship; no officer sits until the captain takes his seat. Maybe that naval formality was something borrowed from the council table of the gods. It is an interesting thought to contemplate.

As soon as Danny and Jeannie were seated, Viracocha and then Neferdor took their seats. A new protocol was set. It was not until Danny, Jeannie, Viracocha, and Neferdor were in their seats that the remainder of the gods would sit.

Viracocha turned to Danny. "You look great! I see Quill got you in shape." He folded his fingers into a fist and gently smacked it into the bulging biceps of Danny's left arm.

However, that was not the purpose of his conversation. Still looking at Danny, Viracocha said, "We are only going to be in this room for a short time. All I want to do is get confirmation of your positions at this table from the Quorum of Gods. We will then move to a more inviting atmosphere and have a feast as we conduct the remainder of the proceedings."

With dignity and grace, Neferdor clarified what Viracocha had just said. She wanted to let all of the gods know that she was at the helm of the ship of ceremony. And with unquestionable authority she declared, "I told my husband that the only room in the pantheon that was fitting for such a grand occasion is the grand dining hall. So that is where we will reconvene and enjoy a more inviting atmosphere and most extravagant feast that the halls of this temple have ever known!"

That was fine with Danny. He had to look past Viracocha and Neferdor to get a glimpse of Jeannie. There she was, holding Zanzee in her lap.

While Danny was staring at Jeannie and her low-cut gown, he got a big lick on his right hand. It was Yellzor, who wanted to let the new god know he had a friend at his side.

When all were seated, Viracocha stood. The buglers sounded off. The drum roll took place. Sergeant at arms Comanzar stood. He stepped to the podium.

"*Hear ye! Hear ye! The supreme god speaks!*"

Everyone stood. Then Viracocha said, "Please be seated."

All took their seats.

"We have one item on our agenda to take care of in the Grand Council Hall."

He paused and looked at each god individually. Then he proceeded. "I move that Danny and Jeannie should be made executive members of the Council of Primeval Gods. All in favor say *aye!*"

There were shouts of joy as all yelled "*Aye! Aye! Aye!*"

There could be no denying that the vote was unanimous.

"Good," said Viracocha. "Now I ask for you to confirm Danny and Jeannie as Keepers of the Books of Life."

Again, he stopped and looked at each seated god individually, and then he said, "All in favor say *aye!*"

Shouts of joy erupted again, and the vote was unanimous approval.

Trumpets blared out again. Two servants stepped forward. They each carried in their outstretched arms obviously heavy objects. They walked to the executive end of the table. Gently they placed what they carried onto the table.

Solemnly, Viracocha said, "Into your trust, Danny and Jeanne, the Council of Primeval Gods places these Books of Life. Throughout the universe, no greater gift is there than the gift of life. It's these books that control who shall and who shall not have the gift of life. You, Danny and Jeannie, are the first gods to have this honor. No other god has ever had such power as is being entrusted to you, Danny and Jeannie."

You could have heard cotton balls drop on the floor as Viracocha spoke. The sensations overpowering Danny and Jeannie were ten million goose bumps, causing their bodies to quiver with emotions that they had never before experienced.

"It is a great honor to present to you these books and entreat you to use them wisely, as life is sacred, and only those who deserve the gift of life should have it, but that is your decision and yours alone."

And there they were—on the red-diamond table—two exquisite objects that were beyond description, comprehension, or value.

Wow! thought Danny as he stared at them. *The gift of life? How does it work, and will it save my parents?*

Maybe it was such a mystery, and then to have that mystery right before your eyes, just waiting to bring you joy, was running through Danny's mind. As he tried to pay attention to the enormity of the ceremony and event that was taking place, something else was dominating his mind—images of two old, feeble people who were not there.

"I must remind you, Danny and Jeannie, that any great honor and power with which you are entrusted also comes with responsibility," said Viracocha.

At this point in his remarks, Viracocha was looking at the faces of the gods who had been with him for eternities. Maybe he was thinking of days gone by and the love of power by the one god closest to him, his son, who had thrust the entire universe into a turmoil and chaos that threatened to destroy the existence of all living creatures. For whatever reason, his next remark hit home with Danny.

"Without balance there can be no order!" Viracocha said as he now turned to face Danny and Jeannie. "Although you have the ultimate control bestowed upon you by this governing body of the universe, not all is possible."

That statement caught Danny's attention, as his mind searched for meaning. *What is he talking about?*

There could be no denying that the object before him had one purpose, and that was to control the gift of life.

Mom and Dad...maybe I can help them! That single thought kept racing around Danny's mind.

Jeannie, on the other hand, had different visions racing through her mind. *Wow! I knew it was all possible, but certainly not this possible…Keepers of the Gift of Life! Wow!*

Most assuredly, Viracocha was well aware of the emotions and thoughts that dominated the two newest gods, who soon would grasp the responsibility and magnitude of the honor bestowed on them.

Viracocha spoke softly. "Not all who have visited the Land of the Dead will have the opportunity to board the boat traveling up the River Styx and return to the Land of the Living."

Now his voice was serious as he ventured on. "Sometimes we make decisions that have consequences. Sometimes we choose to make a decision that goes against the order of the universe."

Viracocha looked at Danny. "Living with decisions that were made in haste can bring sorrow to our souls when gifts of the gods are used unwisely. The Highway of Time is a gift. It brings eternal youth to those who travel it, unless the traveler has been to the Land of the Dead, and then it brings old age and death forever."

No one knew except Danny, Quill, and Viracocha what the supreme god was talking about. But Danny knew all too well that he and he alone had brought upon his parents a one-way ticket to hell.

And on a lighter note, Viracocha said, "Let us retire to the dining hall for the remainder of this ceremony."

Maybe it was time for some humor. Maybe it was time, as they say, for Danny to pull himself up by the bootstraps. For whatever reason, Danny put a smile on his face.

Maybe it was food that Danny had on his mind. And then maybe it was just time to move on. He turned to Jeannie to ask his question, "Jeannie, can you read all that crap that is on that Book of Life Viracocha just gave us?"

Now there was a chuckle from Viracocha as he overheard the conversation and turned so he could listen to Jeannie's reply. "Yeah, Danny. What's wrong with you? Ah! You don't know how to read? You better learn!"

CHAPTER 38

Supreme Honors and Behind the Curtain

Have you ever wondered what was behind the curtain? The saying "What's behind the curtain?" is a cliché that gets overlooked for many reasons, primarily because it can mean so many things. With the welcoming ceremony scheduled to bring Danny and Jeannie into the fold of the primeval gods, does that old cliché have anything to do with the upcoming event?

Danny and Jeannie were at the center of the ceremony. They had just been confirmed as official gods of the Council of Primeval Gods. Yet even more profound, Danny and Jeannie were given the coveted positions of Keepers of the Books of Life. It was those positions and statuses that every god and goddess, other than Viracocha and Neferdor, most wanted.

There was, however, something that was pulling at Danny and causing him sadness. Try as he might, his focus always returned to the same line of thought. *I wonder if they are gone. I hope they didn't suffer.*

He could not shake the images of his parents as old and dying, no longer youthful teenagers in the Scarlet Desert. Instead, his mind was filled with images of them feebly taking their last breaths.

Everyone had moved to the grand dining hall of the pantheon. It could seat and feed over five hundred thousand people at a time. Although there were not that many people there, you could not tell that by the festivities: the gala, the party atmosphere, the dancers, the singers, the entertainers, and the musicians were mixing up a celebration the likes of which the Pantheon of the Gods had never seen. No past celebrations even came close to this event.

Looking out over the mountains of food would make a clan who had just finished their grandma's Thanksgiving dinner want a dozen more helpings.

The feast was about to begin when the buglers interrupted, and those who were anxiously waiting to dive in put down their utensils, as Viracocha was about to speak.

The supreme god's voice soared higher and louder than a chorus of ten thousand singers in a Super Bowl stadium during the half-time show, all singing loud enough so one hundred thousand people could hear them sing. "I wanted a most festive atmosphere when we continued our celebration to honor Danny and Jeannie," said Viracocha as he made his pronouncement. "Never has the Council of the Gods had such as these!" He stopped, asked Danny and Jeannie to stand, and then continued. "They have done what no other has ever even come close to accomplishing."

Viracocha paused. Obviously, he was emotional. He looked at the gods, and forcefully, he asked some hard questions.

"Who of you have lived in the depths of poverty? Who of you have been the sons or daughters of coal miners? Who of you have lost your parents to evil? Who of you have lost your parents to the suffocating death of coal dust? Who of you have been stalked by the vilest of evil creatures? Who of you have fought with demons of limitless evil yet prevailed as the victors and bent the arc of justice to the innocent? Who of you solved the ancient Riddle of Zuron? Who of you stopped the destruction of the universe? Who of you rid the universe of Dark God Zuron? Who of you uncovered a traitor among us?"

A hovering silence stifled the festive mood as Viracocha went on. "There can be no denying Danny and Jeannie's prowess or worthiness to be supergods. They have, through acts of exceptional bravery, valor, skill, and the willingness to lay down their lives for others, achieved what no other god, human, or creature in the universe has done."

The only sounds heard were beating hearts. Jeannie was speechless, lost in a mountain of thought as she listened. Danny, in a million billion years, did not expect this praise from the supreme god.

As Danny listened, for some reason, he could not stop his mind. Try as he might, Danny's mind could not focus on the words being spoken by the supreme god. Danny and Jeannie's journey was at the forefront of his thoughts. There were a few noteworthy moments that flashed to the front of his consciousness. One had been at the funeral for his mom.

Everyone had left except Jeannie, Tony, and me. It was so still in that old church. I was standing next to Jeannie in front of the pews. Jeannie seemed withdrawn, deep in thought, and I knew she was worrying about me. As she was deep in thought, she never expected my question. "Was there a purpose?" I asked her.

The gravity of it was at the core of my anguish, but Jeannie's steadfast vision looked way beyond the surrounding tragedy. She asked, "Our adventure?"

I nodded. "Yes."

Yeah, a gripping silence had filled the chapel as Jeannie paused. With a gentle smile, softly grasping my hands, she said, "Danny, our love story will ring through the ages. And in some distant time, when young people are faced with the harsh reality of tragedy and despair, if they wonder if there's hope for them, someone will ask, 'Have you heard the story of Danny and Jeannie and the pot of gold they found?'"

She did manage to get me to smile as she said, "Oh, my wonderful Danny… if by chance we touch the lives of young people in a time yet to come…if in their struggles they discover from our story that the triumph of the human spirit is possible, then yes, my love! Our adventure had purpose!"

In a voice of power, she ventured on. "The winds of change are blowing, and although a tidal wave on the sea of life has threatened to crush us, we have found the treasure of true love."

I listened, and so it was. In the voice of an angel, she said, "In one year, when we are out of high school, we'll be on our way to having our little green-eyed Danny boys and blue-eyed Jeannie girls. They will fill our cups with more joy and treasure than we could ever dream of. And when they ask us, 'Mommy and Daddy, how did you guys come to be our parents,' we'll answer, 'A pot of gold brought us together,' and then we'll show it to them!"

Yeah, she got my spirits to rise, and then I asked, "Do you think we'll ever escape the clutches of CoalVille?"

She stared at me, and in her mind, I was the picture of the innocence of youth crushed by a murdering monster. Jeannie searched for words of comfort for the teenage orphan she had fallen in love with. Sifting through the bitter sadness that engulfed her soul, she could only fall back on centuries of cultural beliefs that had lifted the spirits of her people. With tears pouring from her eyes, she said in the sweetest of voices, "Oh, Danny, maybe the gods will step in and give us our hopes and dreams of that magical life in a land far away from the miseries of this coal camp."

And I remember so well what I said when I answered with the searching gaze of sadness. Yeah, I said, "I hope so."

It's strange how even when monumental events are underway, such as in the middle of being honored by accolades from a supreme god, your mind finds a way to drift and drift and drift.

And then there was that moment on the bank of the Yellshome River when we first got to Kopaz. I had just lost Tony to a monster. My best friend and buddy, Tony, was brutally murdered by Mochcom, the disciple of Dark God Zuron and was now in the Land of the Dead.

Tears rolled down my cheeks and over my mouth. I was devastated, and the feelings I had were wrenching my soul.

I remember looking at Jeannie. Slowly I said, "I couldn't save both you and Tony from that monster." Stumbling over my words, I added, "I chose you."

Now, a river of tears flowing from her eyes, Jeannie's hand gently reached to touch my cheek. She said with trembling voice, "I'm so sorry, Danny. You did love Tony. He was special in so many ways. Yes, he was a friend to both of us...like no other."

She couldn't stop her fingers from shaking. Searching for consoling words, she sweetly wiped a tear from my eye. "Danny, maybe the gods will step in and help us find our friend in the vast expanse of time."

And with a heart broken by the loss of my friend, I gave her a longing look of sadness and said, "I hope so."

It's funny, Danny thought, *how things turn out. Yeah, it was an incredible journey, but I wonder where Tony and KateLynn are? Are they in the Land of the Dead? I wonder if Peizar, Jerzom's friend, and his sister, Princess Merapondes, are also in the Land of the Dead.*

His journey along the road of life from the son of a coal miner to the second-most-powerful god of the universe was fraught with challenges. There could be no denying that. He and Jeannie alone had ventured on that trail of sorrows, and their tears and joys ended in a triumphant victory that to this very day stands as an ensign of greatness throughout the universe.

Yet there was an image that took center stage in the spotlight of his mind—his parents who were vanishing forever, and it was his fault. All the accolades in the universe could not change that. *My god, what have I done? My parents are gone forever because of me,* thought Danny.

As Danny's head drooped in sadness, Viracocha stopped his speech.

"Danny, what can I do?" the supreme god asked.

It was an unusual question. Danny didn't have an answer. Everyone waited for a response. There was none.

"Well," said Viracocha, "if you have no answer, may I attempt one?" What could Danny say? His hole, figuratively speaking, seemed like it was growing bigger as he stood on its edge and was about to jump in.

Jeannie was getting nervous. She thought, *Danny, please, please don't do this! You can't be ungrateful!*

Viracocha walked to Danny's side. "Do you know the value of the gift of life?" The supreme god did not wait for an answer. He went on. "You have the three items of zedite, and you know their value, right?"

Danny answered. "Yes, I do know the value of the two zedite knives and the solid zedite ball. These three constitute all the zedite in the universe. And there is no value to put on the ownership of the knife of Zuron, as evil has no road to travel unless it possesses that knife."

"Good," said Viracocha. "Now you have a point of comparison. The value of *all* the zedite in the universe is essentially equal in value to *all* the gold in the universe and, as you just said, evil is harnessed. So we can use that as a comparison to something else!"

Compare zedite to what? thought Danny. *What am I to compare that to, that which is of all but insurmountable value, equivalent to essentially all the gold in the universe?*

Danny was about to say something when the supreme god interrupted. "I was going to wait to honor you and Jeannie with the most prized honor that can be bestowed by the gods. In fact, no one has ever been given this honor. You and Jeannie are the first."

Viracocha walked to a golden table on which sat two boxes made of red diamond.

"Please come forward, Danny and Jeannie."

For some reason, Danny had not noticed what was at the side of the table laden with food. It had just looked like part of the decorations.

Viracocha said, "I was going to bestow upon you and Jeannie this honor and show you later, but I'm going to do just the opposite. That is, I'm going to show you first and then bestow the honor."

Now that was totally confusing to Danny and Jeannie. In fact, Jeannie reviewed what the supreme god had just said and tried to make sense of it. She couldn't. It was so foreign that she actually shook her head and then caught herself so she would not appear ungrateful.

"Are you guys ready?" asked Viracocha.

Danny and Jeannie nodded their heads to signify that they were.

"Neferdor, would you do the honors?" asked her husband.

"Most assuredly," said the goddess.

She walked to what appeared to be decorations for the celebration and feast and threw back the curtain.

"*Oh my God*," yelled Danny. "*Mom and Dad! Tony and KateLynn!*"

Like an atom bomb, Danny's mind exploded with feelings of joy that knew no bounds. *The value of all the gold in the universe cannot buy what I am looking at! It's a gift!*

Standing at the front of the crowd of people who had been waiting behind the curtain were eighteen-year-old Johnny and Darla, and right next them were eighteen-year-old Tony and KateLynn. What's more, right next to Johnny was a bright red 1955 Chevy pickup.

Danny was ready to bolt and rush to his parents, but Viracocha stopped him. "Now Danny, the agreement was to show first and then honor you and Jeannie, wasn't that so?"

The trumpets sounded. The drums rolled. It was almost beyond Danny's control to remain part of the solemn proceedings when all he wanted to do was race to his parents. Yet there was wisdom in what the supreme god was doing. Viracocha wanted all to witness, including Danny's parents, Johnny and Darla, the one-of-a-kind honor that was about to be bestowed on Danny and Jeannie.

Yet it was not only Danny and Jeannie who were being propelled into the surreal expanse of the joy of what had seemed all but impossible but also those select few who had had their own incredible journeys and who were now the select group of the old human race. Johnny, Darla, Tony, KateLynn, Jeannie's parents, Peizar and his parents, Princess Merapondes, Princess Aerapondes, the entire royal family of Kopaz, Little Zeb and his parents, and all the children of Danny, Jeannie, Tony, and KateLynn. These were the chosen ones who would start the new human race.

It was the first time Tony had seen KateLynn since they returned from the Land of the Dead, and what's more, it was the very first time he had ever seen his sons. It was likewise the first time that Danny fully comprehended the bond of friendship between Prince Jerzom and his best friend, Peizar, the commoner. Peizar stood next to Princess Merapondes—both had been murdered by the goroms and now were back from the Land of the Dead.

Peizar was like me—poor—and now he stands next to his beloved parents who were also brutally murdered by the evil goroms! thought Danny with compassion in his heart. *Yeah, what a sight to see…Jerzom and Peizar united again, just like Tony and me!*

As it turned out, all had to wait for reunions. It was just the way the supreme god and his wife, Supreme Goddess Neferdor, had planned it.

How can you describe such an event? You can't.

Viracocha said, "Step here." He indicated to Danny and Jeannie where he wanted them to be so all could see them.

Standing next to the golden table with the red-diamond boxes, Viracocha took the lids off. "OK, ladies first."

He motioned for Jeannie to bow her head. He placed around her neck a medallion on a ribbon of golden and silver threads. "Jeannie, I bestow upon you the Medal of the Gods. You are the first ever to receive this great honor."

Likewise, the supreme god bestowed on Danny an equal honor, and when he had finished, Viracocha said, "Now you can kiss your mate."

Now there was a moment of silence as Neferdor stepped into the limelight, and all eyes focused on her as she said, "The next extravagant events to occur in the pantheon will be weddings!"

First she looked at the young Latino boy, Tony, and the girl he had finally managed to get his arm around, KateLynn, who was standing next to him.

Then Neferdor turned her head to look at Jeannie. "So, Jeannie, have you told Danny that illegitimate children are not allowed at the Council of the Gods?"

It was not out of character, even if it was a little cheeky. Jeannie was snickering ever so lightly as she answered, "I told Danny that we'd get in trouble if we messed around, and guess what?"

The supreme goddess smiled at Jeannie's remark and continued. "Well, grand weddings for you and Danny and that young couple over there, Tony and KateLynn, are the next order of business here at the center of the universe."

At that moment, Supreme Goddess Neferdor caught something. It was easy to catch if you were looking for it. Before her were Danny, Jeannie, Tony, KateLynn—and Peizar and Princess Merapondes. It was the look of love that two young people wore when all they could see was each other and nothing else. I guess that is where the old saying "blinded by love" comes from.

Danny and Jeannie followed Supreme Goddess Neferdor's gaze, and it was the look in Peizar's eyes as he looked at Princess Merapondes that caught their attention. Likewise, the fond look of love coming from the young princess as she looked at her brother's best friend, Peizar, was a dead giveaway. Maybe after being brutally murdered and venturing to the Land of the Dead and then through the grace of Supreme God Viracocha and his wife, Neferdor, venturing back to the Land of the Living, love took on a new dimension!

"Hmm…I think the weddings should be expanded to include these two lovers," said Neferdor as she pointed to Peizar and Princess Merapondes. "We will have some beautiful people…just look at them! They will be blessed with glorious bridesmaids and groomsmen!"

The goddess Neferdor smiled at Peizar and Princess Merapondes. "Yes, the weddings of Danny and Jeannie, Tony and KateLynn, and Peizar and Princess Merapondes will raise the standard and give a new meaning to the word love!"

Now Danny could be a little slow on the uptake. This was one of those moments. Danny rolled his eyes and said nothing. He laughed freely so all could hear as he thought, *Jeannie, who jumped in bed with whom, and in whose bed was all that messing around?*

Danny thought his thoughts were private. They weren't. The supreme god who said, "Well, we know what happened in that bed, and so with that revelation, Danny, you may proceed to put your arms around your parents."

The jubilance engendered in Danny had no description or bounds. Yet there was a single thought that crushed all others as he looked at the people who moments earlier had been standing behind the curtain. *Viracocha has just bent the arc of justice to the innocent…my God, how great you are!*

And as he was running to his parents and his best buddy, Tony, there was an image in his mind. It was a note that he had found in Mochcom's house of evil in CoalVille. The words on that note filled his mind: *Fools! You take me for an idiot? No hair. No Tony. No KateLynn forever. Ha ha."*

It was interesting how the supreme god stepped in when least expected. Yeah, as Danny was in a high-speed sprint to reach his parents, Viracocha added in a loud voice, "Forget the hair thing, Danny! Say hi from me to Johnny, Darla, Tony, KateLynn, Terry, Eddie, Soft Wind, Billy Harris, and Tony's mom and dad, and to Kashom's beautiful wife, Star-of-Night, their daughters, Moon-of-Day and Skip-with-Wind, and Kashom's son, Yellow Moon, Zeb's parents, and Peizar's parents!"

When Viracocha had finished listing the names, he said, "Looks like a solid foundation to start all over again, especially with the addition of the little guys and gals that will be legitimate when Neferdor gets these weddings underway and keeps you, Jeannie, Tony, and KateLynn from anymore hanky-panky!"

For all, joy and laughter graced the grand dining hall of the Pantheon of the Gods as all eyes were on the newest god in the universe, Danny.

There were a few moments for touching reunions as Danny hugged his mom and dad. Knowing the significance of the moment, Johnny said, "Danny, your mom and I will wait here as you, Tony, and KateLynn join Supreme God Viracocha and his wife, Supreme Goddess Neferdor."

Danny hesitated and was about to say something when his mother jumped in. "We'll have an eternity to spend together as teenagers, but for now, you are wanted at Jeannie's side."

Darla threw a glance at Neferdor and picked up something. "Danny, it looks like you, Tony, and KateLynn are wanted over there," she said as she pointed.

Feelings he thought he would never have again coursed through Danny's body as his mind raced on. *I've got my best buddy back!*

As Danny walked alongside Tony and KateLynn, his heart was pounding so loudly that the corps of buglers could not have masked its thumping sounds with another blast from their trumpets.

With a sidewise glance at Danny, Tony said, "We have a lot to catch up on…that is, if you want a budding scientist to be your best buddy again?"

All in the grand dining hall heard as Danny replied, "Tony, our friendship is now endless." Then he took a moment to make eye contact with the supreme god and mouthed the words "*thank you!*"

It was only a few moments before four eighteen-year-olds from the Scarlet Desert were standing next to the two most important and powerful gods in the universe. *Wow*, thought Danny as he watched a strange smile grow on Jeannie's face.

Neferdor wanted a few things to happen. She said, "Would the following please step forward. Prince Jerzom and his wife, Little Jeannie, and of course, DannyR. Prince Zeb and his wife, Jeanondes. Little Danny and his wife, Little KateLynn. Little Tony and his wife, Princess Aerapondes. Lord Peizar and his soon-to-be wife, Princess Merapondes."

When all were where the supreme goddess Neferdor wanted them, she said, "Wow! How beautiful! I don't think there could be a better group of young adults to start the new human race! Corrupt politicians, ruthless governments, and religious zealots are finished and no longer control the masses. I'm looking at the rulers of the new human race, and I like what I see!"

As Supreme Goddess Neferdor looked over the group, she instructed them where she wanted them to stand. "This is different...as I know all you kids are married," said Neferdor. She stopped, a smile lighting up her face as she looked at Danny and Jeannie's children. Then she continued. "Now you will have the honor of being in some of your parents' weddings. And as I said, it will be a grand event that will happen soon! I bet I know who Merapondes will have standing next to her as a twin bridesmaids for the wedding of the newest goddess, Jeannie. I'll bet it will be Aerapondes's and Jeannie's girls! And I know also who Jerzom will have standing next to him as his lifelong friend, his brother and a little guy who once did not have a right hand when they as the groomsmen honor the newest god, Danny. I'll bet it will be Peizar, his brother, Kashom, and Zeb!"

Most graciously, the goddess then looked at Little Tony, Princess Aerapondes, Little Danny, and Little KateLynn. "You guys will, I know, have the thrill of honoring your parents, Tony and KateLynn, in their glorious wedding! I can see that much planning is in order for these weddings, which will be the most monumental events to ever take place in our pantheon!"

It was indeed a strange sight. Danny and Jeannie, Tony and KateLynn, and all their children standing with Prince Jerzom, Princess Aerapondes, Princess Merapondes, Lord Peizar, the new ambassador of Kopaz, and little Prince Zeb, who was now eighteen years old.

While the group was coming forward, Jeannie had a moment to reflect. She thought, *It wasn't long ago—at least, that is what it seems like when things were so very different.*

Sometimes, you might say, great minds think along parallel paths. This might have been the case with Danny and Jeannie. For whatever reason, Jeannie's mind was full, and her memory of two very special events, just like Danny moments earlier, had flashed to the forefront of her mind.

I remember, she thought. *It seemed like there could be no bright tomorrows, especially on that awful day in Granite Springs when Danny, Tony, and I were at his mother's funeral. It was only three weeks earlier that we had been at the community church for his dad's funeral. I didn't know what to do. Yeah, Danny was at the bottom of his own private hellhole wondering if our adventures in the desert had meaning. My heart was broken...all I could say was, "Oh, Danny, maybe the gods will step in and give us our hopes and dreams of that magical life in a land far away from the miseries of this coal camp."*

I remember the only words from Danny were, "I hope so."

And then, like the mind likes to do, Jeannie's wandered on also.

I remember that day so well, as if it were yesterday. It was a gorgeous day in the Scarlet Desert—March 24, 1958. His strength was almost gone. His eyes closed. In the softest of whispers, his last words faded. "Stand on all the boxes of treasures you want to take." Then he was lying lifeless on the ground, and he said nothing more. Danny and I were fortunate, through the gifts from the gods, to escape Gorom Mochcom's reign of terror in the nick of time. We landed in Kopaz on the banks of the Yellshome River. There was silence. I looked around.

I whispered as I asked, "Danny, is Tony gone?"

The agony was beyond human capacity. Danny had made a decision to save me and then deal with the haunting reality that Tony was never coming back.

It seemed at the time that the veil of evil would never lift. All I could do was give him hope. I trusted the ways of our people and said, "Danny, maybe the gods will step in and help us find our friend in the vast expanse of time."

Yeah, it was a mountain to climb, and all Danny had was hope. He used his favorite expression. "I hope so."

Now, Jeannie could not stop her smile. Her mind was still in gear. *Yeah, things have changed. Wow! Danny and his "hope so"!*

The goddess Neferdor motioned to Jeannie to step closer. It was like Jeannie's identical twin just waiting to tell her something very wonderful.

When they were where Supreme Goddess Neferdor instructed them to stand, the goddess said, "I must be giddy, as I've already said this, but I'll say it again. You are looking at the core group of people who are the beginnings of the new human race, and I must add," as she reached and took one each of Jeannie's and Danny's hands and said, "they come from the greatest parents of all time!"

That brought smiles from King Dalvin and Queen Neferapondes, Soft Wind and Billy Harris, Tony's parents, Nola and Zeb's dad, Peizar's parents, and of course, Danny and Jeannie, who all had a hand in the beginnings of the new human race.

Revealing a smile that was most unusual for the goddess, she directed her conversation to Danny, Jeannie, Tony, and KateLynn. "How proud you must be of these beautiful children! And now, let us hear from the gods."

Above the sounds of the gala party that was like no other, the corps of buglers stood and sounded off. Comanzar made a statement. "Goddess Neferdor, the gods wish to speak, and their spokesman, Tammuz, is ready!"

All eyes were on Neferdor as she smiled. "Let him speak!"

The tide had turned for not only the universe, Danny and Jeannie, Viracocha and Neferdor, and Zuron but also the god Tammuz. No longer suspected by Viracocha of being a traitor, he was ready with his remarks.

In a booming voice, Tammuz roared with pleasure. "Today, the Council of Primeval Gods has a new standard to reach for. We are privileged to have among us two of the noblest gods. They have traveled a road of sorrow and tears and have sacrificed so much in their journey for others, and now they grace our table."

He turned his head to lock eyes with Danny and Jeannie. "Danny and Jeannie, for as long as our council has been in the universe, which is forever, there have only been four individuals, Supreme God Viracocha and his wife, Supreme Goddess Neferdor, and now you, Danny and Jeannie, who have shown the rest of us the true meaning of sacrifice. You, Danny and Jeannie, have given the ordinary gods a new standard to reach for, and it is my sincere pleasure to be in your company as you sit at the head of our council table."

Then the god Tammuz could not wait longer for his next remarks.

"When those in the vast expanses of the universe are faced by insurmountable mountains of poverty, bleakness, pain, misery, and sadness, someone will ask if they have heard the story of Danny and Jeannie and then tell them this. In the pit of hopelessness and stalked by ancient evil, Danny and Jeannie prevailed against all odds, finding a treasure of gold and precious gems that they did not ransom for pleasure but used wisely in the battle of good against evil to rid the universe of tyranny. Now they sit at the council table of the primeval gods and govern the most precious gift of all, the gift of life. Yes, the story of Danny and Jeannie will stand as an ensign and will shine throughout the ages as a beacon of hope for all those who are searching a way out the depths of despair!"

At that moment, the entire quorum of the primeval gods erupted in shouts. "*Hail, Danny! Hail, Jeannie!*"

As she listened to the shouts of praise, Jeannie encapsulated their journey in a song from her heart, her very own version of *Amazing Grace*, her favorite hymn:

> *Now I am lifted to the skies*
> *On clouds in gentle breeze*
> *I've found my love and won the prize*
> *And sail no bloody seas.*
> > *Amazing grace! How sweet the sound*
> > *That saved a wretch like me.*
> > *In faith I journeyed on and found*
> > *My hopes, my dreams, I'm free!*
> *Throughout ten thousand years and more*
> *A light of hope we'll stand*
> *For those who wish their souls to soar*
> *Love rings through ages grand.*
> > *Amazing grace! How sweet the sound*
> > *That saved a wretch like me.*
> > *In faith, I journeyed on and found*
> > *My dreams fore'er I'll be!*

As the roar of welcome from the cast of gods subsided, Tammuz made his final comments. "I can't wait for the next festivities. With Neferdor in charge, the upcoming joyous affair that we all eagerly await will be the grandest wedding of all time!"

And with that, Supreme Goddess Neferdor looked at Danny and said with pleasure, "You have a lot to catch up on. Your best friend, Tony, is most anxious to be your best buddy again!"

She then turned to Jeannie and said, "Jeannie, KateLynn, your most trusted and dearest friend, has much to tell you!"

A grand party at the center of the universe was about to get underway. Bugles sounded, and Comanzar announced, "Hear ye, hear ye! The supreme goddess of the universe, Supreme Goddess Neferdor, speaks!"

With a smile on her face, and in her stateliest manner, the goddess Neferdor looked at those assembled with a look of triumphant victory as she addressed the entire gathering in a voice of power. "Let the festivities begin!"

And so there was a new beginning on that warm summer day on the planet Volob—the gift of life stood behind the curtain.

Ballads and Songs of the
Kopaz Series

Sunday Morning Pain
Dale Groutage, AKA Johnny Bill

I can hear music, sweet music that grips my soul,
The beautiful sounds—the rhythm of rock and roll.
'Cause there's something about a radio song,
That turns my head, when the DJ says, "Danny, you're on."
Just dreaming of visions, of stardom and fame,
It's only time till the world will know my name.

So I followed my dreams and left my home
Said good-bye my friends and journeyed alone.
Now, I dance with the girls on Saturday night
Just to lift my soul to a brand new height.
We sing and we laugh, drinking lots of beer,
We gather around and yell a big cheer.

On Sunday morning, as daylight draws near,
I'm all alone, but there's silence I can hear.
Like the old man on the bench, sleeping in the park,
Listening to the song of a distant meadowlark.
Did he chase his dreams with an empty bottle near
Just to silence echoes he can no longer hear?

I can't hear the music playing or see the stars of fame,
'Cause I'm listening to the silence of a sleeping city's shame.
On a gloomy Sunday morning, on a sidewalk all alone,

War of the Gods

Makes a body wonder, why I ever left my home.

I'm the boy that's drifting down the road of time,
Chasing dreams of treasure I hope will soon be mine.
I'm a dreamer searching through the darkest night,
Walking down a sidewalk, holding tears from sight.
I know I'll win this race and find my pearl of fame,
In my mind I see a star. Lord, I'll make myself a name.

But now my heart is heavy, carrying this load of pain,
Searching for a rainbow down a lonesome Sunday lane.
Chasing dreams of glory, with lights around my name,
I'm searching for a pot of gold in the cold drizzling rain.
Hoping for a break somehow, I found life's bitter sorrow.
So I prayed, "Lord, where's my hope for tomorrow?"

On a lonesome Sunday morning, in a cold drizzling rain,
I'm sifting through rubble, of rejection and pain.
Searching for a glimmer of hope, I'll make my spirit soar.
Hope will drown the silent echoes, of a sleeping city's roar
And nothing short of madness will lift my soul from sorrow.
In darkest clouds of sadness, Lord, I'll find my fame tomorrow.

I can't hear the music playing, or see the stars of fame,
'Cause I'm listening to the silence of a sleeping city's shame
On a gloomy Sunday morning, on a sidewalk all alone.
Makes a body wonder why I ever left my home.

Dale's version of Amazing Grace

Amazing grace! How sweet the love
That saved my broken soul;
Shine down on me from Heaven above
'Twas grace that made me whole.

> *On jagged trail of tears and sorrows*
> *I saw an endless night.*
> *Through tears I cried, "Are there tomorrows?"*
> *Facing my endless plight.*

Shall I be lifted to the skies
On clouds in gentle breeze,
While others reach to grab the prize
Sailing on bloody seas?

> *Amazing grace! How sweet the sound*
> *That saved a wretch like me;*
> *In faith I journeyed on and found*
> *My hopes, my dreams, I'm free!*

In joy, I'm lifted to the skies
On clouds in gentle breeze
To find my lover and the prize
And sail no bloody seas.

> *Amazing grace! How sweet the sound*
> *That saved a wretch like me!*
> *I once was lost but now am found*
> *Not blind…my love I see!*

All together in heavenly spree

We sail in gentle breeze.
On the sea of life our souls are free
And fear no bloody seas.

> *Throughout ten thousand years and more*
> *A light of hope we'll stand*
> *For those who wish their soul to soar*
> *Love rings through ages grand.*

Amazing grace! How sweet the sound
That saved a wretch like me,
In faith I journeyed on and found
My dreams, fore'er I'll be!

Could It Be There's Magic?

Dedicated to my one and only love, Nancy!

Could it be there's magic in a young girl's soul,
as she watches a boy with her love so whole?
Do you believe that magic gives that boy a thrill,
when she flashes her eyes just to say 'I will'?
There's magic in a young girl's grace,
or why would a smile grow on the young boy's face?
What else but magic would capture his heart,
as he looks to the girl with a yearning that they'll never part?
Does magic light the fire within and set young hearts aglow?
For without the magic, the flame would die, and true love they'd never
know.
With a playful stride and a magical sigh,
she steps to his side, giving him a glance from the corner of her eye.
Ever so gently, she touches his face,
stroking his cheeks with fingers softer than lace.
On tiptoes she stands with her hands just so;
her lips meet his and captures his heart that has no place to go!
Pounding with joy, his heart beats with pleasure;
his first kiss with a girl…it's his newfound treasure.
What else but magic lights the fire within and sets young hearts aglow?
For without the magic, the flame would die, and true love they'd never
know.
There's a moment in time that's just a magical place,
When two lovers are lost in the arms of each other's embrace.

It's magic that lights the fire of bliss and sets young hearts aglow.
For without the magic, the flame would die, and true love they'd never know!

Somewhere, My Love, Tonight

Somewhere, my love, he's out there, searching in the soft moonlight.
I know He hears my beating heart, and lingers for my kiss.
My love will surely lift my soul, from this darkness void of bliss.
My love, he calls to me this night; his love doth make me whole.
In the stillness of the night, I hear him out there call to me;
His faint voice is like the sadness of a weeping willow tree.
I know the sun is setting in a faraway land someplace.
I fear my love is searching but can't find my hiding place.
Starry, starry night, I hope your lights will point the way,
And bring him back to me this day.
In the darkness of the night, my heart is full of pain;
My love, I hear him call my name.
I long to touch his tender face, and keep him close with my embrace.
His sweet eyes light up my soul, when he looks upon my face.
Strong arms that hold me oh so close, lift me to heights of grace.
Is my love lost to the night, searching for me in the soft moonlight?
Now I touch his tender face, and hold him tight with my embrace.
I shall never let him go, strong arms that hold me so.
Smiling at me with sparkling eyes, he makes me laugh with songs so wise.
My love has found me in the night, out here in the soft moonlight.
Starry, starry night, I hope your lights will point the way,
And bring him back to me this day.
In the darkness of the night, my heart is full of pain;
My love, I hear him call my name.

Farewell, My Love

Holding him with close embrace,
His eyes so softly warm my teary face.
I know my love must leave me back in time;
My heart is heavy, carrying tears of pain.
I cry to think how long he won't be mine;
Has my love for him been all in vain?
With just that thought upon my mind:
How long? How long will he be gone?

> *Hold me softly, hold me tight.*
> *Hold me in your arms tonight.*
> *Soon the gods will set you free*
> *And take my love away from me.*
> *Will the road that crosses time*
> *Bring my love back home to me?*

Soon the night will take him far;
My love will be my distant star.
He travels through a time unknown,
In search of answers all alone.
Somewhere out there in a desert's night,
He'll chase his dreams of pure delight.
Fleeting as the dust that's blown,
My love will wander on his own.

> *Hold me softly, hold me tight.*
> *Hold me in your arms tonight.*
> *Soon the gods will set you free*

And take my love away from me.
Will the road that crosses time
Bring my love back home to me?

Now my heart weighs heavy on my soul.
Soon his void will leave me far from whole.
My thoughts keep drifting far away,
Wishing I could be with him each day.
I know that travel on the Road of Time,
Will surely lead to life sublime.
I hope my love comes back to me,
To live in bliss throughout eternity.

Hold me softly, hold me tight.
Hold me in your arms tonight.
Soon the gods will set you free
And take my love away from me.
Will the road that crosses time
Bring my love back home to me?

Zanzee, Jeannie's Mythical Cat

With silky-black fur and sapphire-blue eyes,
Zanzee is a cat divine.
His journey is long, and he never dies,
traveling the highway of time.
There was a season of moments when he lived with pharaohs of old,
gracing their temples of opulent gold.

    Pretty, pretty blue eyes from the gods above,
    You fell from the heavens to bring me your love.
    Now you're my beautiful angel divine.
    You're Zanzee, and you're all mine.

Purring loudly in Queen Nefertiti's lap,
his presence was worshiped by royalty in awe.
None can deny his worth is untold,
for he guards his subjects with ultimate swipe of his claw.
There was a time when he lived with pharaohs of old,
but now he was Jeannie's cat and beautiful to behold.

    Pretty, pretty blue eyes from the gods above.
    You fell from the heavens to bring me your love.
    Now you're my beautiful angel divine.
    You're Zanzee, and you're all mine.

The war of the gods is a mystery to most,
but the mythical cat knows the gods' secrets at will.
He's clever and wise and sees what to do

when evil is lurking and springs for the kill.
Through perilous journey, Zanzee guards Jeannie's life,
and now she sits with the gods and governs without strife.
    Pretty, pretty blue eyes from the gods above
    You fell from the heavens to bring me your love.
    Now you're my beautiful angel divine.
    You're Zanzee, and you're all mine.

Dale Groutage

Dale Groutage was born and raised in Reliance, Wyoming, a poverty-stricken coal camp in the state's southwestern desert. His childhood reading inspired him to pursue a better life, leading to BS, MS, and PhD degrees from the University of Wyoming.

Groutage served as a senior scientist for the US Navy, developing missile guidance and submarine silencing technology. He was inducted into the University of Wyoming Engineering Hall of Fame for his service to his country and honored as one of the top ten engineers in federal government by the National Society of Professional Engineers.

Now retired, Groutage is married with three kids. The former adjunct professor for the University of California and the University of Washington lives in Neenah, Wisconsin.

www.ingramcontent.com/pod-product-compliance
Lightning Source LLC
Chambersburg PA
CBHW060952030726
47503CB00003B/840